The Dead Die Young

DETECTIVE INSPECTOR MARC FAGAN

Book 5

JASON CHAPMAN

OFFWORLD
PUBLICATIONS

Author’s notes

This novel is a work of complete fiction. The names, characters and incidents portrayed are the work of the author’s imagination. Any resemblance to actual persons, living or dead, events or localities is entirely coincidental.

Graphic content warning

This story contains foul language some will find offensive. This book also contains police interview scenes that cover sexual abuse. Some will find upsetting and disturbing.

With Thanks

A big thank you to all my friends and colleagues. Particularly those who I work with. Your faith in me pushes me every day to achieving a dream I have had for over thirty years.

A massive thank you to my beta readers Jacqui and AK for your guidance and input.

And finally, to you, the reader, for giving me the opportunity to tell you my story.

CHAPTER 1

DAY 1

Gordon Avenue – The Sofrydd – South Wales

Detective inspector Marc Fagan surveyed the local landscape. A typical street in the South Wales Valleys. The area was peppered with houses built over the last one hundred and twenty years. A row of miners' cottages overlooked the valley where a massive viaduct once stood. Behind them were several streets lined with houses built in the 1960s, 70s and late 80s.

A portion of the top end of the street had been sealed off. Uniformed officers were going door to door, advising people to stay in their homes. But this didn't stop residents gathering behind the police tape. Some onlookers wore pyjamas and dressing gowns after having been woken by the police.

Two uniforms were walking down the street, jotting down number plates.

Fagan looked up at the three bedroom semi-detached council house. Crime scene investigators were collecting bags of evidence from the house.

Detective Sergeant Sean Watkins appeared out of the doorway, along with PC Stacey Flynn. Both were dressed in forensic PPE.

Through her facemask Fagan could see how distraught PC Flynn was. 'You okay Stacey?' he asked.

'Just about, guv,' Stacey replied, pulling her mask off.

'This isn't your first body, is it?'

'No, guv.' Stacey shook her head, looking back at the upper floor of the house. 'But it is my first child murder.'

'Me and Sean will take it from here. See if those lot have any useful information to offer.' He pointed at the dishevelled group of people watching from behind the police tape.

Watkins read from his notebook. 'The victim's name is Ellie Parry. She's fourteen years old. A neighbour found her this morning around seven o'clock, when she called at the house after hearing a smoke alarm going off. She had a spare key, so she let herself in. She telephoned the police at four minutes past seven.'

'Where are the parents?'

'It's a single parent family. The mother's name is Sophie Parry. The neighbour told us the mother was in Cardiff, partying all night. The neighbour tried several times to ring her, but her calls go straight to voicemail.'

'What about the father?'

'In Ibiza for the past two weeks. He's due back tomorrow. He lives in Brynmawr.'

Fagan looked around the front garden facing the street. Black bags were scattered about on the unkempt lawn. He shuddered, spotting the long tail of a rat burrowing into a bag. 'God, I hate rats. People who pile shit outside their houses don't deserve to live in them.'

A CSI marched briskly out of the front door. She tore away her mask. 'Jesus, it reeks in that house, even with a bloody mask on.'

Watkins continued to read from his notes. 'Stacey was the first response officer, along with another uniform. They arrived at seven fifteen. Twin boys were found in the house. According to the neighbour, they were supposed to be celebrating their fifth birthday today. Their mother was planning a massive party for them.'

Fagan glanced around the filthy garden. An old trampoline was filled with black plastic bags. 'Not the kind of place you'd want to hold a birthday party.'

'One of the boys went downstairs to the kitchen to make some toast. He put the toaster on the highest setting, which is what triggered the smoke alarm.'

'Where are the boys now?'

'Stacey called for backup immediately. Social Services have been and gone. Stacey didn't want the boys hanging around.'

Fagan nodded. 'Good move.'

Another CSI appeared out of the front door. 'Full PPE dress please, DI Fagan.' He glanced back at the house. 'It's hell on earth in there.'

Fagan dressed in appropriate PPE before returning to the house. The hallway to the house was strewn with dirty washing. 'Christ, look at the state of this place. There's cat shit everywhere.'

'The family own two cats,' Watkins explained. 'They scarpered as soon as Stacey and the other uniform turned up.'

Fagan spotted a small pair of underpants caked in shit. 'I don't think this Sophie Parry will win any awards for mother of the year anytime soon.' Through his mask Fagan noticed the distinct smell of marijuana. He stepped into the living room. A large flat screen TV was mounted on the wall. A tatty looking corner sofa and recliner chair occupied one corner. Fagan spotted an ashtray overflowing with spliffs and dogends. Crime scene investigators dressed in their sterile white suits seemed out of place amidst the filth and chaos of the house. Fagan breathed in through his mouth in an effort to blot out the stench. 'How the bloody hell do people live like this?' He pointed at a plate containing the remains of a pizza. Mould had formed on the cheese topping. 'This place reminds of an old girlfriend from Liverpool many years ago. She was a right lazy cow who hated cleaning up. I'm glad I had the good sense to dump her after a few months.'

They made their way to the kitchen, which was a disaster zone. Rubbish was strewn across the worktop. Mouldy bread and other rotting food piled up on a kitchen table. A pile of washing was thrown on the floor in front of an ancient looking washing machine. The resident cats had used it as a litter tray. The back door to the kitchen was open. Dozens of black rubbish bags had been tossed out. Many had been ripped open by cats and vermin.

'Jesus, I'm surprised her neighbours haven't complained.'

'The neighbour's garden next door isn't much better, boss,' Watkins said.

Fagan stepped over the filthy washing and peered through the back door at the adjacent garden. It was full of old sofas and black rubbish bags. He looked back at Watkins. 'Contact the local housing association and tell them to send a team up to this street. They need to see this shitbox for themselves.'

'I'll give it a go, boss. But all these housing associations care about is rent money. My sister lives in Cwmbran on an estate like this. She's always moaning that when she wants something fixed, the housing association takes forever to show up.'

Fagan looked towards the countertop, spotting a battered-looking toaster containing charcoaled toast. He looked towards the kitchen door. 'I guess we better look upstairs.'

They navigated the staircase, which was cluttered with more filthy washing, toys, and cat shit. A snapper was in a tiny bathroom taking pictures. Fagan looked through the door. Discarded cardboard toilet rolls and used sanitary towels littered the floor. Cat piss stains were everywhere.

The main bedroom was a total mess. No wardrobe, just a clothes rail packed with flimsy looking dresses. An ashtray sat on a bedside table, piled with more dogends and used spliffs. The bedroom floor was littered with empty boxes of cigarette papers and spent lighters. They moved on to the next room. The boys' bedroom contained a bunkbed. The ladder to the top bunk was missing a rung. A filthy duvet was pulled back on the bottom bunk, revealing piss stained sheets. The room was littered with MacDonald's containers.

Fagan spotted a half-eaten burger. Fries were scattered on the floor. 'It's a good bet Sophie Parry won't be seeing her sons for a while.'

'That's what Social Services said when they saw the state of this place,' Watkins said.

Fagan walked to the door of the third bedroom, stopping short. For a moment, he hesitated, preparing himself for the scene he was about to face. Finally, he stepped into the bedroom.

CSIs were in the room. One dusting for prints, the other two examining the bed. A vape and several small bottles were on a bedside table. Empty packets of contraceptive pills were on the floor. Empty bottles of WKD were dumped in what appeared to be a laundry basket.

Fagan forced himself to look at the body on the bed. He suddenly grasped why Stacey was so upset.

A young girl, barely dressed, lay on the bed. Her dead eyes stared directly at the ceiling. Long blonde hair splayed out on the pillows. An image of Rebecca lying dead in Bailey Park suddenly flashed across his mind.

The first thing Fagan noticed was the girl had applied makeup, making her look a lot older than her actual age. 'Time of death?'

'I'd say around midnight,' the CSI replied in a mournful tone. He looked at the girl. 'Poor girl is the same age as my daughter.'

'You okay?' Fagan asked.

'Not really. I've attended dozens of murders over the years. Thought I'd seen it all. But this just chills me to the core.'

'Cause of death?'

The CSI pointed at the girl's neck. 'There are signs of strangulation. However, the wounds on the neck aren't severe enough to have caused crushing of the larynx.'

'What about sexual assault?'

'No visible signs, but it's too early to tell. A post mortem will reveal everything.'

Fagan spotted an iPhone charger plugged into a wall socket. 'Where's her phone?'

'Gone,' the CSI replied. 'Chances are the murderer took it.'

'Indicating there's evidence on the phone that could tell us who the murderer is.' Fagan looked around the room, spotting a light mounted on a tripod in the corner. He looked back towards the bed before aligning himself with the tripod. 'Whoever murdered her filmed it.'

'Jesus, that's a dark assumption, even for you, boss,' Watkins said.

'I know,' Fagan replied, looking at the body sprawled out on the bed. 'Our killer filmed the murder and then took her phone.'

'Like a trophy?'

Fagan nodded. 'That's my guessing. This is not your typical murder.'

'There's plenty of people on this street who probably knew her, boss,' Watkins speculated. 'Her neighbour seemed familiar with the girl and her mother.'

Fagan clocked a small plastic bag on the bedside table. The bag contained small blue tablets.

'Looks like she was taking ecstasy, amongst other things,' Watkins remarked.

Fagan glanced at the CSI. 'Do you think the ecstasy could have helped the poor girl on her way?'

'We'll find out when we run a toxicology on her blood.'

Fagan had seen enough. He left the room and bounded down the stairs before emerging into the front garden to catch his breath.

Watkins followed close behind.

Fagan stooped over, clutching his knees, gulping down the fresh air. He glanced at Watkins. 'I served on Merseyside Murder Squad for over thirty years, Sean. Every time a young child is murdered, it hits me like a ton of bricks. I remember the last murder I investigated with Merseyside Police. I ended up belting the father of Aron Miller. Nearly got kicked out of the force for it.' He looked back towards the house. 'I want the bastard who did this strung up. Anyone who murders an innocent child should be put away for the rest of their lives!' Fagan suddenly realised he was shouting. The group of onlookers gawped at him. Fagan composed himself. 'The killer took her phone, which means she probably knew who he was.'

'Pretty grim for the mother to leave two young boys at home with a fourteen-year-old to look after them.'

'These families are ten-a-penny now, Sean. Many of these single mothers have no moral compass. I can't believe the mess that house is in. How the hell they could have lived there is beyond me.' Fagan took a moment to calm himself. He looked at the house. 'Did you say the neighbour let herself in with a spare key?'

'Yeah, but the neighbour also said the back door was open.'

Fagan walked up the road, which was strewn with rubbish bags. A side gate provided access to the garden. 'This is an end house. They usually have larger gardens than the rest of the houses on the street.' He carefully navigated the side garden which led to the back of the house. The smell of rotting food made him feel sick. Fagan pointed. 'There's a gap in the fence. Our murderer could have made their way out of the back door, through the garden and escaped out of the back.'

Watkins activated a map on his phone. 'There's a dirt road on the top there.'

Fagan walked back out of the garden onto the road. 'It's a dead end, but there's a footpath that leads to the back. How far is that dirt track?'

Watkins checked his screen. 'Roughly forty metres.'

Fagan and Watkins followed the narrow footpath, which was peppered with dog shit. They emerged onto the dirt track. 'Where does this track lead?'

Watkins took a moment to answer. 'You can either follow it until it reaches Brookview Farm.' Watkins looked down the dirt track which ran down the rear of the houses on Gordon Avenue. 'Or you can go that way and get back onto a main road.'

Fagan surveyed the ground. 'There are fresh tyre marks on the ground. The terrain isn't too rough. Which means you could get a standard vehicle up here. We're going to need CSIs all across this area.'

'It's a large area to cover, boss,' Watkins remarked, looking out across the landscape.

'First things first. We need to track down Ellie's errant mother. We'll make sure the father is informed by a Family Liaison Officer when he returns from Ibiza.'

'According to the brief conversation I had with the neighbour, the father wasn't exactly the doting dad. He used to see her a couple of times a year. Drop in the odd Christmas present. But mostly kept away.'

'I'm guessing the two boys weren't his,' Fagan said.

'No. The boys' dad is called Alex Philips. Lives in Blackwood. He has regular contact with the boys. Has them every other weekend.'

'Let's go and have a chat with the neighbour,' Fagan said.

CHAPTER 2

Fagan and Watkins walked into the kitchen of a house across the road. A female uniform had been keeping the neighbour company. Helping her deal with the shock of discovering Ellie's body.

Tammy Morris took a long drag from her rolled up cigarette. Her hand shook violently.

'I know this must be traumatic for you, Tammy,' Fagan said attentively. 'We'd appreciate it if you could go through the events this morning, leading up to the discovery of Ellie's body. You've told our officers you heard the smoke alarm going off in the house over the road.'

'I was the only bloody one who took any notice of the smoke alarm,' Morris grumbled. 'No one gives a shit around here anymore.'

'How long have you lived in the street?'

'About five years.'

'How long has Ellie lived here?'

'She's been here all her life.' Morris paused, taking another drag from her cigarette. She glanced out of the window. 'Jesus Christ, I never thought something like this could happen around here.'

'Take your time,' Fagan coaxed.

'I was having a fag out the front this morning. Three people walked by with their dogs. They all heard the smoke alarm, but not one of them took any notice of the bloody thing.'

Fagan sensed resentment in Morris' voice.

'So you had a spare key?'

She nodded. 'Sophie gave me a spare key to feed the cats while she was away.'

'Did she spend a lot of time away?'

Morris suddenly realised she'd said something that might land Sophie in the shit.

'Tammy, it's important you tell us everything,' Watkins said.

'She wasn't a negligent mother,' Morris said in a defensive tone. 'She tried her best to look after those kids.'

'By the looks of the place, Tammy, she didn't do a very good job of it. It's a bit of a mess in there, isn't it?' Fagan said.

'I know how it looks, but Sophie isn't a bad person. She's got a lot of shit going on in her life at the moment. We were going to have someone round next week to clean up the house. She didn't mean to get the house in that state.'

'Does she have a job?'

'No, she had been working part time at the local Londis. But she had to give that up when she became pregnant with the twins. That's when things went downhill. Sophie used to keep that house spotless. She hasn't always been like that. But when she had the twins, the problems started.'

'Problems?'

'With her ex, the father of the boys.'

Watkins checked his notes. 'Would that be Alex Philips?'

Morris nodded.

'What kind of problems was Sophie having with the boys' father?'

'He was applying for a custody order. Or rather that bitch of a mam of his was. Manipulative cow. Made out that she would be able to help her son look after her grandkids. Sophie didn't want to let those boys go. They meant the world to her.'

'And her daughter,' Fagan mentioned.

'What?'

'Her daughter also meant the world to her?'

'Of course.'

'When was the last time you were in contact with Ellie's mam?'

'Last night, she sent me a few messages.'

'She was going down Cardiff, wasn't she?'

Morris nodded.

Fagan grimaced. 'A celebration, friend's birthday, hen party?'

'She went out on the piss with a group of girls from the street. You know, a blowout to relieve stress and all that.'

'Who was looking after the children?'

'Ellie was in the house. I offered to look in on them throughout the evening. You know, make sure the boys went to bed on time.'

'What time did you look in on them?'

'I knocked on the door about eight o'clock. The boys were in bed and Ellie was downstairs watching Netflix. There wasn't any reason to stay. Ellie was a responsible girl.'

Fagan noticed two empty bottles of wine on the worktop. 'Were you drinking last night, Tammy?'

'Yeah, I thought I'd treat myself to a couple of bottles of wine. There's no law against it. I wanted to go to Cardiff with the girls, but I couldn't bloody afford it.'

'What time did you go to bed?'

'I fell asleep on the sofa watching the Kardashians. I woke up about six o'clock.'

'Do you have any children?'

'I have a son. Why?'

'It's just routine questioning Tammy,' Fagan assured her. 'To establish how many people live in close proximity. How old is your son?'

'He's thirty-two.' Caution was evident in Morris' tone.

'Where was he last night?'

'I hope you're not suggesting he had anything to do with what happened to Ellie?' Morris raised her voice.

'No, I'm not. But we have to account for everyone's whereabouts last night. Everyone who lived on this street. I take it your son knew Ellie.'

Morris responded with a slow nod. 'My son was in Newport last night. He was out on the piss with his mates.'

'Is he home now?'

'No, he stayed with a mate in Newport.' Morris glanced at her phone. 'He just messaged me. He's on his way home.'

'What's your son's name?'

'Toby. He's a good kid. Wouldn't hurt a fly, let alone kill

anyone. Toby has learning difficulties. He's been diagnosed with ADHD and autism.'

'But you still let him go out,' Fagan said.

'He's not that bad. He can get about and all that.'

'Okay, let's go back to yesterday. Did you see Ellie's mam before she went out to Cardiff?.'

'Yeah, I was there yesterday afternoon, doing Sophie's makeup and hair. I earn a few extra quid now and then. I do hair and makeup. Everyone's earning a couple of extra quid these days. Especially because of the cost of living.'

'Including selling marijuana.' Fagan looked at an ashtray on the kitchen table. A spliff had been buried under a pile of dogends, but was still visible.

Morris' face flushed. 'I only smoke it occasionally. It helps with stress and my other mental health issues. Looking after a boy with ADHD and autism is really stressful.'

'We found a considerable number of used spliffs in Sophie's house. I take it she was a regular user?'

Morris sighed. 'Yeah, Sophie likes a spliff.'

'What kind of mood was she in yesterday when you were doing her makeup?'

'She was happy, excited to be going out.'

'Did she say what time she'd be home?'

'No, she said she'd be out all night.'

'Does she have any friends in Cardiff?'

'No. Sophie usually stays in the Big Sleep when she goes to Cardiff. It's a cheap hotel near the centre.'

'How often does Sophie go out for the evening?' Watkins asked.

'Not all that often. All of us girls have a blowout every now and then. It helps with the stress of living in this area.'

'Get many problems around here, do you?' Fagan questioned.

'The usual. Kids playing up. Families fighting. No more than you'd get on other housing estates in the Valleys.'

'When you went round to check on Ellie last night, how did she seem?'

'She was okay. Was more than content to watch Netflix and

look after her brothers for the night.'

'What was she watching on Netflix?'

'*Stranger Things*. She loves that show. She's watched it loads of times. I sat with her for about twenty minutes, watching it with her. Then I went back home.'

'While you were there, did you sense there was anything wrong?'

Morris shook her head. 'No, she was messaging friends on social media and watching *Stranger Things*. Before I went, I asked her if she needed anything. She no, and that she was fine.'

'She wasn't upset about anything in particular?' Watkins said.

'No, Ellie was her usual self.'

'What was Ellie like as a person?' Fagan asked.

'Your typical teenager I suppose. Liked her music and YouTube, loved going on TikTok, Snapchat, Instagram and CTC.'

'CTC?'

'Cymru Teen Chat. It's an app for Welsh teenagers. It's got very popular with the kids around here. Ellie was on it last night. She showed me a couple of funny videos.'

'Was she talking to any of her friends on there?'

'Yeah, Ellie was talking to all her friends.'

'Did you know many of Ellie's friends?'

'I know a few of them. They were all on CTC last night chatting with each other.'

'Were you aware Ellie was vaping?' Fagan asked, to gauge Morris' reaction. 'It also appears Ellie was taking the pill.'

'They were to help her with the time of the month.' Morris cut Fagan off. 'She was having heavy periods. So Sophie took her to the doctor, and he prescribed her the pill.' She hesitated. 'As for the vapes, a lot of the teenagers are vaping on the estate.'

'Were you also aware Ellie was taking ecstasy?'

Morris looked shocked. 'No way. Ellie wouldn't dare go near that shit. Yeah, she was wayward. But she'd never touch drugs.'

'Wayward?'

Morris shrugged. 'You know what kids are like these days. They get into all kinds of trouble. Ellie was no different from any other teenager around the estate.'

‘We found a quantity of ecstasy tablets by Ellie’s bed,’ Fagan revealed.

Morris shook her head rigorously. ‘No, Ellie wasn’t like that. She was a decent girl. Unlike some of the other girls. She was streetwise. She knew the dangers of drugs.’

‘How do you mean?’

‘Some parents around here don’t give a fuck about their kids. They just let them do wherever they want.’

‘But not Ellie?’

‘No,’ Morris replied. ‘Yeah, she had typical teenage problems. But nothing to push her into taking drugs. Ellie bothered with the other girls on the street. They used to hang around down the local park. The girls knew drugs were being sold on the estate. But they stayed well clear of that shit.’

‘Any boys used to hang around the park?’

‘Yeah, I suppose. There’s not really much to do around here, other than hang around the park.’

‘Were you also aware Ellie was drinking alcohol last night?’ Watkins asked.

Morris inhaled, realising she wasn’t able to cover for Ellie’s mother anymore. ‘I know how it must look in that house.’

‘It doesn’t look good at all,’ Fagan interrupted. ‘We found vapes, ecstasy, discarded bottles of WKD, plus contraceptive pills in Ellie’s room. All this suggests, she was not only drinking, vaping and taking drugs but also sexually active. Not the life a fourteen-year-old girl should be leading.’

‘She’s not a bad girl. She wasn’t any kind of trouble.’

‘Tammy, listen to me. You saw the way she looked this morning when you discovered her body. The person who murdered her has to be caught as soon as possible. Now I get Sophie is your mate and all. But if you’re covering for her, then it could hamper our investigation.’

‘I’m not lying, honest,’ Morris insisted.

‘Okay, let’s back up. Talk us through everything that happened. When did you first see Sophie and her daughter yesterday?’

Morris thought about the question for a few moments. ‘Early

in the morning. I usually go round for a coffee and a fag.'

'Where was Ellie?'

'Having a shower. Then she came downstairs and had a piece of toast. She was going out with her mates. They usually go down to the park on a Saturday morning. Sit on the swings and just hang about.'

'Did you speak to her?'

'I said good morning.'

'Did she say anything back?'

'Not really. She seemed a bit pissed off. I think just before I arrived she'd had one of her arguments with her mam.'

'Did they argue a lot?'

'More than usual lately. Don't ask me why. I've asked Sophie, but she hasn't said anything.'

'Do you know the names of the girls she hung out with?'

'One of them was Gracie. She lives a few doors down. She knocked on the door to ask if Ellie was going out.'

'How old is Gracie?'

'Twelve, I think. Yeah, I'm pretty sure she's twelve.'

Fagan scribbled notes on his pad. 'Anyone else who might have been at the park?'

'Um, I think Mia and Charlotte were with Gracie when she knocked on the door.'

'How old are they?'

'Charlotte is thirteen and Mia is fifteen.'

'And that's the last time you saw Ellie until you knocked on the door last night?'

Morris nodded.

'How long did you spend with Sophie yesterday morning?'

'Only about twenty minutes. My mam rang to ask for a lift to Tesco in Pontypool.'

'What time did you go around Sophie's yesterday afternoon to do her hair and makeup?'

'About half-past two. Sophie was really hyped about going out. She even had a bitch at me for taking my time. Then I went to do another girl's makeup.'

'Where was Ellie at this time?'

'She was still out with her friends.'

'After you did the makeup for another girl, what did you do?'

'I went to visit a friend in Newbridge.'

'How long were you at your friend's house?'

'About three hours, maybe. I stopped in Sainsburys in Blackwood on the way home to get a couple of bottles of wine.' Morris glanced towards the counter top.

'What time did Sophie go out for the evening?'

'I think she went out about four.'

Fagan pointed at Morris' smartphone on the kitchen table. 'Did Sophie message you before she went out?'

Morris picked up her phone.

Fagan noted how much her hand was shaking.

'Um, yeah, she messaged me at ten past four.' Tammy handed her phone to Fagan.

Fagan read the message. *'Off out now, sweet bitch. Off to get smashed and shag someone. C u wen I c u xxx.'*

Fagan placed the phone back on the table. 'Was Ellie still out when Sophie went out for the evening?'

Morris failed to answer.

'Tammy, did Sophie leave the two boys at home on their own? You just said you were gone for three hours, which means you didn't get back home until after seven o'clock.'

'I dunno. I got home and opened a bottle of wine. Then I went to Sophie's house to check on Ellie.'

'This was around eight o'clock?'

'Yeah.'

'And Ellie was at home?'

'Yeah, I just said so, didn't I?'

'And she seemed her normal, usual self?'

'Yeah. She was happy, watching *Stranger Things*. I watched it with her for a short while before going home.'

'Was she drinking any alcohol? There were several empty bottles in the living room and in her bedroom.'

Morris nodded. 'Sophie went out early yesterday to get her some WKD from the local Londis. It's legal for a child of that age to drink in the house.' She picked up her phone and located the message before reading it to Fagan. *'Got the bitch Ellie some WKD. That should keep her quiet while I get laid, lol.'*

Fagan ran the message through his mind a few times. 'What kind of relationship did Sophie have with her daughter?'

Morris shrugged. 'You know, your typical mother and daughter relationship.'

'You just mentioned they'd been arguing more than usual lately.'

'Yeah.' Morris massaged her temples, yawning.

'Did Sophie often use that kind of language? Referring to Ellie as a bitch.'

'It's just the way Sophie is. She calls everyone bitch or clit.'

'Clit?' Fagan recoiled at the word.

'It's the way she is with everyone.'

'What about Ellie's father?'

'Don't get me started on that twat.' Morris seemed relieved Fagan had switched topics. 'A complete wanker to Sophie and Ellie.'

'Why is that?'

'For the first several years, they had a relationship. But then he started seeing someone else behind Sophie's back and got her up the poke.'

'Do you know the last time Ellie saw her father?'

'Christmas,' Morris answered. 'It only sticks out in my mind because all he could be bothered to do is stick his head around the door and dump twenty quid in the poor girl's hand. She was gutted. All Ellie ever wanted was a proper father.'

'Did you receive any other messages yesterday from Sophie?'

'She sent me this message last night.' Morris read the message. *'Just pulled this lush looking bloke. Going to give him the ride of his life later on, lol.'*

Fagan studied Morris for a few moments before snapping his notebook shut. 'As you can imagine Tammy, we won't want you going out anywhere for the moment. Until our officers are finished. This part of the street will be sealed off for the time being.'

'Okay, as soon as I hear from Sophie, I'll let you know.'

CHAPTER 3

'What do you reckon, boss?'

Fagan looked back at Morris' house, catching her drawing the curtains, talking to someone on her phone. 'A right bullshit fest. She knows way more than she's letting on. Ellie was obviously doing a lot of things most fourteen-year-old girls wouldn't be doing at that age.' Fagan glanced around the street. 'There's a shitload of dirty laundry coming our way, Sean. Housing estates like these are caked with secrets many of the residents prefer to keep secret.' Fagan looked at the house where Ellie was found.

'You okay, boss?'

'I can't help thinking about that tripod and light set up. I'm pretty sure our murderer filmed everything.' Fagan recalled a murder investigation from the early nineties. He shook off the thought. 'Perhaps it's a coincidence the tripod was in the corner of the room facing the bed.'

Stacey walked towards them with a woman. 'Guv, this is Pam. She's got something to tell you.'

Fagan flashed a smile. 'Take your time Pam, how can you help us with our enquiries?'

'I saw someone knocking on their door last night.' Pam pointed towards Ellie's house.

'Did you get a look at the face of this individual?'

'It was too dark to see his face.'

'His face?' Fagan remarked.

'It was definitely a boy. He was wearing a dark-coloured hoodie and dark tracksuit bottoms.'

'Do you think it could have been someone from the estate?' Watkins probed.

Carol nodded. 'Probably one of the boys from two streets down. The boys from that street are always sniffing around that house.'

'Popular are they?' Fagan asked. 'Sophie and her daughter.'

'You must be joking,' Pam scoffed. 'Those two are always causing trouble. I lost count of how many times I've seen them screaming at other people on the street.'

'Including you, by the sounds.'

Pam nodded. 'More than a few times. If they're not arguing with people who live on the street, they're screaming at each other. Let's just say little madam and her mam up the road there aren't all sweet and innocent. A couple of trollops, the pair of them.'

Fagan ignored Pam's criticism. 'Do you recall what time it was when you saw this person knocking on the door?'

'About eleven o'clock. I remember checking the time on my phone. I was just about to go to bed and looked out of my bedroom window. I saw this boy hurrying up the road.'

Fagan jotted down notes. 'And you say the boy could have been from another street?'

Pam nodded. 'I suggest you knock on Carol Osborne's door. Her boys are always causing trouble around here. Think they bloody own the place.'

'Where do they live?'

'Down on Lloyd Avenue.'

'Do you know which of her sons it could have been?'

'Either Simon or Gareth Osborne. They're about the same age as Fanny Adams up the road. She's always causing trouble, that one. Mouthing off to me and other people who live around here. The language she comes out with is disgusting. Her mam isn't much better. Dirty trollop. She was out on one of her benders last night. Probably pulled the first thing with two legs and shagged him. Those two young boys left on their own with a sister who wouldn't give a fuck if they were dead or alive. I've been meaning to phone Social Services on more than one occasion.'

'Why haven't you?' Fagan questioned.

'If I did that, my life wouldn't be worth living. I'd get all kinds of shit from people. Especially her up the road.'

'You mean Sophie Parry.'

Pam nodded. 'She doesn't deserve those poor boys. You only have to look at the state of their garden to know she's not fit to be a mother. The bloody local housing association is useless. I've complained about the state of their house loads of times, but they've done nothing.'

'You get a lot of trouble around here, do you, Pam?'

'All the bloody time from the kids on the estate. They're always fighting or slashing tyres. Gobbing off to people who just want to get on with their lives.'

'Oi, fuck face features!'

Fagan spotted Tammy Morris marching towards them.

Pam rolled her eyes. 'Here we bloody go. Here comes one of the rotten eggs on the street now.'

Morris pointed at Pam as she thundered towards her. 'I suggest you keep your fucking nose out of people's business and let this lot do their jobs.'

'Huh, talking about the pot calling the kettle black. You know everybody's business. Spreading it all over Facebook and Instagram.' Pam glanced at Fagan. 'I'd keep an eye on this one if I were you. Prone to talking through her arse. What have you been telling the police, Tammy? That Sophie is the perfect mother.'

'If you've said anything to land Sophie in the shit, then I kid you not. I'll put you six feet under.'

'Come and have a fucking go then, bitch,' Pam challenged.

'That's enough!' Fagan shouted. 'The both of you can step back and calm down. Or I'll have the pair of you arrested.'

'I'm the one who's calm,' Pam stated. 'It's that bitch there who's the one out of control.'

'I'm fucking warning you, Pam. If you throw Sophie under the bus, then I'll make your life a living hell.'

'And I'm warning you,' Fagan growled. 'If you don't go back inside, I'll arrest you for disturbing the peace.'

Morris glared back at Fagan before giving Pam the middle finger. She stomped back up the road, talking on her phone.

'The biggest gob on the street,' Pam sneered. 'She grasses everyone up to the Social just to get money. There was a couple who moved next to Sophie several years back. Tammy made their lives hell. Pretending to be their friend, then went behind their backs and made up a pack of lies about them. Told Social Services the dad used to force their daughter to sleep naked. And there was never any food in the cupboard to feed her. Then Sophie did a number on them. Scrounging money off them, using their Wi-Fi. Claiming she was hard up and couldn't afford it. In the summer, there'd be twenty of them outside drinking and smoking weed. In the end the couple got fed up and moved away. They complained to the housing association that they were being forced to move because of a nuisance neighbour, but the housing association did bugger all.'

Fagan glanced at the house next door. The front garden wasn't full of rubbish bags. The grass was over knee length and weeds lined the front wall.

Pam pointed at the house. 'They just moved another waste of time single parent in. She's no better. Her house is a total shithole. She's only eighteen and has two young boys already. One of them is four years old. The youngest is always walking around the street wearing nothing but filthy nappies. I caught him out about three weeks ago. It was bloody freezing. He was wearing a filthy nappy and a t-shirt.'

'Who's the father?'

'Someone who's old enough to be her father. Should be locked up.'

Fagan immediately thought of Benny Nelson and his wife, Mon.

'When I saw the young boy on the street, I immediately took him home to his mother. Useless cow didn't want to know. She was wasted on weed.'

'Do you know how old the father is?'

'He's got to be a good twenty years older. Scruffy looking bloke. Greasy hair and barely any teeth in his mouth. He was here yesterday, picking up the boys. She went out on the piss with Sophie and her crony pals.'

'How long have you lived here, Pam?'

'About twenty-five years. It used to be a decent place. I had two young children when I first moved in.'

'Where are they now?'

'My son is at Cardiff University and my daughter works in Asda in Newport. When I first moved in, there were decent families. But then Carol Osborne moved in two streets down. Next thing you know, the kids were too afraid to go out because her boys used to terrorise younger kids on the street. Then the local council handed this estate over to the housing association. That's when they moved in all the benefit scroungers. I've lost count of how many times I've complained.'

'What's the name of the housing association?'

'Merthyr Vale Housing Association.'

Fagan jotted down the name. 'Listen, Pam, I'm going to leave you with my colleague.' He glanced at Stacey. 'She'll take a full written statement off you. Come on, Sean, let's take a look at the local park.'

'A lot of love on this street, isn't there, boss?' Watkins said as they made their way towards the park.

'There certainly is.' Fagan looked around the street. People were walking towards the street where Ellie lived. A man walking his dog glanced at Fagan and Watkins as they walked by. 'I remember my early days with Merseyside Police. We'd patrol the rough areas of Liverpool. The Toxteth riots of 1981 were still fresh in everyone's mind. Residents hating the police. This place isn't much better. Secrets kept firmly behind closed doors. These people are about to find themselves in the media spotlight.'

After a few minutes they reached their destination. The park was relatively small, between the community centre and a primary school. Swings and a roundabout were key features, along with a slide, but nothing else.

Fagan spotted a man with a bucket and a litter picker wandering around the park.

'Oi mate, got a fag you can spare?' A youth of about fifteen years old asked.

'Don't smoke sorry, young man,' Fagan answered politely. 'And neither should you be.'

'Free fucking country, mate.'

'Not if you're under eighteen, it isn't.'

'Who the fuck are you?' The youth scowled.

Fagan pulled his ID from his inside pocket. 'Detective Inspector Fagan, this is Detective Sergeant Watkins.' Fagan recalled the names Pam had given him several minutes earlier. 'Are you Simon or Gareth?'

The youth displayed an expression of surprise and fear. 'Never mind, I'll ask our mam for a fag.' He scurried off.

The man, who was picking up the litter, looked at Fagan and Watkins as they approached. 'Morning gents,' he greeted.

Fagan looked at the bucket that contained several used syringes. 'Get a lot of that around here, do you?'

'A daily hazard, I'm afraid. I'm out here every morning picking up after the people who occupy this park at night. We had an incident last week. A seven-year-old girl fell and caught herself on a used needle.'

'She okay?' Fagan asked.

The man shrugged. 'No idea. She didn't live around here. Her parents were visiting friends who live locally and assumed this park was safe enough to let their daughter play.' The man looked Fagan up and down. 'I take it you're here because of what's going on up the top street?'

Fagan produced his ID.

The man removed his glove and offered his hand. 'Alun Stephens. I run the community centre.' Stephens looked towards a prefab building.

'Can you spare us some of your time?'

'Sure.' Stephens nodded.

Fagan sipped the coffee that Stephens had made him. 'Do you have any help cleaning up the park?'

'I used to, when we started around thirty years ago.' Stephens sighed. 'But then people stepped away. Got fed up with it. Said it was too much hassle. Couldn't park their cars outside because the kids would slash tyres, or break into them.'

'But you've kept going,' Fagan pointed out.

'I've always been determined not to let this place fall to the people that want to ruin it for the younger ones.'

'By the people, you mean the older kids that come in the park?'

Stephens nodded. 'When I first came here, I set up a youth club, so the kids wouldn't have to hang around the streets or the park. That was nearly twenty-five years ago. But over the years, fewer kids came in. Nowadays, if any child is spotted coming in here, they'll get bullied by the other kids.'

'Do the older kids that come in this park give you any grief?'

'All the time. They call me all kinds of names. Pervert, paedo, nonce, kiddie fiddler. None of them have any respect for the adults around here. Their parents don't take any notice if they give you abuse. I've known people who've complained to the parents of the kids, only to get abuse from the parents as well. It's a vicious circle.'

'Still, it's commendable how you've held out for so long.'

'Not much longer, I'm afraid.'

'Why is that?'

'The local council is cutting funding to this place. No one knows its future. And I'm getting too old to wander around picking up after people.' Stephens looked at the bucket of used needles. 'Especially this kind of shit. We have a special bin where addicts can just deposit their needles. But by the time they've shot up, they're too wasted to dispose of them properly.'

'I take it you're a local resident?'

'I am for the time being, but I've just sold my house.'

'People are buying around here?' Watkins asked.

Stephens shook his head. 'The local housing association is buying it off me. I wouldn't let it go for any less than the market value. I've lived here all my life, but now I don't want to stay.' Stephens looked out of the window, across the valley. 'This place has a lot of history. A massive viaduct used to cross this valley. They used to compare it to the Seven Wonders of the World. Even Hollywood has filmed around here.'

'Are you familiar with a local girl called Ellie Parry?' Fagan asked.

'Yeah.' Stephens nodded. 'Ellie used to come in when they ran a nursery here. Her mother would dump her at the nursery every morning. She owed the nursery hundreds of pounds. In the end the nursery refused to take Ellie. I remember one day, her mother, Sophie, got very nasty with the staff. Her daughter never stood a chance.'

'How do you mean?'

'No one starts off being bad when they're born, do they? I believe it's the moulding of the parents that turns children into what they are. Ellie was one of those unfortunate individuals. Sophie was bringing her boys to the nursery until a year or so ago. But there was an incident, so she was banned again.' Stephens took a swig from his mug. 'So, was it her you found this morning?'

'I'm afraid we're not at liberty to say anything at this moment.'

'You don't have to. It's all around the estate already. When something happens around here, it doesn't stay secret for very long. With all the vehicles and CSI you got swarming all over that house. It's obvious you've found a body.'

Fagan looked around the hall. 'We'd like to use this community centre as an incident room and conference centre, if that's possible.'

'Yeah sure. We've had two birthday parties cancel on us this week. This place used to be popular. Now a lot of parents take their kids to Kingdom Come in Abergavenny. We're losing money hand over fist.'

'We'll set a central information room up in Newport. They'll coordinate with the officers assigned to this incident room.'

'How long do you think it will take before you are finished?'

'As soon as we get a positive result.' Fagan finished his coffee and said his goodbyes. He stood out on the street watching life go by.

Watkins appeared by his side. 'What now, boss?'

'We grab Stacey and head back to Newport, and start our analysis. Message Andrew and get him to get the coffee brewing. I'll ask Griffiths to push the panic button and assign more bodies. He'll have no choice, given all the media attention this is about to attract.'

CHAPTER 4

Newport Central Police Station

Fagan gathered together as much information as he could before starting the briefing. Uniforms had collected more witness statements from residents who lived on the same street as Ellie. Fagan read through some of the statements, dismayed by how unpopular Ellie and her mother were.

Watkins had followed the usual drill and bought a load of confectionery from Greggs.

Fagan borrowed a spare whiteboard from the conference room next door. He stuck a large map of the Sofrydd housing estate to the whiteboard.

Watkins, Brooks, and Stacey sat patiently, waiting for him to begin.

'Right then, team. We have a very nasty murder on the Sofrydd estate. Fourteen-year-old Ellie Parry was found this morning at her house. Initial reports reveal she'd been strangled. However, while at the scene, the pathologist cast doubt on the cause of death. Myself and Sean will go to the Prince Charles Hospital in Merthyr this afternoon to get a detailed report.' Fagan paused, glancing at the whiteboard. 'This is going to be a messy one. We've already seen the state of the house where Ellie was found. From what we've heard so far, both Ellie and her mam weren't all that popular on the street. The woman that Stacey spoke with, Pam, didn't seem all that fond of Ellie or her mam. It's of no consequence what Ellie was like in life. Our number one priority at the moment is to catch the killer. There'll be a lot to go through with this. The Sofrydd is a closely knit community. There'll be an outpouring of emotion in the coming days. Which is why we need to nab the piece of shit who murdered Ellie as soon as possible. So let's examine our only lead at the moment.

According to our witness, Pamela Nash, she saw someone knocking on Ellie's door late last night, around eleven o'clock. I think it's safe to assume this individual was Ellie's killer. So, what are your thoughts about the murder?'

'Sexually motivated, sir?' Brooks put forward a suggestion.

'We won't know that until a detailed examination has been carried out. Residents on the estate have given up names of other kids who live on the same street as Ellie. We may learn something from them.'

'Which means there could be a long list of people to interview,' Watkins said.

'What we need to do is start with Ellie's inner circle. Tammy Morris is a close friend of the family. Tammy said Ellie was out with her mates yesterday. Her mam, Sophie Parry, was in Cardiff all evening. She didn't return home last night and was still out this morning. It's only a matter of time before she shows up. What makes this murder disturbing is that two young boys were found at the property along with Ellie's body.'

'Those poor kids,' Stacey said. 'They could have witnessed it all.'

'Agreed,' Fagan said. 'Social Services were up there this morning removing the children. Specialist officers will visit the two boys to find out if they witnessed the events of last night.' Fagan glanced at his notepad. 'The boys' names are Dillon and Ryan.' He pointed at the map of the area. 'Our killer entered the front door of the property. According to our witness, the individual she saw was wearing a dark hoodie and tracksuit bottoms. As for how long they were in the house before Ellie was murdered, that's unclear. I'm adamant the murderer exited through the back of the house, then walked back down the dirt track at the back of Gordon Avenue.' Fagan puffed through his cheeks. 'Once he joins back onto Farm Road, it's anyone's guess.'

'There's a lot of people who live in that area, boss,' Watkins pointed out.

Fagan nodded. 'It's going to be a lot of legwork knocking on those doors, but necessary. We'll also be examining Ellie's home life and lifestyle. From what Stacey, myself and Sean saw in her bedroom earlier, it's obvious Ellie was vaping and drinking alcohol and taking ecstasy. Although given the reaction of Tammy Morris this morning when we mentioned the drugs, this could be a new thing for Ellie. Contraceptive pills were also found in her bedroom. Suggesting Ellie was sexually active.' Fagan inhaled. 'Another element that makes this murder disturbing is that the killer may have filmed the whole thing. A tripod and light were set up in the corner of the room. A phone charger was present in the room. I believe her killer used Ellie's phone to capture the event, and then took the phone.'

'Pretty disturbed if our murderer filmed it.'

Fagan nodded. 'That's why it's important we nab this twat as soon as possible. We'll interview Ellie's closest friends to track her movements yesterday. We also need to find out if Ellie had a regular boyfriend. Detective Inspector Nathan Saddler is up at the Sofrydd estate now, setting up the incident room at the local community centre. I've just received a text from him telling me the media has just arrived. It's safe to say this will be all over the news in the next few hours. Social media will be lit up like a Christmas tree. What we need to do now is find out why our suspect murdered Ellie. Did she know something about him? Was this just a random killing? Or was it premeditated?'

'Given what I saw in that bedroom, guv, I've doubts about whether it could have been a sexually motivated murder,' Stacey said.

'Care to elaborate?'

'The sex could have been consensual. An altercation took place following sex, resulting in her murder.'

'An excellent theory, Stacey.' Fagan inhaled. 'We have to face the facts here. Ellie was a young girl who lived a lifestyle meant for a much older person. She was vaping, drinking alcohol and taking drugs. Tammy showed us the text Sophie Parry sent yesterday.' Fagan glanced at his notes. '*Got the bitch Ellie some WKD. That should keep her quiet while I get laid, lol.* What does that tell us about the relationship between Sophie and her daughter?'

'Sophie had an adult style relationship with Ellie,' Brooks

suggested.

Fagan nodded. 'It looks that way. And because Ellie was drinking, vaping and taking ecstasy, it's possible she was sexually active.'

'I wouldn't be surprised if her mam knew what she was up to,' Watkins threw his penny in.

'Tammy Morris claimed Ellie was on the pill because she was experiencing heavy periods. This also reveals that Tammy knew far more about Ellie's personal life.' Fagan looked at Stacey, who was nodding.

'Some doctors will prescribe young girls the pill if they are experiencing problems with their monthly cycles. But it's hard for young teenagers to be prescribed the pill in Wales, because of all the laws surrounding prescribed contraceptives.'

Watkins stared at his laptop. 'According to the NHS website, you have to visit a doctor in Wales to get prescribed any contraceptive. However, In England you can walk into a chemist and ask for the pill. But you still have to consult with a pharmacist.'

Fagan considered the information. 'Sophie Parry was supplying her daughter with contraceptive pills to ensure she wouldn't get pregnant. The legal age of consent is sixteen. If Ellie had become pregnant, it would have attracted the attention of Social Services.' Fagan glanced at Stacey. 'Did Social Services mention anything about the family already being on a watch list when they picked up the two boys this morning?'

Stacey shook her head. 'No, guv. The two female social workers who turned up this morning took one look at the place and got the boys out of there straight away. They barely spoke to me.'

'Sean, I want you to contact Blaenau Gwent Social Services later on and find out if the family is on the radar. I find it hard to believe that Social Services haven't had contact with them. Given the state of the house, someone must have made a complaint.' Fagan looked at the whiteboard. 'Let's examine the route the killer took after leaving the scene of the crime. According to Tammy Morris, the back door to the property was left open. Our suspect ran down this dirt track that leads onto Farm Road. Which means we're going to need uniform going over the ground at the back of the property. An iPhone charger was present in Ellie's bedroom, but no sign of the phone. If our killer knew Ellie, then he must have taken her iPhone to prevent identification. And considering there's evidence to suggest they filmed the event adds depth and urgency to this case. It's possible he also took other items from the house that could have identified him. We need a search team at the back of the house.'

'We'll need a large team to search the area, boss.'

'And we'll get it, Sean. Griffiths will not want this to drag on. We'll make a statement to the press at five o'clock.' Fagan paused. 'The lives of these people on the street are about to be put under the microscope. We'll need all kinds of community support officers in on this. What do you think the fallout is going to be regarding Ellie's murder?'

'Anger, hatred directed at us,' Stacey remarked.

'That was my thinking,' Fagan agreed. 'When something like this happens, there's always a blame game to play. If our suspect has a criminal background, then the press will ask if this murder could have been prevented. We also need to focus on the area in question. The housing estate has a primary school, social club, park and community centre.'

'According to the police database, forty-eight crimes have been reported in that area this year,' Brooks revealed. 'A mixture of burglaries and several assaults and other incidents. Last month, the police had to confiscate an air rifle from an eight-year-old boy. He had been shooting at passing cars from his bedroom window. His mam claimed he found the rifle at a spot notorious for fly tipping.' Brooks studied the list. 'Two cases of domestic battery have been reported. Both at the house of Carol Osborne.'

'Pam mentioned a family called Osborne this morning. The youth we encountered this morning was probably one of them.'

'Simon and Gareth Osborne. Simon is the eldest. He's the same age as Ellie.'

'A good bet he knew Ellie,' Fagan surmised.

'He was arrested last year for criminal damage. His brother

has been arrested several times for shoplifting. He's thirteen. There are two older brothers, Craig and Daniel Osborne. Both in their twenties and both have spent a term in clink. Craig Osborne was jailed for assault and received eighteen-months in Bridgend. Dan Osborne served a four-year sentence for intent to supply.'

Fagan scratched his head. 'One strategy we'll have to consider here is a voluntary DNA test.'

'On the Sofrydd Estate,' Brooks sounded doubtful. 'Good luck with that. I grew up on the Gurnos. I know exactly what kind of response you'll get when you put the call out for voluntary DNA testing.'

'It's that or round up every male of a certain age on the Sofrydd estate,' Fagan said. 'If we hold a press conference at five o'clock this afternoon and invite as many media sources as we can, it will put pressure on the local community to come forward and help. I think the local residents will want this murder solved as soon as possible. There's many people with problems of their own who won't want to be put under the microscope. The sooner the murderer is caught, the sooner people can get on with their lives. Our top priority is to track Ellie's movements yesterday. According to Tammy, Ellie was there when she popped around for a coffee, around nine thirty. Tammy said good morning but Ellie didn't respond.'

'Tammy reckoned Ellie and her mam may have had an argument prior to her visit,' Watkins said.

Fagan nodded. 'Morris also claimed that Sophie and Ellie were arguing more than usual lately. Something to question Sophie Parry about when she appears. Getting back to yesterday morning. Ellie had a piece of toast. A friend then knocked on the door.' Fagan glanced at his notepad. 'Someone called Gracie. Tammy said she was twelve years old. Two other girls were with Gracie. Their names are Charlotte, thirteen and Mia, fifteen. These three girls are our key witnesses. They were with Ellie yesterday. We'll interview them as soon as we set things up at the community centre. Tammy said she called at Ellie's house last night around eight o'clock. Which means prior to Ellie's murder, these girls are the last people to have seen her alive. At the moment we don't have access to any phone data to give us any kind of picture of events yesterday. We need access to Sophie Parry's phone. To see if she was in contact with her daughter last night.'

Watkins fished his buzzing phone out of his pocket. 'Talk of the devil, boss. Sophie Parry has just arrived at the house.'

Fagan glanced at his watch. 'She took her time. Stacey, get up to the Sofrydd and escort Sophie Parry to Prince Charles Hospital. We need an official identification on the body. Then bring her straight here. Me and you will interview her together. Make sure she knows she's not a suspect. Sean, get on to Blaenau Gwent Social Services. I want to know if the family was on any kind of watch list. Andrew, go with Stacey up to the Sofrydd and give DI Saddler a hand setting up the incident room. As of now, the four of us are the lead team in this investigation. There'll be a ton of people on this by the end of the day, so we need to get our arses into gear.'

CHAPTER 5

Newport Central Police Station

'You okay, guv?' Stacey asked.

'Yeah, I'm fine. Why d'you ask?'

'You haven't mentioned anything about Rebecca's murder trial.'

'It's over a week away, still. I'd put it in the back of my mind,' Fagan remarked.

'Sorry, Guv. Me and Ricky were talking about it last night.'

'I mentioned it to Ricky last week when we had a pint in the King's Head. He avoided the subject.'

'That's just Ricky. It's going to be hard on him. But he knows you'll be there for him.'

Fagan managed a quick smile. 'I don't know why. But when I turned up at that house this morning and saw Ellie, it brought everything back. Ellie looked a lot like Rebecca when she was that age.' Fagan recalled his younger days. 'When we were young, we didn't have the same issues youngsters are plagued with today. There was no internet or social media. It seems the more access the younger generation has to the internet, the more damage it causes.'

Stacey agreed with a nod.

'I don't know why I have to testify. Tim Davis murdered her. It's an open and shut case.'

'That's what we were saying last night. Benny Nelson is also testifying. Ricky is fuming about that.'

Fagan released a snort of derision. 'No doubt Nelson will capitalise on the moment. Like he did with that book of his.' Fagan refocused on the task at hand. 'How did Sophie Parry react when she saw her daughter?'

'Not as upset as I thought she'd be. She even wanted to get

out of there as quickly as possible.'

'What's your thoughts on her?'

'Someone who's keeping a lot of secrets. I asked her to hand over her phone when I arrived at the property. She claims she lost it last night in Cardiff. Apparently it was stolen while she was in a pub.'

'That's convenient for her. And suspicious at the same time.'

'She gave me the impression she may know something about what went on last night.'

'It's too early to jump to any conclusions yet. Hopefully interviewing her will reveal more about Ellie's lifestyle. She was a fourteen-year-old girl with habits of someone a decade older. Sophie Parry will be under the spotlight of Social Services. Especially since she may have left two young children at home on their own to go out on the piss.'

'I can't see Social Services letting her having those boys back.'

'Not with the state the house is in.'

Stacey's phone buzzed. 'The duty solicitor has briefed Sophie Parry. They're ready for us.'

Fagan peeled himself from his chair. 'Come on, let's get our game faces on.'

Sophie Parry chewed on her fingernail. She glanced at Fagan and Stacey as they entered the room.

'How you doing Sophie?' Fagan asked, sitting down opposite.

Parry shrugged. 'I'm a fucking mess. What were you expecting, me to be all smiles?'

Fagan studied her mannerism for a few moments. 'My name is Detective Inspector Marc Fagan. I'm the leading detective on this investigation. You've already met my colleague, Police Constable Stacey Flynn. On behalf of Gwent Police, I'd like to say how sorry we are for your loss. This must be very traumatic for you. So we'll try not to take up more of your time than is absolutely necessary.'

'What's she doing here?' Sophie pointed at the duty solicitor, who sat silently scribbling notes.

Fagan took a moment to answer Parry's question. 'You've

been assigned a duty solicitor because we feel you may need support during this time.'

'As long as I'm not being accused of murdering my daughter?'

Fagan leant back, folding his arms. 'We're not accusing you of anything, Sophie. The duty solicitor is here to advise you on legal matters. If you'd like, we can ask her to leave.'

The duty solicitor threw Fagan a glance, suggesting she wanted that to happen.

Parry took a deep breath. 'No, it's fine. I haven't done anything wrong.'

Fagan nodded, focusing on the file he'd bought with him. 'Constable Flynn has explained the circumstances in which Ellie was discovered.'

Parry nodded.

'Initial reports suggest Ellie may have been strangled. But a full autopsy needs to be carried out to determine the cause of death.'

Parry flinched at the graphic description Fagan had just delivered.

'What we need to do, Sophie, is to establish what happened to Ellie in her final hours. We need you to talk us through us the events of yesterday.'

'I've no bloody idea what happened to her last night. I was in Cardiff, for fuck's sake.' Parry quickly became agitated.

'Sophie, we are not your enemy,' Stacey said calmly. 'This interview is to establish Ellie's movements yesterday. Your friend Tammy has already said Ellie was in the house yesterday morning.'

Parry scratched her nose.

'What time did Ellie get up?'

'I dunno, nine o'clock maybe. I heard her in the shower. Tammy popped around. We had a fag, coffee and a chinwag.'

'What were you chinwagging about?'

'Stuff, you know. The latest gossip on the street and all that. Tammy told me how she was going to do my hair and makeup.'

Fagan looked down at his notes. 'According to Tammy, Ellie came down and had a piece of toast.'

Parry nodded. 'Yeah, I remember now.'

'Did she say anything to you? Did you have a conversation about anything in particular?'

Parry massaged her forehead. 'I think she had a bitch at me because I was going to Cardiff last night.'

'Didn't she want you to go?'

'More like she wanted to go with me and the girls.'

'Did she mention she wanted to go with you?'

'Not really, but she was pissed off I was going out.'

'Is this because she had to stay at home with her two younger brothers?'

'Probably, but it's not like she hasn't babysat before. She's done it loads of times.'

'Tammy said that friends of Ellie's called to see if she was going out yesterday morning.'

'Yeah, I think it was Charlotte, Gracie and Mia.' Parry nodded. 'Yeah, it was definitely those three. They were her best friends.'

'Did Ellie come home for lunch?' Stacey asked.

Parry shook her head. 'No, I didn't see her for the rest of the day?'

'Did Ellie have any money on her for lunch?' Fagan asked.

Parry thought about the question for a few moments. 'I think she had money on her Go Henry card. I put thirty quid on it the other day.'

'Did you have any contact with Ellie throughout the day?'

'I might have, I don't know.' Parry seemed frustrated with the question.

'So you weren't sure if you had contact with your daughter throughout the day? And you're unsure if she had money or not to get lunch. You were going out last night, and you just said Ellie was babysitting. So you must have messaged her before you went out to tell her to come home.'

'Look, my head is in the shed at the moment. I've just seen my daughter lying dead at the hospital. Now you're expecting me to remember everything that happened yesterday. For fuck's sake.'

'Ok, and that's understandable, Sophie. I can't emphasise

enough how sorry we are for your loss. But you have to understand, we need to catch the person responsible for Ellie's murder as quickly as possible. This is already gathering pace on the local news. It's spreading through social media. It will get far worse before things settle down. You are about to be put under the spotlight. We need you to talk us through the events of yesterday. So we have a clear picture of Ellie's movements. Memories are fresh in the mind in the first twenty-four hours. Which is why we need to talk about this now.'

'Okay, okay,' Parry interrupted Fagan. 'She had a shower. She came downstairs. Had breakfast, then went out with her mates. That's the last time I saw her.'

'What time did Tammy arrive to do your hair and makeup?' Stacey asked.

'About half two, maybe.'

'How long did she take?'

'A good hour, I would say. She was taking her time. I had a bitch at her and told her to get a move on.'

'What time were you planning to go out?'

'We were meeting up at four o'clock.'

'Where?'

'At a mate's house.'

'How did you get to Cardiff?' Fagan asked.

'My mate's husband gave us a lift in his minivan.'

'Your mate?'

'Stella, she lives three doors down from me. That's where we were meeting up.'

'How many of you went out for the evening?'

'There were six of us. Me, Stella, Lucinda, Tracy, Abbey and Natalie.'

Fagan jotted down the names. 'Do they live on the same street?'

'More or less. Abbey lives a street down from us. Natalie lives next door to me.'

'Okay, so you were off out about four o'clock. But you maintain Ellie didn't contact you after she went out early in the morning.'

'No, she didn't.'

'Did you make any attempts to contact Ellie?'

'What do you mean, did I make any attempts to contact Ellie? I just told you. Ellie didn't contact me all day.'

'But you must have attempted to get in touch with Ellie. After all, she was looking after the boys for the night, wasn't she? Surely you must have rung Ellie to see if your boys were okay.'

Parry failed to come up with an answer.

'Sophie, did you try to contact Ellie about her coming home before you went out?'

'I might have. Look, I'm hung over. I've just had to identify my daughter's body. Can't this wait?'

'If you want to catch the person who murdered Ellie, then no,' Fagan stated.

Parry ran her hand through her hair. 'I think I messaged Ellie about three o'clock. I told her she had to be home by four to look after the boys.'

'But you didn't wait for her to come home?' Stacey said.

'I called back at the house before I went out.'

'Was she home?'

'I don't know?'

'So you didn't check?'

'The girls were telling me to get a move on. I didn't have time to search the house from top to bottom to see if she was home. I assumed she was in her bedroom.'

'But you didn't check to find out?'

'No, I didn't, okay? Is that the answer you wanted?'

'What we want to know, Sophie, is if your two sons were alone when you went out. Your boys were celebrating their fifth birthday today, weren't they?'

Parry leant back in her chair, glaring at Stacey. 'I know where you're going with this, bitch.'

'And where is that exactly, Sophie?' Stacey sensed her emotions building.

'You're about to make up a load of bullshit about how I'm a bastard of a mother.' Parry leant forward. 'Let me tell you, there are parents on that estate that let their kids do whatever they fucking like.'

Stacey couldn't help herself. 'And you claim to be a decent mother, do you?'

'Do you have kids?'

Stacey took her time answering. 'No, I don't.'

'Then you know fuck all about being a mother. I do everything for those boys.'

'And Ellie,' Fagan added.

Parry glared at him. 'What?'

'Ellie, your daughter. You do everything for those boys, and Ellie.'

'Of course I fucking do.'

'Thing is Sophie, when the police turned up at your house this morning, they had to use facemasks because of the stench.'

'Look, I know the place was a bit of a mess.'

'A bit of a mess!' Fagan expressed astonishment at Parry's candidness. 'Sophie, your house is a total shithole.'

'Careful with your tone, Inspector Fagan,' the duty solicitor warned.

'Ok, let me rephrase. The cats have fouled everywhere in your house. And there are rats scurrying about in your garden. Your garden is also full of rubbish bags.'

'Inspector Fagan, you are here regarding Miss Parry's daughter. Not to cross-examine her on her housekeeping skills.'

Fagan nodded. 'When you got to Cardiff last night, where did you go first?'

'Stella's old man dropped us off in the centre. We had a couple of drinks in The Cottage, then we went to The Prince of Wales.'

'Did you stay there all night?'

'More or less, yeah.'

'More or less?' Fagan pursued.

Parry inhaled. 'There was live music and everything. I met this bloke and went for a few drinks.'

'Where?'

'A place called The Glassworks.'

'What time did you rejoin your friends?'

Parry seemed uncomfortable with the question.

'Sophie, what time did you rejoin your friends at The Prince of Wales?'

'I didn't, okay.' She scratched the back of her head.

'So you spent the night with this man you met in The Prince of Wales?'

'Yeah,' Parry admitted.

'Inspector Fagan, I think we need to end the interview,' the duty solicitor advised. 'It's clear that Miss Parry is too distraught to answer any more questions.'

'Too bloody right I am,' Parry complained.

Fagan hesitated before nodding. 'Fair enough. You can go, Sophie.'

Parry literally jumped to her feet.

'One more thing before you go, Sophie. How did you get back from Cardiff this morning?'

'I caught a train to Hengoed then got an Uber home.'

'What time did the train leave Cardiff?'

Parry shrugged. 'About twenty to seven.'

Fagan smiled. 'Thank you Sophie, you can go.'

Parry fled the interview room.

The duty solicitor calmly packed away her notes before standing and making a passing remark. 'Good luck getting any truth out of that one, Inspector Fagan.'

Fagan puffed out his cheeks, clasping his hands behind his head. 'That woman couldn't be more full of shit if she tried.'

'Every line was a lie, guv.'

Fagan nodded. 'When you picked her up this morning, did she go into detail about her losing her phone?'

'She mentioned it was stolen when she was in The Prince of Wales. How come you didn't mention her phone during the interview?'

'I had a feeling she was lying the moment she opened her mouth.' Fagan's phone vibrated. 'The pathologist wants to see us. Do us a favour. Find out the train times from Cardiff to Hengoed this morning. Then get hold of Cardiff central and ask for access to CCTV.'

'What are you looking for, guv?'

'It might be nothing, but I want to see how much she's lying to us. Check the time that Sophie claims to have caught the train from Cardiff to Hengoed. I want to know why she took three hours to come home. Me and Sean will head up to Merthyr to see the pathologist.'

Stacey stood, steadying herself on the table.

'You okay?'

Stacey managed a smile. 'Yeah, just got up too fast, that's all, guv.'

'After we've done with the pathologist, we'll head back to the Sofrydd. I'm hoping to talk with one of the girls Ellie was with yesterday afternoon.' Fagan gathered his notes and stood. 'Then we'll regroup and have another roundup.'

CHAPTER 6

'What did Social Services have to say about Sophie Parry?' Fagan asked as they drove to Merthyr Tydfil.

'I spoke to someone call Martin Daniels,' Watkins said. 'He's the social worker who was assigned to Ellie.'

'So the family was on the Social Services' radar.'

'It looks that way, and get this, boss. Daniels claimed he visited Sophie Parry and her daughter last week. When I asked him if he noticed anything unusual during his visit, he said no, everything was fine. As a matter of fact, he seemed quite chatty when it came to the family. He said on his last visit he talked about winding down contact with the family.'

Fagan grinned. 'And he didn't say he noticed anything unusual. Which means he's lying. He should have at least mentioned the state the house was in. I'm sure the social workers that turned up this morning to take the two young boys away will have something to say about the state of the house. Question is, why is Daniels lying?'

'I'm going to see him and the head of Blaenau Gwent Social Services tomorrow morning.'

'That should be interesting,' Fagan remarked.

'We've also had another sighting of our murder suspect. A taxi driver said he spotted someone running along the Sofrydd road towards Hafodyrynys around one in the morning.'

'Did the taxi driver give any kind of description?'

'No.'

'Hafodyrynys,' Fagan mused. 'Which puts our suspect at the scene between eleven and one o'clock. What are your thoughts about that, Sean?'

'Our killer may have not been from the area.'

'Exactly, which means we could have to widen our search.'

'Let's not consider that option until we have all the facts, boss. Our killer could have panicked after he murdered Ellie and wanted to get as much distance between him and the victim as possible. There's a search team going over the ground at the back of the house. Our suspect could have tossed Ellie's phone near the back of the property.'

'Or they could have kept the phone.' Fagan remembered the tripod set up from Ellie's room. 'If they filmed the murder, they've kept the phone to watch the video again.'

'Some kind of sick trophy to relive his crime,' Watkins stated.

'Yeah,' Fagan sighed.

Watkins noted Fagan's expression. 'What's your thinking, boss?'

'The only kind of murderer who takes trophies from their victims is a serial killer.'

'Let's not get ahead of ourself, boss.'

'Agreed,' Fagan nodded. 'Did you have time to watch the interview with Sophie Parry?'

'Yeah.'

'What do you reckon about her mother?'

'She's definitely hiding something. She claims to have lost her phone last night while in Cardiff, which I think is a complete pack of lies.'

'Do you think she might know who our murderer is?'

'It's possible, but it was wasn't clear in the interview.'

'Sophie didn't come home last night,' Fagan mused. 'She spent the night with a random stranger she met in a pub. Which says a lot about her character.' Fagan considered the case. 'Ellie was drinking, vaping, taking ecstasy, and sexually active. And God knows how old she was when she started all that. I suspect her mother has given her too much of a free rein. I want all electronic items removed from the house and sent to the Cybercrimes unit.'

'Already been done, boss. There were a couple of tablets in the boys' bedroom.'

'Which means Sophie Parry used the internet as a babysitter. Too many parents do that these days. When you interview Daniels tomorrow, take Stacey along with you.'

'No problem, boss.?'

Fagan pulled his buzzing phone out of his pocket. 'They've found a disused WKD bottle at the back of the property. It's possible he could have taken a bottle from the house.'

'Our murderer has balls, I'll say that,' Watkins stated. 'Had the nerve to take alcohol from the house after murdering Ellie.'

'With any luck, we'll be able to lift fingerprints.' Fagan thumbed the keyboard on the screen. 'We also need access to Tammy Morris' phone. I'll organise another search warrant for a phone. I reckon she's hiding a few secrets about the family. I'll text Andrew, he's still up the Sofrydd.'

'You think she may know more about what happened to Ellie?'

'At this moment, we can't be sure of anything. But given what we already know about the family, I think there's a fair amount of bullshit being spread about. The next step is to examine Ellie's lifestyle more closely. Lift the lid on family life.'

'Do you think that's necessary, boss?'

Fagan nodded. 'You have to wonder what led to her murder. Every time I think about it, I see her mother and other people being a big part of this.'

'How do you mean, boss?'

'How much do you think Sophie Parry was aware of what Ellie was up to? Regarding her drinking, vaping and being sexually active. Think about it. You saw the state of the house this morning. Ellie wasn't exactly going out of her way to keep secrets. It was all laid out bare for everyone to see in her bedroom. The WKD bottles, the vapes, the drugs, and the contraceptive pill packets.'

'You didn't mention any of this in the interview?'

'No, because the moment Parry opened her mouth, I had a feeling she wasn't being truthful. Sophie Parry knew everything that girl was up to.' Fagan paused. 'And probably encouraged it. Then you have the text messages that Parry sent Tammy Morris. She bought the WKD to keep Ellie quiet. Both Parry and Morris even said that Ellie was annoyed that she went out last night. This suggests that Ellie might have gone out with her mam in the past.

Ellie put makeup on last night. She looked older than her actual age. If her mam encouraged all this, then she helped shape Ellie's lifestyle, which ultimately led to the murder of her daughter.'

'What do you reckon happened last night?'

'Ellie was pissed off at her mother for going out. She was stuck at home with her two young brothers. So to entertain herself, she invited the murderer over.'

'What went wrong?'

'That's the mystery here, isn't it? If we had Ellie's phone, it would give us a clearer picture. Her mam claims to have lost her phone last night while in The Prince of Wales in Cardiff. I think that's a total fabrication.'

'I take it you have a theory?'

Fagan nodded. 'Imagine this. Parry and her daughter were in contact with each other last night. Ellie was moaning about her mother going out and not taking her. Parry picks up some random stranger in the pub and boasts to her daughter. Ellie then calls her murderer to come over. Something went drastically wrong.'

'Why do you think she is lying about her phone?'

'I think when Tammy turned up at that house this morning and discovered Ellie's body, the first thing she did was ring Parry. Given the state the house was in there was no time to have a quick clean.'

'She probably phoned Parry to tell her to come home straight away, before phoning the police,' Watkins guessed.

Fagan nodded. 'Tammy waited to get her story straight before phoning the police.'

'That's why you want her mobile phone.'

'Yes. She obviously has knowledge about Ellie's personal life. If she was close to Ellie's mam, then it stands to reason they knew each other darkest secrets. When we mentioned the contraceptive pills found in her bedroom, she mentioned they helped Ellie control her periods.'

'So, she knew a lot about Ellie's personal life.'

Fagan gave a brief nod. 'I reckon she lied about the time she discovered Ellie's body.'

'How did you reach that conclusion?'

'The man who ran the community centre said that it had been all over social media. I know it's a leap but the other resident we spoke to said that Tammy was a bit of a gossip. Spreading street gossip around on social media.'

'Do you reckon she put it up on social media that she found Ellie's body?'

'It's an avenue we're going to have to explore.' Fagan recalled an old murder case. 'Sophie Parry and her daughter remind me of a mother and daughter I investigated while with Merseyside Police. About four years ago, I was assigned to a murder in Southport. The daughter was in her early twenties. The mother was in her mid-forties. They picked up these two blokes and took them home for the night. The mother and daughter are in separate bedrooms. The daughter is having sex with one bloke, the mother is with the other man. They decide to swap over, and that's when all hell kicked off. The man who went with the mother strangled her. The daughter heard her cries for help. But when she tried to get to her mother, the man she was with attacked her. She was able to escape and call the police, who were there in minutes. The two men were caught, but it was too late for the mother.'

'Jesus,' Watkins gasped.

'To cut a long story short, when the daughter was interviewed, she revealed a sordid lifestyle to the police. She would go out regularly with her mother and pick up men from the local bars in Southport. She also confessed that she'd been doing it since she was thirteen, and that her mother encouraged her to be sexually active from a young age. She also painted a dark picture of her mother. Controlling, not wanting her to have a boyfriend or a life of her own. The way she described their relationship was more love rivals than mother and daughter.'

'Where was the daughter's father?'

'There was no father. The mother went out, bought this bloke home, had sex with him and got pregnant. I sat in on some of the interviews with the daughter. I felt sorry for her. The mother had raised her and exposed her to adult material from a young age. Then just touted her out. She even said that when she had sex for the first time, it was with a man in his forties. She remembered his name because they met several times. We tracked him down and he was charged with rape. Still doing time for it. The two men charged with the mother's murder turned out to be Albanian nationals who had got into the country with fake passports. They'd been on the run for three years from the Albanian authorities after being connected with the murder of six women.'

'One hell of a story, boss.'

'And I've plenty more, Sean. My point is, this reminds me of the two women in Southport. Ellie was living a life that wasn't meant for someone her age. And she ended up paying for it with her life. That's why I asked Stacey to get hold of Cardiff Central Station to check for CCTV. When I asked Parry how she got home this morning, she said she caught the train from Cardiff before ordering an Uber.'

'So how did she call an Uber if she had her phone stolen last night?' Watkins questioned.

'That's the sixty-four thousand dollar question.' Fagan flicked the indicator and turned off the road into the hospital car park.

Prince Charles Hospital Merthyr Tydfil

Fagan and Watkins dressed in appropriate PPE and entered the examination room. Fagan dreaded this moment. A similar feeling to entering Ellie's bedroom, where she was found dead earlier that morning.

'Morning, gents,' the pathologist greeted, in a manner that didn't fit the scene. She picked up a clipboard with notes scribbled on an A4 piece of paper.

A sheet had been placed over Ellie's body.

The pathologist walked up to the table, grabbed the sheet and yanked it away.

The shock of seeing Ellie on the table raced through Fagan like an electric current. In his mind's eye Fagan was stood in Bailey Park staring down at the body of Rebecca.

'Boss,' Watkins said loudly, clicking his fingers in front of Fagan.

Fagan snapped out of his trance. 'Yeah, I'm fine.' He looked at the pathologist. 'What have you got?'

'Not a lot at this moment.' The pathologist pointed at the marks on Ellie's neck. 'Our murderer had their hands around the girl's throat. However, the strangulation marks aren't severe enough to have caused her death.'

Fagan nodded. 'What about signs of rape?'

'Nothing yet. Extensive examination has revealed she was sexually active. All the signs of rape such as tearing and bruising are not present. The victim had sex last night, and it was consensual. The murderer's DNA is all over her. Another thing I am certain of is that the victim had sex with more than one individual over the past twenty-four hours.'

'What?' Fagan gasped.

The pathologist nodded.

'How many people exactly?'

'Won't know that until we get DNA samples back.'

'How long before you can get a match?'

'If I fast track it, within twenty-four hours.'

Fagan nodded. 'Do it.' He paused for thought. 'So Ellie invites her killer into her house. They have sex before she is murdered. A taxi driver reports seeing someone in the area about one o'clock. Which means our suspect is in the house for a considerable length of time. He doesn't murder her straight after having sex.'

'Or he did and spent time in the house,' Watkins suggested.

'Given the state of the place, it was impossible to tell whether the house had been ransacked.'

The pathologist pointed at Ellie's wrists and arms. 'It also appears this girl was self-harming. These wounds are fresh.'

'Not surprising, given her lifestyle,' Fagan said.

Watkins pulled his buzzing phone out of his pocket. 'DI Saddler said the incident room is ready and that they're ready to interview Ellie's friends.'

'Hold off until we get there. I want to interview the first one myself. Tell DI Saddler to get a list of every boy on that estate who knew Ellie. One of them is bound to know something.'

'I will conduct a full autopsy of the body later on today before I type up my final report,' the pathologist offered. 'Forensics are sending me more information about the crime scene. Toxicology reports should be back first thing in the morning. Then I'll be able to provide you with a clearer picture of what happened to her in her last hours.'

'Keep me posted.' Fagan turned and hurried out of the room.

CHAPTER 7

Sofrydd Community Centre

Part of the community hall had been set aside for interviews. Social Services and appropriate adult witnesses had been called to assist the police. A stream of people had been coming in all morning, giving names of individuals that they thought might have had something to do with the murder of Ellie. A GoFundMe account had been set up and had raised over two hundred pounds.

Gracie Peacock was accompanied by her mother, Trisha Peacock. She was nervous and visibly upset. A social worker was also present in the interview.

Fagan sat down opposite Gracie. 'Hi Gracie, how are you doing?'

Gracie looked at him, shrugging, before returning to a slouching position. She mumbled something, but Fagan couldn't understand what it was.

'My name is Detective Inspector Marc Fagan. I am investigating what happened to Ellie last night.' Fagan glanced at the social worker. 'I take it this nice lady has talked to you about what happened to her?'

Gracie struggled to nod.

'Okay, we're going to take this slowly, Gracie. If you want to stop, just say.' Fagan smiled at her. 'You okay with that?'

Gracie nodded.

'Now I understand you were with Ellie yesterday. And that you called at her house to see if she was going out?'

'Yeah,' Gracie replied in a mouse like whimper.

'That's great. Can you tell me if you were with anyone when you called at Ellie's house?'

Gracie took her time answering. 'Um, Mia and Charlotte were

with me.'

Fagan smiled at Gracie, jotting down the names. 'Fantastic. Can you remember what time this was?'

'Early, but I can't remember the time.' Gracie wiped away a tear.

Fagan pulled a tissue out of a box and handed it to Gracie. 'It's okay, Gracie, your mam is with you. If you think I'm asking questions that are upsetting you, then you can take a break.'

Gracie blew her nose on the tissue.

'How was Ellie when you called at her house yesterday?'

'She was okay.'

'Was she sad about anything in particular? Had something upset her in any way?'

'No, she was her normal self.'

'You're doing brilliantly, Gracie,' Fagan praised. 'After you had called at Ellie's house, what did you do?'

'We went straight down the park.'

Fagan pointed at a window with a view of the small park. 'Over there?'

Gracie nodded.

'So you were just hanging around?'

'We were sitting on the swings just chilling.'

'I love chilling,' Fagan said. 'Sitting with my feet up. Watching the telly. Nothing better than just hanging around, is there? Do you girls like to watch the telly?'

Gracie smiled and nodded.

'Yeah,' Fagan said enthusiastically. 'What do you like to watch on the telly?'

Gracie thought about the question. '*Stranger Things* and *Cobra Kai*.'

'I heard Ellie likes *Stranger Things*. I don't know what that is, sorry.'

'It's a programme about a girl with special powers.'

'Wow,' Fagan responded. 'I wish I had special powers. Do you know what I'd do if I had special powers, Gracie? I'd go around and catch all the bad guys who did horrible things and lock them all up. Wouldn't it be cool if we could do that? The world would be a much safer place.'

Gracie nodded.

'What is *Cobra Kai*?'

'It's a telly show about karate.'

'Really. Are you good at karate? Does this *Cobra Kai* teach you about karate?'

'No,' the social worker interrupted. 'It's a TV show based on characters from a film called *The Karate Kid*.'

'I remember the *Karate Kid*,' Fagan said, glancing at the social worker. 'They've made a TV series out of it?'

The social worker nodded.

'Just goes to show how old and wrinkly I am, doesn't it.'

Gracie giggled at Fagan's comment.

'So you hung around on the swings yesterday morning?'

Gracie nodded enthusiastically.

Fagan could tell she was gaining confidence. 'And you were talking about your favourite telly shows.'

'Yeah, we were just saying how much she fancied Robbie from *Cobra Kai*.'

'Good looking, is he?'

Gracie blushed before nodding.

'I used to fancy a singer called Kate Bush,' Fagan confessed.

Gracie sang the main line from *Running Up That Hill*.

'That's a brilliant song. It's great to see the kids of today still know that one. It's super old.'

'It's from *Stranger Things*,' Gracie revealed.

'I'm going to have to watch that now.'

'It's not really for grown-ups.'

'Okay.' Fagan nodded. 'I've a mate called Jamie. He's my age, but he hasn't grown up. He still loves to watch *Star Wars* and other stuff.' He refocused. 'So you were hanging around on the swings in the local park?'

Gracie nodded.

'Do you know how long you were there for?'

'Ages.'

'I used to hang around the park when I was your age. Me and my mate Graham.' Fagan stopped, suddenly remembering his friend.

'Inspector Fagan,' the social worker called out his name.

Fagan snapped out of memory lane. 'Sorry, I was remembering an old friend from long ago. So you were sitting around chilling. Talking about boys off the telly. Do you girls talk about boys a lot?'

Gracie blushed again before nodding.

'We all used to do that. Me and my mates used to talk about the girls at school we liked. Was it just you girls in the park, Gracie? Was there anyone else who was hanging about?'

Gracie thought about the question. 'Some boys from the estate turned up.'

'Did they talk to you?'

'Yeah, but we didn't want to talk with them.'

'I don't blame you. I didn't want to talk to girls when I was young.' Fagan inhaled. 'Did you stay in the park long after the boys turned up?'

Gracie took a moment before nodding.

'How long were you in the park for?'

'I don't know.'

'An hour, maybe, two hours?'

'It could have been, I don't know.'

'My daughter has learning difficulties,' Gracie's mother revealed. 'She has trouble with numbers.'

'I hated maths at school,' Fagan revealed. 'All those numbers really gave me a headache. Okay, so did Ellie speak to any of the boys?'

Gracie seemed hesitant in answering.

'Gracie, are you okay?' the social worker asked.

Gracie stared at Fagan.

Fagan had seen that look before. The look of a young child who was terrified. 'Gracie, listen to me. You won't get into trouble. This conversation is between the four of us, okay.'

Gracie nodded.

'Why don't we start with the names of the boys that turned up at the park yesterday? Can you do that?' Fagan hovered his pen over his notepad.

Gracie took her time. 'There was Morgan, and Falon. Jake was there and Taylor.'

Fagan scribbled furiously. 'You're doing excellently, Gracie. Your mam is so proud of you.'

Gracie's mother put her arm around her daughter. 'I am proud of you, my lovely.'

'So, Jake, Taylor, Morgan and Falon are all boys who live on the estate.'

'Um, Jake lives down the road in Hafodyrynys.'

'What happened when they turned up? Did they talk to you straight away?'

'No, they hung around by the climbing frame.' Gracie paused, looking at her mother.

'It's ok sweetheart, you can tell this policeman,' Gracie's mam coaxed.

Gracie took her time. 'We were sat on the swings. Then one of the boys came over.'

'Which boy was that?'

'Taylor.'

'What's Taylor's second name?'

'Richards.'

'Brilliant. Did he say something to you that might have upset you?'

'He had a go at Ellie.'

'Why did he have a go at Ellie?'

Gracie started to tear up.

'Gracie, would you like us to stop?' Fagan asked.

Gracie took a few moments before shaking her head.

Fagan nodded. 'Okay, in your own time, Gracie. Can you tell me why Taylor started arguing with Ellie?'

'It was something she posted on CTC.'

'CTC,' Fagan repeated. 'That stands for Cymru Teen Chat, doesn't it?'

Gracie's mother nodded. 'All the kids are using it these days. If you ask me, it's worse than Snapchat, Instagram and WhatsApp.'

'Why's that?'

'It's supposed to be a safe place for kids to hang out online. But it's caused nothing but trouble. Gracie is always getting abuse.'

'What kind of abuse are you getting, Gracie?'

Gracie looked very uncomfortable with the question.

'It's okay to talk, Gracie,' Fagan encouraged. 'No one is going to find out what you said.'

Gracie's mother spoke again. 'The boys on the estate have been saying lots of nasty things to the girls. It's caused no end of problems between the parents. I don't even want to live around here anymore. That Taylor Richards is one of the worst ones.'

Fagan looked at Gracie's mother. 'Why is that?'

'He's been saying things to the girls that have terrified them. Plus, he's been in trouble with the police because of indecent messages he sent to a girl last year. He was arrested twice because he said some disturbing things. A family used to live several doors down from him, but had to move last year. He threatened their daughter. Said he was going to rape her and slit her throat at the same time.'

Fagan could see how upset Gracie was getting. 'Gracie, it's okay. You're safe with us. No one is going to hurt you. I promise. Do you understand?'

Gracie nodded through the tears.

'So, Taylor had a go at Ellie, did he?'

'Yeah.'

'Are you able to tell us what he said?'

'Taylor came over and started gobbing off at Ellie.'

'What was he gobbing off about?'

'He said that Ellie had been slagging him off on CTC.'

'Are you able to say what Ellie was supposed to have said to Taylor?'

'It's okay, sweetheart. Taylor won't be able to hurt you,' Gracie's mother assured her.

Gracie drew a long breath. 'Um, Ellie made fun of Taylor because he shared a picture with her the other night. And when she was at the park, she shared it with us.'

'A picture?'

Gracie looked at her mother.

'Go on, you can tell this nice policeman.'

'He sent a picture of his willy to Ellie. She made fun of him, saying he had a small one.'

The weight of Gracie's words hit Fagan like a lead weight. For a moment, he was too shocked to speak. 'How old is Taylor?'

'Fifteen,' Gracie's mother answered. 'Fifteen bloody years old and he's pulling shit like this. His mother doesn't give a toss what he does. A few of us had a go at her last year when Taylor was sending vile messages to the girls on the estate.' She pointed at her daughter. 'He even told my daughter he was coming round to murder me. I was bloody livid with the boy. I went round to his mother's house and had a right go. All she did was tell me to fuck off. That's when a group of us told the police. You lot took your time doing something about him.'

'Cases involving harassment online can be very difficult to pursue. Often there are arguments on both sides.' Fagan looked at Gracie. 'When Ellie made fun of Taylor, how did he respond?'

'He went ballistic,' Gracie replied. 'He told Ellie that he was going to get her. He said he knew her mother was going out last night and that he would be round to give her a good sorting.'

Fagan scribbled furiously. 'Did he say anything else?'

Gracie nodded. 'He said he would show her exactly how big his willy was.'

'I have one more question for you, Gracie. Then we can wrap it up. Can you remember what Taylor was wearing when you saw him in the park yesterday?'

Gracie thought about the question. 'He was wearing a hoodie.'

'Can you remember what colour it was?'

'Black,' Gracie answered after a brief silence.

Fagan nodded. 'Listen, Gracie. I think we're going to finish for now. I think you have been fantastic. You've been very brave. We're all so proud of you, especially your mam.'

Gracie's mother embraced her daughter, kissing her on the forehead. 'I am so very proud of you, sweetheart. I'll take you out next Saturday and you can have your nails done.'

'Wow, I wish I was having my nails done,' Fagan said.

Gracie giggled.

'You and your mam can go now, Gracie. I don't want you worrying about anything. The police will fix everything, I promise.'

The social worker remained seated.

Fagan scanned his notes before burying his hands in his face. 'I can't believe this.'

'We have to deal with shit like this every other week,' the social worker remarked. 'It's becoming a real problem.'

'Do you know much about this Cymru Teen Chat?'

'It's causing an uproar at the moment throughout the Valleys. I work for Monmouthshire Social Services. We've had dozens of complaints relating to this app. It's supposed to be just for teenagers. But there are adults using it to sell drugs and send sexually explicit images. Last year I read an article in the Western Mail. It's supposed to be linked to several suicides throughout South Wales. I hope you're going to arrest this Taylor Richards.'

'I'll have a chat with my colleagues first before we can make our next move.'

The social worker nodded before standing. 'You're going to have your work cut out for you, Inspector Fagan. Especially around here. You could be opening a can of worms you won't be able to shut.'

'I'll keep that in mind. But right now, all I care about is finding out who murdered Ellie Parry.'

'Good luck,' the social worker said before walking away.

Fagan hit the speed dial on his phone. 'Sean, gather the troops. We may have our first suspect.'

CHAPTER 8

Newport Central Police Station

Fagan drained the last of his coffee. It was his second cup in half an hour.

Watkins, Stacey and Brooks had gathered a wealth of information from officers at the community centre and were sorting through witness statements and other information they had accumulated over the last few hours.

Fagan glanced at the clock on the wall. 'Right then, time is ticking away on this one, guys. The press are camped up the Sofrydd. I am due to give a statement in a few hours. So let's sort through what we have and hopefully make some progress.' Fagan glanced at his tablet. 'I've interviewed twelve-year-old Gracie Peacock. Gracie called at Ellie's house yesterday morning. She said there were two other girls with her. Charlotte Mason and Mia Probert. DI Saddler is due to interview Charlotte Mason. Other officers will interview Mia Probert later on today. My interview with Gracie Peacock turned up a lot of information. It would seem that Ellie was arguing with a boy called Taylor Richards. And the boy threatened to get Ellie back. Sean, what have you got?'

'Fifteen-year-old Taylor Richards lives on Keir Hardie Terrace. Already got form. He's been interviewed eight times for sending threatening messages to girls who live on the estate. Some messages he sent are very explicit for someone his age. He's been on a police watch list for three years. Last year, he was questioned regarding a girl from Pontypool. He was arrested after the girl claimed he had ordered her to send explicit pictures of her and her friend. When she refused, he threatened to go around to her house and rape her and her mother. Taylor was arrested and released on bail. While all this was going on, he threatened to kill another girl he met on a gaming website. He then tracked her down on WhatsApp and ordered her to take pictures of her self-harming.'

'Sounds like a right bag of shit,' Fagan stated. 'According to Gracie, Richards approached the girls and started arguing with Ellie.' Fagan checked his notes. 'Gracie said Richards sent Ellie a picture of his penis. Ellie mocked the size of his penis in front of the other girls.' Fagan inhaled.

'You okay, guv?' Stacey asked.

'No, I'm not,' Fagan responded. 'We have a fourteen-year-old girl who is living the life of someone much older. Plus, what I'd call a fifteen-year-old sexual predator sending mucky pictures to underage girls on the estate.'

Watkins kept on reading. 'His mother claims her son has severe learning difficulties and a host of mental health problems.'

Fagan sighed. 'Is it me or has every kid on that estate got learning difficulties?'

'Could be a schizophrenic,' Brooks suggested.

'Which makes him unpredictable. The initial pathologist's report states that Ellie had been self-harming. Fresh wounds were present on her arms and wrists. What's the betting Richards has been encouraging her to slash herself?'

'There's always something in the South Wales Argus about children and self-harming, and having access to graphic online images and videos. There are loads of stories making the news these days about underage children sharing sexually explicit pictures of themselves.'

'Gracie mentioned something called Cymru Teen Chat,' Fagan said. 'It's a social networking app the kids are using these days.'

Watkins tapped away on his keyboard. 'Cymru Teen Chat was started nearly five years ago by a seventy-year-old Newport entrepreneur, Russel Connor. This is interesting, boss. There's a charity that is trying to ban the app.'

'Why?'

'This charity claims the app has been responsible for a spate of suicides over the last three years.'

'I spoke to a social worker this morning. She mentioned

reading about the app being linked to suicides.'

'Connor started the app in December 2019, just before Covid came along. The app grew in popularity. By July 2020, it had nearly a quarter of a million users throughout Wales. In March 2022, the first suicide linked to the app happened. Eleven-year-old Holly Jones took her own life. Her dad runs a charity called Safe Children Wales. Michael Jones has been campaigning for the app to be banned and Connor to be investigated. According to this information, police have interviewed Connor about the app.'

'Anything come of it?'

'No, boss. Connor released a statement in December 2022 after more allegations were made. He said that Cymru Teen Chat was safe to use. Connor has also taken a restraining order on Jones. Last year Jones gained access to an award ceremony at the Celtic Manor. Connor was being given the Welsh Businessman of the Year Award when Jones burst on stage and belted him. The South Wales Argus ran a piece on it. Jones claims he had been in contact with over a hundred parents concerning the app. Parents whose children had suffered severe bullying and harassment while using the app. Connor didn't press charges for assault, but took out a restraining order.'

'Let me get this straight. This app has been allegedly responsible for a spate of suicides over the last few years, but they didn't flag up on any police database.'

Stacey carried out a quick search. 'At the end of 2022, an investigation was launched. It lasted seven months, but the police couldn't find anything suspicious. According to this, Chief Constable Paul Griffiths claimed that after a seven-month investigation, no evidence linking the suicides to the app could be found.'

'If the teenagers on the Sofrydd estate are using the app to send explicit photographs, then Connor needs to be put on the radar. Sean, see if he's available to talk with us. I wouldn't mind a chat with him. Let's get back to the murder of Ellie. Gracie's description of Richards' clothing matches our suspect last night, seen entering Ellie's house. Richards had an argument with Ellie yesterday morning. He leaves the park and spends the rest of the day planning how he can get revenge on Ellie.'

'Premeditated murder, boss,' Watkins suggested.

'It depends how pissed off Richards was with Ellie, humiliating him in front of his mates and the girls. And considering his background there's more than enough to put him in the frame. He's been known for sharing explicit images.' Fagan paused. 'I can't get that tripod and light out of my head. I'm certain whoever filmed Ellie filmed her murder.'

'That sounds a little extreme, even for Richards,' Brooks considered. 'There been nothing to indicate any kind of video has been shared on social media.'

'You're right, Andrew. According to the pathologist, Ellie had a sexual encounter last night. But there were no signs of rape. Which means sex was consensual. Not only that, but the pathologist believes Ellie could have had multiple partners over the past day or so.'

'Which suggests that Richards may not be our murderer,' Brooks said.

Fagan nodded. 'We can't arrest Richards and accuse him of murdering Ellie until we have something concrete. However, since he has form and was seen arguing with Ellie yesterday, we can bring him in for routine questioning.' Fagan glanced at the map of the Sofrydd Estate. 'We know the murderer entered the front of the house. Our witness confirms that. They left through the back garden and made their way down the rear of the houses onto the main road. We have another witness report from a taxi driver saying they saw someone running towards Hafodyrynys. Our suspect could have gone in two different directions. They could have headed back towards Pontypool or towards Crumlin. We need to pull CCTV footage from the main set of lights at the Crumlin junction. Speaking of CCTV, where are we at with CCTV footage from Cardiff?'

'I've been on to Transport Police Wales, guv,' Stacey revealed. 'They've sent a couple of uniform to Cardiff Central to look at their CCTV footage.'

'Keep on to them. I've a feeling we'll turn something up. What did you think about Ellie's mam?'

'Piece of work. Out on the piss last night with her mates. Leaving two young boys alone. Definitely a regular occurrence with her.'

'Plus, we've reason to suspect she lied about her phone. She said she ordered an Uber this morning to take her home from the railway station. Although she didn't have a phone to call an Uber. The question is, why did she lie?'

'Perhaps she knew the killer,' Watkins remarked. 'Wanted to put as much distance between her and what happened to Ellie as possible.'

'That's a good point, Sean.'

'What about the neighbour, boss? She was definitely covering for the mother.'

Fagan nodded. 'She's close to the family, which means she's bound to know all their dirty laundry. You could tell by the way she was talking this morning. She was hiding a lot of stuff. Especially regarding the lifestyle of both Sophie and her daughter.'

'I think Sophie Parry knows she won't be getting her kids back,' said Stacey. 'Not with the state the house was in. Plus the materials found in Ellie's bedroom. Vapes, alcohol, drugs and the contraceptive pills. I don't think she was too bothered about anything when we interviewed her. She didn't even seem very upset when I went with her to identify Ellie's body. When the pathologist pulled back the blanket, Sophie just nodded and said it was her. She was more concerned about getting back outside for a fag than grieving for her daughter.'

'If she lied about having her phone stolen, I've a feeling we'll be pulling her in again,' Fagan said. 'I'm guessing there's a lot of damning information on her phone that might shed light on what happened to Ellie.'

'Transport Police Wales said they'd get back to me in the few hours.'

Fagan nodded. 'Right, let's gather all we have together and prepare something for the press. I'll go up to the community centre on the Sofrydd and issue a statement. Sean, I want you and Andrew to pick up Richards. Make sure everything is in place before we interview him. Stacey, keep nagging the Transport Police in Cardiff.'

Sofrydd Community centre

Although he'd made announcements to the media many times before, Fagan rehearsed his statement before he faced the press. Local BBC and ITV were in attendance. Along with the South Wales Argus, Western Mail and several national newspapers. The BBC and ITV Wales had been running the story on their websites. A candle lit vigil had been organised for Ellie for later that evening at the community centre. The GoFundMe appeal had reached over £1,500 in donations.

The crowd of journalists waited patiently.

'Good afternoon, ladies and gentlemen. Thank you for attending this briefing. I am Detective Inspector Marc Fagan. I am here to provide you with an update on the horrific events that unfolded on the Sofrydd Estate early this morning.'

'At approximately 7:20am this morning, officers from Gwent Police were called to a property on Gordon Road. Upon entering the house, our officers made a harrowing discovery, which was the body of a young girl in an upstairs bedroom. Crime Scene Investigators were immediately summoned, and a full-scale investigation is now underway.'

'I can confirm that the victim has been formally identified as fourteen-year-old Ellie Parry. This devastating loss has shocked not only her family and friends, but the entire community. On behalf of Gwent Police, I extend our deepest sympathies to those who knew and loved Ellie. Our hearts go out to you during this incredibly difficult time.'

'While a forensic examination has already taken place, I must stress that we are not in a position to release details on the cause of death at this stage. Further examinations will be conducted later today, which will shed more light on Ellie's final hours. What I can tell you is that we are treating Ellie's death as suspicious. Every resource available is being utilised to find those responsible.'

'I want to take a moment to address the local community. I

urge you not to engage in speculation, especially on social media. Rumours and unverified information can severely hamper our investigation and cause unnecessary distress. Instead, I encourage you to channel your energy into supporting one another and helping us find those responsible for this horrible crime.'

'The local community centre is open for anyone who needs to talk, and our Community Support Officers are on standby to assist in any way they can. The local church has also opened its doors to provide comfort and a space for reflection during these trying times.'

'Uniformed officers from our neighbourhood policing teams will be present in the area over the coming days. Offering support and ensuring that everyone feels safe. I cannot stress enough the importance of community cooperation in situations like this. We currently do not have any suspects in custody, but I implore anyone with information, no matter how small or seemingly insignificant, to come forward. Your information could be the key to solving this case.'

'Finally, we are issuing an urgent request for local men to voluntarily provide DNA samples. This step is critical in narrowing down our investigation and bringing justice to Ellie and her family.'

'We will continue to keep you updated as the investigation progresses. Thank you.' Fagan stood and left the room. He reached into his pocket and pulled out his phone..

'Boss, Richards is down at Newport,' Watkins revealed. 'His mam is kicking up a fuss about her son being brought in for questioning.'

'I'm on my way.'

CHAPTER 9

Newport Central Police Station

'Everything Okay?' Fagan asked, noting the look on Watkins face.

'Not really, boss. We've had nothing but shit since bringing in Richards in.'

'Being a bit of a handful, is he?'

'I wish. It's his bloody mam. She's the one who's being vocal. Uniform had to threaten her with arrest when they turned up at their house. She refused to let them take Richards in. Even the duty solicitor has had a moan.'

'Let's get this over with. With any luck Richards will give us something to go on.'

Julie Richards glared at Fagan and Watkins as they entered the room. 'Where the fuck have you lot been? We've been sat in here for over half an hour.'

The duty solicitor shot her a disapproving look.

'We're sorry to have inconvenienced you, Mrs Richards,' Fagan said in a polite tone.

'Like fuck you are,' Julie responded. 'You dragged us down here to accuse my son of murder. Well, for your information, he had fuck all to do with murdering that slut. If you ask me, she had it coming.'

Fagan stared at Richards' mam. 'And why is that?'

'Everyone knows what that dirty little slag is like on the street. You lot will treat her like she's some kind of innocent victim.'

'Mrs Richards, despite your opinion, a fourteen-year-old girl has been murdered. Now, are you going to let your son answer our questions?'

'You had no right to arrest him!' Julie shouted.

'He wasn't arrested Mrs Richards. We're only questioning him because we have a witness who saw him arguing with Ellie yesterday morning.'

Julie rolled her eyes. 'Here we bloody go. What's that trollop and her merry band of bitches been saying now?'

'Show some respect will you Mrs Richards.' Fagan's patience wore thin. 'That trollop you refer to was brutally murdered last night.'

'My son didn't fucking murder her.' Julie glanced at her son. 'Tell them Taylor. Tell these arseholes you had nothing to do with it.'

'Another insult like that, Mrs Richards, and I'll have you removed from this interview,' Fagan growled. He focused his attention on Richards. 'Taylor, listen to me. You'd be doing yourself a favour by helping us catch whoever did this to Ellie. Do you understand?'

'I didn't kill her!' Richards protested.

'There, he said he didn't kill her.' Julie stood. 'Let's go Taylor. You've told them what they need to know.'

'Mrs Richards, you have two choices. You can either sit back down or I'll have you removed from this interview. We can find another appropriate adult to sit with Taylor.'

'Sit down mam,' Richards requested in a quiet tone.

Julie pointed at her son. 'Don't you dare say anything that will land you in the shit? I've had a gutsful of your antics.'

Richards stared at Fagan. A distraught expression painted a picture of his sadness at what had happened. 'I didn't kill her, honest.'

'Okay, that fine,' Fagan said calmly. 'Could you tell us where you were last night, around eleven o'clock?'

'I was round my mate's place.'

'What's your mate's name, Taylor?' Watkins asked.

'Jake Salford.'

Watkins scribbled the name. 'Where does Jake live, Taylor?'

'Hafodyrynys.'

'What were you doing?'

'We were on the Xbox and listening to some tunes.'

'What time did you leave your mate's house?'

Richards shrugged. 'Dunno, late.'

'After midnight?' Fagan said.

Richards thought for a moment before nodding. 'Yeah, it was about three o'clock before I left Jake's house. His dad came into his bedroom and had a moan about how late it was. He mentioned the time, and that we were making too much noise.'

'There, he's supplied an alibi,' Julie waded in. 'Now we can leave?'

'Not until we've asked your son a few more questions,' Fagan replied.

'When do we get a fag break? The stress is killing me?'

'Mrs Richards, your son is not under arrest. He's just supplied an alibi. Which I'm sure will go a long way to clear him of any wrongdoing. But we do have questions. The longer you sit there and interrupt, the longer it will take.'

'Fine, ask a bloody way. Just make it quick.' She bit into a nail.

Fagan looked down at his notes. 'Yesterday, Taylor, you were seen in the park by the community centre. One of Ellie's friends said that you were arguing with her.'

Taylor nodded. 'Yeah.'

'Something to do with a picture you sent Ellie the other night.'

'Jesus bloody Christ. What have you been putting online now?' His mother groaned.

Fagan ignored her. 'According to a witness, you sent a picture of your penis to Ellie. When you turned up at the park yesterday morning, Ellie made fun of the picture you sent her.'

Richards squirmed at Fagan's words.

'And who made up that bullshit?' Julie demanded to know. 'One of the bitches she hung around with? Let me guess. Gracie Peacock, Charlotte Mason or Mia Probert. All fucking little trollops in their own right. That Gracie Peacock has been caught thieving from the Londis no end of times. Charlotte and Mia always putting on a display for the boys on the estate.'

'Taylor, did you send a picture of your penis to Ellie?'

Richards inhaled before nodding. 'But it was just for Ellie to see. I didn't think she was going to share it.'

'What did I fucking tell you about doing that?' Julie exploded.

'Now you've gone and landed yourself in the shit again. Jesus, I don't know how much more I can take of your bullshit.'

Fagan went on the attack. 'Let me ask you this, Mrs Richards. What was your son doing out until three in the morning?'

'What?' Julie answered with a confused look on her face.

'Why did you let your son stay out so late?' Fagan glanced at Richards. 'How old are you, Taylor?'

Richards inhaled. 'Fifteen, I'm sixteen next month.'

Fagan focused on his mam. 'Fifteen years of age and you're letting him stay out all hours of the night. What were you doing last night, Mrs Taylor?'

'Huh, probably on Plenty of Fish,' Richards mocked.

'Piss off, don't start on me,' Julie chastised her son.

'Well you are, mam. You're always on it. All your phone does is ping all day long.'

'Taylor, it's important that you answer our questions,' Fagan said before Julie launched a defence. 'Tell me about the argument you had with Ellie yesterday morning when you were at the park.'

Taylor stared back at Fagan for several seconds. 'I was in love with her,' he confessed.

'Ellie?' Fagan said.

Julie rolled her eyes. 'Jesus Christ, Taylor, have you got shit in your eyes or what?'

'That's the trouble with you, mam. You're always judging people.'

'I don't have to judge her. You know what she's like.' Julie corrected herself. 'Or was like. It wasn't exactly a secret. And don't get me started on that of a mother of hers, dirty slag.'

'If you say you were in love with her, Taylor, then why the argument?' Watkins asked.

'She wasn't supposed to have shared that picture.'

'I get it.' Fagan nodded. 'I'll show you mine, if you show me yours.'

'No.'

'Thing is, Taylor, you've got a long track record of posting indecent pictures online.'

The duty solicitor glanced at Fagan.

Fagan looked at his file. 'You've been arrested on several occasions for threatening behaviour and sending indecent images of your genitals.'

'This is all a load of bollocks. You just want to stitch him up for something he didn't do,' Julie argued.

Again, Fagan ignored her. 'One of the girls said that you told Ellie that you were going to show her exactly how big your penis was. And that you knew her mother was going out last night.' Fagan checked his notes. 'You said you were going around her place to give her a good sorting.'

'My son has just told you he was round a mate's place last night and that he had nothing to do with the murder,' Richards' mam countered.

Fagan continued to ignore her. 'What did you mean by going around to give her a good sorting?'

'She wasn't supposed to have shared that picture. She took the piss out of me in front of all her mates.'

'Did that make you very angry?' Watkins asked.

'Yeah, but I didn't mean it. As I just said, I was at a mate's house.'

'What do you mean by saying you were in love with Ellie?'

'We were going to run away.'

Richards' mam glared at her son. 'Run away, are you for real? And where were you thinking of going?'

'Anywhere,' Richards responded. 'We're pissed off living on the Sofrydd.'

'Were you and Ellie in a relationship?' Fagan asked.

Taylor hesitated before nodding.

'How long had you been going out with Ellie?'

Taylor shrugged. 'A few weeks.'

'Jesus Christ, Taylor, you can do better than that,' Julie sighed.

'You're going to have to give us a bit more, Taylor. A few weeks isn't long enough to decide to run away together.'

'We started going out at Easter,' Richards said.

'So several months, then? Longer than a few weeks, don't you think?'

Richards nodded. 'We just got talking one day. There were just two of us.'

'Go on,' Fagan coaxed.

Richards glanced at his mother. 'We're so pissed off with living on this estate.'

'Did you have sex with Ellie?'

'No.' Richards shook his head. 'I wanted to but Ellie always said no.' He glanced at his mam. 'We're both pissed off with living around here.'

'Everyone is fucked off, Taylor,' Julie moaned. 'You think I enjoy living up the Sofrydd? You know I've applied to the housing association for a new place. But they keep sticking two fingers up at us.'

'Taylor, listen to me,' Fagan refocused. 'It's very important we find the person who murdered Ellie. You were part of her life. Do you have any idea who could have murdered her?'

Richards ran his hand through his hair. 'We had an argument last week.'

'About what?'

'I saw her talking to someone in the street.'

'Do you know who Ellie was talking to?'

Richards gave his mother a sheepish look before cautiously nodding. 'Owen Woods.'

'For fuck's sake!' Julie exploded for the second time. 'What did I tell you about going near that twat?'

'I didn't go near him, mam. I just saw him talking to Ellie.'

Fagan scribbled the name. 'Who is Owen Woods?'

'He's the local crack dealer, that's who,' Julie answered.

'Mam!' Richards shouted.

'What, you think I give a shit if I throw him under the bus? Prick has been a menace for years.'

'Does he live locally?'

Julie nodded. 'Lives a few doors down from us on Keir Hardie Terrace.'

'How do you know he sells crack?'

'Everybody knows it. He doesn't exactly make it a secret. He sells everything.'

'Ecstasy?' Watkins asked.

Julie nodded. 'He even got put away for it. But is hasn't stopped the twat. He uses that app the kids are using to sell shit.'

'Would that be Cymru Teen Chat?'

'Yeah, that's the one.'

'How old is he?'

'Must be in his mid-thirties.'

Fagan noticed the look on Richards' face. 'Taylor, if you know something, then you need to tell us. I know you've been in trouble in the past for sending indecent images to various girls.'

'Stick to the crime, Inspector Fagan,' the duty solicitor stated.

'What were you arguing about with Ellie?'

'She was going to buy some tabs off him.'

'Ellie told you this, did she?'

'Yeah,' Richards nodded. 'She never did anything like that before. I know she's bought vapes off Owen, but never drugs. She even said only losers take drugs. That's why I was arguing with Ellie. I told her she was stupid doing it.'

'Did she buy any ecstasy from Owen Woods when you saw her talking to him?'

'No, she had no money.'

'Did she tell you why she was going to take ecstasy?'

'She said it would help with her depression.'

'She was going through a difficult time?'

'Yeah. Ellie and her mam were always arguing.'

'Do you know what the arguments were about?'

'Ellie said that her mam always used to be on her mobile phone, talking to men.'

'Everyone knows what that slut of a mother of hers is like,' Julie said. 'Sophie Parry is the biggest bike on the estate. I sometimes felt sorry for Ellie.'

'Why's that?' Fagan asked.

'Despite all her flaws, it's no surprise the way she turned out the way she did. Her mam hasn't exactly done a brilliant job at bringing her up. We've lived on the Sofrydd as long as they have. I remember when we went to Ellie's eighth birthday party at the community centre. When I asked her what she wanted to be when she grew up, she said she wanted to be a pole dancer. What kind of eight-year-old wants to be a pole dancer? Her mother even brought her a pole for her bedroom. Used to film it on her mobile and share it on Facebook. Bloody disturbed if you ask me.'

'Taylor, when you left the park yesterday, do you know if Ellie was still there?'

Richards nodded. 'We all left, because the girls were talking to this boy on CTC.'

'Cymru Teen Chat?' Watkins asked.

Richards nodded.

'Do you know who they were talking to on CTC?'

'This boy, they've been talking to him for a few weeks.'

'Do you know the name of this boy?'

Richards shook his head. 'Not his real name, just his nickname.'

'Which is?' Fagan pursued.

Richards took a moment to recall the name. 'Shadowcaster. Ellie and her mates were always talking about him. I had an argument with Ellie. Said she was spending too much time talking to him.'

'What happened after you had the fight with Ellie?'

'We all spit up and I went round Jake's house.'

'And you were there until early this morning?'

'Yeah. I came home and went to bed until mam woke me and told me about Ellie.'

Fagan looked at Julie. 'What time do you find out about Ellie?'

'About half six this morning. It was all over WhatsApp. Tammy Morris was bragging about it.'

Fagan glanced at Watkins. 'And you say this was about six thirty this morning.'

Julie pulled her phone from her pocket and activated the app. She handed Fagan her phone. 'It was about six thirty when she started to spread the gossip.'

Fagan stared at the messages that had been exchanged before giving Julie her phone back. He looked at her son. 'Taylor, if there is anything else you remember about yesterday. I want you to call me.' He slid his contact details card across the table.

'You are free to go.'

Julie was the first to spring to her feet. 'Jesus, I'm dying for a fag.'

'What do you think, boss?'

'There's a lot of tall tales being told on that estate. A lot of people covering for others. We'll send a couple of uniform around to arrest this Owen Woods. I'm fuming about Tammy Morris posting Ellie's murder on social media before phoning the police.' Fagan pulled his phone from his pocket to check the message that had just come through. 'CCTV from Cardiff Central has produced results.' Fagan looked at the clock on the wall before nodding. 'Looks like it's going to be a late one.'

C H A P T E R   1 0

Fagan swigged back a mouthful of the extra strong coffee he had asked Brooks to make for him. If there was one thing Brooks was guaranteed to make, it was strong coffee.

Stacey held a tablet and was looking at a large flatscreen monitor. 'Cardiff Police have really come through for us, guv. This footage was taken this morning at Cardiff Central Train Station. The train Sophie Parry boarded pulled in at platform two.'

Fagan watched the screen. Sophie Parry was speaking on a mobile phone. 'So much for her claiming she had her phone stolen last night.'

Parry was pacing up and down the platform.

'She looks like she's having an intense conversation with someone,' Watkins remarked.

Parry thumbed the phone screen for a moment before tapping it.

'She's phoning someone else,' Brooks speculated.

Parry spent another several minutes on her phone.

'Watch this next bit,' Stacey instructed.

Parry walked by a rubbish bin and tossed her phone in.

'Before you're wondering, guv, we've already recovered the rubbish bag. Station staff empty the bins throughout the day and store them in a shed at the end of the platform before Cardiff City Council takes them the next morning. It's only a matter of time before we find the missing phone.'

Fagan glanced at Stacey, smiling. 'Nice one.' He looked back at the screen, noting the timeframe in the corner. 'Hang on a minute. This footage was captured at eleven minutes past six this morning. What time did you arrive at Parry's house up the Sofrydd?'

'The call came in at five past seven. We were there within ten minutes.'

'What did Richards' mam just say to us, Sean?'

'She reckoned Tammy we was bragging about finding Ellie on a WhatsApp group.'

'About six thirty according to her phone she showed us.' Fagan glanced at the timeframe on the screen. 'Which means there's a significant amount of time between Tammy Morris discovering the body and calling the police. What was she doing during all that time?'

'She was phoning Sophie Parry, obviously,' Brooks said.

'But why did she take so long to notify the police?'

'Trying to get their story straight, probably,' Stacey considered.

Fagan processed the information. 'The moment Morris phones Parry to tell her she's discovered Ellie's body, Parry knows she's in the shit. She knows her two young sons are also in the house.' Fagan glanced at Watkins. 'We know that Sophie Parry is already on the radar of Social Services.'

'I'll be speaking with the social worker first thing in the morning, boss,' Watkins said.

'But why the long wait?' Fagan questioned, looking back at the screen.

'You think Sophie Parry knew who murdered her daughter, boss?'

'I didn't think so at first. But now it's something we're going to have to consider. Sophie isn't stupid. She knew she would be questioned by police over Ellie's murder. She knows that her life is about to be put under the microscope.' Fagan glanced at the video that was set on repeat. 'Look how she is on the phone. She doesn't look all that distraught. When we questioned her earlier, she showed little emotion about her daughter's murder. You would have thought, as a mother, she'd been in pieces. There's still a lot we don't know about Ellie's last movements. We know she met up with friends yesterday morning. She went to the park, where they encountered a group of boys, including Richards. An argument ensued between Ellie and Richards.'

'After which he said they went their separate ways,' Watkins added.

'Richards also mentioned someone called Owen Woods. According to Richards' mam he's the local crack dealer.'

Watkins tapped on his keyboard. 'Got a ping on the police database. Thirty-four-year-old Owen Woods. Has a string of offences as long as your arm. Jailed in 2010 for supplying cocaine and heroin. Spent just under two years in Cardiff.'

'That's not long,' Fagan pointed out.

'He was only caught with a small amount. Since then he's been convicted of possession on nine occasions. Everything from weed to ecstasy. Also been caught driving without insurance four times.'

'The very fact ecstasy was found with the body gives us probable cause for arrest. I want to know every step Ellie took yesterday. She went out in the morning and met up with friends in the park. The boys arrived and some kind of confrontation took place. All this happed in the morning. We need to start tracking her movements throughout the afternoon.' Fagan watched the replay of the video. 'Sophie Parry throws her phone away after being told her daughter is dead.'

'Parry didn't arrive at her house until twenty past eleven,' Stacey said. 'I was there for eleven thirty to take her to Prince Charlies to identify the body. It only took several minutes before we headed back to Newport.'

'That's four hours after police discovered Ellie's body,' Fagan said.

'The train to Hengoed station in Blackwood leaves Cardiff at six thirty-five and arrives ten past seven. Hengoed train station has two CCTV cameras. One overlooking the platforms and the other monitoring the carpark. I gave the times to Transport for Wales. They sent me these two clips.' Stacey tapped on her tablet. 'They were taken just after the train arrives at Hengoed.'

Fagan watched the train pulling up to the platform. Passengers hurried from the train the moment the doors opened.

'There.' Stacey pointed at the screen. 'Sophie Parry exits the train and heads straight for the car park.'

'She could have ordered the Uber while she still had her

phone on her in Cardiff.'

'No,' Stacey answered, gesturing towards the monitor. She tapped on the tablet and another video played. 'This is video footage taken of the carpark at Hengoed.'

Fagan watched Parry climb into a Nissan Juke.

'I've already run the plates. The car is registered to fifty-six-year-old Mandy Parry. She lives in Talywain.'

'Mother?' Fagan guessed.

'Yeah.' Stacey nodded.

'The train gets in at around ten past seven. Which means there's a four-hour gap between Parry leaving the train station and arriving at the house. Not only that, but Parry lied to us twice. First, she tells us that her phone was stolen while she was at The Prince of Wales Cardiff last night. And again this morning, when we interviewed her. She said she caught an Uber from the train station to the house.' Fagan pondered the information. 'Why lie about everything? I mean, she was in Cardiff last night. So it's not like she's high on our suspect list.'

'She obviously knows she's in a lot of shit. Not only regarding her daughter's murder,' Watkins said. 'But also the state the house is in. And let's not forget she left two young boys unattended.'

'Let's pull her in. Along with Tammy Morris and Mandy Parry. They're obviously part of what's going on here. Where are we with everything else?'

'Surprising result from your DNA request at the press conference a few hours ago,' Brooks revealed, 'Over one hundred men have submitted DNA samples, including Tammy Morris' son Toby.'

'I'll message labs and tell them to fast track results. Sophie Parry deliberately threw her phone in the bin. Considering she's lied about losing her phone, I'm going to apply for a warrant to examine it.' Fagan picked up his pen and notepad. 'Let's see what bullshit Sophie Parry is about to spout.'

CHAPTER 11

Newport Central Police Station

Sophie Parry stared at the wall in the interview room. Fagan could tell she'd been crying. But he could also tell her sorrow was for herself and not for her murdered daughter.

Parry had been silent since she had been brought in by the police.

The duty solicitor scribbled notes.

Fagan glanced at the notes he had written. 'It would appear, Sophie, that you haven't been totally honest with us regarding last night's events.'

Parry remained silent.

'Can you recall telling us what happened to your phone earlier?'

Parry took a moment to answer. 'I, uh, lost it in Cardiff last night. It was stolen. I already told you.' Her voice trembled.

Fagan tapped on the screen of his tablet. 'I'm showing Sophie Parry footage taken from Cardiff Central this morning. It shows her talking on a mobile phone. She is seen talking for a considerable length of time before throwing the phone into a rubbish bin.' Fagan leant forward, interlocking his fingers. 'Sophie, is this the phone you say you had stolen last night?'

Parry pursed her lips and glanced at the duty solicitor. 'No comment.'

'You are on the phone for approximately half an hour, making two phone calls before chucking it in the bin. Cardiff Police have recovered the rubbish bags and they will recover the phone. So there is no point denying it, Sophie. Can you tell us who you were talking to on the phone?'

Parry remained silent.

'Sophie, who were you talking to?'

'Tammy phoned me,' Parry confessed.

'What time was this?'

'About ten past six.'

'You blatantly lied to Constable Flynn this morning when she asked you about your phone.'

Parry briefly made eye contact with Stacey, sitting by the side of Fagan.

'You realise you could be charged with perverting the course of justice,' Stacey explained. 'You lied on purpose about having your phone stolen last night. And you lied to us about calling an Uber from the train station. When it was your mam who picked you up.'

Parry glared back at her. She'd not realised that she had dragged her mother into the mess she had created.

'We have two more officers interviewing your mam as we speak, Sophie,' Fagan revealed. 'We also have Tammy Morris in custody, who will be questioned about your daughter's murder. Look, we know you were in Cardiff last night. Officers up the Sofrydd have spoken to your friends who were out with you last night. They have confirmed this. So we're not accusing you of murdering your daughter. But you need to help us out here. The more you stay silent, the deeper the hole gets you've dug for yourself.'

'Your two sons are with Social Services,' Stacey said. 'I take it you want to see them again?'

Parry wiped tears away before nodding. 'Yeah,' she rasped.

'Then you need to help us,' Stacey said in a firm tone.

'Why did you lie to Constable Flynn earlier today about having your phone stolen?' Fagan queried.

Parry seemed to take forever to answer the question. 'I, uh, was afraid.'

'Afraid of what?'

Parry ran her hand through her hair. 'I don't know.'

'You don't know, or don't want to tell us?'

'Everything is so fucked up.'

'When was the last time you saw your daughter alive?'

Parry inhaled. 'Yesterday afternoon.'

'Can you recall what time this was exactly?'

Parry struggled to answer. 'About three o'clock, I think.'

'You think,' Fagan remarked.

'Look, I'm sorry, okay. I had no idea what was going to happen.'

'When we interviewed you earlier, you told us you didn't have any contact with Ellie after she went out with her friends yesterday morning.'

'No comment,' Parry answered quickly.

Fagan's phone buzzed. He looked at the screen. 'I've just received a message from colleagues in Cardiff. They have found your phone. Cyber forensics will examine it.' He glanced at Parry. 'This is the same phone you claimed you had stolen.'

'No comment.'

'You've already told us that Ellie didn't have contact with you after she went out with friends. Now you're saying you had contact with her. Which is it Sophie?'

Parry glared at him. 'No fucking comment.'

Fagan shook his head. 'Is this how it's going to play out, Sophie?'

'You've already told me I had nothing to do with my daughter's murder. I don't know why you've dragged me down here again.'

'You've been brought in for questioning because you lied to us earlier about your phone and catching an Uber. And now you've confessed that you had contact with Ellie yesterday. When you've already told us you didn't see her after she went out yesterday morning. That's three times you've lied to us. And since a murder is involved here, you could face a charge of perverting the course of justice. Which could involve a jail sentence. Is that what you want, Sophie? Is that what you want for those boys?'

Parry remained silent.

'Did you know your daughter was using drugs?' Stacey asked.

The question shook Parry to her core. She glared back at Stacey. 'No.' She shook her head. 'Not, Ellie. I've told her a thousand times to stay away from that shit.'

'A quantity of ecstasy pills were found by her bed.'

'I'd know if Ellie was taking something, I swear,' Parry stated. 'Besides, I don't think she had any money to buy that sort of thing.'

'You obviously didn't know.'

'Trust me, if Ellie was using drugs, I would have known.'

'Because you smoke cannabis. Is that what you're saying?'

'It's to help with my mental health issues.'

'The pathologist is going to supply us with a detailed toxicology report tomorrow. It should tell us if Ellie had drugs in her blood during the time of her murder. Were you aware your daughter was self-harming?'

Parry nodded. 'Ellie was vulnerable, prone to doing all kinds of things.'

'All kinds of things, like engaging in underage sex?' Fagan recalled the case in Southport he had told Watkins about. 'Did you know your daughter was sexually active?'

'No comment.'

'Multiple semen samples were found during the initial examination.'

'No comment.'

'Do you have any idea who could have murdered Ellie?'

'No, I swear,' Parry insisted.

'Could it have been someone she knew, someone she was close to?'

'I don't know.'

'Someone on the estate?'

'Honestly, I've got no bloody clue!'

'Did you know she was in a relationship with Taylor Richards?'

'That little twat,' Parry scoffed. 'There's no way Ellie would have anything to do with him.'

'That's what Richards claimed when we interviewed him earlier. We also know that he had an argument with Ellie yesterday. One of her friends has told us the argument was regarding an indecent image Richards had sent to Ellie.'

Parry became enraged by Fagan's reveal. 'You fucking wait until I get my hands on him because of what he did to Ellie. He's always been like that. I knew it would be a matter of time before he'd do something. His mother is a psychopath. Been meaning to give that bitch a good slapping. He's already been in trouble for sending porn to the girls on the estate.'

'Richards had an alibi for last night,' Stacey said.

'What do you mean, an alibi?'

'What we mean, Sophie, is that Richards had nothing to do with Ellie's murder. He claimed he saw Ellie talking with someone called Owen Woods a week or so back.'

'That piece of shit,' Parry seethed. 'He supplies drugs to the entire Sofrydd estate.'

'We know Woods has convictions for supplying drugs. And we know he's been convicted of dealing ecstasy. Which was found by the side of Ellie's bed.'

'I've told Ellie loads of times to stay away from that twat.' Parry became distraught. 'Why would she do that?'

'Perhaps she was angry with you,' Fagan suggested.

Parry looked at him.

'Did you buy Ellie alcohol before you went out yesterday afternoon?'

'You can drink in the house at fourteen,' Parry ranted.

Fagan nodded. 'Yes, you can. We found an empty bottle of WKD at the back of your house. We believe it could have belonged to whoever murdered Ellie.'

'Then why don't you arrest that drug dealing bastard?' Parry ranted.

'A warrant is being processed. Let's focus on the last time you spoke to Ellie. You just said it was about three o'clock.'

Parry nodded. 'Uh, yeah. She had just come from her mate's house. She was having a go at me for going out to Cardiff.'

'Was she with anyone?'

Parry nodded. 'One of her mates was with her. I think it was Charlotte.'

'According to your friend Tammy Morris, Ellie wanted to go to Cardiff with you. You even suggested this when we spoke to you earlier.'

'Yeah, she did.'

'Did you often take her out to the pub?' Stacey asked.

Parry glared back at Stacey. 'We'd go to Wetherspoons occasionally, that's all.'

'Is that why you bought the WKD, to shut her up?'

'It wasn't like that.'

Fagan checked his notes. 'Tammy Morris showed us a text she received from you yesterday morning.' He read the message. '*Got the bitch Ellie some WKD. That should keep her quiet while I get laid, lol.*'

Parry squirmed in her chair as she heard the message read out loud.

'How would you describe your relationship with Ellie?'

'How do you mean?' Parry seemed surprised by the question.

Fagan glanced down at his notes. 'The text you sent Tammy yesterday morning shows you had a very adult relationship with your daughter. Did you call her a bitch often?'

'No.' Parry struggled with her next line. 'Look, I'm not a terrible mother, okay. Is that what people have been telling you up the Sofrydd? That I'm a shit mam, and I don't deserve children. Let me tell you, everyone who lives on that estate has secrets, everyone.'

'Do you get on with your neighbours?' Stacey asked.

'Some of them.'

Stacey refocused on the reason Parry had been brought in for questioning. 'So why did you lie about your phone being stolen?'

'I was scared, okay.'

'You've just said this, Sophie. What are you scared of?'

Parry remained silent.

'Listen, Sophie, you're not doing yourself any favours by clamming up. Now either you tell us why you chucked your phone away, or cyber forensics will find out.'

'Because of the stuff I've got on there,' Parry blurted out.

'Stuff?' Stacey questioned.

'You know, stuff you lot might want to do me for.'

'What kind of things do you do on your phone, Sophie?'

Parry shrugged. 'You know, play games, funny videos. Stuff on Facebook and things.'

'Things?'

'You know, rude pictures.'

'Do you have anything inappropriate, like pornographic material?'

'Look, I get all kinds of shit, okay. People send me some fucked up stuff.'

'But you don't delete any of it, instead you keep it.'

'Yeah,' Parry admitted.

'Do you share anything with Ellie? Is that why you chucked your phone away?'

Parry sobbed. 'I'm not a bad mam, honest. Things are so fucked up at the moment.'

'Why did you take so long to come home?' Fagan asked. 'Tammy phoned you before she phoned the police, didn't she?'

'I had to get my head straight,' Parry cried. 'I didn't know what to do.'

'So you claim you last had contact with your daughter yesterday afternoon around three o'clock?'

'Yeah. We had a bitch fest with each other.'

'Because she wanted to go to Cardiff with you?'

'Yeah.'

'And she never had contact with you after you went to Cardiff.'

'No.'

'Did you at least try to check on her throughout the evening?'

'No.'

'Why not?'

'Because I knew she was capable of looking after the boys.'

'This is despite the fact that you weren't sure if Ellie was home when you went out.'

'Look, you don't have to rub it in. I know I fucked up. I'm sorry, okay.'

'You should have come straight home, instead of going to your mam's for over three hours. Now you've dragged her into this.'

'I know,' Parry sobbed.

'DI Fagan, I suggest we end this interview,' the duty solicitor requested. 'Miss Parry clearly needs time to process what has happened over the last twenty-four hours. Detaining her will have a negative impact on her mental health.'

Fagan considered the request before nodding. 'Okay, you are free to go, Sophie. But please be aware we will interview you again. We'll be analysing all your phone data. If we find you have lied to us again, you will be questioned, *again*.'

Parry struggled to nod. 'Okay.'

Both left the interview room.

'I think it's finally sinking in what happened to her daughter last night. But I still think she's holding back.'

'Why?' Stacey asked.

'I don't know, and that's the thing. She knows we now have her phone.'

'What do you reckon cyber forensics will find on her phone?' Stacey asked.

'I would imagine a shit load of material she doesn't want us finding.' Fagan gathered his notes. 'We'll interview Tammy Morris and have a round up before calling it a day.'

CHAPTER 12

Newport Central Police Station

Tammy Morris looked withdrawn as she was led into the interview room. The duty solicitor was a tall, stringy man with glasses.

'You understand why you have been brought in this evening, Tammy?' Fagan asked.

'Not really,' Morris grunted.

'You told us you rang the police as soon as you discovered Ellie's body. This was at approximately five past seven this morning.'

'I did,' Morris claimed.

Fagan shook his head. 'We know you phoned Sophie before you phoned the police. CCTV footage taken at Cardiff Central Train Station shows Sophie Parry talking to you at ten past six this morning. Sophie Parry has already confirmed you phoned her before you phoned the police. We also have your phone which has confirmed this. From what little time we've had to analyse your phone we've discovered you and Sophie exchanged twenty messages throughout the evening.'

'That stupid bitch!' Morris shouted. 'I told her to keep her mouth shut.'

'When you heard the smoke alarm, what did you do?'

'I went to get the front door key for Sophie's house to let myself in.'

'And what time was this, exactly?'

Morris massaged her forehead. 'I'm not sure. It was early.'

'What time is early?'

'Just gone six.'

'Then what did you do?'

'I waved a towel to turn off the alarm, before checking on the boys.'

'Where were they?'

'They were in their room, asleep.'

'So the smoke alarm was going off all around the house but didn't keep the boys awake? Obviously, one of them made the toast.'

'Well, yeah, maybe. I can't remember. It's too much for me to recall.'

'According to our first responders, you said that one of the boys got up to make some toast.'

Morris nodded. 'Yeah, that's right. I remember now.'

'After you checked on the boys, what did you do?'

'I went to check on Ellie.'

'When you discovered Ellie was dead, why didn't you call the police straight away?'

Morris hesitated. 'Her mam needed to be told before you lot.'

'Tammy, you didn't phone the police until five past seven. That's over an hour after you discovered Ellie's body.'

'Jesus, I was trying to calm Sophie down. She was distraught. I told her she had to come home straight away.'

'Sophie took over three hours to come home,' Stacey mentioned.

'It's a long way from Cardiff.'

'Not by train. It's a forty-minute journey. We already know she spent the next three hours with her mam in Talywain.'

'What did you expect? She just found out her daughter had been murdered.'

'All the more reason to come home straight away,' Fagan said. 'Why do you think she threw her phone away?'

'I don't bloody know. I'm not a mind reader.' Morris became agitated.

'How did she react once you had told her Ellie was dead?'

'How do you think? She was beside herself. I could barely calm her down.'

Fagan pushed a tablet in front of Morris. 'I'm showing Tammy Morris footage of Sophie Parry at Cardiff train station.'

Morris stared at the video.

'As you can see, Tammy, she doesn't look like a grieving mother. What were you talking about on the phone?'

'What do you think? We were talking about Ellie.'

'So you found Ellie's body and the first thing you did was phone Sophie.'

Morris nodded. 'Yeah.'

Fagan pointed at the tablet. 'And her reaction was a calm one?'

'None of you know Sophie the way I do. I know she seems unemotional, but trust me, she's hurting.'

'Why did you announce you had found Ellie's body on WhatsApp before phoning the police?'

Morris seemed to panic at the question. 'I, uh, wanted to let everyone know what had happened.'

'But surely you must have known the police need to be informed before everyone else.'

'Look, I'm sorry, okay. I know what I did was wrong.'

'Did Sophie know what you did?' Stacey asked.

'Yeah, it was her who suggested it.'

Stacey was horrified at Morris' answer. 'Let me get this straight. Sophie Parry told you to announce that Ellie had been found dead on social media.'

'Yeah.'

'Insensitive of you, wasn't it?'

'You would have kept it quiet.'

'In order to catch the killer as soon as possible,' Fagan countered. 'What you did Tammy, was alert the killer who could be anywhere by now. You want Ellie's murderer caught, don't you?'

'Of course I bloody well do,' Morris barked.

'Then why did you take your time calling the police? Why didn't you call them before phoning Sophie and posting it on social media?'

'I panicked. I didn't know what else to do but phone her mam. I know I shouldn't have put it on WhatsApp. I admit to that.'

Fagan stared at her for several seconds before asking his next question. 'When we interviewed you this morning, you claimed you last saw Ellie yesterday morning when you went to see Sophie. However, Sophie claims her daughter returned home around three yesterday afternoon. You've already stated you were at Sophie's house around that time doing her hair and makeup. Did you see Ellie?'

'Yeah,' Morris confessed.

'How did she seem?'

'Pissed off that her mam was going out to Cardiff. They had a row and Ellie stormed out. Sophie reminded her she had to be back by four to look after the boys.'

'What did Ellie say?'

'She told Sophie to fuck off and that she wouldn't be home.'

'How did Sophie react?' Stacey asked.

'She didn't. Sophie was used to Ellie telling her to fuck off all the time. She was determined not to let it spoil her night.'

Fagan glanced down at his notes. 'You exchanged twenty messages throughout the evening. Your phone data confirms this.'

Morris buried her head in her hands.

'Sophie Parry messaged you about nine o'clock last night. Claiming she had met someone.' He read the message aloud. *'Just pulled this lush looking bloke. Going to give him the ride of his life later on, lol.* You responded to her text. *Go for it hun, you deserve it. Especially what you have been through with that bitch of a daughter of yours. Besides after tonight we'll be set.* What did you mean by that?'

Morris inhaled. 'Sophie and her daughter had been arguing lately.'

'About what?'

'Everything. School, her mental health. Ellie claimed she was being bullied at school.'

'What did you mean by after tonight we'll be set?'

'No comment.'

'According to your phone records, you also made a phone call to your son this morning. You were on the phone for about twenty minutes. What did you talk to him about?'

'I told him what happened to Ellie.'

Fagan located a text message on his tablet. 'You messaged your son around nine thirty this morning just after myself and DS Watkins spoke to you. You told him not to come home, otherwise he'll be in the shit. What did you mean by that?'

'No comment.'

'I don't get it. What do you and Sophie Parry have to gain by lying to us?'

'My son has learning difficulties. He won't understand what's going on. That's why I told him to stay away.'

'Once again, Tammy, you had plenty of opportunity to call the police to inform them you had found Ellie Parry dead. But instead you chose to spread more gossip.'

'Okay, I'm sorry.'

'The only thing you have told the truth about is that your son was in Newport last night.' Fagan glanced at his phone. 'Toby has given a DNA sample.'

An expression of horror flashed across Morris' face. 'You what?'

'Toby, your son gave a DNA sample.'

'He didn't murder Ellie. I told you earlier on this morning. Toby was in Newport.' The expression of horror morphed into an expression of rage.

'Tammy, is there something you wish to say to us?' Fagan asked.

'No,' Morris answered abruptly.

Fagan decided to wrap up the interview. 'Just one more question for you Tammy. Is there anything you wish to say to us before we examine your phone further?'

'No,' Morris responded in a confident tone. 'I've nothing to hide.'

'Okay, well, you're free to go.'

Morris stood up.

'Do you have any other electronic devices in your house?'

'I've got an iPad.'

'You need to stay off social media for the time being, Tammy. It's imperative that you don't post anything that could hamper our murder investigation.'

'Okay,' Morris agreed.

'I don't believe this,' Fagan stated. 'She's full of shit, just like Sophie Parry. Did you see the look on her face when I told her about her son offering a DNA sample?'

Stacey nodded. 'Definitely more going on here than meets the eye, guv.'

Fagan agreed with a nod. 'Come on, let's have one more meeting before we call it a day.'

CHAPTER 13

'Right, team, before we hand this over to the night crew, let's have one last look at the information. Have there been any recent developments?'

Watkins glanced at his phone. 'Labs have had a result with fingerprints taken from the WKD bottle found in the field at the back of the house. They belong to Owen Woods. Police have already knocked on his door, but he's not home. They questioned his dad, but he didn't have a clue where his son might be. They have also searched Woods' bedroom and taken away several items of clothing.'

'Bastard has already done a runner,' Fagan seethed. 'No thanks to Tammy plastering Ellie's murder over social bloody media. What was your impression of Sophie Parry's mother when you interviewed her?'

'Not much, boss. Very loud. Claimed all the time her daughter was with her, she was inconsolable. But she seemed elusive with answers to certain questions we asked her about her granddaughter.'

'Such as?'

'We asked her about Ellie's personal life. She seemed to distance herself from her daughter when we asked if she knew Ellie was drinking and vaping. I did a quick check on Mandy Parry. She was questioned about a domestic disturbance last year at her daughter's house. Apparently, Sophie Parry made a call to the police, claiming that her daughter was out of control and threatening to kill her. No one was arrested, but police referred the family to Social Services.'

'Here's the plan tomorrow. I'll go and see the pathologist to see if he has any more information on the circumstances in which Ellie was murdered.' Fagan glanced at Watkins. 'You and Stacey will head up to Blaenau Gwent Social Services and question them about what they knew about Ellie. Sophie Parry didn't seem very inconsolable when she was with us. I've a feeling when we look through her mobile phone data we'll find a lot more.' Fagan walked over to the whiteboard and scribbled Woods' name. 'It looks like Owen Woods could be a front runner in our list of murder suspects. His fingerprints were on the empty bottle of WKD found at the back of Ellie's house.'

'Should we put out a press release stating that Woods is our number one suspect, guv?' Stacey ask.

'No. If he did murder Ellie, the question we have to ask ourselves is why? Because ecstasy was found at the scene, it's safe to assume that Woods supplied her with the drugs.'

'Her mam was adamant Ellie didn't do drugs. Tammy Morris also said Ellie wouldn't do anything like that,' Stacey said. 'He could have murdered her because she threatened to grass him up.'

Fagan nodded. 'Our priority is to find Woods.' Fagan glanced at the whiteboard. 'I suggest we pull his father in for questioning. With any luck, he may give us something to go on.' Fagan glanced at his watch. 'Let's call it a night. It's going to a be a busy day tomorrow.' Fagan's phone buzzed. 'Shit,' he cursed, realising who had messaged him.

'You alright, boss?' Watkins asked.

Fagan hesitated before nodding. 'Yeah, I'm fine. Just got a text from Griffiths. He wants an update on the investigation. I've got to pop into Cwmbran HQ on my way home.'

CHAPTER 14

Gwent Police HQ – Llantarnam - Cwmbran

'Working late tonight, sir,' Fagan commented, taking a seat in Griffiths' office.

'I've a lot of things to catch up on, DI Fagan,' Griffiths said in a tone that made Fagan feel unsettled. Griffiths locked eyes with him. 'How's the murder investigation going?'

Fagan sat down. 'At first looked like an open and shut enquiry. But we have been bogged down by a wall of lies. The mother of Ellie Parry has lied to us from the beginning and other residents on the street haven't been exactly truthful.'

'So in other words, you haven't any real leads yet.'

'We have one suspect to arrest. A man who lives on the estate where Ellie lives, Owen Woods, is a person of interest. He has plenty of form as a known dealer. We've found evidence linking him to Ellie's murder. An empty bottle of WKD has been found at the back of the house with Woods' fingerprints. Unfortunately Woods has done a runner. Officers will interview his father. Hopefully, he'll be able to help us locate his son. I'm confident it's only a matter of time before we catch him.'

'What do you mean by a wall of lies?'

'Ellie was a girl with a complex family and social life. We've established she led a life that was meant for someone much older. Her mother seems emotionally unattached to her. She took her time returning from Cardiff when she was told about her daughter's murder. She has lied to us regarding her relationship with her daughter. At this point I don't think she had a role to play in Ellie's murder. But she has a lifestyle that is chaotic and was already on the radar of Social Services. They took her children away from her this morning.'

Griffiths remained silent for a few moments. 'I'll assign extra officers to the murder team. It's imperative that we catch the murderer as soon as possible. I don't want the public losing faith in our ability to tackle crime in that area. We are under increasing pressure to tackle crime in the Valleys. The press has been hammering on me about this murder. The Sofrydd is synonymous with crime. Intelligence suggests locals will react negatively if Ellie Parry's killer isn't caught soon.'

'I'm confident my officers with apprehend Woods soon enough,' Fagan said.

'How are you holding up?'

Fagan sensed where the conversation was going. 'I'm fine, sir.'

'I'd just like to remind you that you're due to take the stand next week.'

Fagan nodded. 'Yes, I am well aware of this, sir.'

'Are you certain this won't affect your judgement regarding the current murder investigation?'

'No, it won't affect any decisions I make regarding the Investigation of Ellie Parry's murder. In fact, I've been meaning to ask why I need to give evidence.'

'It's a routine statement you'll be giving in court, DI Fagan. I'm sure you've been on the stand many times before during your career with Merseyside Police.'

'Indeed, I have, sir.'

Griffiths hesitated. 'You've been with Gwent Police for eighteen months now. How do you think you have settled in?'

'I have eased into the job, sir. I have a strong and very capable team around me.'

'The reason I'm asking is because of your recent arrest of the First Minister, Lloyd Bevan. The Senedd has Gwent Police under the microscope regarding this matter.'

'I know my actions will have lasting implications, sir. However, given the information I had obtained and the death of Martin Cooper, I felt Bevan needed to be brought to justice for his role in the murders of Dafydd Collier and Sean Price in 1985.'

Griffiths nodded slowly. 'I want you to tread carefully from now on, DI Fagan. When you first joined us, I said that Gwent Police doesn't need maverick detectives.'

'And I don't intend to step over any lines, sir,' Fagan countered.

'Good,' Griffiths answered abruptly. 'Keep me informed on how the murder investigation is proceeding.'

Fagan stood and looked across at a table in Griffith's office. An old black-and-white photo took up centre place. Fagan recognised Bob Benson in the photo. He was dressed in his Chief Constable's uniform.

Griffith caught Fagan looking at the photograph. 'Something wrong, DI Fagan?'

'No, sir,' Fagan replied before hurrying out of the office.

CHAPTER 15

The Cantreff – Abergavenny

'Evening Fagan,' Jackie greeted. 'You're late tonight. I was about to shut the doors. Jamie is pissed off with you for missing the quiz night.' She poured a pint and placed it on the bar.

Fagan picked it up, bolting it down. 'It's been one of those days, Jacks.' Fagan savoured the taste of the beer.

'I saw the press conference you gave on Wales Today earlier. Shitty stuff going on up the Sofrydd.'

Fagan nodded. 'I've had to deal with all kinds of people today. Including a mother who doesn't give a shit her daughter has been murdered. All she's done is tell me a pack of lies all day. And the young girl who was murdered hasn't exactly got a good reputation. The amount of people coming in and slagging her off has been unbelievable. I don't understand her mother and the lack of empathy for her murdered daughter.'

'There's a lot of parents like that in this town. They let their kids do whatever they want. I had to chase a group of girls away from the beer garden the other day. They had the nerve to ask this bloke to go in and buy them a load of drinks. Abergavenny is a nice enough town during the day. With its cafe culture and all the festivals throughout the year. But pull away that layer of icing. Once the night comes, it turns into a different place. Fortunately, I don't get any trouble in here. But a few of the other pubs are always attracting trouble on the weekends. Then there was a massive brawl at the fair last May.'

'I didn't expect so much change while I was in Liverpool.'

'Do you remember the fair when we were kids?'

Fagan drained the last of his pint and handed it back to Jackie. 'Yeah, brilliant days, weren't they?'

'I know a few girls who lost their virginities to those fair boys.

And nearly all of those girls were underage. I remember when we all used to sit on the waltzers. The fairground boys used to come around and chat us up. Most of them were in their twenties or thirties. Most of us girls were only fourteen or fifteen. An old school friend of mine, Nancy Proctor, ran off with one of them. Her dad went ballistic, caught up with her in Crickhowell. A few months later, she was up the duff. Haven't seen Nancy in years. Will have to look her up on Facebook to see what she's up to these days.'

'I remember Jamie and Dean being addicted to Space Invaders and Asteroids. Jamie used to steal out of his mam's purse when the fair was in town.'

'Oi,' a voice came from the doorway. 'I hope you're not running me down, Fagan.'

Fagan turned around, spotting Jamie Evans. 'No, I was just telling the truth. You told me you always used to thieve from your mam.'

Evans nodded. 'Our mam used to be the only one with money in the house. Our dad used to blow all his wages in the betting shop.'

Dean Tyler walked in behind Evans.

'Dean, what are you doing in town?'

Tyler looked glum 'The other half and me are going our separate ways. I'm glad I still own our mam and dad's house in Llanfoist or I'd be homeless.'

Fagan chuckled. 'With the money you have.'

'You know the old saying, Fagan. Money isn't everything.'

'We were just talking about the fair and what it was like when we were young,' Jackie said.

'The good old days,' Evans said. 'I spent a fortune in those arcades. Especially on the video games. I had to top score on Pac-Man in one of arcades. Do you remember when Outrun came out?'

Tyler nodded. 'I loved that game, and Afterburner.'

'I used to love that *Star Wars* game, the one with vector graphics. I've got it on my computer, still addictive.'

'I had a wander round the fair in September,' Jackie said. 'Just to see what it was like. Load of crap now, all the arcades have gone, and the rides cost a fortune.'

'You're in court next week, aren't you?' Tyler asked.

Fagan nodded slowly. 'Ricky's girlfriend reminded me this morning. Rebecca has been playing on my mind lately. Especially now I know I'm going to be facing off against Nelson's lawyer, who's defending Tim. I don't get how he's able to afford him.'

'Benny has made a shitload of money off that pack of lies he published and the TV and newspaper interviews,' Evans said. 'He's still living in our street. I don't know why he doesn't just fuck off.'

'Sounds to me like he's trying to rub it in. Probably why he's got his solicitor defending Tim.' Fagan took a deep breath.

'Have you had any contact with Tim?' Jackie enquired.

Fagan shook his head. 'After I arrested him, he was processed by the system. I've seen the interviews with him.'

'Is there any chance that Tim will get off with Bec's murder?' Jackie asked.

'He'll plead manslaughter. And put it down to diminished responsibility.' Fagan recalled the moment he arrested Davis. 'When I arrested him, he claimed he didn't mean to kill Rebecca. He just wanted to talk to her. He said she told him she wanted to reconnect with me.'

'What about Justin Pike?' Tyler asked. 'He helped Tim dump Rebecca's body in Bailey Park.'

'Justin will probably get time served. He wasn't there when Tim murdered Rebecca.'

'Stupid sod,' Evans stated. 'He should have never have screwed Benny's wife. Now he's lost everything.'

'The man had been single for years, Jamie,' Jackie stated. 'I'm sure if you were in the same position and some twenty-five-year-old handed it to you on a plate, you wouldn't say no.'

'I wouldn't if Benny the perve Nelson has been anywhere near her. Besides, I'd never do the dirty on Daisy.'

'What about the other things we found out during Rebecca's murder investigation?' Tyler asked. 'About Benny's mother being in a mental asylum. You also mentioned Danny Llewellyn's disappearance.'

'None of which have any relevance to Rebecca's murder trial,' Fagan pointed out. 'And as for Danny's disappearance, that's just a theory.'

'I know. But you have to admit, the murder trial will be weird, because Benny will be called as a character witness. Him and Tim never got on. He's been bragging about it on social media.' Tyler handed Fagan his phone. 'See for yourself.'

Fagan stared at the screen. 'Piece of shit. Thinks he can do anything he wants.'

'What are you going to do, Fagan?' Jackie asked.

'There's not a lot I can do, Jacks. I've been told I have to turn up and take the witness stand.'

'You don't suppose Benny is out to get you, do you, Fagan?'

'How d'you mean?'

'You said it yourself when you came back to Abergavenny. You set a series of events in motion. Perhaps that's why Benny is using that fancy solicitor of his. To rattle your cage. I reckon he's scared of you.'

'Why is that exactly?'

'If Benny has more secrets to hide, the last thing he wanted was you coming back to Abergavenny and bringing them to light. We all know what he was like back in the day. You told us what George told you last year about what Benny and Bob Nelson did to Graham and those other boys at Forest Coalpit Dorms. Benny Nelson should have gone down years ago. You're the one person who could make that happen, Fagan.'

'Nelson needs to make a mistake before I can do anything about him.' Fagan took a swig from his pint.

'I've been talking to a few girls who had encounters with Nelson back in the day. They're more than willing to come out and talk about what Nelson did.'

'Trouble with that, Jacks, is he's got that fancy lawyer. He'll cut anyone to shreds who makes any accusations. Especially since Nelson has made a shitload of money from that book and all the TV interviews he's done. Until Nelson himself confesses to something, there's nothing to charge him with. If one of the girls you know who had encounters with Nelson back in the day comes forward, it would take forever to process. You can't go round accusing people of things these days.'

'So what's happening up the Sofrydd?' Evans asked, changing the subject. 'Pretty nasty murder.'

'Yeah,' Fagan nodded. 'I've had to deal with some real characters.'

'The Sofrydd estate is a smaller version of the Gurnos, if you ask me,' Tyler pointed out.

'I don't get it with parents today. They don't seem to give a shit about what their kids are up to.'

'That's modern living for you, Fagan,' Jackie said. 'Most parents want to do their own thing. When I was bringing up my two, the internet was still new. So I got to spend the time I needed with them to make sure they didn't get up to mischief. Nowadays, as long as the parents are getting benefits, they don't give two shits where their kids are.'

'What do you know about Cymru Teen Chat?' Fagan asked Tyler.

'It's a social media app set up just before the pandemic came along. Allowing teenagers across Wales to connect with each other during lockdown. I've read a few bad things about it. They reckon there's a lot of controversy surrounding the app. I've heard rumours it's used for drug dealing and other illegal activities like sharing images of children. The site owner, Russel Connor, claims the website is safe to use. I'd been meaning to have a look but never got round to it. My tech company is too busy worrying about AI at the moment. They're really making leaps and bounds in that field. It's hard to keep up with.'

'I wouldn't worry about AI,' Evans remarked. 'It's not that clever.'

'Since when have you been an expert in AI?' Tyler asked in a mocking tone.

'I read up on stuff.'

'I wouldn't be so sure, Jamie,' Fagan said. 'They did a bloody good job of bringing Alex X back to life after she had been murdered back in the 90s.'

'Carl the conspiracy theorist is always banging on about AI. Says it's going to be like *Terminator* in another ten years.'

'How many times have I told you, Jamie?' Tyler groaned. 'Don't listen to that silly bastard. I remember all the bullshit he spouted during the pandemic.'

'So how's Melissa?' Jackie asked, winking at Fagan.

'Melissa is fine, thanks.'

'Melissa as in Melissa Knight?' Tyler questioned.

'Yes, what about her?'

'Nothing,' Tyler said, holding his hands up. 'Jamie didn't say anything about you seeing her. She was stunning at school.'

'She's still a stunning-looking woman now.' Fagan smiled.

'You lucky sod, Fagan. She's been living in America for the past few decades, hasn't she?'

'Yeah.'

'It's about time you finally got laid,' Evans said. 'You've been back in Abergavenny long enough.'

'I didn't come back here to get laid. And me and Melissa just bumped into each other in Morrisons a while back.'

'And you've been out with her a few times.'

'We enjoy each other's company.'

Jackie poured four shot glasses and lined them up on the bar. 'Let's have a drink and remember Rebecca, shall we?'

Fagan looked back at her and nodded silently.

Jackie picked up her shot glass. 'To Rebecca. May she find peace and justice in the days ahead.'

CHAPTER 16

DAY 2

Blaenau Gwent Social Services

'We appreciate you seeing us today. I'm Detective Sergeant Sean Watkins. This is Constable Stacey Flynn.'

Janice Blackmoor introduced herself. 'This is my lead social worker, Martin Daniels. I'm the section head for special needs families for Blaenau Gwent Social Services. We were all devastated when we heard the news about what had happened to Ellie Parry. We hope you catch the murderer as soon as possible.'

'Did you know the family well?'

'I was Ellie's social worker,' Daniels revealed.

'What kind of person was Ellie?' Stacey asked.

Daniels considered the question for a few moments. 'She was a troubled teenager,' he reflected. 'Her mother struggled with mental health issues. And Ellie's father didn't want to have a relationship with his daughter. A really sad state of affairs that is repeated all too often.'

'Did you visit Ellie regularly?' Watkins asked.

Daniels nodded. 'Yeah, I was there just last week.'

'How was Ellie when you visited her?'

'She seemed fine at the time of the visit.'

'So there were no issues with her. You didn't have any concerns.'

'Nothing particular springs to mind. We had the usual chat, how she was and how were things at school.'

'What other things did you talk about when you used to visit Ellie?'

'All sorts of things. Her friends, her social life, what she liked to do in her spare time. Her hopes for the future.'

'What did she like to do in her spare time?'

'The usual, you know, hanging out with friends, listening to music. The things teenagers do these days. She was your typical happy-go-lucky girl. Ellie had dreams and ambitions about being a singer. She had a wonderful voice. I've heard her on several occasions. I encouraged her to take part in singing competitions and take singing lessons. She had a powerful voice.'

'Was she having any difficulties at school?'

'Unfortunately, Ellie had been suspended several times from her school over the past two years. We've been in contact with the school. She'd have outbursts in class and swear at the teachers, throw things about, walk out of the classroom.'

'Did you ever talk to Ellie about her behaviour at school?'

'Social Services visited the school frequently over the last year. We've had several meetings with staff at the school. We talked about several options to improve Ellie's behaviour at school. Ellie's bad behaviour comes in waves. Her singing ability helps with her mental health issues. We call it singing therapy.'

'Did Ellie have any concerns when you visited her last week?'

'She was her usual self. She was a bit down on issues at school and other things like her home life. She confided in me she didn't want to live in the street anymore.'

'What kind of relationship do you have with Ellie's mother?'

'Like her daughter, Sophie Parry is a troubled individual. Relying heavily on antidepressants to get her through day-to-day life. Sophie has experienced deep trauma in her life. She hasn't got the best relationship with her mother. When she was thirteen, her father died of a drug overdose. This event has affected her ever since. She told me once that she had a deep connection with her father. And when he died, it devastated her. She still misses him to this day. We offered her a counselling service, but Sophie refused.'

'Why do you think that was?'

'Sophie was resentful towards Social Services. Following the death of her father, she was taken into care. Albeit temporarily. Her mother had difficulty dealing with Sophie.'

'When you visited Ellie Parry last week, did you notice

anything unusual?' Stacey asked.

'How do you mean?'

'What kind of condition was the house in when you arrived?'

'It was well kept. Ellie was a very tidy girl. She was proud of her bedroom. It was a place of comfort for Ellie. An escape from her troubles.'

Stacey glanced at Watkins.

'Did Ellie ever talk to you about personal problems?' Watkins asked. 'Issues with other teenagers on the street?'

'The kids on the Sofrydd are always bickering with each other. But Ellie didn't mention she was having problems with any of them.'

'Has Ellie ever seen a child psychologist? To talk about personal problems that may be bothering her.'

Blackmoor shook her head. 'We didn't think Ellie's behaviour warranted a child psychologist. Her behaviour was manageable. We were making progress with her. We even talked about winding down the visits. From once a week to once a month.'

'When did Sophie Parry first come to the attention of Social Services?'

Blackmoor considered the question. 'It was January last year. We were called following an incident at Sophie's house. Ellie had threatened to stab her mother with a kitchen knife. The police were called, and they referred the family to us.'

'You didn't think the incident was serious enough to take Ellie and Sophie's sons into care?'

'No, we carried out a full assessment of family life and decided it was best if the family stayed together. The family was typical of most families living in that area. Sophie was without a job, so that didn't help matters. They were always struggling for money. Sophie is a heavy smoker. We've tried to help her quit the habit, but we were unsuccessful.'

'Do you know why Ellie threatened to kill her mother?'

'I think it was something to do with the fact that Ellie wanted to go on a trip with her friends to Newport.'

'How would you describe Ellie's relationship with her mother?'

'It was turbulent at times,' Daniels replied. 'But overall, I'd say it was your typical mother-daughter relationship. They'd do things together. They'd go out shopping together. I'd say they had a very close relationship.'

'What about Sophie Parry's sons?'

Blackmoor smiled. 'Two lovely boys. Very popular at the local nursery. I believe they were due to celebrate their fifth birthday in the next week or two. Sophie was planning a big party for them.'

'So there was no cause for concern.'

'No, not at all.'

'We'd like access to all records relating to Ellie Parry,' Stacey requested.

Blackmoor pursed her lips. 'Certain parts of her file are confidential because of ongoing internal reviews. I can provide you with a summary instead.'

'A summary would be fine for now, but we're going to need access to detailed records in time,' Stacey said. 'A detailed background history will help our officers build a better picture of what kind of person she was.'

Blackmoor shook her head. 'I'm sorry, but we cannot divulge any detailed records on Ellie Parry at this time until we've run our own investigation. Because of what happened to Ellie, we have to make sure we did everything in our power to help the girl.'

'Investigation into what?' Watkins asked.

Blackmoor looked directly at him. 'Social Services have a duty of care to all its charges. Given what happened to Ellie, we need to go through all our records to determine whether her murder could have been prevented. When something like this happens, it's always easy for people, the press and the police to point the fingers at Social Services. It's imperative that we carry out a full investigation to see if we could have helped. As a matter of fact, Ellie was due to go on one of our respite trips.'

'What is a respite trip?'

'It's a new programme we started up earlier this year. Children under the care of Blaenau Gwent Social Services are taken out of their environment and given a short break for a weekend. Usually a place in the country. Something totally different from their usual surroundings. We find that this helps with dealing with their mental health issues.'

'How long will it take you to conduct your investigation so that you can give us a full report?'

Blackmoor glanced at Daniels. 'As you will understand, DS Watkins, investigations like these take time.'

'How much time?'

'As long as it takes.'

Watkins closed his notebook. 'We'd appreciate it if you'd let us have a full copy of your report as soon as you've conducted your investigation.'

'Yes, that shouldn't be a problem,' Blackmoor stated. 'We'll let you know as soon as we've finished.'

Watkins and Stacey left the office.

'What do you reckon?' Stacey asked.

'The biggest bullshit fest I've heard in a while,' Watkins replied. 'So far, just about everyone has spun a pack of lies.'

'Why? What's the point? When everything will eventually come out.'

'There's obviously a lot of shit going on in that street. Sophie Parry has done nothing but lie from the start. She knows she's in a lot of shit. But the woman is too stupid to realise that. Tammy Morris has also lied to us. I can't believe she posted on social media about Ellie before contacting the police. What does that say about the woman?'

'Why do you think Social Services are lying?'

'Probably to cover their own arses. It's obvious they haven't seen Ellie Parry in a while. I'm guessing they're like every other Social Service department in Wales, overworked. Ellie probably dropped off their radar months ago. Daniels told a blatant lie about how he only visited Ellie last week. You saw the state their house was in. No one's been there in months. And as for Sophie having a loving relationship with her daughter, that's a bunch of bullshit.'

Stacey thumbed through the pictures on her phone, stopping on a picture of her with her mum. 'I sometimes wonder what my life would have turned out like if my mam hadn't had died. My father was a dealer and my brothers. They made mam's life hell. I was in foster care for a while before my nan and grandad took me in. I hated foster care. Looking back, I could tell the foster carers were just doing it for the money and nothing else. I was so glad when my nan and grandad turned up. They gave me the life I should have had with mam.'

Watkins threw Stacey a sidewards glance. 'Any regrets about turning evidence against your dad?'

'Nope.' Stacey shook her head. 'If it wasn't for him, my mam would still be alive today. He didn't give a shit when she died. Neither did my brothers. They were too busy living the dream. Fast cars, piles of money, endless holidays. All from making people's lives a misery with drugs. It was harrowing to see the ecstasy by the side of Ellie's bed yesterday when we entered the house. Such a pretty young girl with her life ahead of her. There were times yesterday when me and the guv interviewed her mam, when I wanted to leap across the table and punch her in the gob. When I took her up to Prince Charles in Merthyr to see Ellie, she didn't show one hint of emotion. I remember when I found my mam's body in that squalor of a house we used to live. I still haven't got over it. I'm just glad my nan and grandad were there to pick up the pieces with me.' Stacey's phone pinged. 'Cyber forensics wants to see us. They've analysed the information on Sophie Parry's phone.'

'Now it's about to ramp up,' Watkins remarked. 'The boss should be in Merthyr now, getting results from the pathologist.'

CHAPTER 17

Prince Charles Hospital Merthyr Tydfil

The pathologist looked up as Fagan entered his office. 'DI Fagan, I was just about to call you.' She pulled a folder from a desk drawer and handed it to Fagan. 'A full report on the Ellie Parry murder.'

Fagan pulled the report from the folder.

'Further examination of her body revealed that there was no sign of rape.'

'So, sex was consensual?'

The pathologist nodded. 'But that's only the beginning. I found signs of a struggle. There were small traces of skin underneath Ellie's fingernails. When I spoke to you and DS Watkins yesterday, I mentioned our killer had his hands around Ellie's neck for a considerable length of time.'

'So they had sex and after, our suspect murders Ellie.'

'No,' the coroner shook her head. 'The toxicology report revealed there was a significant amount of ecstasy in Ellie's blood. The bruises on Ellie's neck were consistent with strangulation. But not severe enough to suggest that our killer had violent intentions. In many strangulations I've seen, the larynx is usually crushed, indicating a violent act. Here, the bruising on the larynx isn't severe enough to prove she met a violent end. However, because of the amount of ecstasy she had taken, her heart rate would have sped up enough to bring on a heart attack.'

'Is that what killed her?'

'I'm certain of it, yes.'

'Could this have been some kind of sex game that went wrong?'

'It's possible. In the thirty years I've been a pathologist, I've come across eleven cases of this kind of act. Where a man has accidentally killed his wife or partner through strangulation while having sex. The last one I investigated was last year, a man in his 50s. Choked his wife to death while having sex with her.'

Fagan glanced at the report. 'But there were traces of skin found under Ellie's fingernails. If this was some kind of sex game, perhaps Ellie decided she didn't like it. And fought against whoever it was she was having sex with.'

'That's the way I see it,' the pathologist said. 'However, there is more, and this is where it gets weird. Following Ellie's murder it would appear our suspect stayed for a while.'

'Revelling in his crime, I would imagine.'

'Forensics found semen on the bedsheets and on Ellie's clothing. It looks as if our murderer masturbated over her body.'

'Jesus,' Fagan gasped.

'There were trace elements of gravel found on the bedsheets. Showing that he was standing on the bed at the time of masturbation. If you ask me, DI Fagan, this was a very careful and choreographed murder.'

'A premeditated murder.'

'But it's going to be hard to prove.' The pathologist paused. 'And this is where it gets super weird.'

'How?'

'I've found something that's made me consider a serial killer may be at the centre of this.'

'A serial killer.' Fagan could hardly believe what he was hearing. 'How have you reached that assumption?'

'Labs have analysed the semen samples I sent them. It would appear the victim had sex with at least three men within the past forty-eight hours. Labs found one match straight away. There's a national database for unknown DNA samples. It's where deaths have taken place, but DNA found at each scene remains unknown. While looking through the database, I came across four deaths in the past four years. In all the cases an autopsy was performed. Semen samples were taken. The mystery DNA sample I found from Ellie's body matches DNA from the four other deaths. But there is no name matching the sample.'

'How old are the victims?'

The pathologist tapped the keyboard on her laptop. 'They range between nineteen and twenty-two. The first victim lived in Manchester. The second victim lived in Peterborough. The third in Swansea and the fourth in Warwick.'

'Anything connecting all four women?'

'They were all students.'

'So whoever our murderer is, he's targeting students.'

'And there's where you hit a wall.'

'Why?'

'The deaths were all put down to suicide.'

'Suicide?' Fagan questioned.

The pathologist nodded. 'Two died of an overdose. One hung herself in her dorm and the other slit her wrists in the bath.'

Fagan glanced at the pathologist. 'So the girls who died were all in contact with whoever murdered Ellie Parry?'

'Yes. The semen samples found on Ellie and her clothes and bedsheets match DNA found on the other girls, who had one thing in common at the time of their deaths. They all had sex with the person who murdered Ellie. Three of the deaths have occurred in the last eighteen months. The first death occurred on March 16, 2020.'

Fagan considered the information at hand. 'A week after that, the country went into lockdown because of Covid.'

'Which means our killer had to pause his activities. The next death occurred in December 2022, when the country was recovering from Covid. Then after that, June 2023, then January this year.'

'Let's back up here. We have four other deaths with DNA samples matching the sample found at Ellie's. But the deaths have been put down to suicide.'

'Yeah.'

Fagan ran the information through his mind. 'If we are dealing with a serial killer, then he's taken things to the next level.'

'How do you mean?'

'Four of the girls committed suicide, but Ellie was partially strangled. She is the fifth victim, and the first murder victim,'

Fagan said. 'Her death is the second in Wales. Suggesting our suspect could be a resident. The moment I stepped into that bedroom and saw the body, I had a feeling this was no ordinary murder. There was a tripod and lighting. Plus, the murderer took Ellie's phone.'

'This is a weird one,' the pathologist remarked.

Fagan glanced at the report. 'Ellie was his first actual victim. Which means if we don't catch him soon, he will grow more confident.'

'He's a fledgling killer finding his feet.'

'I need you to e-mail me a full copy of this report so I can pass it on to the rest of my team.' Fagan stood. 'I'll head back to Newport for a team briefing. As soon as your contact lets you know about the other two DNA samples, text me the information.'

'Will do.'

Fagan inhaled. 'This has just taken things to the next level.'

CHAPTER 18

Tarian – Regional Cyber-Crimes Unit – Newport

"We've recovered a sizeable chunk of information from Sophie Parry's phone. She was in contact with her daughter until just after midnight last night.' Edwin Corke revealed.

'Something to add to the bullshit she's been spinning?' Watkins rolled his eyes.

'It appears they were arguing for most of the day and well into the night. There are some really nasty exchanges between Sophie and her daughter.'

Watkins read one of the messages. *'You're a vile cunt.'*

'I have to admit, I was shocked when I read some of these messages. This certainly isn't a normal mother and daughter relationship.'

'Ellie wanted to go with her mam to Cardiff,' Stacey mentioned. 'By the looks of some of these messages, Ellie was really pissed off with her mam.'

Watkins stared at the screen, pointing. 'Her mother's boasting she's just picked up some bloke in a pub. The Prince of Wales.'

'Ellie's responded by saying that she's going to get in contact with someone called Shadowcaster off CTC,' Corke said. 'And that she's going to invite him round to her place.'

'Shadowcaster,' Watkins stated, looking at Ellie. 'During his interview yesterday, Taylor Richards mentioned someone called Shadowcaster. He said that Ellie and her friends were talking to him on CTC the day that Ellie died. Richards also claimed he had an argument over this Shadowcaster.'

'Ellie invited her murderer over. The poor girl had no idea what was going to happen to her,' Stacey said.

Corke picked up a tablet with a sticker marked evidence.

'We've also had a look at the boys' tablets the forensics recovered from the bedroom. If you think the text messaging was bad between Ellie and her mother, this will definitely make you shudder. We've examined the tablets found in the boys' bedroom.'

'What have you found?' Watkins asked.

Corke tapped the screen. 'That's the trouble with the internet these days. Too many parents use it as convenient babysitter. Are you ready for this?'

'Go on,' Watkins invited.

'You would have thought that any young child with a tablet would look at kids' videos on YouTube or play simple games. I'm afraid it isn't like that with these two boys. They were accessing illicit pornographic material.'

Stacey clasped her hand over her mouth and closed her eyes. A wave of emotion cascaded over her.

'You okay Stacey?' Watkins asked.

'I'm sorry. I can't look at this. This is just too much for me to handle.'

Watkins nodded. 'No worries, I'll meet you back at the office. The boss should be back soon. He'll want to be updated on what he's missed this morning.'

Stacey hurried out of the room.

'The material these boys were exposed to is pretty fucked up,' Corke revealed. 'Both tablets we recovered have no child locks on them. Sophie Parry is just giving them a free rein on this.'

'What kind of mother lets her two young sons access hard core porn? They're only five years old, for Christ's sake.'

'Unfortunately, it's all too common these days. We have cases nearly every week of young children accessing pornographic material. It's turned into an epidemic. Tarian cyber-crimes unit has even employed child psychologists.'

'What about this Cymru Teen Chat?'

'Don't get me started on that.' Corke let out a snort of derision. 'Russel Connor, the man who runs it is an arrogant prick. He claims this app is safe for all teenagers to use. Everything is encrypted on it. The software uses facial recognition technology to unlock it. I banned my son from using it last year. It was causing him to self-harm and have thoughts of suicide.'

'I was doing a little reading yesterday,' Watkins said. 'Cymru Teen Chat had been blamed for a spate of suicides in 2022. A team was assembled to investigate, but nothing came of the investigation.'

Corke nodded. 'I was part of the team heading up the investigation. It was cut short because Chief Constable Griffiths reckoned it was costing too much to run. One of the senior detectives on the investigation was Detective Sergeant David Padfield. He was pissed off when they closed down the investigation. He put in a complaint about the investigation being closed. Russel Connor, who owns the software, has a lot of influence in the Senedd.'

Watkins couldn't help smiling. 'The Senedd is having problems of its own right now.'

Corke nodded. 'I saw the First Minister being arrested live on TV. Fagan had some balls walking onto that Senedd floor and arresting him. I never liked the man, especially when he introduced that stupid twenty mile an hour speed limit.'

Watkins studied this screen. 'It looks like Sophie Parry was arguing with her daughter for most of the day. Ellie was begging to go to Cardiff with her. But Sophie's telling her to fuck off.' Watkins inhaled. 'Shit, if only we had Ellie's phone.'

Corke nodded. 'We have Ellie's phone number, and are checking to see which network she is with.'

'I need you to e-mail me information about Sophie Parry's phone straight away. The boss is going to want to see this. We'll have to interview Sophie Parry again. That woman has done nothing but string us along ever since this investigation started.'

'Ellie Parry's murder is generating a lot of interest on social media. The amount of conspiracy theories being spouted is unbelievable. It's like people have got nothing better to do than to jump on the latest bandwagon and just start spouting crap. and they claim it's all about free speech. Half the people who come up with this shit don't even know the meaning of free speech. They can't tell the difference between saying something sensible and being a complete dickhead.'

'Call up the last text message Ellie sent her mam,' Watkins requested.

Corke clicked on the mouse.

'Jesus,' Watkins gasped, staring at the text message. *'Do you want me to film it and upload it to FansOnly?.'* Watkins shuddered. 'According to the pathologist, Ellie had sex within the past twenty-four hours.' Watkins inhaled. 'Ellie invited her murderer over. A tripod and light were set up in the corner of the room. DI Fagan is right. The man who murdered Ellie did film it. Jesus, this is dark.'

'Ellie was fourteen, wasn't she?'

'Yeah.' Watkins nodded.

'I'm guessing whoever Ellie had sex with before she died was much older.' Corke pointed at the screen. 'Perhaps he found out Ellie's actual age and didn't want her bragging about having sex with an older man. Perhaps she threatened to grass him up. Triggering him to murder her.'

'The pathologist is still unclear how she died.' Watkins mulled over the information. 'What time did Ellie last text her mother?'

Corke studied the screen. 'Eleven minutes after midnight.'

Watkins looked at his phone that had just buzzed. 'My boss is on his way back from Merthyr. I'd better get all this and get it up to the office upstairs. He's going to want to see everything. I want you to e-mail me everything you've discovered on Sophie Parry's phone.'

'Yeah, sure.' Corke replied. 'Have you got at least half an hour more you can spare? There's a lot more on this phone you need to see before you brief DI Fagan. And I should warn you, it gets a lot darker.'

'Show me,' Watkins instructed.

CHAPTER 19

Newport Central Police Station

Watkins stood next to a large screen TV, holding a tablet. 'There's a shitload to go through here, boss. Finding Sophie Parry's phone has opened another can of worms, and a very disturbing one at that. Cyber forensics uncovered a wealth of information on her phone that gives us insight into her life and the life of Ellie. Which I'm sad to say is more disturbing.' Watkins paused. 'Sophie Parry, thirty-six years of age. It's turns out that Sophie has a FansOnly account.'

'FansOnly?' Fagan questioned.

'It's a social media platform that lets individuals share explicit images and videos. Not to be confused with OnlyFans, which is another site that lets individuals share their private lives. OnlyFans has come under heavy criticism from people who want it taken offline. A few years ago, the owners of the site changed their online platform.'

'So they toned down their graphic content.'

'Basically, yeah. You still get people on the platform showing explicit images and stuff like that, but they're not allowed to take it any further. FansOnly, however, has taken another path, a much darker path.'

'Let me guess, pornographic?'

Watkins nodded. 'Yeah, and FansOnly have no strict guidelines on who's allowed to show what. Literally anything goes on this site. Sophie Parry has an account with them. She's been uploading sexually explicit images and videos. And it gets more disturbing than that. Whereas OnlyFans allow just one person to have one account. FansOnly allow a person to open an account and let four other people take part.'

'So it's like a group thing, then?'

Watkins nodded. 'Campaigners have been trying to shut down the site since 2020. The owner has been accused of letting content providers show really explicit material. The site has also been linked to other activities. Drug traffickers are known to be using the site. Sophie Parry opened her account in July 2020, during the darkest days of the pandemic, when everyone was in lockdown. She has three thousand subscribers. She's uploaded over six thousand videos and pictures. Parry features in most of the content. Videos and pictures.' Watkins paused, taking a deep breath. 'However, cyber forensics says that she also uploaded over seventeen hundred images and videos are of Ellie. Most of which are of graphic content.'

'Jesus, Sophie Parry was pimping out her own daughter,' Brooks stated.

'Please don't tell me that Sophie Parry was in some of those videos with her own daughter,' Fagan groaned.

'No.'

Stacey massaged her forehead. 'Makes me sick to my stomach.'

'Where is this website based?' Fagan asked.

'In the Philippines.' Watkins answered. 'It gets worse, boss. The site was established by a man called Paul Decker. He's a convicted paedophile here in the UK. Moved to the Philippines in 2009 where he became a tour operator for sex tourists.'

'How is he able to run a website that has this shit on it? Hasn't the UK Cyber Division been able to block it?'

'The National Crime Agency has been trying to crack this website since it was first established during lockdown. But so far they've been unsuccessful. According to our cybercrimes division, the website uses sophisticated software. The site has a three-tier membership system. Basic, Premium and Platinum memberships. Basic membership gets you access to pornographic material. Images and videos, nothing more. Premium membership allows you to message content providers, albeit on a limited basis.'

'What do you mean by that, Sean?'

'Premium Members can message content providers and ask

them to do stuff. Content providers set the price. But there is a price cap on what members can pay.'

'And platinum membership? What does that allow members to do?'

'Just about anything they want. Platinum membership allows subscribers live access to content providers. Unrestricted two-way communication. And there is no price cap. Members can pay content providers as much as they want to perform different acts. The more explicit the act, the more content providers can charge. Also, Platinum subscribers are the only ones allowed to view their content. Because of the sophisticated software the website uses, the National Crime Agency can't get a location on any of its members in the UK. From what little information I've been able to gather from our cybercrime unit, the NCA believe there are at least fifteen thousand members in the UK. Over seven thousand members have platinum membership. FansOnly boasts it has seventeen million subscribers worldwide. The NCA has tried to set up accounts to crack this website, but every time they set up an account, it's deleted almost immediately.' Watkins paused. 'Do you want to hear the best part, if there is such a thing?'

'Let's hear it.'

'Paul Decker was jailed for eight years in 1993, following the successful conviction of a paedophile gang in Swansea.'

Fagan's heart skipped a beat.

Watkins hesitated before saying his next line. 'Decker was a serving Detective Sergeant with South Wales Police. Decker, along with twenty-three other men, including local politicians and two other serving police officers, were convicted of a series of crimes, including possession of child pornography and sexual activity with children. Their conviction was part of a police investigation called Operation Julie.'

'I've heard of that.' The name triggered a memory in Fagan's mind.

Watkins tapped on his tablet and looked at the TV screen. 'Operation Julie was launched in 1992. Twelve-year-old Julie Mann was found in Cromwell Street in the Mount Pleasant area of Swansea. She'd been subjected to torture, sexual abuse, and strangulation. The story made national headlines. Despite the publicity, Jullie's murderer was never caught.'

'Is the case still open?' Stacey asked.

'It's still considered as a cold case. It opened up a can of worms for local authorities and South Wales Police. Exposing public figures, local politicians and serving police officers.'

'Right, okay,' Fagan interrupted. 'Before we get sidetracked here, let's focus on Ellie and finding her murderer. What else did you find on Sophie Parry's phone?'

'A string of text messages between Ellie and her mam. They didn't have your typical mother-daughter relationship. The language they use shows their relationship was very adult. Whether you like it or not, boss, this also has to do with that website. Last week, she had an argument with her daughter. In one message, Ellie said that Sophie was destroying her life and didn't give a shit. Sophie responds by telling Ellie that the money she earns keeps her in luxuries.'

'Luxuries,' Fagan mocked. 'I'd hardly describe them living in the lap of luxury, judging by the state of the house. If Sophie Parry was earning money from this website, she'd be able to afford a cleaner.'

'I've traced records and text messages going back at least three years. Most of the text messages use simple decryption software cybercrimes were able to decipher. Are you ready for this? Sophie Parry and her daughter were both engaged in a sexual relationship with Toby Morris, Tammy Morris' son.'

'What?' Fagan exclaimed.

Watkins stared at his tablet. 'It goes a long way to explain why she threw her phone in the bin at Cardiff Central. Some of the messages exchanged between Sophie and her daughter regarding Toby Morris are pretty explicit.'

'Jesus, what the hell is going on up the Sofrydd? I want Toby Morris pulled in ASAP,' Fagan demanded, taking stock of the information. 'So, Sophie Parry has been having a sexual relationship with Tammy Morris' son. Ellie has also been having a relationship with him. Didn't Tammy Morris mention her son has learning difficulties?'

'Yeah,' Watkins nodded. 'When we interviewed her earlier, she said he had autism and ADHD.'

'Sophie Parry has been sharing graphic images of her fourteen-year-old daughter. I want her arrested and dragged back down here immediately.'

'I'm on it, sir.' Brooks hit the speed dial on his phone.

'Let's go back to the day that Ellie was murdered. We know her mother was going out that evening to Cardiff with a bunch of other girls from the street.'

'Ellie and her mother messaged each other over a hundred times throughout the day Ellie was murdered. We've also found out Ellie was using Cymru Teen Chat throughout the day. She mentioned this in several messages she sent to her mam.'

'What time was the last message sent?'

'Around four minutes past midnight.'

'According to a taxi driver, he saw someone running away from that area about one in the morning. Running down Sofrydd road towards Hafodyrynys. So, Ellie was murdered somewhere between midnight and one o'clock. Any luck on locating Owen Woods?'

'Not yet, boss.'

'We've yet to determine the last person to see Ellie alive, guv,' Stacey remarked.

'Unless you count Tammy Morris, who claims she looked in on Ellie in the evening when she returned from her friend's house. Ellie was supposedly watching Netflix. And that's assuming Tammy Morris is telling the truth. The fact we know her son was engaged in a sexual relationship Sophie and Ellie adds another layer to this investigation. That woman has already lied to us multiple times. At this point I think we should take everyone's statements with a pinch of salt.'

Brooks checked his phone that had just pinged. 'Search teams have found an iPhone on waste ground at the back of the house.'

'That has to be Ellie's phone,' Fagan said, rubbing his hands together. 'We need to get that phone to cyber forensics as soon as possible.'

Watkins checked his tablet. 'Ellie sent two messages to her

mam just after midnight. The first message says, *He's here. I'm gonna have the ride of my life, unlike you, who will be too pissed to remember what you've done in the morning.* Ellie sent her mam a second message. *Do you want me to film it and upload it to FansOnly?*'

'It makes sense now. The tripod and the lighting.'

'Sophie Parry doesn't respond. However, between quarter to six and ten past six the following morning, Sophie Parry sends four messages to Ellie's phone. She even rings her three times.'

'Unaware that her daughter was already dead. Let's hear some of the messages.'

'*How did it go last night? Did you film it?* That text was sent at a quarter to six. Five minutes later, Parry sends another message. *Oi, clit, wakey, wakey. How did it go last night? I hope you put on a decent show. You know we're going to make a shitload of money. Enough to set us up for the next few years.* Then, at five past six, Parry sent another message. *FFS Ellie, answer your fucking phone, clit.* Sophie tries to ring Ellie twice after that before sending one last message. *Fine, b like that u selfish cunt.* We know that Tammy Morris first contacted Parry around that time to tell her Ellie was dead.'

Fagan puffed out his cheeks. 'I find it almost impossible to wrap my head around this. Okay, I will not go into too much detail, but my visit from the pathologist has turn up some disturbing results.' Fagan paused. 'There's a possibility Ellie could have been the victim of a serial killer. DNA evidence found on Ellie's body has been linked to four other deaths.'

'You're sure about that, boss?'

Fagan nodded. 'But for now, let's concentrate on Ellie. According to her last text message, Ellie asks her mam if she wants her to film her having sex with the murderer. Ellie filmed her own murder, Sean. The whole tripod and light setup. This doesn't strike me as a heat of the moment murder. The poor girl had no idea what was going to happen. Our suspect stayed in Ellie's house for some time.'

'The two boys could have witnessed it,' Stacey said.

'Agreed.' Fagan responded. 'Specialist officers will interview them tomorrow to find out if they saw the killer in the house. But our priority goal has to be Ellie. Right, this is what we'll do. Me and Sean will wait for Sophie Parry to turn up. After that we'll interview Toby Morris about his relationship with Ellie and her mother. Andrew, I want you to get down to the cyber division and drag everything off Tammy Morris' phone. I also want to know the moment they access Ellie's phone.' Fagan reflected on the past twenty-four hours. 'This started off as a straightforward murder. However, we have uncovered other crimes which is going to make this more complex. Let's get cracking.' He glanced at Stacey, looking towards the door. 'I need a quick word.'

Stacey breathed the fresh air outside the police station.

Fagan handed her a cup from the coffee machine in the canteen. 'It's better that what Andrew makes.'

Stacey accepted the cup. 'Thanks.' She took a sip.

'Are you okay with investigating this case?'

'Not really, guv.'

'I can tell it's having an effect on you.'

Stacey watched the traffic passing the police station. 'I don't know why. Ever since I saw Ellie the other day, it's triggered so much emotion.'

Fagan inhaled. 'No matter how many murders you investigate, you never get used to a child murder. Plus the fact we've examined Sophie Parry's phone it's opened another can of worms.'

Stacey sipped from her cup.

'I want you to do me a favour. I'm sending you on a side quest.'

'Side quest?' Stacey quizzed.

'I want you to pull the casefile on Operation Jullie.'

'The case that Sean just mentioned.'

'Yeah.'

'Is there a specific reason you want to see the casefile, guv?'

'If Paul Decker was part of the operation, I want a list of all the other officers involved in the operation, including those arrested with him.'

'Yeah, sure. Anything in particular you're looking for?'

'I won't know that until you pull the casefile.'

'I should be helping out on the murder of Ellie Parry,' Stacey countered.

'And you will be,' Fagan assured her. 'Pull the casefile, analyse it, and let me know if there are any discrepancies.'

'Okay.' Stacey nodded.

C H A P T E R 2 0

Newport Central Police Station.

'Interview with Sophie Parry. Present in the room is Sophie Parry and the duty solicitor David Tucker. Interviewing officers are Detective Inspector Marc Fagan and Detective Sergeant Sean Watkins. Sophie, I need to remind you of your rights. But, it may harm your defence if you do not mention when questioned something which you later rely on in court. Anything you do say may be given in evidence. Do you understand the rights I have read to you?'

After several seconds Parry nodded. 'Yeah.'

Fagan swiped his tablet. A picture appeared on a large screen monitor. 'I'm showing Sophie Parry a picture of her mobile phone recovered from Cardiff Central train station. Is this your mobile phone, Sophie?'

Parry glanced at the picture on the screen. 'No comment.'

'Extensive examination of your phone has revealed a series of text messages you sent your daughter the day before yesterday. Can you remember what you said when we asked when was the last time you had contact with Ellie?'

'No comment.'

'You told us you last had contact with Ellie before you went to Cardiff. Around three o'clock in the afternoon.' Fagan glanced down at the information on the tablet. 'The information we recovered from your phone revealed you and Ellie exchanged a hundred and twenty-five messages throughout the day. These include messages you exchanged throughout the evening. I'd like to remind you we've interviewed you twice, Sophie. In the first interview you claimed you had no contact with Ellie after she went out in the morning, the day she was murdered. In the second interview, you claimed to have had contact with Ellie before you went out to Cardiff. But these text messages prove you were in contact with Ellie all day and well into the evening. In fact, you were in contact with her right until the moment she was murdered.'

'No comment.'

'One of the last messages Ellie sent you was at two minutes past midnight.' Fagan paused before reading the message. '*He's here. I'm gonna have the ride of my life, unlike you, who will be too pissed to remember what you've done in the morning.*'

Parry stared at the wall. 'No comment.'

'Doesn't it disturb you that your daughter notified you that her murderer had just turned up?'

'No comment.'

'You were arguing with Ellie all day. The day she was murdered. You exchanged verbal insults with her. You called her some really nasty names. Names, no mother should be calling their daughter. Ellie was equally disturbing in her responses to your messages. Sophie, listen to me carefully. Help us out here. Don't you understand? Your life is more or less over. You've lost everything, your two boys, your daughter, you've no future. When did it all go wrong between you?'

Parry glanced at Fagan. 'No comment.'

Fagan tapped the tablet. 'While conducting an examination of your phone, our cyber forensics team found other material. Material of a disturbing nature, a graphic nature. The information on your phone revealed you had a FansOnly account.'

Parry ran a trembling hand through her hair. 'No comment.'

'You've uploaded over six and a half thousand sexually explicit pictures and videos over a four-year period. According to this information, you created the account in July 2020 during lockdown.'

'No comment,' Parry responded with a defiant tone.

'Seventeen hundred and fifty-two photos and videos you uploaded featured your daughter Ellie.' Fagan checked his notes.

Parry buried her face in her hands.

'These videos featuring your daughter are of a graphic and sexual nature. The videos stretch back over a two-year period.

How old was Ellie two years ago, Sophie?'

'No comment.'

'You've done nothing but lie over the last two days, Sophie. Why? Doesn't Ellie deserve better? Doesn't she deserve justice? Or are you just going to sit there and pretend like you had nothing to do with this?'

'I didn't murder my fucking daughter!' Parry yelled. 'I didn't know what was going to happen. How would I have known? I was in Cardiff. You have to believe me. I had no idea what was going to happen.'

'Sophie, do you have any idea who murdered your daughter?'

'No, I swear!'

'Let's look at this text, shall we? The last but one message she sent you.' Fagan read the text. '*He's here. I'm gonna have the ride of my life, unlike you, who will be too pissed to remember what you've done in the morning.* Do you have any idea who Ellie was referring to?'

Parry shook her head. 'No.'

Fagan glanced at his tablet. 'During the afternoon, Ellie mentions someone called Shadowcaster, and that she was inviting him over later that evening.'

Parry stared back at Fagan with an expression etched with fear.

'It couldn't have been anyone on the estate, could it?'

'I don't know. Ellie had a new bloody boyfriend every other week. I couldn't keep up with her.'

'Were you jealous of Ellie?'

'No,' Parry snorted.

'How did you pay for the hotel you stayed in?' Fagan checked his notes. 'The Big Sleep.'

Parry hesitated before answering. 'Cash.'

'Who paid?'

'The bloke I was with. Everyone pays by cash at the Big Sleep. Especially those who have been shagging behind their partner's back.'

'Did he leave you any contact details so that we can verify your whereabouts?'

'No,' Parry replied. 'It was a one-night stand, not a full on relationship. In the morning we parted ways.'

'What time was this?'

Parry scratched the bridge of her nose. 'It was early, before six o'clock.'

'Let's go back to your account, on FansOnly. You signed on to the website in July 2020. Why?'

'Everyone was in lockdown,' Parry answered. 'You couldn't go out anywhere. Fucking government telling you to stay at home. Don't go out, don't mingle with anyone. It was driving me up the fucking wall. The police were constantly patrolling the estate to make sure no one was outside and talking to each other. It was like a fucking prison. I got so fed up with it. I was going stir-crazy, stuck in the house all day long. All there was to do was watch Netflix or surf the internet. I got so bored with Netflix.'

'Is that when you came across the website, FansOnly?'

'Yeah,' Parry nodded. 'I heard this girl from Tredegar was making a shitload of money every month from it.'

'Doing what?' Watkins asked.

Parry rolled her eyes. 'What do you bloody well think?'

'Posing nude in front of the camera?'

'Yeah,' Parry replied. 'That's when I set up the account. I posted a couple of videos online. I didn't really think much of it. Everyone was doing something during lockdown. People going on YouTube and doing stupid things, making a fortune. That Joe Wicks was making a bloody fortune with his stupid exercise videos.'

'So you thought you'd have a go at doing something?' Fagan guessed.

'Yeah,' Parry admitted. 'I posted a couple of short videos and half a dozen pictures. I didn't think anything would come of it.'

'But?'

Parry reflected for a moment. 'My videos and photos made two hundred quid. People started messaging me from all over the world. Asking me to make more videos. So I turned out videos. The more videos I made, the more money I'd make. At one point I was making a couple of hundred quid a week. It was so easy to make money just by posing in front of a camera. It was better than getting benefits from the government.'

'But you still claimed benefits, while you were making money off FansOnly.'

'Everyone's doing something these days to make extra money. Benefits aren't enough to keep me going.'

'You could have got a regular job like everyone else, Sophie,' Watkins suggested.

'What, and have to answer to some dickhead of a fucking manager? Who doesn't know their arse from their elbow, I don't think so.' Parry hesitated before continuing. 'I wasn't making as much money as some girls on there. I mean, look at me, I'm not exactly Marilyn bloody Monroe, am I? I heard some of the girls on there were making up to fifteen grand a month. Getting their kit off and doing other things.'

'Other things?' Fagan asked.

'Don't be so bloody naïve. You know what I mean.'

Fagan nodded. 'You mean more hardcore stuff?'

'Yeah. It all started off pretty tame, you know. Stuff like get my baps out for a couple of old codgers in America. Blokes would ask me to go full nude. I thought, what harm could it do? I mean, it wasn't like they were in the same room. They couldn't touch me or anything. It was easy money. And I was in control of everything. I turned down loads of freaky stuff blokes would ask me to do. They wanted me to go with women and men, but that just wasn't my thing, you know.'

'So what was your thing?'

'Just normal stuff, you know, showing my tits, flashing my fanny. Playing with myself.'

'That's normal, is it?' Fagan asked.

'I was earning money from it,' Parry defended herself. 'By the end of the first year of the pandemic, I was making around two hundred and fifty quid a week. It was a full-time income. I didn't have to do much. It's not like I had to do physical work. Or get up and leave the house to go to a dead-end factory job. I only had to make one video a week and post a few pictures, and bang, a couple of hundred quid in the bank. Thank you very much.'

'Did Ellie know what you were doing?'

'No, whenever I posted videos, I made sure it was late at night, early in the morning, before Ellie got up or while she was still asleep. Or with her mates down the park. It was difficult because the schools were shut. But I kept everything under wraps. I didn't even tell my mates what I was doing.. But I couldn't help myself after a while. It became addictive. Just get your tits out for a couple of minutes and make a couple of hundred quid extra a week?' Parry inhaled. 'And then, things went all to shit.'

'How so?'

'This bloke, two streets down from me, subscribes to the website. He came across a few videos of me. The twat posted them all over social media. Next thing I know, I was in the shit with just about everyone. Tammy, the girls on the street. My mam came around and wiped the floor with me. Gave me this lecture about how she brought me up not to do that kind of thing.' She paused for thought. 'Then one of the boys that Ellie hung around with showed her the videos.'

'What was Ellie's reaction?'

'She was fuming with me. Said that it was wrong what I was doing. But I carried on. It was bringing the money in. I didn't see that I had any other choice.' Parry paused for a few moments. 'One night, I got pissed as a fart. After I went to bed, Ellie got hold of my phone. She knows my password and everything.'

'Let me guess, Ellie logged on to your FansOnly account?'

Parry nodded, but said nothing.

'For the record, Sophie Parry is nodding. What happened?'

'She posted pictures of herself topless. I remember seeing the pictures the next morning. I was absolutely livid with her. I banned her from her phone, her tablet, even the TV. We had a major screaming match about it. I told her she wasn't going anywhere near any phone until she was thirty. I got this app that blocked all her devices from the internet.' Parry inhaled. 'A few days later, ten grand was deposited into my bank account. I never had that much money paid into my bank before. It was like a scratch card win. That's when Ellie said this bloke from Russia told her he'd pay ten grand if she sent more pictures. I told Ellie that she wasn't going anywhere near my phone ever again. I changed the password and everything so she couldn't get access to my phone.'

'Despite being paid ten grand, you kept your FansOnly account,' Watkins pointed out.

'I was making money off it. I wasn't just going to shut it down. I would have lost over a thousand quid a month. I became reliant on that money. Suddenly, I could afford the little luxuries in life, you know? Take the kids out. Buy them clothes. Get stuff for Christmas.'

'Couldn't afford a cleaner though, could you?' Watkins remarked. 'Why did you let the house get into such a mess?'

'I don't know. I just let things get on top of me.'

'What about the other graphic content Ellie appears in?' Fagan asked. 'There are over seventeen hundred videos and pictures of Ellie?'

Parry composed herself. 'The money dried up. I was earning less every month. I panicked. The only way I could earn more money was to do other things, take it to the next level. Ellie knew we were struggling for money. That's when she suggested making a video to put it up on the website. I refused at first. I told her to fuck off. There was no way I was doing that. But I was weeks from getting another payment from the Social. I had no money. I tried to borrow money from people and my mam, but they all turned me down. I didn't even have enough to buy milk, bread or food for the kids.'

'That's when you caved,' Fagan said.

Parry nodded. 'I couldn't see any other way out. I had no food for the boys. I was afraid if anyone found out, they'd call Social Services. Tammy is a fucker for doing that. She grasses everyone up.'

'I thought Tammy was your best mate.'

Parry released a snort of derision. 'If she knew she could get money, she'd stab me in the back without even thinking about it. She's grassed loads of people up over the years.' Sophie sounded resentful.

'What happened?'

'Me and Ellie had a long talk about what she suggested. I said she could make one video to get us out of the mess we were in. After, I would shut my account down. We made sure it wasn't anything too disturbing. Just a minute-long video of her dancing in the nude. When we posted the video, it got a stupid number of views, mostly foreigners. The next thing I knew, I had twenty-five grand paid in my bank account. It was like winning the lottery. The relief I felt when all that money just dropped into my account. I took Ellie to Cardiff, we bought some clothes, makeup, we booked a holiday to Turkey. I bought loads of toys for the boys and clothes and other stuff. It was like nothing I'd experienced before. Like a rush of adrenaline.'

'But you still didn't shut down your account,' Fagan said.

'No,' Parry admitted. 'I thought I was in control. I posted more videos online of just me doing stuff. People were asking me to do new stuff, so in order to keep the money coming in, I upped my game. The money started coming in again. Things were great for a while. I wasn't struggling. I could afford things for the kids. Me and Ellie would go out together. We became closer. But again, after a while, the money ran out. I ended up earning less than a hundred quid in a month. I lost subscribers as well. I was back to being skint all over again. That's when the owner of the website messaged me. He said that if I upgraded my account to FansOnly Platinum and posted more videos of Ellie, I could make a fortune.'

'What did you say to him?'

'I told him to fuck off. My daughter wasn't for sale.' Parry hesitated. 'But the money ran dry again. So we made some more videos of Ellie.'

'Do you remember the name of the person who e-mailed you?'

Parry thought for a short while. 'Paul, something.'

'Decker?'

Parry nodded. 'Yeah, that him.'

'The last message Ellie sent you on the night she was murdered says, *Do you want me to film it for upload later on?*' Fagan looked at Parry. 'Were you encouraging your fourteen-year-old daughter to have sex with someone, and upload it to

FansOnly for financial gain?'

'No comment.'

'Sophie, do you have any idea who murdered Ellie?'

'No, honestly.' Parry's expression suddenly changed.

'Sophie, do you remember something?' Watkins asked.

'A few months ago Ellie started talking to this boy on Cymru Teen Chat.'

'Did she tell you the boy's name?'

'No, she didn't know. On CTC they all used nicknames. This boy told her he'd seen some of the videos on FansOnly. They've been talking for a while.'

'How long was a while?'

Parry tried to remember. 'A few months back, maybe.'

'Do you know the nickname of the boy?'

'I'm not sure. I think it was the Shadow or something like that.'

'We just mentioned Shadowcaster,' Fagan reminded her.

'Yeah, that's him, Shadowcaster.'

Fagan looked at the tablet. 'Just after eight o'clock in the evening Ellie said she was going to invite him over the evening you went to Cardiff. The individual calls himself Shadowcaster.'

Parry nodded. 'That's the one Ellie was talking to.'

'It's looking pretty obvious this person was responsible for Ellie's murder. Sophie, do you have any idea who it could have been?'

'No, I swear, why won't you believe me?'

'Because Sophie, you've lied. Do you understand? You've lied about everything. You said you had your phone stolen, but you didn't. You lied about when you last saw Ellie on the day she was murdered.'

'DI Fagan, can I suggest we end this interview?' The duty solicitor requested. 'As you can see, Miss Parry is in no shape to answer any more of your questions.'

Fagan considered the proposal and ended the interview. 'You will be released on police bail, but we will interview you again. Our cyber forensics team will analyse all the messages you exchanged with Ellie on the day she was murdered.'

Parry hauled herself out of the chair and left the room.

Fagan leant back in his chair, clasping his hands behind his head, considering the information in front of him.

'Quite the interview, boss.'

Fagan nodded. 'There's a part of me that feels sorry for her, Sean.'

'How so?'

'Desperation, addiction. The desire to live a dream lifestyle. Why do people sell drugs? They do it for the lifestyle, fast cars, holidays abroad, money, women. It's literally living the dream. Being financially independent is what many people want these days.'

'Doesn't make it right though, boss.'

'I'm not saying it makes it right, Sean. But Sophie Parry was sucked into a world she could never get out of. And her daughter was lured in and ended up paying with her life.'

Watkins phone pinged. 'Toby Morris is being processed at the front desk.' He pulled his buzzing phone from his pocket. 'Labs have been in contact. Two of the DNA samples have been identified. One matching Toby Morris. The other matching Owen Woods.'

'Jesus, now we have question somebody else about Ellie's lifestyle. Let's get information from Tammy Morris' phone so we can hit her son with it.' Fagan paused for thought. 'Didn't you mention a GoFundMe account has been set up for Ellie?'

'Yeah, they did.' Watkins checked his phone.

'Is there any information who started the account?'

Watkins studied the information he'd just found. 'Surprise, surprise, boss. The account was set up by Tammy Morris.'

'That bloody woman has no morals whatsoever. You grab that information from Tammy Morris' phone and I'll look over Ellie's casefile.'

Watkins stood and left the room.

Fagan produced his wallet and located the old photo of him and Rebecca. He smiled, remembering better times.

C H A P T E R 2 1

Newport Central Police Station.

Fagan ran through the interview start-up process.

Toby Morris sat on the other side of the table with the duty solicitor, looking terrified and fidgeting nervously.

'You've been arrested, Toby, because the DNA sample you provided yesterday was found at the murder scene. This DNA evidence proves you were having a sexual relationship with Ellie Parry. Can you explain why you submitted a DNA sample?'

'I didn't murder her. That's why I did one of those thingy tests.'

'A DNA Test?' Fagan said.

Morris nodded.

'But in doing so, you've implicated yourself with the crime of having a sexual relationship with a fourteen-year-old girl,' Watkins pointed out.

'I didn't murder her, I swear,' Morris stated. Panic clear in his tone.

Fagan studied Morris' mannerism. 'Let's talk about your relationship with Sophie Parry and her daughter Ellie. How long have you known them?'

Morris shrugged. 'A few years, maybe.'

Fagan looked down at his notes. 'Your mam says you moved in approximately five years ago.'

'Yeah.' Morris nodded.

'So Ellie Parry was around nine years old when you moved opposite her?'

'I guess, yeah,' Morris replied in a quiet voice.

'Could you speak more clearly, please, Toby, for the benefit of the recording,' Watkins requested.

'Yeah,' Morris spoke louder.

'Did your mother strike up a friendship with Sophie Parry straight away?' Fagan asked.

'Yeah.'

'What about you?'

'No, I never bothered with them at first.'

'At first?'

'I thought Sophie was too gobby. She was always mouthing off to everyone in the street. I think that's why our mam liked her so much, because our mam can be gobby as well.'

'According to data gathered from your mam's phone, Toby, you started a relationship with Sophie Parry around three years ago. Is that true?'

Morris shifted in his chair, clearly uncomfortable with the question that Fagan had just asked him. He glanced at the duty solicitor. 'Is this where I say no comment?'

'You are free to give whatever information you want to give, Mr Morris. Unfortunately, I cannot tell you what to say. I can only advise you.'

Morris looked back at Fagan. 'No comment.'

'The messages exchanged between you and your mother clearly show that you were involved in a sexual relationship with Sophie Parry. These messages go back over a three-year period. Tell us how your relationship with Sophie began.'

'I don't know,' Morris responded.

'You don't know or don't want to tell us. Which is it, Toby?'

'It was long ago now, okay, I can't remember.'

'Three years ago is not that long, is it Toby?'

'We were still in lockdown, but Sophie and our mam didn't give a shit,' Morris explained. 'Sophie had barbecues at the back of her house so the police wouldn't see when they drove by. She'd invite everyone.'

'Including you?'

'I only used to go because our mam used to make me go.'

Fagan concluded that Morris' reactions to his questions showed this was the first time he had been questioned by the police. Fagan also got the impression that Morris was under his mother's thumb. 'Let's take it slow, shall we, Toby?'

Morris nodded. 'Okay.'

'How did you begin a relationship with Sophie Parry?'

'It was when we were having a barbecue round Sophie's house.'

'Go on.'

'Everyone had just found out that Sophie had been posting naughty pictures on that website.'

'FansOnly,' Fagan said.

Morris nodded. 'Yeah, that's the one.'

'Do you ever go on this website?'

Morris shook his head. 'No, I don't bother with anything like that. Our mam always says things like that are bad.'

'What things were they saying to Sophie when you were at the barbeque?'

'Our mam said she was mad doing it. Some of the other girls said they wouldn't mind doing it, but were too scared. Sophie asked me what I thought of her nude pictures.'

'What did you say?'

Morris hesitated. 'I said she had a nice pair of tits.'

'How did Sophie react?'

'She, uh, said I could have a grope if I wanted.'

'Sophie Parry said that in front of everyone?' Watkins asked.

'Yeah. That's when our mam said he could do with a good grope.'

'Did you feel embarrassed?'

Morris nodded. 'My mam is always showing me up in front of other people. She enjoys it.'

'Can I ask you a personal question, Toby?' Fagan said.

Morris shrugged. 'If you want.'

'When did you first have sex with a woman?'

'Is that question really necessary, Detective Inspector Fagan?' the solicitor asked.

'It is, yes,' Fagan countered. 'Toby, can you answer the question, please?'

'Sophie,' Morris replied.

'Sophie Parry was the first woman you've had sex with?'

Morris sniffed. 'Yeah.'

'What happened exactly?'

'We were round Sophie's house having a barbecue. People had been sharing pictures around the estate, nude pictures of Sophie. I said she had a nice pair of tits. She said I could give them a grope if I wanted to. That's when our mam said he could do with a good grope.'

'And then what happened?' Fagan asked, noting that Morris had repeated himself.

'The girls got more pissed.'

'Were you the only bloke there?'

Morris nodded.

'What happened?'

'Everyone went home. It was just me, our mam and Sophie left.'

'What about the children?'

'The boys were in the house. Ellie was over at her friend's house having a sleepover.' Morris paused. 'Our mam and Sophie were giggling and looking at me. Our mam said she'd look after the boys for the night.'

'Leaving you and Sophie alone.'

'Yeah,' Morris replied with a sheepish undertone. 'Sophie said she was getting cold and we should go inside and have a nice cup of coffee. Um, so we went in and um.' Morris stopped talking.

'Go on Toby, we're listening,' Fagan encouraged.

'We were, uh, sat on the sofa. Sophie was saying how good looking I was. She asked why I hadn't got a girlfriend.'

'What did you say?'

'I dunno. I can't remember. Sophie started to cwtch up to me.'

'You mean she came on to you?'

'Yeah. She was pissed as a fart. She started kissing me. The next thing I knew, we were in bed together.'

Fagan glanced down at his notes. 'Tell us about your relationship with Ellie.'

'I didn't murder Ellie,' Morris responded rapidly. 'Honestly, I was in Newport the other night. I was out on the piss with my mates. You can ask them.'

Fagan held his hand up. 'Slow down, Toby. We're not accusing you of murdering Ellie. However, your DNA was found on Ellie's body.'

Morris inhaled. 'Look, I know it was wrong, but our mam and Sophie made me do it.'

'What do you mean by that, Toby?' Watkins said.

'They made me and Ellie get together.'

Fagan's stomach turned somersaults. 'Are you saying that Sophie Parry and your mam encouraged you to pursue a sexual relationship with Ellie?'

'Yeah.'

'When did this start?'

Morris thought for a few moments. 'Not long after, I started seeing Sophie. One night when we were all round Sophie's. We were all talking. Sophie joked her daughter fancied me.' Morris paused. 'That's when our mam and Sophie said they were off down the pub.'

'Leaving you and Ellie in the house alone.'

'Yeah.' Morris admitted. 'The boys were with their dad for the weekend. I knew it was wrong, but I couldn't help myself.'

'When was the last time you had sex with Ellie?'

Morris thought for a few moments. 'The night before last. She came over.'

'How did she seem?'

'She was upset. Ellie had a massive bust up with her mam.' Morris became distraught. 'I didn't murder her, honestly,' he sobbed.

Fagan stared across the table at him. 'I think we're done here, Toby. We'll end the interview. However, you will be questioned in due course about your sexual activity with Ellie Parry. Do you understand what I've just told you?'

Morris nodded. 'I'm sorry. I never meant any of this to happen. It was all our mam's fault. She made me do everything.'

'You're free to go Toby.'

Morris and the duty solicitor left the interview room.

Fagan took a deep breath. 'I tell you what, Sean, the more people we interview, the more fucked up this becomes. It makes me think about that case in Southport I told you about. When I interviewed the daughter following her mother's murder, she revealed how controlling the mother was. She'd been forced to have sex with older men from a young age.' Fagan looked towards the door. 'In many respects, Toby Morris is just another victim here. It's obvious he's vulnerable. His mother controls most of his life. You've seen what Tammy and Sophie are like. They're both narcissists in many respects. Controlling their kid's behaviour. But when interviewed, they act as if they're victims. Tammy seems like the overbearing mother who has shielded her son from the world.' Fagan glanced at the tablet. 'There are thousands of messages Tammy and her son have exchanged over the past few years. Just scanning through them, you can tell that Tammy is very much in control of his actions. I'll see if our cyber department can pick up on anything incriminating before we interview Tammy Morris again.'

'Pretty fucked up stuff, boss,' Watkins remarked.

'There are so many layers to this, Sean. When someone is murdered, people don't realise the complexities of the circumstances. I've investigated hundreds of murders during my career. Some of them have been open and shut cases. But others have dragged on. Peeling away layer after layer. Exposing the ugly side of family disputes.'

A knock on the door jolted Fagan from his train of thought.

A young police constable peered around the door. 'Sorry to you bother you, sir? There's a woman at the front desk claiming to have information about Ellie Parry.'

'Did she say what kind of information it was?' Fagan asked.

'I'm afraid not. She insisted on talking to the senior detectives involved in the murder case.'

Fagan nodded. 'Keep her at reception. Give us half an hour and we'll have a chat.'

CHAPTER 22

Newport Central Police Station

Fagan approached the woman in her late fifties, offering his hand. 'Hi, thanks for coming in to speak with us. I'm Detective Inspector Marc Fagan. This is my colleague, Detective Sergeant Sean Watkins. We understand you've got information you'd like to share with us regarding Ellie Parry.'

The woman smiled back, shaking Fagan's hand. 'I'm Ruth Sutton. I used to be a social worker for Blaenau Gwent Social Services.'

'Used to be?' Fagan said, raising an eyebrow.

Ruth nodded. 'I quit the job last December. Had a gutsful.'

'Why was that exactly, Ruth?'

'Because of the bullshit I had to put up with. Blaenau Gwent Social Services is run by a bunch of idiots who have no clue what they're doing.'

'What information have you got regarding the murder of Ellie Parry?'

'It's not information about Ellie's murder. But if Blaenau Gwent Social Services listened to me, Ellie would still be alive.'

'Okay, Ruth, we're listening.'

'I was Ellie's social worker last year. We were referred to the family by the police. I was part of a dual team. Martin Daniels was my partner.'

Watkins glanced at Fagan. 'He's one of the social workers me and Stacey interviewed this morning.'

'A friend of mine who still works for Blaenau Gwent rang me earlier. She told me that the police had been there this morning to interview Martin and Janice.'

'Janice Blackmoor,' Watkins said.

'Yeah,' Ruth nodded. 'She's head of Social Services at Blaenau

Gwent. But she hasn't got the first bloody clue on how to run it. All Janice gives a shit about is reaching targets. And her bonus every year. Loads of people have quit because of her.'

Fagan sensed resentment in Ruth's voice. 'By any chance, Ruth, are you one of these people?'

'Yeah,' Ruth admitted.

Fagan sighed. 'So you've turned up today to slag off Social Services.'

'I'm not slagging anyone off. I'm telling the truth. Ellie would still be alive if they followed my recommendations. Instead, they just ignored them.'

'What were those recommendations?'

'I recommended that Ellie and the two boys should have been removed from Sophie Parry's care.'

'Why was that?'

'Because I didn't think she was a decent mother. She was incapable of looking after those children properly. I spent six months with the family. At the end of my time, I concluded she wasn't a competent mother. All she gave a shit about was herself. She was always pretending to be the victim.'

'When did you first have contact with the family?'

'January last year. The family was referred to us by the police. Following an incident where Ellie threatened to stab her mother.'

'And when you turned up at the house, what did you find?'

'The family was in disarray. Sophie claimed to be struggling because she was out of work. She always said she was skint all the time. But I got the impression she had money coming in from somewhere.'

'Would this somewhere be the website called FansOnly?'

'Yeah, but I only found out after I quit my job.'

'Did you quit your job because of the lack of action by Blaenau Gwent Social Services?'

'Mainly, but it was loads of other things. We had hundreds of cases as part of our workload. Staff were struggling. We were losing people right, left and centre. Because they can't cope with the workload. Blaenau Gwent Social Services is swamped with cases. None of the social workers get time to review cases properly. They're told to get on with the job, review cases within a short amount of time, and move on to the next. Some of us complained to Janice, but she didn't want to know. The woman isn't even a qualified social worker.'

'What was your impression of Sophie Parry when you first called in on the family?'

'She was a waste of space. Not capable of looking after those children properly. The house was a total shithole for a start. I got hold of the local housing association and they sent a team of people to clean up the house. But within a month, it was back to being a shithole again. Sophie's excuse was that she had no motivation. She said every day was the same for her, a struggle to get through. No matter how hard I tried to work with her, she didn't want to know. She'd just sit there on her phone all day long. Most of the time, Ellie had to cook for the boys. I called in other people to help her become a better person. But she remained the same. That's when I had doubts about her capability of being a mother.'

'Did you ever visit any of the fathers of the children?'

'I talked to Ellie's father once. He wasn't exactly the doting dad. He had another family. He told me he didn't have time for Sophie or his daughter. Said they were both more trouble than they were worth. He claimed Sophie had poisoned her daughter against him. She told Ellie her dad didn't want to know her.'

'What about the boys' father?'

'He was applying to have custody of the boys but wasn't getting anywhere with it. Because he had criminal convictions, he was finding it very difficult to get custody. He generally loved those boys and wanted them out of that house. Mainly because of the condition it was in all the time. And then there were the people that Sophie associated with.'

'What kind of people were they?'

'Not the type you'd want to know. Her neighbour across the street, Tammy Morris, is a troublemaker. Plus, there's her son, Toby Morris, who had an unhealthy relationship with Sophie Parry.'

'By unhealthy relationship, I take it you mean sexual?'

Ruth nodded. 'Sophie Parry didn't exactly keep it a secret. I had a conversation with Toby Morris one day. It didn't take me long to realise he had learning difficulties.'

'What about Ellie?'

'What about her?'

'Were you aware Ellie was having a sexual with Toby?'

Ruth responded to Fagan's question with a shocked expression. 'No.'

'What about your colleague, Martin Daniels? What was his impression of Sophie Parry?'

'Let's just say that Sophie Parry made more than an impression on Martin.'

'What do you mean by that?'

'Sophie wasn't stupid. She knew I didn't like her. So she set about undermining my working relationship with Martin.'

'How did she do that?'

'By screwing him,' Ruth responded.

Watkins glanced at Fagan. 'Martin Daniels was having a sexual relationship with Sophie Parry. Is that what you're saying, Ruth?'

'Yeah, but again, I didn't find out until after I quit the job. I didn't rate Martin as a decent social worker. He was another social worker that wasn't really qualified to do the job.'

'How did he get the job?'

'Janice Blackmoor had already worked with him. But I don't know where. After I quit, a friend of mine got in touch. That's when she told me that Martin had been screwing Sophie Parry.'

'How did your friend find out?'

'Martin was brazen enough to tell her. She reported it to Blackmoor.'

'Was he disciplined for this?'

'No. Martin was Janice's favourite.'

'What was your relationship with Ellie Parry like?' Fagan asked.

'It was a good relationship. I really liked Ellie, and she started to open up to me towards the end. At first she was closed off, very shy. I think she was afraid of opening up to me because of what her mother might have said. I got the feeling that she was hiding stuff from me. Sometimes she would suffer from a really deep depression. And other times she'd be on such a high, it was hard to bring her down. After six months, we had a major review on family life. I recommended the children should be taken into care and Sophie Parry should be given limited access to them.'

'I've a feeling there's a but coming somewhere, Ruth.'

Ruth nodded. 'Because Martin was the senior social worker, I was overruled. That's when I'd had enough. So I quit the job. It was shortly after that I found out about Martin and his relationship with Sophie Parry.'

'Do you know if they were in a relationship for long?'

'It was only a fling that lasted a few months, so my friend told me. Sophie Parry knew he was the senior social worker. By screwing him she knew she could get me off her back. Martin was already married. But that didn't stop him from going behind his wife's back all the time. They say hindsight is a wonderful thing. Looking back, it was obvious that Martin was a bit of a predator.'

'What do you mean by that?'

'Martin had the choice of any casefile. He always used to choose the casefiles where the families had single mothers. He always established a friendly relationship with the mother. Again, it was only after I finished I found out he was screwing a lot of the mothers he was supposed to be working with. When I found out he'd been having a relationship with Sophie Parry, I made a complaint to Janice Blackmoor. But she just dismissed it. She even wrote a report on me, saying I was a former disgruntled employee out for revenge.'

'Do you have any evidence to prove any of what you've told us?'

Ruth inhaled. 'Only from what I've been told. Look, I know it seems like I'm tittle tattling. But Ellie and the boys should have been removed. About six months before we were assigned to the family, there was an incident at a nursery on the Sofrydd estate. One mother phoned Blaenau Gwent Social Services to complain about Sophie Parry's boys. Apparently, one of the boys tried to strangle a two-year-old girl.'

'Do you know if Sophie Parry was interviewed by Blaenau

Gwent Social Services?'

Ruth nodded. 'She was, but nothing came of it. According to Sophie, she claimed boys will be boys. Shortly after that, she pulled them out of nursery.'

Fagan scribbled notes. 'This is really helpful, Ruth. Thanks for coming in today.'

'I know I've said nothing really useful that will help you with your murder inquiry. But I had to get this off my chest. If they listened to me, Ellie would still be alive. When I saw what happened on the news, I couldn't stop crying. I feel so guilty for not being able to help Ellie or them boys.'

'And I feel for you, Ruth,' Fagan said. 'Social Services should have acted on your report after you submitted your recommendation to have the children removed. Did they tell you why it had been turned down?'

'Martin claimed I had a grudge against Sophie. Because she had three children. I once confided in Martin that me and my partner could not conceive children. I reckon he told Sophie this, and she used the information against me. She even e-mailed Social Services and complained that I was being bitchy with her all the time. I was only doing my job. We're trained to be straight with the people we have to deal with, not friendly. That's why many people take us the wrong way. As if we just want to remove every child who's having problems. It's not like that. We have to be professional at all times.'

'I know how you feel,' Fagan sympathised. 'We'll take everything you've said today into consideration and add it to the mounting information we're getting regarding Ellie.'

'How close are you finding Ellie's murderer?'

'We are working as hard as we can to find the person responsible for Ellie's murder,' Fagan said. 'Thank you for coming in today, Ruth. Much appreciated.' Fagan handed her an information card. 'If you think of anything else, contact me.'

Ruth took the card and left.

Fagan studied the notes he had scribbled. 'Another layer to this case, Sean.'

'When I interviewed Daniels yesterday, he gave out the wrong vibes. He didn't come across as a social worker. If you don't mind, boss, I'd like to run his name through the police database.'

'Yeah, sure, if you think it'll turn up something.'

Watkins' phone buzzed. 'Police have just arrested Owen Woods. He was in Swansea.'

'Finally,' Fagan stated. 'Perhaps now we'll get some proper answers.' He glanced at the clock on the wall. 'It will take a few hours to process Woods and get him up here for an interview. Let's get something to eat.'

CHAPTER 23

Newport Central Police Station

Fagan started the recording process. 'Interview with Owen Woods, present in the room, are Detective Inspector Mark Fagan, and Detective Sergeant Sean Watkins. Also in the room are Mr Owen Woods and the duty solicitor Michael Prichard.' Fagan glanced down at his notes. 'Could you tell us where you were between the hours of eleven o'clock and one o'clock the night before last?'

'No comment,' Woods answered.

'We have a witness who saw you entering the house of Ellie Parry around eleven o'clock on the night she was murdered.'

'No comment,' Woods repeated.

Fagan inhaled. 'Owen, your DNA was found on the body. Did you have sex with Ellie Parry?'

Woods hesitated. 'No comment.'

Fagan leant forward, interlocking his fingers. 'Owen, semen samples were found at the scene of the crime. Your DNA is a perfect match for those samples. So there's no point in sitting there denying everything.'

Woods rubbed his nose and made brief eye contact with Fagan. 'No comment.'

'What happened, Owen?' Watkins asked. 'Why did you kill her?'

'I didn't kill her,' Woods rumbled, looking Watkins in the eye.

'DNA doesn't lie, Owen. You had sex with Ellie Parry the night she was murdered.'

'I didn't murder the girl, okay?' Woods protested.

'But you had sex with her, didn't you, Owen?'

'No comment.'

'Do you know how old Ellie Parry was, Owen?'

'No comment.'

'Ellie Parry was fourteen years old. Do you understand what kind of trouble you are in?'

'Did you supply her with the ecstasy?' Fagan asked.

'No comment.'

'Owen, listen to me. You're not doing yourself any favours by sitting there and denying everything. You're a known dealer on the estate, Owen. Everyone knows you supply drugs to the kids. Several witnesses have come forward and claimed that you sell vapes to the local teenagers that hang around the park. Your DNA sample was already on our database, Owen. You had sex with Ellie Parry the night she was murdered.'

Woods wrung his hands in an agitated manner.

'All we want is the truth, Owen. Now I will ask you again. Did you murder Ellie Parry?'

'No, I fucking didn't,' Woods seethed. 'I fucking didn't touch her, I swear.'

'But you had sex with her.'

Woods rocked back and forth in his chair. 'No comment.'

'Do you know what people hate more than a drug dealer, Owen?' Watkins said. 'It's a paedophile. Semen samples matching your DNA were found on Elli Parry's body. Can you explain how that is possible?'

'No comment.' Tears trickled down Woods' cheeks.

'If you don't tell us what happened between you and Ellie Parry, Owen, you will be charged with murder. Do you understand?' Fagan stated.

'I didn't murder her,' Woods whimpered. 'I just.' He stopped speaking.

'You just what, Owen?'

'We just got chatting, that's all.'

'What were you chatting about?'

'You know, stuff.'

'What's stuff, Owen? What were you talking about?'

'She was just telling me how pissed off she was.'

'Did you supply her with the ecstasy?'

'No comment.'

'Owen, don't do this to yourself, mate. You're already in enough shit. Did you supply Ellie Parry with ecstasy the night she was murdered?'

'No comment.'

'Owen, we're going to be here all day, aren't we, mate?' Fagan sat back in his chair, folding his arms. 'You need to wake up to the situation you've put yourself in. A fourteen-year-old girl was murdered on the estate the night before last. And so far, you fit the bill for that murder. DNA evidence points to the fact that you had sex with Ellie Parry prior to her murder. A witness saw you going into Ellie's house around eleven o'clock that evening. We've already searched your house. A hoodie and tracksuit bottoms matching the description worn by our suspect were found at your property. So you see, Owen, it's not looking good for you, is it, mate? Now just tell us the truth. Did you murder Ellie Parry?'

'No,' Woods insisted. 'I didn't lay a fucking finger on her!'

'But you called her to her house around eleven o'clock.'

Woods ran his hand through his hair.

'Were you at Ellie Parry's house around eleven o'clock?'

'Yes, okay, I was there,' Woods confessed.

'Did you have sex with Ellie Parry?'

Woods sat silent.

'Owen, listen to me. Not only will you be charged with sexual activity with a child. But you will also be charged with the murder of Ellie Parry. Plus, you will be charged with supplying her with the ecstasy. Do you understand?'

'I didn't murder her!' Woods hammered his fist on the table, causing the duty solicitor to jolt.

'If you didn't murder Ellie Parry, then what time did you leave the property?'

Again Woods remained silent.

'Owen, how long did you spend at Ellie Parry's house?'

'I can't remember.'

'You can't remember or you just don't want to tell us.'

'I didn't murder Ellie Parry. Why won't you believe me? I didn't murder her, I swear!'

'But you had sex with her,' Fagan persisted. 'Semen samples matching your DNA were found on Ellie Parry's body. So don't sit there and deny everything. You had sex with Ellie Parry the night she was murdered, didn't you?'

Woods buried his face in his hands.

'There's no way out for you, Owen. Do you see the situation you've put yourself in?'

'Okay!'

Fagan shrugged. 'Which one is it, Owen?'

'Yes, we had sex. Is that what you want to hear?'

'Was this the first time you had sex with Ellie Parry?'

'Yes! I'm no paedophile, okay.'

'Ellie Parry is fourteen years old, so yes, that makes you a paedophile, Owen. You know the legal age of consent in the UK is sixteen.'

'I'm not stupid, okay? I know what it is.'

'But you had sex, despite knowing her age. Why?'

'She had no money.'

'Money for what?'

'What do you bloody well think?'

'The ecstasy?'

Woods nodded. 'Yeah.'

'So, in exchange for money for the ecstasy, you had sex with her?'

'I didn't start it, if that's what you're thinking. She came on to me. Started flirting and everything.'

'And you responded.'

'Oh, come on, what would you have done?'

'I'm a copper, not a drug dealer or a paedophile,' Fagan remarked dryly.

The word paedophile made Woods flinch.

Fagan nodded. 'Yeah, you can live with being a drug dealer, can't you, Owen. But being a paedophile, that's something you'll never be able to live with. Your life is now in ruins.'

'She came on to me strong. She wouldn't leave me alone.'

'So what? You just obliged, did you? You just thought, oh, I'm going to get laid here.'

'I'm not a fucking paedophile, okay?'

'But Ellie was fourteen. That makes you a paedophile, Owen. Do you understand?'

'Fuck!' Woods cursed.

'Let's back up here. Can you tell us how you ended up at Ellie Parry's house the night she was murdered?'

Woods hesitated. 'She rang me.'

'So, Ellie, had your phone number?'

Woods nodded. 'Yeah.'

'Did you have contact with her prior to the night she was murdered?'

'Yeah, she started talking to me a couple of weeks ago.'

'Did you have much interaction with Ellie Parry before the night before last?'

'No, not before a couple of weeks ago.'

'Okay, so you turned up at her house, you had the ecstasy on you, then what happened?'

'Ellie was telling me how she just had an argument with her mam.'

'Her mam was in Cardiff.'

'Yeah, I know. They were texting each other. Ellie was pissed off that she couldn't go to Cardiff with her mam.'

'Do you know Ellie's mother?'

'Yeah, everyone on the estate knows Sophie Parry. Or rather, every bloke on the estate knows Sophie Parry. She's shagged most of them. Plus, she's all over FansOnly.'

'How do you know this?'

'Word gets about, you know.'

'But you never had a relationship with her.'

Woods released a snort of derision. 'I wouldn't touch that ugly bitch with a barge pole.'

'What time did Ellie call you?'

Woods considered the question. 'About eight o'clock.'

'But you didn't turn up at her house until eleven.'

'I was getting the gear she needed.'

'Where did you get the ecstasy from?'

Woods clammed up.

'Owen, where did you get the ecstasy from?'

'No comment,' Woods replied defiantly.

'Okay, if that's how you want to play things, Owen,' Fagan inhaled. 'So, Ellie Parry called you around eight o'clock.'

'Yeah.'

'Did she ask for the drugs straight away?'

'We had a bit of a chat before she got on to the subject of the ecstasy.'

'Was this the first time you supplied Ellie Parry with ecstasy?'

'Yes, it was. She usually avoids me.'

'So she knows you're into drug dealing?'

Woods nodded. 'Ellie and her mates would shout abuse whenever I walked past the park. They'd call me a loser and a twat.'

'Okay, so Ellie called you around eight o'clock. You had a chat before she asked you to get her some ecstasy tablets.'

'Yeah.'

'You went out, acquired the drugs, and returned to the estate.'

'Yeah.'

'How long did it take you to get hold of the ecstasy?'

'An hour, maybe,' Woods answered.

'So you didn't go straight back to Ellie's house?'

'No.'

'When you turned up at Ellie Parry's house, what happened?'

'She was pissed off. She just had an argument with her mam. Her mam was telling her to fuck off.' Woods hesitated. 'When she rang me earlier, Ellie said she just wanted a little pick-me-up. The booze her mother had left her wasn't giving her enough of a buzz.'

'And that's when she asked you for the drugs.'

'Yeah.'

'How long did you spend chatting when you turned up at Ellie's house?'

Woods shrugged. 'Several minutes, maybe.'

'And then?'

'I asked her how she was going to pay for the drugs.'

'What did she say?'

'She said she had no money.'

'What did you do?'

'I told her if she had no money on her, she wasn't getting any gear.'

'How did she react?'

'She was pissed off with me. She said she wanted the tabs as a little pick-me-up. Something to really get her buzzing.'

'What did you do?'

'I went to leave. But she stood in the doorway, she stopped me from leaving.'

'You could have pushed her out of the way. I mean, you're pretty fit, by the look of you. Why didn't you just push her aside and leave the house?'

'Because she was coming on to me. She was dressed up to the nines. Short mini skirt, stockings, high heels, little top.'

'Turned you on, did it?'

Woods took his time, eventually nodding. 'She looked a lot older than fourteen, I can tell you that.'

'So you didn't resist when she came on to you?'

'I tried honestly. I said I knew how old she was. I said I wasn't interested in young girls.'

'And then?'

Woods took a deep breath. 'She came towards me and stuffed her hand down my jogging bottoms. She shoved her tongue down my throat.'

'Where did you have sex?'

'She was so pissed off with her mam, she dragged me into her bedroom and we just got on with it.'

'So you had sex with her in her mother's bedroom?'

Woods nodded.

'For the benefit of the tape, Mr Woods is nodding.'

'How long were you at the house?'

'About half an hour. I was going out later that night.'

'Where were you going so late at night? All the pubs would have been shutting at midnight.'

'I was going down to Swansea. There's a few clubs there that don't shut until eight o'clock in the morning.'

'When did you first hear about Ellie's murder?'

'Yesterday morning, I heard about it on social media. Tammy Morris posted it on WhatsApp.' Woods hesitated. 'I knew I was in the shit. Which is why I took so long to come home. I wanted to get my story straight. You have to believe me. I didn't murder her.' Woods paused, remembering the night before. 'After we, you know, did it, Ellie was texting someone on Cymru Teen Chat.'

'And you know this for a fact, do you?'

'Yeah,' Woods replied. 'She said she was going to get ultimate revenge on her mam.'

'Did you know what she meant by that?'

'Ellie was having a massive argument with Sophie on Facebook. They were texting each other. Sophie was boasting she'd just picked a bloke up in a pub and she was going to shag him all night long. Ellie was fuming. Earlier on when we were chatting, Ellie told me that her mother had become jealous of her.'

'Why is that?'

'Because she was the better looking one. Her mother had let herself go a bit. Started to get all saggy. Ellie was a tall girl for her age. She hung around the park with her mates. She was always dressed in skimpy clothes. Even in cold weather. I knew what she was like, you know. She had a reputation with the boys on the street.'

'Do you know if Ellie was having a relationship with anyone on the street?'

'She was seeing loads of boys. If you want to question anyone, I suggest you talk to Toby Morris.'

'Tammy Morris' son?'

'Yeah.'

'Do you know him?'

'We used to go drinking together. One night, when Toby was pissed as a fart, he boasted he had shagged Sophie Parry. He'd spent the weekend at her house. He also claimed that he had sex with Ellie. And had broken her in. He reckoned that Ellie's mam told him to do it.'

'How long ago was this?'

'About three years ago, maybe. I also know he kept on seeing Ellie and her mother.'

Fagan sensed the urge to vomit.

Woods broke down and sobbed. 'I know I fucked up. I know it was wrong. I was only there to give her the pills. I thought I could make a couple of extra quid.'

'When you left Ellie's house the night before last, did you take a bottle of WKD?'

'Yeah,' Woods nodded.

'Why did you leave through the back of the house?'

'I was meeting a mate. I met him at the back. I didn't want to get seen coming out of Ellie's house. There's a lot of nosy people on that estate who would have grassed me up to her mam.'

'So you drank the WKD and chucked it away?'

'Yeah.'

'Interview terminated,' Fagan said, tapping the stop icon on his phone.

'What happens now?'

'At the moment, Owen, you are our only suspect. I know you maintain you didn't murder her, but you still had sex with her prior to her death. Until we find other evidence that points to another suspect, you'll be remanded in custody.'

A uniform entered the room and escorted Woods out. The duty solicitor scribbled some notes before leaving.

'Pretty fucked up, if you ask me, boss,' Watkins commented.

'I was thinking a same thing, Sean,' Fagan sighed. 'Woods seemed more than eager to throw Toby Morris under the bus.'

'What's the next move?'

'Contact the labs and tell them to go over the sheets and duvet cover from Sophie Parry's bedroom.'

'What's your thinking, boss?'

'I don't think Woods murdered her. But until we find the evidence to clear him, he'll have to remain in custody. We need to interview Sophie Parry again. There's a hell of a lot of information to go through. We'll have a break, then meet up with the team for an analysis. See if we can come up with another suspect.'

'Like the serial killer you mentioned earlier.'

'Yeah,' Fagan nodded. 'Ever since I saw that tripod and light, it's been bugging me. It's like I said this was no ordinary murder. We need to piece together everything we have. I'll look over the report the pathologist e-mailed me. We need to keep this under wraps.'

Watkins checked his newsfeed on his phone. 'According to the Argus, the crowd funding page Tammy Morris set up has made fifty grand.'

'Jesus, the nerve of that woman. I told her to stay off social bloody media.'

'Loads of people will donate, considering the publicity it's generating.'

'Yeah, and Sophie Parry will be vilified the moment it's revealed that she's been pimping out her daughter on FansOnly.' Fagan considered the new information. 'We'll leave it for now. If we try to shut down the fundraiser, we'll come across as dickheads.'

CHAPTER 24

Newport Central Police Station

Fagan looked at the whiteboard. 'Okay team, it would seem that we have our first suspect in custody. Thirty-five-year-old Owen Woods, a convicted drug dealer. Woods called at Ellie's house around eleven o'clock the evening she was murdered. His motive was to supply her with the ecstasy we found at the scene of the crime. According to Woods, Ellie claimed she had no money to pay for the drugs. Woods said he tried to leave the house. But Ellie came on to him and they ended up having sex in Sophie Parry's bedroom. Woods claims he was at Ellie's house for approximately half an hour. After he left, Woods headed down to Swansea.' Fagan paused. 'Unfortunately, there's a problem. Even though Woods is a suspect, we will end up releasing him. This is because of what I was told by the pathologist earlier. We have identified two DNA samples found on the body. Belonging to Woods and Toby Morris. We also have another DNA sample that has been linked to four other deaths.'

'Then why are we holding Woods, if you don't mind me asking, sir?' Brooks questioned.

'Because we have to be seen doing something, Andrew. I just put out a brief statement to the press. That should keep them happy for a while. Since this murder investigation was first launched, we've been fed nothing but a pack of lies by key witnesses and those close to Ellie. Sophie Parry lied about having her phone stolen in Cardiff the night her daughter was murdered.' Fagan checked his notes. 'According to Parry's phone records, her daughter messaged her at eleven minutes past midnight. Stating that someone had just turned up at their house.' Fagan read the text message. *'He's here. I'm gonna have the ride of my life, unlike you, who will be too pissed to remember what you've done in the morning*. She messages her mother three minutes later. *Do you want me to film it for upload later on?* I think it's safe to say Ellie was talking about her murderer. During his interview Woods claimed Ellie was talking to someone on Cymru Teen Chat. When we interviewed Taylor Richards yesterday, he said that Ellie and her friends were talking to someone called Shadowcaster the day she was murdered. Ellie also mentions Shadowcaster in some of the messages she sent her mam.' Fagan glanced at Watkins. 'Didn't you say Cymru Teen Chat has been linked to a spate of suicides over the past three years?'

Watkins looked at his laptop screen. 'According to the investigation into the suicides, there was no link found with the Cymru Teen Chat app. However, Detective Sergeant Dave Padfield made a complaint when the investigation was closed.'

'How many suicides were there?'

'Thirteen in the spate of nine months. The first suicide was Holly Jones. She took her own life on the 15th of March 2022. Between March and December 2022, there were twelve other suicides. Holly's dad, Michael Jones, has been campaigning for the app to be shut down. He set up the charity Safe Children Wales in February 2023.'

'I want a chat with Padfield. He obviously found something that warranted further investigation. Send him an e-mail, Andrew. We'll draft DS Padfield into the extended murder investigation team. It looks as if we're going to shift our investigation to this Cymru Teen Chat. I don't want to hold Woods for too long. Otherwise we'll start getting flak for it.'

'Russel Connor is giving a presentation at Cardiff University later on, boss,' Watkins revealed.

'That should be interesting,' Fagan mused. 'We'll pop a long and have a chat with Mr Connor. Someone is going to have to visit Social Services.'

'I'll do that guv,' Stacey offered.

Fagan nodded. 'Thanks Stacey. Take young Andrew with you.'

'I meant to say, boss. I got a result on Martin Daniels earlier. I also got a hit on Janice Blackmoor. They were both interviewed in 2014 regarding allegations of abuse at a care home for vulnerable people. According to this news article I found, the South Wales Argus sent a reporter undercover to the care home in Risca. The paper reports they were approached by a former member of staff, who claimed both physical and sexual abuse was going on at the home. Daniels was pulled up after the parents of a vulnerable woman made an allegation against Daniels. They claimed he'd been sexually abusing their seventeen-year-old daughter. But because of the mental state of the girl, the charges were dropped. The Crown Prosecution Service couldn't find enough evidence to charge Daniels. Janice Blackmoor was running the care home at the time and was also questioned by police regarding the behaviour of staff there.'

'It will be interesting to see what Daniels has to say. When did Ruth Sutton say Daniels was having a relationship with Sophie Parry?'

'Last year.'

'Go downstairs to cybercrimes. See if they've found any communication between Parry and Daniels last year.'

Watkins hauled himself out of his seat. 'I'll be back as soon as I can.'

Fagan looked at the whiteboard. 'Let's get back to the time of the murder. According to Owen Woods he left Ellie's house at around eleven thirty. Ellie messaged her mam at twelve minutes after midnight.' Fagan glanced at his phone screen. *'He's here. I'm gonna have the ride of my life, unlike you, who will be too pissed to remember what you've done in the morning.'*

'The killer has to be local,' Stacey suggested.

Fagan nodded. 'It's a forty-minute gap between Woods leaving the house and Ellie messaging her mam her killer had arrived.'

'Are you going to share any information on your theory about a serial killer being on the loose in the South Wales Valleys?' Brooks asked.

Fagan handed Brooks a file. 'Four girls have died since March 2020. DNA found at each scene matches DNA found on Ellie's body. Each pathologist's report states that the girls had sex with someone within twenty-four hours of death. However, the deaths weren't logged as suspicious because each girl had committed suicide. The DNA matches up with Ellie and the four other deaths. It's too much of a coincidence. Girl number one, Amy Davies. Found dead in her dorm just outside Manchester. She hung herself. The pathologist's report states she had sex with someone twenty-four hours prior to death. The second girl, Danielle Jacobs, was found just outside Warwick. Another university student. She took a massive overdose. The next is Sarina Meadows, another overdose. Lived in Swansea. The fourth death was Amber Fletcher. She slit her wrists in the bath.'

Brooks studied the file. 'It says here all the girls had a FansOnly account.'

Fagan nodded. 'Amy Davies was from Port Talbot, Danielle Jacobs was from Chepstow, Sain Medows was from Holyhead and Amber Fletcher was a Newport girl. They were uploading sexually explicit images. He's using FansOnly as a hunting ground.'

'He's hunting Welsh girls,' Stacey said.

Fagan nodded. 'Yeah, and because he was at Ellie's house within forty minutes of Woods leaving proves our killer is relatively local to the area.'

Brooks carried out a quick search on his computer. 'Merthyr is about thirty-five minutes away. And at that time of night, you could easily shave five minutes plus off your travel time.'

'A taxi driver saw someone running down the Sofrydd road towards Hafodyrynys,' Fagan said.

Brooks studied a map on his screen. 'If he was running down the Sofrydd road, he would have come out onto the A472, Hafodyrynys road. He could have headed back towards Crumlin or Pontypool.'

'Any luck on the traffic cams at the Crumlin junction?' Fagan asked.

'No, guv,' Stacey replied. 'Uniform contacted the Highways Agency yesterday. The traffic light system on the junction is about to undergo a massive overhaul, which means all the cameras have been switched off.'

'He could have headed back to Pontypool, sir,' Brooks

suggested.

'Because of DNA samples found at the scene the other night, I'm adamant it has to be this Shadowcaster. Apart from the fact the other girls took their own lives, it's the same MO. He has sex with the girls prior to their deaths. But in Ellie's case, he stayed to finish the job. He knew she took the ecstasy.'

'What's his motive?' Stacey asked.

'The same as any other serial killer. To keep killing.'

'Have you ever had to deal with a serial killer, guv?' Stacey asked.

Fagan nodded, recalling an old casefile. 'Back in the 90s when I was a snotty-nosed detective constable, we had three bodies turn up on the banks of the Mersey in the space of a month. We used to get bodies washing up regularly. But the difference in these three cases was that they hadn't washed up. They'd been deliberately dumped.' Fagan reflected. 'Anyway, we identified all three bodies as working girls. The thing that made this killer so sadistic was that he was targeting heavily pregnant women. Each of the victims had their baby cut out of the womb and laid next to the body. Just left to die.'

Stacey clasped her hand over her mouth and closed her eyes.

'We worked the case for months with no leads. It was quickly established that the killer had medical experience. He would snatch the girls off the street, drug them, before cutting them open and taking out the unborn child and leaving it to die next to the mother. Anyhow, just when it was decided the killings were an out of the blue event, he killed again. The body was recovered from a bedsit in the Liverpool suburbs. When we entered the bedsit, we found the killer had scrawled a message in blood on the wall.' Fagan paused. 'I will keep on killing. And that's what he did for an eighteen-month period. Our head of department, Detective Chief Inspector Leslie Chapman, pulled out all the stops to catch the killer. He'd worked the Yorkshire Ripper case back in the seventies. So he had the experience. But the killer was always one step ahead of us. There was speculation that the killer was on the force. But no one could prove it. For eighteen long months, he killed over and over. Each time a heavily pregnant woman. The killer taunted us, daring us to catch him. He pushed us all to our limits. We'd patrol the red-light districts of Merseyside, offering the girls on the street support. But none of them wanted it. The case almost broke us. Especially a Detective Sergeant who was working the case. What we didn't know at the time was that DS Jack Daw was in a relationship with a prostitute. Her name was Jane Kelly. She was the last victim. The murderer took his time with her. Torturing her. I remember being called to the scene where she was found. DS Daw was with me. We both thought it was just another victim. When Jack Daw saw who it was who had been murdered, he broke down. The killer would send us messages. When he snatched Jane Kelly, he tortured her for hours. She told him everything about her relationship with Jack. Following the murder the killer sent Jack a message, saying that like Jack the Ripper, it was only fitting that she was going to be the last victim. But in years to come, he would return.'

'Mary Jane Kelly,' Brooks stated.

Fagan looked at him.

'She was believed to have been the last victim of Jack the Ripper.'

'Know a lot about Jack the Ripper, do you, Andrew?' Fagan questioned.

'It's a bit of a hobby of mine, sir. I go to regular discussions about him in Pontypool.'

Watkins breezed into the room holding some sheets of paper. 'Got something boss.' He handed Fagan one of the sheets. 'The social worker, Ruth Sutton, wasn't lying to us. Sophie Parry was having a relationship with Daniels. Look at what Parry says to him in one of the messages.'

Fagan read the message aloud. *'If you get that bitch Ruth Sutton off my back, I'll fuck you into oblivion.'*

'Daniels sent that reply.' Watkins pointed at the sheet of paper.

'No worries babes, I can't wait to eat your pussy, morning, noon and night.'

'Jesus,' Stacey said. 'No wonder they didn't want to hand Ellie's casefile over to us.'

'What are we dealing with here?' Fagan questioned.

'Well, it looks like Martin Daniels lied to us about everything.'

'Yeah, but let's look beyond that for a moment,' Fagan said. 'We have evidence that Ellie was murdered by a serial killer. Plus, she was a vulnerable young girl who was being abused. Sophie Parry has lied to us from the start. She lied to us about losing her phone. She hid the fact that she had a FansOnly account and that she'd been using Ellie to make money. Tammy Morris has also lied to us.'

'In order to protect her son, who was involved in a sexual relationship with both Sophie and Ellie,' Stacey added.

Fagan nodded. 'All this has been uncovered because of Ellie's murder. If the events of a few nights ago hadn't happened, Sophie Parry would have carried on with FansOnly. Sophie thought she was in control of her life.' Fagan glanced at Stacey. 'Remember what she said to us when we questioned her about her FansOnly account? She was confident she was safe. Because it was just posing in front of a camera. It's not like any of her fans were in the same room. What she didn't count on was Ellie attracting the attention of a serial killer.' Fagan paused. 'What time is Russel Connor giving that talk at Cardiff University?'

Watkins clicked on a mouse. 'In about an hour and a half, boss.'

'Right, okay, Stacey and Andrew will pay Social Services a visit and cross-examine Daniels about his relationship with Sophie Parry. Me and Sean will head down Cardiff and talk to Connor about his social networking app. Then we'll wrap things up for the day. First thing tomorrow morning, we'll have a team briefing. DI Saddler will have a full account of his interview with Ellie's friends. So we'll be able to put more of this puzzle together. Hopefully, they will have pulled information of Ellie's phone so we can add that into the mix. We'll speak to DS Padfield about the investigation into the spate of suicides connected with Cymru Teen Chat.' Fagan glanced at his watch. 'I'll e-mail Griffiths and tell him we need to hold Owen Woods for the maximum time. So, we have ninety-six hours from now to catch a serial killer. So let's get cracking.'

Stacey and Brooks headed for the door.

'Oi, you two,' Fagan called out.

They both turned.

Fagan pointed at them. 'I'm recommending you two for detective training. By the end of the year, I want you both bumped up to Detective Constables.'

Stacey nodded while trying to suppress a smile. 'We'll call in on cybercrimes downstairs to see if they have any more on Parry's phone we can question Daniels about.'

Watkins threw his jacket over his shoulder and followed them out of the door.

Fagan thumbed through his contacts on his phone. 'Hey Melissa.'

'Marc, is everything okay? Don't say you're about to stand me up tonight,' she teased.

'No, I'll just be a little late. I need your help with something. Hope you don't mind if I bring work with me.'

'No, not at all.'

Fagan smiled. 'Great, I'll see you at nine.'

CHAPTER 25

Blaenau Gwent Social Services

'Why are you here again?' Martin Daniels aired a tone of annoyance as Stacey and Brooks sat down. 'I have a meeting in less than an hour.'

'We're here asking a few routine follow-up questions,' Stacey said, pulling her phone from her pocket. 'How would you describe your relationship with Sophie Parry?'

'I thought we talked about this earlier. It was amicable. We got on. We were working together to help Ellie and her problems.'

'So, there was nothing more to your amicable relationship?'

Daniels rolled his eyes. 'Here we go. Don't tell me, someone has been to see you, slagging me off.'

Brooks nodded. 'A former social worker has talked to detectives. She claims she was forced out, because she had made a recommendation that Sophie Parry's children should be removed from the family home. You overruled that decision.'

'I bet it's Ruth Sutton who you've spoken to. I overruled her decision because it would have done more harm than good removing the children from the family home.'

'And you still maintain that your relationship with Sophie Parry was strictly professional?' Stacey maintained a calm tone.

'Yes.'

'When me and my colleague spoke to you earlier, you said the last time you visited Sophie Parry was last week. You also claimed her house was in order and there was nothing wrong.' Stacey thumbed her phone, holding it up. 'As you can see, Mr Daniels, Sophie Parry's house is far from tidy. The social worker you just mentioned, Ruth Sutton, told detectives that Sophie Parry could not keep a tidy house, despite offers of support. Would you care to explain to us why you lied to us earlier on?'

Daniels seemed like a rabbit caught in spotlights.

Stacey took advantage of his silence. She located a message Parry and Daniels had exchanged *'If you get that bitch Ruth Sutton off my back, then I'll fuck you into oblivion.* This is just one of over two hundred sexually explicit messages you and Sophie Parry exchanged last year. So why have you lied to us about your relationship with Sophie Parry?'

'Let's just back up here, shall we? Sophie Parry came on to me. I didn't make the first move.'

'No, but you made the second move. Which was to start an inappropriate relationship with someone who was on the radar of Social Services. You said it yourself, Mr Daniels. Sophie Parry was a vulnerable woman.'

'In 2014, you were interviewed regarding an incident at a special needs home in Newport,' Brooks stated.

'Nothing came of it,' Daniels replied in a defensive tone. 'When you work in social care, you have to put up with all kinds of accusations.'

'But why did you think it was perfectly okay to carry on an inappropriate relationship with Sophie Parry?'

'Look, if you are here to accuse me of something, I suggest you stop right there. I am entitled to a solicitor if you are about to accuse me of the murder of Ellie.'

Stacey held up her phone. 'We're not here to accuse you of murder, Mr Daniels. However, the evidence here is as plain as a nose on your face. You were having an inappropriate relationship with Sophie Parry. What I want to know is how did it start? You just said she came on to you.'

'Sophie Parry is always coming across as a victim. A vulnerable woman who can't cope with life. If you want my honest professional opinion, she's nothing but a narcissist.'

'So why didn't you report her inappropriate actions towards you?'

'Look, we're all vulnerable in our own way, okay.'

'Is that how you see yourself, Mr Daniels?' Brooks asked. 'A vulnerable individual. So, why are you a social worker?'

'I know it was wrong what I did. I was glad when she lost interest in me.'

'How did your relationship with Sophie Parry start?'

'It was a difficult case to start off with. Ellie was very closed off.'

'Did you have any ideas why she was like this?'

'No.'

'Did you know that Sophie Parry had a FansOnly account?'

Daniels took time answering. He eventually nodded. 'Yeah. That's how she reeled me in. She showed me one of her videos that she had made for FansOnly. She said that I could taste the merchandise.'

'Did Sophie Parry show you any other videos?.'

'Well, yeah, a few. I don't subscribe to FansOnly.'

'Were you aware that Sophie Parry was posting videos of her daughter Ellie on the site?'

Stacey's words were met with a stunned expression. 'What do you mean, Sophie Parry was posting videos of her daughter on FansOnly?'

'Sophie Parry had uploaded over seventeen hundred sexually explicit pictures and videos of her daughter.'

Daniels held up his hands. 'I kid you not. I knew nothing about this. I'm many things, but not a paedo.'

'We're not suggesting that, Mr Daniels,' Stacey remarked.

Daniels took a few moments to consider his situation. 'Shit, I should have seen that coming.'

'You should have seen what coming?' Brooks asked.

Daniels took a moment to answer. 'When Sophie Parry was first referred to Social Services, it took time to connect with her. It was almost like we were an inconvenience being there. In the first few weeks of us contacting that family, it was strictly professional.'

'When did it become unprofessional?' Stacey asked.

'Ruth, the other social worker, took the boys and Ellie out for the day. They went up to Big Pit.'

'Leaving you and Sophie alone.'

'Yeah,' Daniels admitted. 'We were just having this frank

conversation about Sophie struggling with money. Because we hit it off so well, Sophie confided in me about her FansOnly account. She claimed she was making a couple of quid extra, just to keep her head above water. That's when she showed me a video.'

'And you didn't think to tell Sophie Parry that it was not appropriate to show you that video.'

Daniels massaged his forehead. 'I was going through a low period myself in my life.'

'What low period were you going through, Mr Daniels?'

'My wife and I were constantly arguing. The usual things, money, kids, life in general.'

'So, suddenly, Sophie Parry looked like the better option, did she?' Brooks said.

'What? No!' Daniels shook his head. 'I was having a moment of weakness.'

'Did you have sex the day she showed you the video?'

'No,' Daniels replied. 'When I got home later that day, me and my wife had a massive argument. I was really low. Sophie Parry messaged me later that evening. She sent me another video. That's when she said, if I wanted, I could taste the merchandise.'

'When did you start your affair with Sophie Parry?' Stacey asked.

Daniels took a moment to answer. 'It was a couple of days after. Ellie was with friends, and Ruth was with the two boys and their father. It wasn't even a registered call.' Daniels admitted. 'Me and the wife had just had another argument. Sophie Parry messaged me. She claimed she wanted to talk to me about the progress Ellie was making with Social Services. When I turned up at the door, she seemed really hyped up. She comes out with this bullshit story. Something about how our relationship was going, and how I was the only man in her life at the moment that really trusted her. She said she would turn her life around. Get a job and all that stuff. She'd even had a massive clear-up of her house. It looked really tidy.'

'Is that when you had sex with her?'

Daniels inhaled and nodded. 'It's only looking back. I realise it was all bullshit. After a few weeks, she started getting down. Sophie and Ruth didn't get on. Ruth thought she was an unsuitable mother, always lying to Social Services. That's when Ruth suggested that the children should have respite.'

'What is that?' Brooks asked.

'It's where children are put into temporary care with fosterers. It gives both children and parents breathing space. Anyway, we had a meeting to discuss a way forward for the family. That's when Ruth suggested respite care. Sophie went to pieces. She phoned me up one day crying, threatening to commit suicide. She begged me to intervene.'

'Did you tell Ruth Sutton what Sophie did?'

'No,' Daniels admitted. 'I know I should have. However, we were having an intense relationship. So I recommended the children should stay with Sophie. Ruth went ballistic. That's when she told Social Services to shove the job.'

'But you carried on the affair,' Stacey surmised.

'For a while,' Daniels revealed. 'But then Sophie distanced herself from me. Once she knew Ellie or the boys wouldn't be taken away, she didn't want to know me anymore.'

'She used you, in other words.'

Daniels nodded. 'I turned up at her door this one time and she told me she wanted a rest. I asked her why and she said her head was too in the shed to have a relationship. I tried to talk her out of it. But she got really pissy with me. She threatened that if I kept pestering her, she'd tell my wife everything. She also threatened to tell Social Services what was going on between us.'

'But you carried on the visits.'

Daniels hesitated before shaking his head. 'No.'

'But you claimed earlier you last saw Sophie Parry last week.'

'I lied, okay. Look before we go any further. I didn't know what Sophie Parry was up to regarding her daughter. But when she threatened to destroy my life, I knew I couldn't keep on visiting her. Even in an official capacity.' An expression of regret flashed across Daniels' face. 'Guess I should have listened to Ruth.'

'Yes, you should have,' Stacey said. 'Instead, you've been falsifying reports for over six months. You realise this is going to cost you your job once all this comes out.'

Daniels nodded. 'I've already handed in my notice.' He reached into a desk drawer and pulled out a folder, handing it to Stacey. 'The full report on Sophie Parry and her family. Including Ruth's recommendation that the children should have been taken into respite care. I know I'm going to be in a lot of shit about this. When I found out about what happened to Ellie, I knew it was over.'

Stacey took the file. 'We appreciate your cooperation in this matter.' She stood and headed towards the door with Brooks.

'One more thing,' Daniels called after them.

Stacey turned.

'When you see Sophie, tell her I'm sorry.'

Stacey nodded. 'I will.'

CHAPTER 26

'Want to know something interesting, boss?' Watkins said, staring at his phone.

'What's that, Sean?' Fagan aggressively flicked the indicator and pulled into the fast lane of the M4 motorway. 'People who hog the middle lane piss me off, big time.'

'Russel Connor has form for GBH.'

'Really.'

Watkins nodded. 'I just ran his name through the police database. Connor was jailed in 1993 for GBH. He was given a two and a half year sentence.'

'Not really anything significant there, Sean.'

Watkins gave Fagan a sidewards glance. 'But here's the best bit. At the time of his arrest Connor was working at Vine Road Studios just outside Monmouth.'

'You're joking.'

'Thing is, there's nothing here about who he assaulted.'

'There should be something.'

'Nope.' Watkins shook his head. 'All it says, that he was sent down in July 1993.'

Fagan considered the information. 'Alex X was murdered in the summer of 1993. The night of the Brit Awards.'

'She was, yeah.'

'Where and when was Connor arrested?'

Watkins thumbed the phone screen. He broke out into a broad grin. 'At the Agincourt Hotel. On the 27th June 1993.'

'Two days after Alex X was murdered,' Fagan recalled the murder investigation. 'Has Connor got a profile page on Wikipedia?'

Watkins carried out a quick search. 'Here we go, boss. Russel Connor, born 1954. Is a Welsh entrepreneur and innovator known for his pioneering work in video graphics during the 1980s and subsequent advancements in computer software and artificial intelligence. Born in Newport, South Wales, Connor's career has spanned several decades and has left a lasting impact on the music, entertainment and technology industries. Connor began his career at Vine Road Music Studios in 1976, where he gained recognition for revolutionising video graphics techniques in music videos and television commercials. His innovative approach not only enhanced visual storytelling but also set new standards for creative expression in media production during the burgeoning digital age. Building on his success in video graphics, Connor transitioned into the software industry, founding and leading a prominent computer software company. Under his stewardship, the company became synonymous with groundbreaking technology and software development. Pioneering advancements that pushed the boundaries of what was thought possible in early AI applications and computer programming.'

'It doesn't say anything about his stint inside?' Fagan queried.

'No, boss,' Watkins continued. 'In recent years, Connor has focused on fostering meaningful connections among young people through his latest venture, Cymru Teen Chat. This online social media platform has garnered widespread acclaim for its innovative features designed to enhance communication and community-building among Welsh youth. By leveraging his expertise in technology and his deep understanding of social dynamics, Connor has created a platform that not only connects young people but also empowers them to share ideas and experiences in a safe and supportive environment.'

'Sound like a bunch of bullshit to me.'

Watkins carried on. 'Russel Connor's contributions to the fields of technology and social media have earned him many accolades, including the prestigious Welsh Businessman of the Year award. His visionary leadership and commitment to innovation continue to inspire both aspiring entrepreneurs and seasoned professionals alike. Outside of his professional endeavours, Connor is known for his passion for classic arcade games and his avid interest in UFO phenomena.'

Fagan burst into laughter.

Watkins also found it hard to keep a straight face. 'He lives in his hometown of Newport, South Wales, where he remains actively involved in community initiatives and philanthropic efforts aimed at supporting local talent and fostering innovation in technology. Russel Connor's career trajectory mirrors that of iconic figures like Steve Jobs and Bill Gates, blending technical expertise with a visionary approach to business and social impact. His ongoing commitment to pushing the boundaries of technology and fostering meaningful connections among young people underscores his status as a leading figure in both the Welsh and global tech communities.'

'So, as well as being a bit barmy, believing in aliens, Connor fancies himself as being the next Bill Gates. Does his police record say where he served time?'

'Cardiff.'

'What's the betting he knew about Alex's murder?'

'You reckon he could have found out about the murder and confronted Dillon Powell or Frankie Jordan about it?'

'It's a possibility.'

'Going off on a tangent, aren't we, boss, interviewing Connor?'

'Not really,' Fagan said. 'When we have a briefing tomorrow, we should find out about Ellie's activities on Cymru Teen Chat. Hopefully, the labs will have pulled something useful off her phone so that we can move forward with all this. DI Saddler will also tell us what his team has discovered. With any luck we should make significant progress.'

'If it was a serial killer that murdered Ellie, what's the likelihood of us catching him?'

'I couldn't tell you, Sean,' Fagan answered. 'But there's a connection between four other deaths and Ellie's. And the fact Cymru Teen Chat has been linked to a spate of suicides adds another layer to our investigation. I'm even having trouble keeping up.'

'FYI, boss, Tammy Morris has raised seventy grand on a crowd funding website.' Watkins was staring at his phone screen.

Fagan rolled his eyes. 'I'm sure she'll donate whatever is left over to charity after they've paid for Ellie's funeral. I don't get some people. What makes them tick? It's hard enough to figure out what makes a person want to commit murder.'

'Do you reckon Tammy Morris could have known about Ellie's mam posting pictures and videos of her daughter on FansOnly?'

'It wouldn't surprise me. That woman lied to us about her son having a sexual relationship with Ellie and her mother. Sophie Parry manipulated him into bed and encouraged her daughter to pursue a sexual relationship at eleven years old. What I don't get is why carry on the lies? Tammy is raising money on a crowd funding website to make money and nothing else. It makes you wonder what happened to her morals as a mother.' Fagan paused. 'When we have our briefing tomorrow morning, all the investigation teams will gather and look at the evidence. Hopefully, we'll be able to put something together that will bring us one step closer to her killer.' Fagan flicked the indicator to turn off the motorway.

CHAPTER 27

Cardiff University

By the time Fagan and Watkins arrived, the auditorium was already full. They had to stand at the back.

'Russel Connor is very popular,' Fagan remarked, looking around the packed lecture hall.

Watkins stared at his phone screen. 'According to his website, he's giving a speech, a questions and answers session, followed by a book signing.'

'We'll wait until he's finished with his book signing before having a chat.' Fagan sensed his phone buzzing in his pocket. Unknown number flashed on his screen. 'I'll be back shortly, just got to answer this, Sean,' he said, heading for the door.

'DI Fagan, I'm DCI Gethin Lewis.' The voice on the other end introduced himself. 'I was wondering if we could have a chat about your enquiry regarding Operation Julie.'

Fagan stayed silent.

'It's okay, DI Fagan. I'm not reprimanding you for instructing Constable Flynn to open the case file. It flagged up in an automatic e-mail. But it is important I speak with you. Meet me at the new police station in Abergavenny tomorrow morning.'

Fagan nodded, 'Of course, sir.'

'Eight o'clock sharp,' Lewis said before hanging up.

Fagan returned to the auditorium.

As Russel Connor stepped out on to the stage, he was met with a rapturous applause. He looked at his audience, smiling. 'Thank you for attending this session this evening, ladies and gentlemen.'

The lights dimmed, leaving Connor silhouetted in a spotlight circle. The room plunged into silence for a few moments before being replaced by an ambient futuristic sounding melody.

'Imagine a world where your online safety is paramount. Where teenagers across Wales can go online and not have to worry about any kind of threat. Where you can connect with friends, share your passions, and explore new interests in a secure environment designed just for you. A platform that utilises the latest AI security software to ensure the safety of its young online users. Ladies and gentlemen, I give you, Cymru Teen Chat 2.0. The revolutionary app created for young people throughout Wales.'

A projector whirred to life, displaying images of the Welsh valleys.

'Our app is dedicated to providing a safe and engaging online haven for teenagers aged 13 to 17. The race to create an online platform for the younger generation is heating up. Companies around the world are competing. We have created an online platform that will push the boundaries of technology. Cymru Teen Chat 2.0 stands out by combining innovative technology with a user-friendly interface, making it the go-to app for teens who crave both security and excitement.'

More enthusiastic applause echoed around the auditorium.

Connor smiled at his audience. 'However, Cymru Teen Chat 2.0 isn't just about pushing technological boundaries. It's about creating a community where teens can thrive, express themselves, and build meaningful connections. Our new improved platform allows users to add photos, emojis, video and sound. Using some of the most advanced AI profiling software in the world, users can create customised avatars and personalised profiles. Young people can truly make their online presence unique and reflective of their individual personalities. Thus immersing themselves in an online world where anything is possible. But it doesn't stop there. Cymru Teen Chat 2.0 is working with partners from major industries, including several UK based gaming companies. These collaborations are bringing exclusive gaming content and special events directly to our users. Making Cymru Teen Chat 2.0 not just another social platform, but a hub for entertainment and innovation. All these innovations are under the watch of advanced AI technologies. Artificially intelligence based technologies that can pick up on the slightest threat. Our real-time AI moderation system ensures that inappropriate content is instantly filtered out. Cyber bullying will soon be a thing of the past. Cymru Teen Chat 2.0 will be a safe and welcoming environment for all young users. Cymru Teen Chat 2.0 is so advanced our AI based system can analyse tens of thousands of conversations all at once. It can detect cyber bullying and deal with it instantly. This unparalleled level of security means that our users can focus on what matters most. Connecting with friends, exploring new interests, and enjoying their time online without worry. Thus giving parents of teens across Wales peace of mind. With robust parental controls and privacy settings, parents can customise their teen's online experience, ensuring they stay safe while enjoying all the app offers. Cymru Teen Chat 2.0 is forever looking towards the horizon of the future. Besides our online platforms we are developing new technologies. Hardware that can connect to your personalised environment and create an experience that transcends anything you've experienced on any social media platform.'

The projector screen displayed an image of a woman using a virtual reality headset.

'Imagine a future where your Cymru Teen Chat profile can seamlessly integrate with cutting-edge devices, offering a multi-sensory experience that brings the digital world to life like never before. Where you can touch the digital world and interact with virtual objects just like real-world objects. All this from the safety and comfort of your own home. Ladies and gentlemen, welcome to the future. A future where Cymru Teen Chat leads the way in blending technology and social interaction, creating a safe, innovative, and immersive experience for the next generation. Thank you for joining us on this exciting journey.'

The audience rose to their feet, clapping.

Fagan glanced at Watkins. 'I don't know about you Sean, but this Connor comes across as more of a cult leader that some sort of tech guru.'

'I was just thinking the same thing, boss,' Watkins said loudly, while clapping.

'Then why are you applauding him?'

Watkins stopped clapping.

Connor held a questions and answers session for the best part of an hour.

Fagan messaged Melissa that he'd be a little later than he said he'd be.

After another three quarters of an hour, Fagan and Watkins approached Connor.

A frustrated looking assistant ushered enthusiastic fans away.

Connor looked at Fagan and Watkins. 'If you have questions, gentlemen, you should have asked them during the Q and A session.' He yawned and stretched out his arms.

Fagan stared at Connor before speaking. 'I have a few questions, Mr Connor, if you don't mind.' He produced his ID. 'DI Fagan and DS Watkins with Gwent Police.'

Connor seemed mildly irritated the police had showed up after his presentation. 'It's been rather a long day for me, gentleman. If you speak to my assistant, you can schedule an appointment for later this week.'

Fagan admired Connor's arrogant attitude. 'I'm afraid that won't be possible. We're kind of on a clock to catch a murderer.'

'Are accusing me of this murder, DI Fagan?'

'No, of course not, Mr Connor. But we know the victim in question was using your app the day she was murdered. We have reason to suspect she was in contact with her killer the night she was found dead in her home.'

'What teenagers get up to on Cymru Teen Chat is their business, not the business of my company.' Connor stood. 'Now if you'll excuse me, gentlemen, I want to get home.'

'So, what you're saying is, you've better things to do than help the police?'

'What I'm saying, DI Fagan, is that it's impossible to help you at this time.'

'But you do have access to data regarding those who use your software,' Fagan pursued.

Connor disguised his irritation with a smile. 'Our policies are very strict. We protect our users' privacy. Even if I wanted to help, I can't just hand over personal information. The software that our app uses is run by AI. This is why it's become so popular. The AI that runs the app prevents human intervention.'

'But what happens when you want to change your app?' Watkins asked.

'The AI makes the changes. That's what makes our app stand out from every other social media app.' Connor grinned. 'Mark Zuckerberg and Elon Musk are shitting themselves right now.'

'Why is that?' Fagan enquired.

'Because I'm about to launch the app worldwide next year. It's going to revolutionise social media beyond anything seen before.'

Watkins leaned forward. 'A fourteen-year-old girl is dead, Mr Connor. And all you can think about is becoming the next tech billionaire. I'd say you are a man without morals.'

Connor's smile vanished. 'I'm not without compassion. I feel for this girl and her family, truly, I do. But the system is run by AI, that's why it was created. To prevent human intervention. The AI runs the software and the website.'

'And what happens if we apply for a court order?' Fagan challenged.

Connor chuckled. 'You can get ten court orders if you want. It won't make any difference.'

'Why create a system if you can't control it? Isn't that a little dangerous?'

'I haven't created a Terminator robot hell bent on wiping out the human race.'

Fagan pressed on. 'There must be something you can do. Who created to the app?'

'I came up with the concept before enlisting a group of talented computer engineers.'

'Where are they based?' Watkins asked.

'The Philippines,' Connor replied abruptly. 'Which is why you'll have trouble with your court orders.'

'So what you're saying is, you don't have access to the

software because it's based in the Philippines?'

The frustration returned. 'I just told you. The software is run by AI.'

'Designed by engineers in Philippines,' Fagan added. 'Who have access to information the police need in order to catch Ellie's Parry's killer.'

'And how do you suppose you are going to get a court order out to the Philippines?' Connor questioned.

'Is that why you set up a company in that part of the world?' Watkins asked.

'Everyone is setting up companies in the Far East. It's cheaper and more efficient.'

'Efficient for you, Mr Connor, but nor for our police investigation. We need access to data regarding Ellie Parry's account. We know she had one.'

Connor sighed, rubbing his temples. 'Look, DI Fagan, I sympathise with your situation, but my hands are tied. Our app has robust encryption and security measures in place. Those measures are controlled by AI, which utilises sentient programming to govern its systems. Even I don't have direct access to user communications. That data is analysed and encrypted to protect privacy. That's why we switched everything over to AI. It's impenetrable, I'm afraid.'

Fagan interjected, with a sharp tone. 'Are you telling us there's no way to track who Ellie Parry was speaking to on your app?'

Connor hesitated. 'I'm saying it's not straightforward. Our user data is stored on secure servers controlled by AI.'

'Yes, you've been shoving that down our throats for the past few minutes.' Fagan's frustration mounted.

'Look, I can make some enquiries. See if there's a way to bypass the AI protocols. But it will take time.'

Fagan's eyes narrowed, sensing Connor was withholding something. 'Time is a luxury we don't have, Mr Connor. Every moment we waste, or rather you waste, the killer gets further away.'

'It's not my intention to waste the time of the police, DI Fagan.

I just said I'd make some enquiries.'

'And you're sure you've told us everything.'

Connor leaned back, crossing his arms defensively. 'I've told you everything I can. I will contact you immediately if I find something.'

Fagan and Watkins exchanged a glance. Watkins changed tactics, his voice softening. 'Mr Connor, we understand there are things you cannot help us with. But a young girl's life was taken. Any delay could cost us crucial evidence. Please, reconsider. Help us find her killer.'

Connor's expression softened slightly. 'I'll see what I can do,' he said quietly. 'No promises, but I'll look into it. That's all I can offer right now.'

Fagan nodded. 'Thank you, Mr Connor. We appreciate any help you can provide.'

Connor stood. 'Now if you'll excuse me, gentlemen, I want to head home.'

As they stood to leave, Fagan couldn't shake the feeling that Connor knew more than he was letting on.

'What do you reckon, boss?'

'More bullshit, Sean. Connor is another in a long line of people who have fed us bollocks over the past few days. Connor, Sophie Parry, Tammy Morris, have lied to us to protect their little secrets.'

'What do you think Connor is lying about?'

'Judging by what he fed us, just about everything. I may not be all knowing about computers, Sean, but I know enough that what he just fed us is a bag of bollocks.' Fagan glanced at his phone screen. 'We'll call it a day. There's a major briefing tomorrow. With any luck we'll piece more together and get one step closer to Ellie's killer.'

CHAPTER 28

Sundarbon Indian restaurant - Abergavenny

'You okay Marc? You've hardly said a word since we got in here,' Melissa remarked.

Fagan snapped out of his trance. 'Sorry Melissa, my mind is wandering.'

'Tough day?'

Fagan nodded and sighed at the same time. 'You could say that.'

'You're investigating the murder up the Sofrydd, aren't you?'

Fagan looked at Melissa, who smiled back at him.

'Jackie phoned me earlier. She wants to meet up. We got talking about you.'

Fagan frowned.

'Just talking, not gossiping,' Melissa assured him.

'I think most people are still surprised to see me back in Abergavenny. Although I've been back for over a year.'

Melissa agreed. 'I've bumped into a few people from the good old days. One person I spoke to actually thought I was dead.'

'You'll be surprised at what people say about you when you move away.'

'Do you want to tell me about your day?'

'It's been a bit of a crap past few days. Lies and deceit surrounding the murder of a fourteen-year-old girl.'

'Who's been lying to you?'

'For starters, the mother,' Fagan revealed. 'The night her daughter was murdered, she was out on the piss in Cardiff. She lied about her mobile phone, claiming that it'd been stolen while she was in a pub. But she was picked up on CCTV, throwing her phone into a bin at Cardiff train station. When forensics examined her phone, they found a load of obscene videos, including videos of her daughter. She's got a FansOnly account and has been uploading sexually explicit videos of both her and her daughter.'

'Jesus,' Melissa gasped.

'We've also found out that the girl had sexual relationships with other men on the street. Including the son of her mam's best friend.'

'Sign of the times, I'm afraid, Marc.'

'Yeah, I'm slowly learning that.'

'Can I ask you a personal question?'

'Yeah, you can ask me anything, you know that, Melissa.'

'How old were you when you lost your virginity?'

Fagan almost spat out a mouthful of chicken curry. 'I'm not sure what that question has to do with the price of cheese, Melissa.'

Melissa chuckled. 'Sorry, I didn't mean to catch you off guard.'

Fagan wiped his mouth. 'I don't really remember. It was so long ago.' He thought for a few moments. 'I was probably fifteen. But for the life of me, I can't remember who it was. I don't think I felt the earth move or anything like that.'

Melissa smiled back, taking a sip of wine. 'Jane Trask, that's who.'

'How an earth would you know that?'

'Because she told me when we came off the summer holidays.' Melissa recalled the year. '1979, to be exact.'

Fagan could feel the blood pumping into his cheeks. 'Bloody hell, that's embarrassing.'

'It was all over the walls of the girl's toilets,' Melissa teased. 'You and Jane were the talk of King Henry.'

Fagan buried his face in his hands. 'I can't believe I'm hearing this over forty years down the line.'

Melissa laughed again. 'You shouldn't be ashamed of the past, Marc.'

'I'm not,' Fagan reflected. 'But we were kids, and probably knew it was wrong. Just out of curiosity, how old were you when you lost your virginity?'

'I was twenty-two,' Melissa answered casually. 'It was after the family moved to New York. I was studying at Columbia university. I met this handsome American, and we got together for a few years before parting. When I was at school, I knew a lot of my friends who lost their virginities. My father was very strict. He was also a school governor at King Henry. He used to say they'd talk about the behaviour of the kids at school. A friend of mine, Susan Jones, became pregnant at 13. He knew what my friends were like back then. I remember inviting some friends over. Do you remember where I used to live, Triley Mill Hotel?'

Fagan nodded.

'I invited some friends over and they invited a few boys along. My dad went ballistic. I remember him frogmarching everyone out.'

Fagan looked back down memory lane. 'I did a lot of stupid things back in the day. Things that landed me in a young offenders' prison for two years. When I left Abergavenny, I didn't expect to return.'

'Why did you come back home?'

'There was nothing for me in Liverpool. Following my mam's death my long-term relationship ended. So I thought, what the hell.'

'A lot has changed, hasn't it?'

'Yeah,' Fagan agreed. 'So much has been knocked down or built upon. Cooper's Filters. The old Llantilio Pertholey school is now a house. And Pinches the bakery has gone. They used to make the most amazing custard tarts.' Fagan's thoughts turned to Rebecca.

'It wasn't your fault, Marc,' Melissa said, noting the look on Fagan's face.

'Is it that obvious?'

'Rebecca's death is bound to affect you.'

'Yeah, but I don't want to sit here and spoil our evening together by talking about a long-lost love.'

'Marc, we're both grownups, who have seen our fair share of tragedy in our lives,' Melissa reassured him. 'Because of the careers we chose. But we have one thing in common. We have been able to handle things no ordinary person could.'

'I guess we both have a dark streak in us.'

'Maybe,' Melissa agreed. 'Do you think Tim will get convicted of murder?'

'He'll go for a manslaughter charge.'

'What about Benny Nelson?'

'Arrogant prick,' Fagan mocked.

'You arrested him before you arrested Tim. When you should have questioned Tim first. And that's me not judging you, Marc.'

'I know,' Fagan sighed. 'Benny Nelson was the reason I had to leave Abergavenny. When I saw him for the first time in nearly 40 years, the loathing I had for him in 1985 was still there. Nelson hadn't changed. He was still the same as ever. Arrogant, thinking he can get away with anything. And then he strung us along, pretending that he had murdered Rebecca. All the time that lawyer of his making out that we were in the wrong. Also, factor in Tim, who snapped when he found out I was coming home.'

'Marc, I know what you're doing. You are not to blame for Rebecca's murder.'

'But I am. If I hadn't had come back to Abergavenny, she'd still be alive.'

'Consider this. How do you know Tim wouldn't have done the same thing if you hadn't had come back home? From what Jackie had told me he'd been violent to her in the past. Tim even put Rebecca in the hospital. If there's one thing I discovered during my time in New York. It's those who have murdered people were always going to go down that path. Tim would have eventually snapped.'

'But I was the catalyst,' Fagan said.

Melissa shook her head slowly. 'No Marc. Tim's rage was the catalyst, not you.'

Fagan scooped up some rice from his plate.

'Getting back to the subject we were just discussing. Youngsters today are just as promiscuous. However, the internet has added a whole new level.'

'It has,' Fagan agreed. 'The internet has been the biggest problem during this investigation.'

'What did you want my help with?'

'There's evidence to suggest that we may be dealing with a

serial killer.'

'Go on, I'm listening,' Melissa said, breaking off a small piece of poppadom.

'Four other deaths have occurred over the last four years. In each death the same semen sample was found. However, the four other deaths were concluded as suicides. All the girls had sex with the same man within twenty-four hours of their death. But with victim number five, the murderer actually took part in her death by starting to strangling her. The pathologist has revealed she had taken enough ecstasy to bring on a heart attack, though.'

'What are your thoughts?'

'I think he knew she was dying. So he didn't have to put his hands around her throat in a manner that suggests strangulation.'

'Making it look like some sort of sex game that went wrong.'

'Yeah,' Fagan nodded. 'Help me out here, Melissa. A serial killer who has the power to convince others to take their lives without actually touching them. Is such a thing possible?'

Melissa nodded. 'Absolutely, although it's still a relatively new concept. Just before I left New York, the police were having to deal with at least a dozen cases across the state. All involving young people who had taken their lives for no reason. But New York Police believed all the victims were in contact with cyber serial killers.'

'What kind of person are we up against?'

Melissa considered Fagan's question. 'First off, your killer will be very intelligent. He doesn't have to be intelligent in the sense he's been educated in a university or college. There's a lot of knowledge to be gained off the internet these days. He'll be calculated, choosing his victims carefully. Trawling social media. One of the problems with social media these days is that people are too open about their personal lives. And that's what your killer will feed on. Young women or girls who are content with exposing their vulnerabilities to others. He'll pick a target, make contact, pretending to be like-minded and understanding the individual. Gaining their trust. He'll analyse what they say to him. And pick up on their weaknesses and vulnerabilities. Your killer will trawl a lot of pages associated with mental health issues.'

'I had someone look for pages on Facebook today,' Fagan mentioned. 'There are hundreds of them. Claiming to help people with mental health issues.'

'A fertile hunting ground for any serial killer in the modern age. He'll be someone who can read people. When you have the ability to read people, you know what makes them tick. He'll come across as very understanding and a loyal friend. Gaining access to a victim's psyche. The more his next victim reveals, the more he can manipulate them. Until it reaches a stage where he can make them do whatever he wants. It's like how sexual predators work online. He'll be an expert in psychological manipulation. Slowly isolating his victims from their usual support networks. Convincing them that people around them are toxic and that he is the only one who understands them. It could take weeks or months to do this. But the end game is always the same, convincing his victim to take their own lives.'

'But what does he gain out of it if he can't be there to take part in their death?'

'What does any serial killer get out of killing?' Melissa asked. 'Pleasure. Fred and Rose West loved to torture their victims for sexual gratification. And when they were no longer sexually gratified, they killed them. Then moved on to the next victim. Upping the stakes. Ensuring their next kill would be even more sexually gratifying. Ian Brady and Myra Hindley killed for kicks. They loved torturing their victims before killing them. And then you have Peter Sutcliffe, the Yorkshire Ripper who would cruise the streets at night looking for his next victim. Most of whom were prostitutes. One of the easiest target categories for any serial killer. No one is going to miss them. And so we come to your serial killer. Someone who can kill at a distance. He's also taunting the police.'

'How so?'

'You say the killer had sex with four of the victims within twenty-four hours of their deaths?'

'Yeah.'

'And their four other deaths were put down as suicide.'

Fagan nodded.

'He's taunting the police because he has gone unchecked until now. As far as the police are concerned, all the victims before Ellie committed suicide.'

'Yeah, it was only when the pathologist was running a DNA scan did he make the connection with the four other victims.'

'He'll be full of himself now. Watching you scurry around. Trying to figure out who murdered Ellie. It's been all over the Welsh news for the past few days. This alone will give the killer more confidence. I wouldn't be surprised if he's already picked out his next victim. He'll want to test the police to see how long it will take them to catch him.'

'Are you saying he wants to be caught?'

Melissa nodded. 'There have been cases where serial killers have killed purely out of wanting to gain notoriety or infamy. Comparing their actions with the actions of other serial killers. Sort of like a macabre competition to see who can kill more. And how long they can keep on killing before they are caught? So chances are he's already chosen his next victim, and he's preparing to set up the kill. Because of all the news media publicity, it's motivating the killer to speed up his kills. He's confident because he can kill at a distance, which makes it harder for the police to catch him.'

'I want you to liaise with our team and provide a profile for our killer.'

'Of course, Marc. Anything I can do to help.'

Fagan smiled at her. 'We'll finish our meal before heading back to my place. I'll show you everything I have.'

Melissa winked at him playfully. 'I'm up for that.'

CHAPTER 29

Abergavenny Police Station

'DI Fagan,' Detective Chief Inspector Gethin Lewis approached, shaking his hand. 'Glad you could come in so early.'

'It's not a problem, sir,' Fagan responded, while looking around him.

'It's a little small, I know. It's more of a satellite station. If a major incident happens, we have room for portable buildings to be brought in. I couldn't get an office. Have you had breakfast?'

'Just a cup of coffee, sir,' Fagan replied.

'We'll pop over the road to the Brewers Fayre. They have an excellent buffet breakfast menu.'

'Fine by me, sir,' Fagan said.

After they had piled their plates, Fagan and Lewis found themselves a spot in the restaurant. At that time of the morning there were hardly any people around to eavesdrop on their conversation.

Fagan noted Lewis had ordered a double whisky.

'So how are you finding your hometown after moving back after so long?'

Fagan looked out of the window at the new police station. 'Some things have changed and others have remained the same.'

Lewis munched on a hash brown, looking in the same direction. 'The reason I've called you so early, DI Fagan, is because I need your help. Can I ask why you pulled the file on Operation Julie?'

'While investigating a murder up the Sofrydd, we've discovered the mother of the victim had a FansOnly account. She'd uploaded pictures of her fourteen-year-old daughter. The site is run by a former copper who is a convicted paedophile. He was jailed after Operation Julie exposed a paedophile ring in

Swansea. A former Abergavenny copper Bob Benson helped crack the case.'

'Bob Benson was Chief Constable of South Wales Police when a gang of paedophiles was exposed in the early nineties. It all started with Operation Julie. Thing is, Bob Benson wasn't what I would call squeaky clean.'

'You think Bob Benson may have been hiding something?'

Lewis nodded. 'Benson threw a lot of people under a bus to save his own skin. He had a lot of dirt on people that could get him out of being part of what was happening.'

'I'm vaguely familiar with Operation Julie,' Fagan said. 'I found reference to it while investigating the murder of Alexandria Xavier.'

'In January 1992, the body of twelve-year-old Julie Mann was found in an upstairs bedroom of a terraced house in Cromwell Street, Swansea. This was following a four-day search for the girl. A post-mortem revealed she'd been raped, tortured and finally strangled. A massive police investigation was launched to find the murderer. I was part of that investigation,' Lewis revealed. 'Unfortunately, the investigation was flawed from the start. Three of the serving officers investigating the murder were part of a paedophile gang operating throughout South Wales. They spent months putting police off the trail. By the time the bent coppers were exposed, it was impossible to catch Julie Mann's killer. Certain information surrounding Julie Mann's death has been withheld from the press.'

'What kind of information?' Fagan asked.

'I was one of two detectives who entered the property after uniform had found the body. The other detective was DS Paul Decker.'

'One of the serving officers who was later convicted,' Fagan said. 'And now running FansOnly.'

Lewis nodded. 'Her hands were tied and she was gagged. It was obvious she'd been there for days. The walls of the room had been soundproofed. So no one could hear her screams as she was tortured. In the following days, during the initial investigation, we kept one major detail from the press. A video camera and tripod had been found in the room where Julie was found. But the tape from the camera was missing.'

'They filmed her murder,' Fagan guessed.

Lewis nodded. 'Lots of publicity was generated because of the murder. But information about the camera being found was suppressed. The investigation dragged on for months. We were getting nowhere. Always hitting dead ends or false leads. One day, out of the blue, a woman came into Swansea Police station with her daughter, who was four months pregnant. The daughter was thirteen. Her mother wanted to report that she'd been raped. Not only that, but she'd been raped by a serving police officer. A Detective Sergeant by the name of Peter Norman, who was part of the investigation team into Julie Mann's death. I was the detective that took the girl's statement. But instead of sharing the information with the rest of my team, I took the information to the lead detective, Detective Chief Superintendent Tony Blake. Blake was a decent copper. An old school copper who despised bent coppers. He took me into his confidence and told me he suspected the murder investigation into Julie Mann's death was being hampered. Blake claimed the investigation was being manipulated by officers at the top.'

Fagan guessed what was coming. 'Bob Benson was South Wales Police Chief.'

'Yeah.' Lewis nodded. 'Blake had suspicions Benson knew a lot more about Julie Mann's murder than he was letting on. He also believed that Benson was a nonce. Benson knew some very shady people back in the day. Crooked politicians and other bent coppers in top positions, including another former Chief Constable, Owain Lance.'

Fagan recalled what George Walker had revealed to him a year earlier. 'Benson was a copper in Abergavenny for about two decades. Then he climbed the ladder rapidly.'

'He first gained notoriety at the Battle if Six Bells in 1985. In 1986 he was bumped up the ladder to Inspector. He moved to Swansea. How much do you know about Benson?'

'More than I care,' Fagan said. 'When I came back to Abergavenny last year, I discovered he was part of a group of men who took part in a sexual assault at a dormitory in the Black Mountains.'

'You know this for sure?'

Fagan nodded. 'I had a friend who took his own life in November 1980. He was one of the victims. I spoke to his father about it last year. Just before Graham died, he confessed everything to his mam and dad. All but one of the victims are dead. Four, including my friend took their own lives.'

Lewis considered the information Fagan had revealed.

'Can I ask, sir, what's all this has to do with me?'

'You've made waves, DI Fagan. Your arrest of the First Minister, Lloyd Bevan, turned heads. Along with the exposure of Detective Chief Superintendent Clive Warren.' Lewis expressed a wry smile. 'I've been wanting the bring that bastard down for years. There were a few of us who knew he was a bent copper. But proving it was another thing. And then there was the murder of Alex X. It's safe to say you have a few admirers high up in the force.'

'That's kind of you to say so, sir.'

'A taskforce is being assembled across South Wales,' Lewis said. 'It covers all the Valleys, the Cardiff Bay area, along the Gower coast and Pembrokeshire. We're also expanding into mid Wales counties like Powys. It's under the radar at the moment. Primarily because we don't want to attract the wrong type of copper. There has been a spate of corrupt officers that have been exposed over the last ten years across the UK. The Welsh Minister for Justice Rory Smith wants to establish this taskforce to deal with crimes that are proving difficult to solve. Everything from cold cases to county lines drug trafficking. I was speaking to Smith the other day. Your name came up in the conversation. He wants you to be part of this new taskforce.'

'I'm honoured you'd consider me for being part of this team. However, I came back home to settle back down in my hometown. I'm not sure I'd be happy with leaving Gwent Police.'

'You won't be,' Lewis assured Fagan. 'This new taskforce will be operating on a when needed basis. We call on officers for specific crimes that we feel they'll be able to assist. And right now, DI Fagan, we want your help to solve the murder of Julie Mann back in 1992. We believe that because you solved the mystery of Alex X, you're more than qualified to take this on.'

'I'm currently working on solving the murder of Ellie Parry, sir. I can't just walk away from an active murder investigation. And now there's a serial killer on the loose in South Wales.'

'I know,' Lewis said. 'Let me explain. Last night you interviewed Russel Connor about his social media platform.' Lewis noted Fagan's expression. 'Don't worry, DI Fagan, we haven't been following you. However, one of our officers was at Cardiff University last night, keeping tabs on Connor. So he reported that you and DS Watkins spoke with him last night.'

'Can I ask why you've been keeping tabs on Connor?'

Lewis produced his phone. 'The National Crime Agency has been working with my team investigating the social media app created by Connor.'

'Why?'

'Because Cymru Teen Chat has a connection with FansOnly,'

'The website being run by your former colleague, Paul Decker.'

'Yes. Decker and Connor served time together in Cardiff prison back in 1993. Connor served two years for assault.'

'I did a background check on him yesterday,' Fagan said. 'The police file doesn't say who Connor assaulted.'

'That's because a gagging order was slapped on the press.'

'Because?'

'The person who Connor assaulted was Dillon Powell.'

Fagan nodded. 'He knew what happened to Alex X.'

'We made the connection when Powell was arrested for her murder last year. When Connor was released from prison, he had over fifty thousand pounds in his bank account.'

Fagan processed the information. 'You think Connor knew about Powell murdering Alex and went after him?'

Lewis nodded. 'Powell was in hospital for two weeks with severe injuries.'

'To silence him, someone paid Connor to keep him quiet,' Fagan speculated.

'My money is on Frankie Jordan,' Lewis guessed. 'He paid him the money to stop him from going to the press. So that he could carry on the illusion that Alex was still alive.'

'Right, okay, so what's the connection between Connor's social media platform and Decker's FansOnly website?'

Lewis fished his phone from his pocket. 'The National Crime Agency has been trying to crack FansOnly for the past few years. It's become a hub for uploading illegal images and videos of underage girls.' Lewis located a photograph on his phone and handed it to Fagan. 'Last year, the NCA sent undercover officers out to the Philippines. They were following Russel Connor. He met with Paul Decker. We've been able to confirm they are working together. Connor has been taking videos and images of young girls from his social media platform and supplying Decker with content. Both their companies are based in the Philippines.'

Fagan shrugged. 'Why not just bring Connor in for questioning?'

'Because it's been almost impossible to gather evidence suggesting anything was going on.'

Fagan considered the new information he'd been given. 'The mother of the murdered teenager I've been investigating has a FansOnly account. When we examined her phone, we found that she'd been uploading sexually explicit videos of her daughter to FansOnly. We've also discovered Ellie Parry was in contact with the killer the night she was murdered. And they were having a conversation through Connor's social media platform.'

'Did Connor reveal anything to you last night when you interviewed him?'

'No, but he tried to dazzle us with a load of technical jargon. I don't know much about computers, but I know what he was talking about last night was utter crap.'

'We want you to pull Connor in for questioning.'

'And how am I supposed to do that exactly, sir?'

'You recovered Ellie Parry's phone, didn't you?'

'Yes,' Fagan replied.

'Then with any luck you'll find evidence on there that will give you enough cause to bring Connor in for questioning.'

'Cyber forensics were examining it yesterday. They should have some information for us today. We have a major briefing this morning to discuss the case. All departments will be meeting to see if we can make a significant step forward.'

'We're hopeful you'll be able to find something, DI Fagan. And you'll be able to bring Connor in for questioning. The reason the National Crime Agency is staying out of it for the moment is they believe Decker is clever enough to know he's being watched.'

'If we pull Connor in for questioning, he might shut down on us. What makes you think Gwent Police can make a difference?'

'You can make a difference. In the past twelve months, you've solved two very high profile cold case murders. You're more than qualified to get the information we need out of Connor.'

'I'm flattered you have faith in me, sir,' Fagan stated. 'If I can get the information you want, what are your goals?'

'We want to bring down Paul Decker and his kiddie porn empire. But it's difficult because he's living out in the Philippines. And the Filipino Police aren't exactly bending over backwards to help us out. Decker is living in a remote location, and is being protected by the local militia. He has backers from around the world who pump money into his website. If you can bring in Connor and get him to reveal information, that could help us in our fight. We know he has access to the inner workings of both Cymru Teen Chat and FansOnly.'

'I knew he was bullshitting me last night.'

Lewis reached into his laptop bag. 'This is the report on Julie Mann's murder. I want you to study it for a few days. I'm hoping you will see something we missed.' Lewis paused. 'For over thirty years, that murder has plagued me. Last year, her mother died. I made her a promise that I'd keep on investigating her death and catch the man responsible for her murder.'

'Who else can I talk to about this?'

'At the moment, no one. We just want you to go over the case file.' Lewis glanced at his watch. 'I have to go. Read the file and I'll be in touch.'

CHAPTER 30

DAY 3

Newport Central Police Station

'Thank you for all attending this briefing, ladies and gentlemen,' Fagan said loudly.

The room full of people focused their attention on him.

'We are in day three of the Ellie Parry murder investigation. What I want to do this morning is discuss the relevant information we have so far. I would like all department heads to share the information with the lead investigation team. Our goal here is to establish known facts. There's a lot of false information floating around about Ellie's murder. This morning, I'll be revealing some information for the first time. All officers involved in this investigation will be e-mailed a full summary of what we know so far. This is now a major news story, so the pressure is on. We need to establish a clear timeline of Ellie's activities on the day she was murdered. DI Saddler will walk us through what we know about her movements, interactions, and messages she sent to her friends and her mam. We have gathered a lot of information from witness statements.' Fagan looked at Saddler. 'I understand there is CCTV footage pulled from the primary school next to the park.'

Saddler nodded. 'Footage has been recovered and analysed. It confirms what Ellie's friends have told us. They were in the park for approximately twenty minutes before a group of boys turned up.'

Fagan nodded, refocusing on the whiteboard. 'We'll also be discussing Ellie's evening activities, focusing on the time leading up to her murder. After we have a solid understanding of Ellie's movements, our goal is to identify any gaps in the timeline or new leads we can pursue immediately. Let's focus on Ellie's last day to uncover any clues that might lead us to the killer. We need to set a solid foundation for discussing the other critical aspects of the investigation.' Fagan briefly locked eyes with Melissa. 'We have a leading psychologist who has joined us this morning. This is Doctor Melissa Knight. She is a leading expert in serial killers.'

Everyone in the room exchanged shocked expressions.

'Yeah, I know, this is new information for most of you. But until yesterday, we assumed this was just an individual who had killed once. We have since found evidence that the killer has been involved in four other deaths over the past four years. My team is still piecing all the facts together.' Fagan glanced at the whiteboard. 'First off, let's go over Ellie's movements the day she was murdered and what she did throughout the day. According to her mother, Ellie got up around nine o'clock, had a shower, came down for breakfast. Her mam, Sophie Parry, was planning for a night out in Cardiff. The e-mail you will receive contains messages sent between Ellie and her mam. It's obvious their relationships on that day was strained. I should warn you. Some of the messages exchanged between Sophie Parry and her daughter are very graphic.' Fagan refocused his attention on the whiteboard. 'At approximately nine thirty in the morning, Sophie Parry's friend, Tammy Morris, called at the property. According to Morris, Ellie was still in the house when she arrived. Morris claims she said hello to Ellie when she came down for breakfast. But Ellie didn't respond. Morris believed Ellie had been arguing with her mam before she arrived. But she didn't go into any details about what Ellie had been arguing with her mother about. One of Ellie's friends knocked on the door.' Fagan pointed at a name. 'Twelve-year-old Gracie Peacock called at the house to see if Ellie was going out. Gracie was with two other girls.' Fagan checked the board again. 'Mia Probert and Charlotte Mason. I interviewed Gracie Peacock, who recounted Ellie's movements that morning. According to Gracie, Ellie and her friends went down the park. It was not long after when a group of boys turned up.' Fagan glanced at Saddler. 'DI Saddler will give us an insight on an altercation that took place between Ellie Parry and one of the boys who entered the park, Taylor Richards.'

Saddler stood and walked to the whiteboard. 'CCTV footage

shows Ellie and her friends entering the park around quarter to ten in the morning. They were there for at least twenty minutes before a group of boys entered the park. There's at least ten minutes of CCTV footage, which shows the two groups being separate. According to one of Ellie's friends, Charlotte Mason, Ellie messaged Taylor Richards. During an interview with DI Fagan and DS Watkins, Richards revealed he was in a relationship with Ellie Parry. According to Richards, they'd been in a relationship since Easter. According to Charlotte Mason, Richards approached Ellie, argued with her. The argument was about a picture that Ellie had shared on Cymru Teen Chat with her friends.' Saddler paused. 'The picture in question is of Richards' penis.'

'They were sharing mucky pictures. Is that what you're saying?' A uniform asked.

'Yes,' Saddler replied.

'How old is Richards?'

'He's fifteen years old.'

'So he's being charged,' the uniformed continued.

'Richards has a track record for distributing indecent images. He's been questioned about his activities several times before. He's notorious for convincing young girls to send him indecent images of themselves. Richards has also threatened several girls if they refused to send him illicit pictures. So far, no case has been brought against Richards. However, the CPS are now looking for a way to charge him with the creation and distribution of indecent images of children. This will be a separate investigation.'

The uniform shook her head. 'I don't get kids today, I really don't.'

'This has turned out to be a really disturbing case for all those involved,' Fagan said. 'Details have been revealed about Ellie's personal life. We know she was living a life meant for someone much older. Her mother was aware of this and was actively encouraging it.'

Saddler continued. 'According to Ellie's friends, the argument between her and Richards got very heated. At one point, Richards went to hit Ellie. That's when the other boys came over to join the group. There were three other boys. Their names are Noah

Simpson, Callum Skinner and Jake Salford. Both Salford and Skinner intervened in the argument. Skinner and Salford stopped Richards from hitting Ellie. Other officers have interviewed the boys. They have stuck to the same story. CCTV footage shows the boys leaving the park half an hour later. Around eleven o'clock Ellie and her friends head over to Hector Avenue where Mia Probert lives. At approximately twelve thirty Mia Probert is picked up by her father, Nigel, who lives in Abergavenny. Ellie, Gracie and Charlotte head over to the park near Hafodyrynys football pitch. They meet up with two other friends. Evie Preston and Isha Aston. According to her friends, Ellie was annoyed with her mam. The data retrieved from Sophie Parry's phone reveals Ellie was in contact with her mam all afternoon. When Sophie Parry was first interviewed, she claimed she didn't have any contact with her daughter after she went out the day she was murdered. However, dozens of messages were exchanged. Ellie attempted several times to convince her mam to let her go out that evening with her to Cardiff. But every time Sophie Parry told Ellie that she wasn't going anywhere. Some of the messages exchanged between Sophie and her daughter were very graphic. Over a hundred messages were exchanged between Sophie and her daughter that day. Thirty-four messages contain language that most fourteen-year-olds wouldn't use. Ellie calls her mam a cunt several times for not letting her go out to Cardiff.'

Shocked whispers reverberated around the briefing room.

'Ellie and her friends were in the park until about three thirty. Then both Evie and Isha parted company and went home. Ellie, Charlotte, and Gracie headed back to the Sofrydd estate. Gracie returns home, leaving Charlotte and Ellie. According to Ellie's mam, Ellie returned home at half-past three in the afternoon. Charlotte claims she was with her. We also have another statement from Tammy Morris. She was doing Sophie Parry's hair and makeup when Ellie returned home. Ellie and her mother had an argument about Cardiff. Both Tammy Morris and Charlotte witnessed the argument.'

'So they didn't exactly keep their disputes private,' a plainclothes detective said.

'No,' Saddler shook his head. 'We have several witness statements from residents, revealing both Ellie and her mam had many arguments in public. One street resident said she had seen them having shouting matches in the street.' Saddler paused, taking stock of what he had revealed. 'Ellie and Charlotte headed for Charlotte's house. Ellie stayed there until seven o'clock before returning home. A witness saw Ellie entering her house around ten past seven.'

Fagan stepped forward. 'We have another witness who spotted Ellie talking to a girl on the estate before she got home. We have yet to discover who that girl is.'

'During the time she was at Charlotte's house,' Saddler continued, 'she messaged her mam thirty-six times. The messages they exchanged were very graphic. Tammy Morris said she called in on Ellie around eight o'clock. Ellie was watching Netflix. After Tammy Morris left the house, Ellie called Owen Woods and asked him to supply her with ecstasy. Owen Woods arrived at the property around eleven o'clock. In his interview with DI Fagan and DS Watkins, Woods confessed to having sex with Ellie in exchange for the drugs. Ellie Parry's phone is currently being analysed by cyber forensics.' Saddler glanced at Cyber CSI Analyst Edwin Corke.

Corke nodded. 'We're still pulling data off her phone. From what we've seen so far it's pretty grim stuff. She kept a personal diary that is full of harrowing entries.' He made eye contact with Fagan. 'I'll be in touch with your team within a few hours.'

Fagan nodded, taking up position in front of the whiteboard. 'Thank you for that analysis, DI Saddler. There is a lot of information to go through here. As DI Saddler explained, there is a three-hour gap between Tammy Morris leaving and Owen Woods turning up at Ellie's house. From the information we recovered from Sophie Parry's phone, it appears within that three-hour gap Sophie and Ellie carried on arguing. Just after eight o'clock, Ellie messaged her mam saying that she was going to invite someone called Shadowcaster over. DI Saddler's interview with Ellie's friends revealed this Shadowcaster had a Cymru Teen Chat account. Sophie Parry also revealed to us that

Ellie had met this boy online and that he had told her he'd seen some of her videos on FansOnly.'

'Can I interrupt, sir?' a junior detective asked. 'What do you mean by that exactly? Are you saying Ellie Parry had a FansOnly account?'

'What I'm saying is, her mam had a FansOnly account and had uploaded over seventeen hundred graphic videos and images of Ellie. Sophie Parry opened the account during lockdown and has uploaded over seventeen hundred videos of Ellie and herself. Whoever murdered Ellie Parry not only had a Cymru Teen Chat account but also a FansOnly account. When I went to see the pathologist for a full report, he had found evidence that Ellie's killer was connected with four other deaths. Showing we could be dealing with a serial killer.' Fagan looked at Melissa. 'I also have reason to suspect that this Shadowcaster could be involved in the deaths of thirteen other young girls. Doctor Knight will explain more.'

Melissa flashed a smile before stepping in front of the whiteboard. 'Good morning. Before I begin, I'd like to introduce myself. I am Doctor Melissa Knight. I spent over thirty years working with various New York City Police departments, tracking serial killers. I've analysed the information DI Fagan sent me. Ellie's murder is linked to four other deaths since 2020. However, the other victims all committed suicide. Semen samples recovered reveal they had sex with the same man. That man was at Ellie's house the night she was murdered. It's clear to me the perpetrator we are dealing with is a master manipulator. Capable of exploiting vulnerable women online. He's using Cymru Teen Chat and FansOnly, as a hunting ground. Four of the girls who have died had both a CTC and a FansOnly account. The man we are dealing with is extremely confident. He is able to talk to girls and able to get them to reveal all kinds of secrets and vulnerabilities. Our killer uses keywords like life and death. He will alienate his victims from loved ones, convincing them that everyone around them is toxic. Once he has the victim's trust, he will encourage them to self-harm. All the women who have died had a medical history of self-harming and depression. The autopsy report on Ellie has concluded that she suffered a massive heart attack because of the ecstasy she had taken. However, the killer helped her on her way by strangling her. With the other women, it's not clear if he was present during their deaths or convinced them to take their own lives while talking to them online. What I am sure of is this person has probably convinced others to commit suicide.' Melissa looked at Fagan. 'Cymru Teen Chat has been linked to a spate of suicides in the last four years. All the data is available on the police database for you to study.' Melissa stepped away from the whiteboard.

'I want you all to go over the casefile you have been e-mailed. And come to me if you think you have a lead on how we can catch this person,' Fagan said, scanning the room. 'Let's get back to work and catch this man before he kills again.' Fagan looked towards a plainclothes detective in the corner of the room. 'DS Padfield, I'd like a quick chat, please.'

CHAPTER 31

Fagan waited until the room had emptied before he spoke to DS Padfield. 'You were involved in the investigation into Cymru Teen Chat a while back.'

Padfield nodded. 'Yeah, it was a disturbing trend. Thirteen young girls took their lives.'

'What were their ages?'

'Between twelve and fifteen years of age.'

'You lodged a complaint when the case was shelved. Why?'

'Because I thought the suicides were all linked to Cymru Teen Chat.'

'But Griffiths still shut down the investigation.'

'Yeah, it pissed me off big time. I even approached him about the matter. But he basically fed me a load of bullshit about not having the resources to continue running the case.'

'How did you come across the case in the first place?'

'A man called Michael Jones contacted the South Wales Police shortly after his daughter took her own life in March 2022. He said that Holly had gone from a happy pre-teenager to a sullen, depressed girl. She'd spend hours in her bedroom. Her school life was affected. She'd be up all night on her phone. Jones said he'd attempted several times to take her phone off her. But she became violent towards him. In the end, Jones had no choice but to pull his daughter out of school because of her abusive behaviour towards teachers and other pupils.'

'What made Jones think his daughter's death was connected with Cymru Teen Chat?'

'When I interviewed Jones, he said it took several weeks after his daughter's death to go through her phone. When he spoke to me he said that what he found traumatised him.'

'How?'

'Holly kept a personal diary on her phone. She wrote it in the last weeks of her life. It was packed with entries that spoke of suicide and how depressed she was. When Jones accessed her messages, he found one entry particularly disturbing. Holly had been talking to another app user on CTC. Slowly but surely, he had manipulated Holly into taking her own life. That's when Jones went to the police. Cybercrimes had already had several complaints regarding CTC. When Tarian tried to access the app on Holly's phone, her account was deleted.'

'How is that possible?'

'The cybercrimes analyst told me it was only possible at the software end of the app.'

Fagan considered what Padfield had revealed to him. 'So, Russel Connor has access to the software.'

'Let me guess,' Padfield said, reading Fagan's expression. 'You've spoken to Connor, and he's fed you a load of crap about not having access to the software because it is being run by an AI generated operating system.'

Fagan nodded. 'Yeah, that's exactly what he told me.'

'It's all a load of bollocks. The reason he shut down Holly's account was to cover his tracks. Make sure no one could connect Holly's death with the app.'

'Holly's dad didn't happen to know who she was talking to on the app, did he?'

Padfield nodded. 'Shadowcaster. The same user you just mentioned in the briefing. By December 2022, there'd been more suicides. Michael Jones contacted me again. Said he'd been contacted by other parents whose kids had taken their own lives. All linked to CTC and all the girls involved had been in contact with the Shadowcaster. I went to my Chief Super and told her about my suspicions regarding the deaths. She gave the go ahead to launch an investigation. That's when Michael Jones launched his charity, Safe Children Wales, to protect children online. By May 2023 last year, thirteen girls had taken their own lives. I analysed each case. They were so identical. Your colleague, Doctor Knight, mentioned a lot of Shadowcaster's characteristics. The linguistic structure this Shadowcaster used. The psychological manipulation to get the girls to isolate themselves from their friends and families. I spoke to all the families of the victims. Until they started using Cymru Teen Chat, they were all normal. But once they started to use the app, they became very different people. When I analysed each suicide, I found so many similarities. The timing and frequency of app usage were consistent with all the victims, indicating a calculated approach by this Shadowcaster. The victims until then shared common characteristics such as age, social status, and psychological profiles, suggesting they were specifically targeted. Thing is, every time we accessed each victim's phone, the CTC app would shut down. It was almost like the software designers knew we were trying to gain access to the app. We'd be able to view the accounts for a short while, but then they would just shut on their own. That's when I went to confront Russel Connor about the app.'

'He tried to dazzle you with tech jargon, did he?'

Padfield nodded. 'Fed me a load of bullshit about not having access to the software.'

'Because it's controlled by AI,' Fagan stated. 'You should have heard the pile of crap he fed me and DS Watkins last night.'

'Another thing we found when examining the victims' phones is they kept diaries in the last weeks of their lives. They'd e-mailed their entries to the suspect responsible for the suicides. Trouble is, when we tried to gain access to the e-mail address they sent their diaries to, we were blocked.'

'Who was the e-mail provider?'

'We don't know. It wasn't a regular e-mail address like Hotmail or Gmail.' Padfield inhaled. 'In July last year, the operation was shut down.'

'Why?'

'That's what I'm still wondering. It was under the orders of Chief Constable Griffiths. When I went to meet with him, he told me the case had been shut down because of lack of evidence. I remember handing him the casefile with all my finding, linking the suicides to CTC. I had a lengthy chat with him. Gave it my all to keep the investigation going.'

'What did Griffiths do?'

'He told me it would take too many man hours to investigate the case fully. And any links I had made between the suicides and the app were coincidental. This is despite the evidence being overwhelming. My Chief Super had retired a few months before the case was closed. I thought about taking it higher to the Commissioner. But in the end I had to drop it. Griffiths can be a bit of an arsehole if you try to sidestep him.'

'Griffiths didn't review the casefile himself.'

'No, he didn't want to know, which I thought was odd.'

Fagan studied Padfield's expression. 'There's more, isn't there?'

'Yeah, but,' Padfield sighed.

'But what?'

'It depends on how much I can trust you.'

'Dave, you can trust me. You think there's a leak somewhere, don't you?'

Padfield nodded. 'Every time I handed information over to Tarian, the case would dry up. Like I just said, we'd have access to the account briefly, but mysteriously it would just shut.'

'Someone in Tarian must be feeding information back to Connor,' Fagan speculated. 'He's shutting down the app at his end to prevent information about his social media app being exposed.'

'That's exactly what I thought. In the space of four years, Connor has earned over three hundred million quid from that app. The media often describe him as the Steve Jobs of Wales. He even dresses similar. I've collected so much information on the case. Statements from the parents and friends of the victims. Every time I got close to finding out who this Shadowcaster was, the lead went cold. And every time it happened was when I had handed over the victim's phone to Tarian, the Welsh cyber Crimes Unit.'

'Do you have anyone specific in mind?'

'No.' Padfield shook his head. 'Whoever is leaking information isn't stupid enough to get caught.'

Fagan thought about what he'd just learnt.

'I know I sound shitty by saying this, but I'm glad it's kicked off again,' Padfield confessed. 'Ellie Parry didn't deserve what happened to her. But now there's evidence linking her death with the others. Those at the top won't be able to dismiss it.'

'I think whoever murdered Ellie has made his first mistake,' Fagan said.

'How?'

'He's been killing from a distance until he turned up at Ellie's house.'

'If you want to find out more, talk to Michael Jones, the father of the first victim. He's got all the information needed to piece this together. Just before the case was shut down, I gave him a complete copy of the casefile.'

'You leaked the casefile.' Fagan was unimpressed.

'If you want to report me, go ahead,' Padfield said in a defiant tone. 'There were so many unanswered questions and so many leads to follow up. I helped Michael Jones set up his charity. I'm still in contact with him. If you want, I can tell him you want to interview him.'

Fagan considered the proposal for a moment before nodding. 'I understand your reasons for handing information to Jones. Sometimes as police officers we have to do things that aren't by the book.'

'Like arresting the First Minister during his speech for an independent Wales.'

Fagan recalled the moment he marched onto the Senedd floor and arrested Lloyd Bevan.

'You've made as many enemies as you have allies,' Padfield remarked.

'Noted,' Fagan said. 'Give me Jones' contact details.' He glanced at his watch. 'I'll head out and have a quick chat.'

CHAPTER 32

Pen-y-Fai – Bridgend

By the time he'd reached Michael Jones' house, Fagan felt he was going off track, and that he should turn around and head back to Newport. He sat in his car for a few minutes debating with himself. Finally, he climbed out and walked towards the front door of Jones' house.

The door opened, revealing a tall, thin man with receding hair. Jones had already spotted Fagan approaching. 'DI Fagan, I take it?'

Fagan offered his hand. 'I appreciate you meeting with me. I won't take up much of your time.'

'It's nice that the police have a renewed interest in Holly's death.'

'I'm actually investigating a murder that took place three days ago.'

Jones nodded. 'Dave Padfield messaged me. Something about a murder in the Valleys.'

Fagan nodded. 'Yeah.'

'Come in, I've just boiled the kettle.'

Fagan sat in a spacious living room, which had been turned into a shrine. Dozens of photographs of Holly hung on the walls, placed on sideboards and shelves. There were cushions on the sofa with Holly's smiling, angelic face.

'I know, it's a bit much,' Jones said, entering the living room with two mugs of coffee.

'Not at all. It shows how special she was to you.' Fagan also noticed an array of wedding photos. 'Is your wife here?'

'I lost my wife in the first year of Covid. It came over her quickly. Within three weeks she was gone.'

'I'm sorry for your loss.' Fagan realised the gravity of the situation. A man who had lost both his wife and daughter.

'Elaine had so many underlying health conditions.' Jones looked at a photo of his wife cuddling up to her daughter. 'When she died, Holly was devastated. She was so close to her mam.'

'And you.' Fagan pointed at several photos of Jones with his daughter.

'Holly had so much love to share with everyone. She loved doing just about everything. She was so active. When Covid hit, we immediately went into self-isolation because of Elaine's health issues. We thought we were doing everything right, you know. Washing our hands, keeping distance. Ordering stuff online. I was able to work from home.' Jones stared at a wedding photograph. 'But it wasn't enough.' He closed his eyes.

Fagan could tell he was holding back a tsunami of grief.

'At first, the symptoms were just mild. Elaine dismissed them as just a light cold.' Jones inhaled. 'But she got worse until I had no choice but to call an ambulance. When they came, the paramedics said we couldn't go with her to the hospital because of the infection rate. Holly was hysterical. All she wanted was to be by her mam's side. For the next ten days, we had to ring the hospital every day for a progress report. At first, Elaine seemed to get better. Holly was full of hope that she'd be coming home soon. I'd constantly watch the news for updates on the pandemic. Each day bought more grim news about infection rates and death rates. Finally, we had the phone call we'd been dreading. Elaine had slipped into a deep coma. They said we could come to the hospital. But all they gave us was ten minutes to say our goodbyes.' Jones looked at Fagan. 'How do you say goodbye to someone you've planned to spend a lifetime with?'

Fagan couldn't find a suitable answer.

'Holly was in pieces. A nurse had to drag her away from Elaine's bed. Two days later, we got the call. Elaine had passed away.'

'I'm so sorry.' Was all Fagan could say.

'There were only four allowed at the funeral. Me, Holly, and Elaine's mam and dad. It was the darkest day of our lives. In the months following Elain's death. Holly struggled. The school was shut, so all she could do was talk to friends online. When her school opened again, they provided a counsellor. It helped. Holly perked up. In January 2022, she started using that Cymru Teen Chat app. At first I thought nothing of it. Holly told me it was a new app and better than the other apps she had been using. Her behaviour changed rapidly. Suddenly she was quick-tempered. She'd say inappropriate things. We argued when I mentioned she was spending too much time on that app.'

'Dave Padfield said she became violent towards you when you tried to take her phone,' Fagan said.

'Yeah. She took a swing at me on several occasions. Threatened to smash everything in the house. She got nasty with the things she'd say. Holly blamed me for Elaine's death. She would constantly say she wished I had died and not her mam. The school contacted me. They said that Holly's behaviour at school was unacceptable. So I had to pull her out. She would spend all day in her bedroom. I lost count of how many screaming matches I had with her. I reached out to both sets of grandparents. They tried to speak to her. But by that time she was too far gone.' Jones composed himself. 'This one day, she came downstairs and said she was going out. She told me she was meeting up with friends. By that time, I had had so many screaming matches with her, I began to despise her. Two days later, I knocked on her bedroom door. I hadn't seen her in hours. I could usually hear her using the bathroom. At first I thought she'd gone out.' Jones wiped away a tear.

'It's okay, Mike. Take your time.'

'When I couldn't get an answer, I opened the door. The first thing I noticed was her phone, on a tripod, facing the bed. And then I saw her, just lying on the bed, motionless.' Jones finally broke down. He looked at another photo of his wife and daughter. 'I failed, I failed to protect them both,' he sobbed.

Fagan was lost for words.

Jones blew into a handkerchief. 'I've told this story a thousand times.'

'It's fine, Mike.'

Jones fought back another wave of tears. 'It took me about

six weeks after her funeral to pluck up the courage to go into her room. Without Elaine and Holly in the house it seemed so empty.' Jones looked over at an armchair. A small Jack Russell terrier lay on the chair. Its large eyes spoke volumes. 'We got Holly the dog a year before Covid came along. Blu was the centre of Holly's life. She loved her so much, especially after Elaine died.' Jones paused. 'I knew I had to face that room again, so I went in. That's when I pulled her phone off the tripod. I charged it up. There were so many pictures of her and her mam.' Jones paused briefly 'I accessed her Cymru Teen Chat account. She was in contact with just one person on there.'

'Can you give a name?'

'Shadowcaster.'

Fagan nodded. 'We have evidence this person who calls himself Shadowcaster could be responsible for other deaths.'

Jones nodded. 'I looked through all her messages she had exchanged with this Shadowcaster. It was obvious she was being manipulated. The more she revealed to him, the more he fed on her emotions. He even claimed he'd lost both his parents during the pandemic. That's how he prayed on her. I went to the police. But there wasn't much of a case to answer. Dave Padfield took interest in the case. He said he'd seen a few online articles warning of the dangers of Cymru Teen Chat. That's when I contacted the Western Mail about Holly's death. They ran an article I had prepared for them. A few days later, I got a call from Connor's solicitor. He said, if I made any more libellous accusations about Cymru Teen Chat, I would face legal action. They tried to slap some sort of gagging order on me. Connor even offered me thirty grand to stay silent.'

'He tried to pay you off,' Fagan responded with surprise.

'Yeah, but I told him to shove the money up his arse. A few months after the article was published, I received messages on Facebook from two parents who had both lost their daughters. When we compared notes, there were similarities with all our experiences. All three girls had been in contact with Shadowcaster. He had engaged in conversation between them weeks before their deaths. As 2022 came to a close, twelve girls had committed suicide. At the start of 2023 there was another suicide. Although the police were now investigating the deaths, the media was keeping quiet.'

'Probably terrified of getting sued by Connor,' Fagan guessed.

'That was my thinking.' Jones got up and walked over to a sideboard, pulling out a file. 'This is the information DS Padfield gave me just before the investigation was shut down. This is a copy. I left out one disturbing part of the case.'

'What's that?'

Jones took a deep breath. 'When I charged up Holly's phone, I found the last video she had made. She left a video suicide note.'

Fagan was too horrified to speak.

'All the girls who killed themselves did this.'

'Can I ask, Mike? How did Holly die?'

'Paracetamol overdose, along with a bottle of gin she'd drunk. Thing is, I never kept alcohol in the house.'

'You said she went out two days before she died.'

Jones nodded, trying to hold back another wave of tears.

'So who bought her the painkillers and alcohol?'

'Dave Padfield reckoned it had to be her killer. All the girls who killed themselves all drank alcohol and took painkillers.'

'What about your assault on Connor last year?'

'I read in Wales On Sunday, Connor was being honoured with a Welsh Businessman of the Year Award. When I read the article, it pushed me over the edge. So I drove to the Celtic Manor in Newport to confront him. There are videos on YouTube of the event. After the police arrested me, I was released on bail. Connor's solicitor contacted me and stated that Connor wasn't pressing charges. But he had filed a restraining order against me. I've been trying to raise awareness of the dangers of teenagers using Connor's app. But sometimes it feels like no one is listening.'

'Well, I'm listening Mike,' Fagan assured him.

'Does that mean you're going to open the case again?'

Fagan nodded. 'We have firm evidence to suggest the murder a few days ago is linked to all this.' He pointed to the casefile. 'However, the case was closed, which means I'm going to come under a lot of fire from my superior when I reopen it. But we need to catch this Shadowcaster as soon as possible before he kills again.' Fagan stood.

'I appreciate you coming down here today.' Jones looked out of the window. 'Bridgend has seen its fair share of tragedies over the years. Fifteen years ago there was a spate of suicides. They reckon that was because of the internet. But no one could prove anything.'

'I had better head back to Newport.' Fagan held up the file. 'I promise you we'll bring this Shadowcaster to heal.' Fagan's phone buzzed.

'Boss, where are you?'

'I'm on my way back, Sean.'

'Cybercrimes have just given us the full details of Ellie Parry's phone. They've also pulled more information of her mam's phone.'

'I'll be there within the hour, Sean.'

CHAPTER 33

Newport Central Police Headquarters

Fagan hung his coat on the back of his chair. 'Where are we at with everything?'

'Pulled some interesting stuff from Ellie's phone, boss,' Watkins revealed. 'Forensics came across a diary she kept.'

'Was she using Cymru Teen Chat the day she died?'

Watkins nodded. 'That's what forensics reckons, boss. However, they could not access her account because it's been shut down.'

'There's no bloody way AI can do that. I suspect our little chat with Connor last night prompted him to cover his tracks.' Fagan recalled his conversation with Michael Jones.

'You planning on bringing him in?'

Fagan displayed a frown. 'Unless we have probable cause, we can't do anything. Besides, he'll surround himself with a wall of expensive solicitors. However, I think there's enough cause to bring him in for a routine questioning. I'll make that call after this briefing.'

'Before we consider that, sir,' Brooks said, 'isn't it possible the killer could have wiped the app when he took her phone?'

'It's possible, yeah,' Fagan sighed.

'We've also got hold of Ellie's full medical records,' Stacey announced. 'In December 2022, Ellie had an abortion.'

'An abortion?' Fagan queried. 'Her mother never mentioned that when we interviewed her.'

'Another secret she's been keeping, guv.'

Fagan nodded. 'Let's bring her in again. And this time, I'll lay everything on the line to her.'

'The family was referred to Social Services in January last year following an incident at Parry's house.'

'Yeah, Ellie apparently threatened to stab her mam.'

'This is really going to blow the investigation wide open now that we have her diary,' said Watkins. 'She started to write it in February 2021.'

'We were still in lockdown mostly,' Fagan recalled.

'The diary Ellie kept on her phone reveals the full extent of her relationship with her mam.' Watkins handed Fagan a tablet. 'Her first entry was on the 21st of February 2021.'

Fagan read the entry aloud. *'Me and mam had a massive argument today. I hate that bitch sometimes. I never do anything right. She's always complaining about something I've done. God, I hate lockdown. It's driving me crazy. Want to get out, get away.'* Fagan digested the information. 'Very mature for her age.' He swiped the tablet, scanning a few more passages. 'Ellie had a very turbulent relationship with her mam. They were constantly arguing.' Fagan spotted something. 'Ellie speaks about her first sexual encounter with Toby Morris.' He began to read. *'Mam and Tammy made me and Toby get together last night. They were going on about it all day. It really hurt at first. Toby said he was sorry and that his mam was always on to him.'*

'You were right, boss. Tammy Morris is domineering.'

'What a total bitch,' Fagan stated. 'She said her son has learning difficulties. That was obvious from the interview Morris gave yesterday. Yet his mam encouraged him to have a sexual relationship with an underage girl. And now he'll face time in prison for it.'

'It's the world we live in, sir,' Brooks remarked. 'This murder has uncovered an ugly truth about what goes on behind closed doors.'

Fagan continued to look through Ellie's diary. 'Here we go. March 2022 is when Ellie uploaded those first pictures to FansOnly.' He read the passage. *'Really helped mam today. We've been skint for weeks. I know I shouldn't have put those pictures on mam's FansOnly account. But I'm so fed up with mam having no money. We're so poor. All the other girls on the Sofrydd have nice clothes. This bloke paid me ten grand to send him photos of me naked. It wasn't a big thing. All I had to do was pose in front of the phone. Mam had a massive meltdown. She downloaded an app to stop me from using my phone and everything. Bored to tears now.'* Fagan read the entry through again. 'This entry confirms what Sophie Parry revealed to us. Some bloke from Russia paid her ten grand for the pictures of Ellie.' Fagan continued reading. 'This entry is a few months further on. *We're skint again. Mam is pissed off. She's been posting loads of pics. But no one is paying for them. We're constantly arguing about money. I'm going to have to help her out again. Don't know whether this is a good thing, but we need the money.'*

'She's having doubts,' Stacey said. 'Ellie said it there. She doesn't know if it's a good idea?'

'What did Parry tell us when we talked about her FansOnly account, Sean?' Fagan asked.

'She said she and Ellie had a long chat about whether she should be posting videos.'

Fagan nodded. 'They came to an agreement and posted another video.' Fagan looked back at the tablet and read another passage from the diary. *'Mam got paid twenty-five grand for my video. Happy days. Been to Cardiff. Got some really nice dresses. Charlotte had a bitch at me about my new clothes, jealous cow. Mam booked a holiday to Turkey. Can't wait. Got a stunning costume.'* Fagan scanned more entries. 'She goes into detail about all the things her mother has brought her.' Fagan cleared his throat. *'Went to Victoria's Secret in Cardiff. Mam brought me some gorgeous underwear. She says it will make me look more stunning when I make more pictures for her. My video has had a stupid number of views. Some of the blokes creep me out. One bloke asked me to go to his house so he can take me from behind. Getting creeped out by all the messages mam is getting. Loads of blokes wanting to come over and have a go on me.'*

'Jesus, that's fucked up shit,' Brooks stated.

Fagan looked at him. 'You okay, Andrew?'

Brooks shook his head. 'I grew up on the Gurnos. I remember the police showing up at a house across the street. There were loads of us in the street, watching the police dragging this bloke from his house. I was too young to know what was going on. Later on, my mam told me the man had been taken away because he was doing naughty things to the twin girls that lived there. They were three years old.'

Fagan trawled through more entries in the diary. 'Ellie writes about her growing anxiety about posting more pictures. He read another passage. *Mam made me pose for more nudes today. I'm getting fed up. I don't like what some of the blokes are asking. Creepy things. Tammy suggested me and Toby should pose together.* For fuck's sake,' Fagan seethed. 'This confirms it. That bitch across the street knew what Sophie was up to.'

'It's possible she could have been sharing the money, boss,' Watkins remarked.

'Agreed. Remember what Parry told us? Tammy Morris would grass everyone up on that estate. Pamela Nash said that Morris had made allegations against a former neighbour of Sophie's and they moved away because of it. Parry also told us that when everyone found out about her having a FansOnly account, she was chastised over it.'

'Tammy must have known that Sophie Parry was posting videos of her daughter and threatened to go to the police,' Stacey explained. 'They are very close. People share all kinds of things.'

'It's possible,' Fagan mused. 'But Sophie Parry doesn't seem like the sharing kind.'

'Tammy's son was having a relationship with Ellie,' Stacey mentioned. 'So it stands to reason Sophie could have told Tammy that if she grassed her up, she'd grass on Toby.'

Fagan considered what Stacey said. He looked back at the tablet and kept on reading. He glanced at Stacey. 'You're right, Stacey. Ellie mentions it here.' He read the entry. *'Tammy did my hair today for a session. She said I should be more adventurous with my poses. It would make more money if I did it with someone. Toby said I shouldn't be doing it. Toby is sweet. He really cares for me. Mam is constantly bitching at me for not doing enough. Getting fed up with it now. Don't want to do it anymore. I was sick twice today.'* Fagan read through the last part again. 'Ellie wrote this in November 2022. She became pregnant at twelve years old.'

'Toby Morris must have been the father,' Watkins said. 'Ellie only mentions Toby Morris in her diary.'

Fagan nodded pointed at his tablet. 'He was, Ellie says in an entry. She told Toby she did a test. Ellie also writes further entries. It says here that her mam found out she was pregnant in December 2022.' Fagan cleared his throat. '*Mam has found out. We had a screaming match. Toby told his mam. I want to keep the baby but mam says to get rid of it. I'm so fed up. Can't stand what mam is making me do. More pictures, more videos. Loads of blokes creeping me out. The things they want to do with me. Mam said to make more money I will have to do it with someone.* Jesus.' Fagan stated.

Stacey looked through Ellie's medical records. 'According to this, she had the abortion on the 15th January last year.'

Fagan read another entry. 'This one is from January last year. *I feel so sick after coming out of the abortion clinic. Mam is saying she needs to take more photos of me. The money is starting to go down again.*'

'Looks like her mam is using Ellie as some sort of cash cow,' Stacey remarked.

'It does,' Fagan agreed, before continuing to read. *'Loads of blokes asking mam if they can do it with me. I feel so alone. I don't want this to go on. I hate her so much. Tammy said I need to go on the pill to stop getting pregnant again.'* Fagan inhaled. 'So it was Tammy who suggested she go on the pill. When we interviewed her the morning they found Ellie's body, she claimed that Ellie had been experiencing heavy periods.' He processed the information. 'There's a timeline developing here, isn't there? Starting in 2021 when Ellie first starts her diary. When was the incident where the family was referred to Social Services?'

Brooks glanced at his laptop. 'According to records, the police were called to the address on January 20th, 2021. They labelled it as a domestic. Ellie threatened her mother with a kitchen knife. Tammy Morris was questioned about the incident. Mandy Parry was also questioned.'

'Does it give a reason why Ellie threatened her mam with a kitchen knife?'

Brooks stared at the screen. 'No, it just said police were called to a domestic on the Sofrydd estate in January last year.'

'Did they question Ellie?'

'Yeah, according to Ellie, her mother had a meltdown and phoned the police because she was having an argument with her.'

'So, it doesn't say if a knife was recovered from the scene.'

'No,' Brooks said after a brief scan of the incident record. 'Ellie was screaming at her mother when the police arrived, threatening to end her. But according to the attending officers, there was no knife anywhere. There's also a short audio recording of the 999 call Sophie Parry made.'

'Let's hear it, Andrew.'

Brooks clicked on the mouse, and the audio played. Sophie Parry sounded hysterical as she asked for the police.

'You can barely make out what she's saying,' Fagan remarked, straining to understand Parry's hysterical rant. A young girl could be heard shouting in the background. 'I'm guessing that's Ellie in the background, but you can't make heads or tails of it.' The call lasted for less than a minute before Parry ended the call. Fagan looked back at the tablet containing extracts from Ellie's diary. He scrolled down the entry list. 'These entries get shorter. Ellie is desperate to put an end to her mother's abuse.'

'No wonder the poor girl was self-harming,' Stacey said.

Fagan spotted something. 'This could be it. This entry is dated May this year. *Just started talking to this amazing boy on CTC. So much in common with him. Makes me feel alive. Cannot tell mam otherwise she'll hit the roof.*'

'Sounds like Sophie Parry is preventing Ellie from forming relationships,' Watkins said.

'Here's another entry,' Fagan said. *'Had a long chat with Shadowcaster today.'* Fagan looked up from his tablet. 'It's him. She's just confirmed it.' He checked the date on the entry. 'Ellie made this entry in June.' Fagan carried on reading. *'I'm totally in love with Shadowcaster.'* Fagan stopped reading. 'We need this prick's real name if we've any chance of catching him.'

'Without access to Ellie's Cymru Teen Chat account, we're dead in the water, boss,' Watkins grimly remarked.

'You're right, Sean. But it gives us something. Andrew, I want you to contact the parents of the four other girls linked to the DNA found on Ellie's body. Find out if their daughters ever mentioned someone called Shadowcaster before they died.'

'Bit of a longshot, sir,' Brooks said. 'Not everyone keeps a detailed diary like what Ellie kept.'

'I know, but it's worth a go.' Fagan looked at the tablet, reading another entry. *'Mam took my phone off me earlier, to see if I was doing anything I shouldn't be. Too stupid to know I'm keeping a diary. One day, I will tell everyone what she's been doing. One day I'll be free. I know Shadowcaster is there for me. He's my rock.'* Fagan stopped reading. 'This Shadowcaster has gained her trust.'

'Ellie mentions how controlling her mother is,' Stacey said. 'Sophie Parry checks her daughter's phone regularly.'

'Aye, probably because she doesn't want Ellie telling anyone what she's been up to.' Fagan scanned more of the entries. 'Right, this is what we're going to do. Me and Stacey will interview Sophie Parry again.' Fagan looked at Watkins. 'I want you and young Andrew to pull Tammy Morris in and question her regarding her involvement in this.' Fagan massaged his brow.

'You okay, boss?'

'Just about.' Fagan glanced at his tablet. 'I just don't understand how Sophie Parry thought she could get away with this. Pimping out her own daughter is beyond evil. And why did she do it? So she could make a couple of quid extra.'

'I'm guessing Sophie Parry thought that because it was behind closed doors, she'd be able to get away with it,' Stacey explained. 'Ellie looked a lot older when she applied makeup. Sophie thought that if she could keep doing this, Ellie would make her a lot of money in the long run. Especially when she turned sixteen. If you ask me, her mother would have upped her game by getting Ellie to engage in sex with other people.'

Fagan digested Stacey's commentary. 'Let's look at messages exchanged between Ellie and Sophie in the days leading up to her murder. I've a feeling we'll find something more we can hit Parry with when we interview her.'

CHAPTER 34

Newport Central Police Station

Sophie Parry drummed her fingers on the table nervously as Fagan ran through the interview start-up process. Fagan stared across the table for several seconds, studying her posture. 'Well, here we are again Sophie,' he sighed. 'More lies, more deceit.'

'No comment,' Parry stated, glaring back at Fagan.

Fagan tapped a tablet, pushing it towards Parry. 'I am showing Sophie Parry a picture of an iPhone recovered behind the property where Ellie Parry was found. Do you recognise this phone, Sophie?'

Parry stared at the wall, unwilling to look at the image on the tablet.

'Sophie,' Stacey said calmly. 'Could you please look at the image on the tablet.'

Parry rubbed her nose. 'No comment.'

'Sophie, all we want you to do is look at the image.'

Parry glanced at the ceiling with a defiant expression. 'No comment.' She looked at her nails.

Fagan decided he wasn't playing games with her. 'The phone found at the back of your property belonged to your daughter. Our cyber forensic team has retrieved damning information from the phone.'

'No comment,' Parry repeated.

Fagan focused his attention on Ellie's diary. 'Are you aware your daughter kept a diary?'

Parry stared back at Fagan before glancing at the tablet for a few moments. She looked at the interview room wall, sniffing. 'No comment.'

'You didn't know, did you?'

'No comment.'

'She's been keeping a diary since 2021.'

Parry shook her head. 'No comment.'

'Ellie goes into detail about her misery of having to pose nude for your FansOnly account,' Stacey said. She looked down at the tablet and read aloud. *'Nothing I do is good enough. Every time I complain, mam just tells me to shut the fuck up.'*

'How would you describe your relationship with your daughter?' Fagan asked.

'No comment,' Parry said quickly.

Stacey read another passage. *'I feel so alone. I can't do this anymore. There has to be a way out.'*

'When you were taking pictures of Ellie for FansOnly, did you know what you were doing was illegal?' Fagan questioned.

'No comment.'

'Were you even aware how miserable Ellie was? That you were putting her through hell?'

Parry cleared her throat. 'No comment.'

'Doesn't it bother you how miserable she was?' Stacey asked.

Parry remained silent. She leant back in her chair, folding her arms.

'Ellie constantly talks about her misery. She also says she told you repeatedly she didn't want you to take any more pictures of her. What was your response?'

'Why didn't you want to listen to her, Sophie?' Fagan asked. 'Was it because she was making a shitload of money for you?'

Parry inhaled. 'No comment.'

Fagan took it up a notch. 'Tell us about the abortion Ellie had in January last year?'

Parry frantically scratched the back of her head.

Fagan continued. 'Was it Toby Morris' baby?'

Stacey could see how the remark had rattled Parry. 'According to Ellie, she wanted to keep the baby.' She looked down at the tablet. *'I'm pregnant, finally a way out of this hell I'm trapped in. Mam and Tammy won't be able to use me. I'll get as far away as I can.'*

'Must have really pissed you off when you found out she was pregnant,' Fagan stated. 'I mean, as time wore on and the baby bump showed, it meant you running out of money. Also attracting attention from the wrong people, namely the police and Social Services. How did you get away with taking her to the doctor to arrange an abortion? Did you play the victim in the doctor's surgery, Sophie? The hard done by mother who was struggling to control her daughter who was out of control. We have witness statements from residents on the estate. Many have said that Ellie was abusive towards them. A trait she obviously picked up from you. You're not exactly popular on that estate, are you? It was a perfect cover for you, wasn't it? I mean, take her down to the doctor, give him a sob story. He arranged for Ellie to have an abortion. Giving you the opportunity to carry on your sordid activities. Make more money off Ellie.' Fagan switched gear again. 'What about your relationship with Martin Daniels?'

'No comment,' Parry replied aggressively.

'When Ellie had her abortion last year, it tipped her over the edge, didn't it? Is that why she threatened to kill you? In a blind panic you phoned the police. So, when Social Services turned up on your doorstep, you had to come up with a plan. A plan to get them off your back. Is that why you went after Daniels? Manipulate him into bed. After all, you couldn't have Social Services breathing down your neck. You were making so much money posting pictures of Ellie. You got to know Daniels very well. He was the Jack the Lad type up for anything. So you seduced him. You acted as a honey trap to stop Social Services.'

'You realise this is pure speculation, DI Fagan,' the duty solicitor point out.

Parry glanced at her before focusing her attention on Fagan. 'Yeah, this is all speculation.'

'But we've already spoken to Martin Daniels,' Stacey pointed out. 'He's told us everything. How you lured him in and had sex with him. Daniels revealed to you he was having marriage difficulties. So you thought you'd put yourself forward as the better option. But you knew you couldn't carry on with the affair, because of what you were doing on FansOnly. When Ruth Sutton recommended your children should be taken into foster care, you gave Martin Daniels a sob story about not being able to manage without your children. So you manipulated Daniels into blocking her attempt to remove the children from your care.'

'When Ruth Sutton's recommendation was blocked,' Fagan continued, 'you realised Martin Daniels became a liability. So you broke off the relationship. When he wanted to know why you didn't want to know any more, you threatened to go to his wife and tell her all about the affair. You also threatened to tell Social Services that you were having an affair with him. You had the power to end his marriage and his job. With him out of the way you were free to carry on.'

'How did Tammy Morris become involved in all this?' Stacey looked down at the diary. 'According to Ellie, Tammy used to prepare her hair and makeup before you took pictures. You know, make her look much older. I'm sure a lot of the blokes who saw these pictures thought she was older than fourteen.'

'No comment,' Parry said in a wavering voice.

'Yeah, she was fourteen years of age,' Fagan said, noting Parry's expression. 'You will be charged with creating indecent images of children and distributing indecent images of children.'

'I'm not a fucking pervert!' Parry blurted out. 'It's not like I sexually abused my daughter.'

'No, you didn't,' Fagan agreed. 'But what you don't understand, Sophie, is that you exposed Ellie to perverts who wanted to do just that. Ellie mentions it in her diary.'

'No one knew where we lived,' Parry argued. 'I kept her safe.'

'You kept her safe,' Stacy remarked. 'So how did she end up being murdered?'

The question shattered Parry as tears tumbled down her cheeks. 'You fucking bitch. You've no idea what it is to be a mother.'

'I'm pretty sure my concept of being a mother differs from your idea.'

'PC Flynn, was that comment necessary?' the duty solicitor asked. 'As you can see, Miss Parry is regretful of her actions.'

'Are you Sophie?' Fagan pursued.

'I'm sorry. I never meant for any of this to happen.'

'So why did you let it continue? I mean, the first time Ellie got hold of your phone and took those pictures you told us you banned us from all her devices.'

'I did,' Parry insisted.

'So why did you agree to let Ellie upload a minute long video of her dancing naked?'

'I had no money. I was desperate.'

'But you knew it was illegal.'

Parry was unable to answer.

'Sophie,' Fagan persisted. 'You knew what you were doing was illegal.'

'Yeah.'

'Why did you carry on?'

'Why do you bloody well think? Because of the money.'

'But you knew it was wrong,' said Stacey.

'You've no fucking idea,' Parry ranted.

Stacey returned the statement with a confused expression. 'What d'you mean? I have no idea.'

'What I mean is, you have no fucking idea what it's like to be at the bottom.'

'At the bottom of what, Sophie?'

'Having no money, always struggling to make ends meet.'

'But that's your choice, Sophie,' Fagan stated with little emotion. 'You chose to live life on the dole. Everyone has a chance to work and thrive. But you just sat back, sat on your arse and claimed every benefit going. And on top of all that, you used your daughter as a cash cow. A way to make money.' Fagan could sense his temper getting the better of him. He looked at the tablet. 'Let's examine the messages you and Ellie exchanged the day she was murdered. The first message she sent you was around a quarter past ten that morning.' Fagan read the message through before reading it aloud. *'I'm coming to Cardiff tonight, whether or not you like it.'* Fagan glanced at Parry. 'Your response. *Fuck off, clit. If you think you're coming tonight, you can think again.* Ellie messages you back. *You cunt, after all I've done for you.* You respond by saying, *You do fuck all but moan and bitch at me.* Ellie then responds. *Perhaps I should moan and bitch to the police.'* Fagan glanced at Parry. 'You message her back. *If you do that, we'll miss out on all the money we're about to make tonight. I'll end up in prison and you'll end up in foster care. Is that really what you want?*. Ellie responds, *Fuck you, bitch.'* Fagan looked at Parry. 'What do you mean by missing out on all the money you're about to make?'

'No comment.'

'Let's examine the last text Ellie sent you. *Do you want me to film it and upload it to FansOnly?* Was she planning to film herself having sex with someone?'

'No comment.' Parry shook her head defiantly.

'Were you encouraging your daughter to produce a sexually explicit video and upload it to FansOnly?'

Parry pursed her lips. 'No comment.'

'Was Shadowcaster the man Ellie was supposed to have had sex with the night she was murdered?'

'You have no idea what I've been through. What they made me do!' Parry ranted. 'I had no bloody choice.'

'Who are you talking about?'

'The dickheads that run FansOnly.'

'You need to tell us everything, Sophie,' Fagan stated. 'It's the only way we'll be able to catch the person who murdered Ellie. And any help you give us will reduce the sentence you will receive.'

Stacey observed Parry's reaction.

'I didn't mean for it to go this far,' Parry began. 'When Ellie uploaded those pictures, I was genuinely pissed off with her. I banned her from all her devices. I stopped her using the internet and everything. We had a massive chat about what she'd done and how it was wrong. I told her she was only twelve years old and it would attract all kinds of unwanted attention. I told Ellie if the police and Social Services found out what she'd done, she'd be taken into care, her brothers would be taken into care, and I'd be slung in jail. At the time, she was genuinely sorry for what she'd done. But a few days before, I was moaning how skint we were all the time. There are families on benefits going away twice a year, and I couldn't even afford a trip to Barry Island, let alone

Spain or Turkey. And then, a few days after Ellie posted those pictures, ten grand was paid into my bank account. At first, I wasn't going to spend a penny of the money. I thought about giving it away to charity. Or just leaving it in the bank account. But I was scared that the benefits office might find out about me having money, so I spent it.'

'What did you spend it on?'

Parry shrugged. 'I paid off credit card bills with it. I bought Ellie some nice clothes and makeup. I bought myself some new clothes. I bought the boys some toys and clothes. For the first time in God knows how long, we weren't struggling. Suddenly I could afford to live again. I was making a bit of money myself off FansOnly. But after a while it got harder and harder to make money. When I first started it, it seemed like a good idea. I know there are people out there who'd be really disgusted with what I do to make money. The thing is, there are loads of girls throughout the Valleys doing it. You'd be surprised with what's going on behind closed doors. I know at least two couples near me who film themselves having sex and upload it to FansOnly.'

'I suggest we take a break, DI Fagan,' the duty solicitor requested. 'It's clear that this interview is having an effect on Ms Parry's mental health.'

Fagan considered the request before nodding. 'Okay, we'll take a break.'

Parry and the solicitor left the room.

Fagan clasped his hands behind his head and yawned. 'I tell you what Stacey, this is turning into a right shitshow, isn't it?'

Stacey nodded. 'Yeah. I don't think this brings us any closer to finding out who murdered Ellie, though.'

'No, it won't. A can of worms has been opened that can't be shut. When all this comes out in the media, and trust me, it will. Sophie will serve time in prison. When she comes out, there's no way she'll be able to return to the Sofrydd.'

'Tammy Morris also,' Stacey added.

Fagan nodded, before looking down at his phone that had just buzzed. 'Speak of the devil. Sean and Andrew are about to interview Tammy Morris about her part in all this.'

CHAPTER 35

'Interview with Tammy Morris,' Watkins began. 'Present in the room are interviewing officers, Detective Sergeant Sean Watkins and Police Constable Andrew Brooks. Also present is the duty solicitor Sarah Bedford.'

'When did you find out that Sophie Parry was uploading indecent images of her daughter to FansOnly?' Brooks asked.

Morris shrugged. 'A couple of years ago.'

'How did you find out?'

'A boy on the estate shared a video of Sophie.'

'That's not what we meant, Tammy,' Watkins said. 'What we want to know is when did you find out that Sophie was uploading images and videos of her daughter?'

'I'm not saying anything,' Morris stated.

'A bit late for that, isn't it? We've already interviewed your son. He has confirmed that you encouraged him to pursue a sexual relationship with Sophie.'

Morris chewed her lip.

'Then you and Sophie encouraged him to have a sexual relationship with Ellie when she was just eleven years old.'

'That was all Sophie's doing, not mine,' Morris whinged. 'She was the one who led him on. She was the one that jumped into bed with him.'

'And you never thought to question your best mate about having a relationship with your son.'

'They were both adults. They knew what they were doing.'

'Not entirely. Toby has learning difficulties.' Watkins glanced at his tablet. 'According to our records, you're a former drug addict. You were convicted for possession in 1989.'

'I kicked that habit years ago.'

'But not before you became pregnant with Toby in 1991. You

were rushed to the hospital after an overdose.' Watkins looked up from the tablet. 'I'm surprised Toby survived. It goes a long way to explain why he has learning difficulties. Drug and alcohol foetal syndrome can affect people long into their lives.'

'When I gave birth to Toby, I turned things around. I gave up the drugs and made a go of my life.'

'According to a diary that Ellie kept, you used to do her hair and makeup before Sophie took pictures of her before uploading them.'

Morris shook her head. 'That little bitch is lying.' She stopped talking.

'Yeah,' Brooks nodded. 'That little bitch you're referring to was murdered the other night.'

'I had nothing to do with it,' Morris insisted.

'Ellie's kept a diary, Tammy. She details your involvement in all this.'

'Was Sophie giving you any of the money?'

'She'd chuck me a couple of quid now and then.'

'Just to shut you up,' Watkins suggested.

'I wasn't going to grass her up. I'm not like that.'

'The reason you never grassed Sophie up is because Toby was having a sexual relationship with Ellie. Something he's now going to be convicted for. Ellie also writes in her diary that it was you who suggested she should go on the pill.'

'Fuck off!' Morris shouted. 'It was all Sophie's doing. She took the pictures, not me.'

'But you knew what she was doing, and you took part by making Ellie look a lot older. That way, you wouldn't arouse suspicion. You could carry on with your sordid enterprise. Thing is, Tammy, both you and Sophie had attracted the attention of a prolific killer. He stalked Ellie online. Contacted her through Cymru Teen Chat. And he murdered her.' Watkins paused.

Morris buried her face in her hands.

'If the events of the other night hadn't had happened, it's likely you and Sophie would have carried on.'

'I'm sorry,' Morris sobbed.

'You knew how miserable Ellie was.' Watkins looked down at

his tablet. 'According to one of Ellie's diary entries, she had spoken to you and begged you to tell her mother to stop.'

'Sophie became obsessive with making money from FansOnly. When I found out about Ellie being on there, I told Sophie she shouldn't be doing it. I told her to stop, or I would tell someone what she was doing.'

'Is that when she threatened to grass Toby up?'

Morris nodded. 'Amongst other things.'

'Other things?' Brooks enquired.

'I was ready to go to the police, honestly.' Morris paused. 'But Sophie paid me two grand to shut me up. She said we could make a shitload of money selling pictures of Ellie.'

'Two grand is more than a couple of quid, isn't it?' Watkins said.

'I was skint.'

Watkins rolled his eyes. 'That's what Sophie said when we interviewed her about her FansOnly account.'

'I wanted to tell someone.'

'But you couldn't because of your son, Toby.' Watkins paused. 'Why did you and Sophie encourage your son to pursue a sexual relationship with Ellie?'

'That was all Sophie's doing.' Morris hammered a clenched fist on the table.

Watkins swiped the screen on the tablet. 'No Tammy, you were equally suggestive. We've been going through your messages with Toby. This message is dated August 2021. *Me and Sophie are going out on the piss. The boys are with their dad. It's time for you to make a woman of that little bitch.'*

Morris stared down at the table. Grasping the gravity of her situation.

'Why?' Brooks asked.

'I don't know,' Morris whimpered. 'Things got out of hand.'

'Yes, they did, Tammy,' Watkins said. 'You and Sophie have destroyed lives. Your life is now over.' Watkins checked the GoFundMe account. 'I see people have donated over ninety thousand pounds to your GoFundMe appeal.'

'I wanted to give Ellie a decent send off. She deserved that.'

'You set up this account on the day Ellie was murdered,' Watkins remarked. 'You knew the media attention this would attract. So what was the plan? Make one final score from Ellie. Pay for a decent funeral, then you and Sophie split the money down the middle?'

Morris nodded. 'When I found Ellie, I knew she was dead. I panicked and phoned Sophie straight away to tell her what had happened. At first, she didn't believe me. Said I was full of shit. That's when I took a picture of Ellie and sent it to Sophie.'

'What was Sophie's reaction?'

'She was fuming. Sophie was more concerned she wouldn't be able to make any more money. Sophie screamed Ellie was a selfish twat. And that she killed herself just to spite her. We knew we'd have to phone the police to tell them what happened.' Morris hesitated. 'That's when Sophie told me to set up the GoFundMe account.'

'Before you'd even phoned the police?' Brooks said.

Morris nodded. 'Sophie said she was going to chuck her phone. Because of all the stuff she had on there.' Morris expressed a look of rage. 'The stupid bitch. She should have dumped her phone where no one could find it.'

Watkins inhaled. 'Interview ended.'

'What happens now?'

'You'll be charged with making indecent images of children.'

'I didn't make those images,' Morris protested. 'That was all Sophie's doing. I had nothing to do with uploading them.'

Watkins pointed at his tablet. 'But you did Ellie's hair and makeup before each session. Ellie states this clearly in her dairy.'

Morris stared at the tablet. 'Yeah.'

'This will come out eventually, Tammy. Both you and Sophie will be the most hated women in the Valleys. You'll be up there with Karen Matthews and Maxine Carr.'

The solicitor led Morris out of the room.

'Jesus, I think I'm going to throw up,' Watkins said.

'A real shit show,' Brooks remarked.

Watkins glanced at his phone. 'I'll send the boss this recording. He's due to have another interview with Sophie Parry.'

CHAPTER 36

Fagan restarted the interview process and gave a short recap of where they were in the interview. 'Okay, Sophie, so you spent the ten grand. You stopped Ellie from using the internet, what made you crumble?'

'I was running out of money again. I was down to my last couple of hundred quid.' Parry hesitated. 'When Ellie posted those first pictures, the number of fans I had shot up. These blokes would ask me to put more pictures of Ellie online. They said they'd pay me good money. I'd tell most of them to fuck off. Honestly, I didn't want to put any more pictures of Ellie online.'

'Something must have changed your mind,' Stacey said.

Parry thought for a moment. 'One of the girls who lives two streets down from me was boasting about how she was going to Turkey for two weeks. She has six kids. She claims all the benefits going.'

'What's her name?' Fagan asked.

'Lisa.'

'Were you jealous of Lisa?'

'Yeah, I was,' Parry admitted. 'She has three fucking holidays a year. Anyway, about a week after that, I was skint again. No matter how much I try to save, I just can't make my money last. That's when Ellie came to me and said she'd make a video.'

'You obviously turned her down,' Stacey said.

'Of course I bloody well did,' Parry barked, raising her voice. She stared at the interview room wall. 'When I had that ten grand paid into my bank account, it felt so good. It was a real adrenaline rush. But when the money ran out, I felt really low. Especially when Lisa came to me bragging about how she was going away for two weeks. When she left, I just broke down and started crying. That's when Ellie came into the living room and asked me what the matter was. I said to her we were out of money again and I was weeks away from getting paid any benefits. She said nothing at first. She just went back upstairs to her bedroom. A couple of hours later, she came back downstairs and said that she would make a video so we could make some money.' Parry put her hand up. 'I said no way are you fucking doing that.'

'But you did it anyway,' Fagan said.

'I had no bloody choice!' Parry shouted. 'I tried to lend money off my mam, off Tammy. But they all said no. I was on my fucking knees. Ellie said we should upload the video. She'd already made it on a mobile phone. Filmed herself in her bedroom, dancing to one of her favourite songs. We talked for hours about it. We reached the decision.'

'Which was upload the video,' Fagan said.

'Yeah,' Parry replied. 'I said to Ellie, if we made decent money I'd shut down the account and that would be the end of it.' Parry hesitated. 'Within a day of me uploading that video, it had over two million views worldwide. I thought we'd make similar money to what we made before. But three days later, twenty-five grand was dumped into my bank account. It took my breath away. I had money again. Like before I paid off the credit cards, treated Ellie and the boys and booked a holiday. It was brilliant,' Parry reflected. 'I even went boasting to Lisa about the holiday I'd booked.' Parry hesitated. 'Then it went all to shit.'

'Why?'

'I was ready to shut down my account. I thought the money would help get me out of the shit with all my debts. I was looking for a part-time job and to get back on my feet. You know, do the things that normal people do. About a week after I got paid, the bloke who runs FansOnly e-mailed me.'

'This is Paul Decker?' Fagan quizzed.

Parry nodded. 'He told me if I uploaded more pictures and videos of Ellie, I could make a shitload of money. I told him to piss off. And shut my FansOnly account.' Parry ran her hand through her mousy blonde hair. 'But he wouldn't leave me alone. A couple of weeks after I shut my account, he e-mailed me and claimed he knew how old Ellie was and would post the video to the police.

And that I'd be arrested.' Tears washed down her cheeks. 'I had no choice.'

'Didn't you think about coming to the police?'

Parry shook her head. 'I thought the moment I told the police they'd be at my house taking the kids away.'

'So you reopened your FansOnly account?'

'It was never shut down. I'm thick as shit, but even I realised Decker kept it open.'

'What did you tell Ellie?'

'I said that I couldn't find a job and that the only way to make money was to post more videos and pictures.'

'And she readily agreed, did she?'

Parry hesitated. 'At first, yeah.'

'And then what?'

'After a few months, she didn't want to do it. She said it was wrong.'

'But she was right, wasn't she?'

'Yeah, she was right. I know I fucked up. You don't need to keep reminding me. One day, we had a massive argument about it. Ellie refused to make any more pictures or videos.'

'What did you do?'

'I went into panic mode. I contacted Paul Decker and told him that Ellie was refusing to have any more pictures and videos taken of her.'

'What did he say?'

Parry released a snort of derision. 'He wrote back and said it was too bad and that he was going to send videos and photos to the police. That's when I told Ellie the truth.'

'What was her response?'

'She was fuming with me. I don't blame her. But in the end Ellie agreed to make more photos and videos.'

Fagan pointed at his tablet. 'You must have known how miserable she was. It's all in the diary she wrote.'

'I tried to stop, honestly, but I had no one to turn to.'

'You could have turned to the police, Sophie,' Stacey pointed out. 'You could have come to us for help.'

'You'd have locked me up and thrown away the key,' Parry

speculated.

'No,' Fagan stated. 'We could have helped you. You were obviously being manipulated by Paul Decker.' He inhaled. 'But the fact that you let it carry on for over two years now implicates you in this crime. All this information we've gathered from your phone and Ellie's phone will go to the prosecutor. They'll look at all this information and have a field day. Your life, Sophie, is now over. You've lost everything.'

'How did Tammy get involved?' Stacey asked. 'She did Ellie's hair and makeup before you took photos and videos of her.'

'Ellie let slip to Toby what she was doing.'

'What was his response?'

'Tammy's son has learning difficulties. He's too stupid to know that what we were doing was wrong. But he told his mam, anyway. That's when Tammy came around and had a right go at me. She threatened to go to the police.'

'What did you say?'

'I said that if she did that, I'd tell the police that Toby was involved in a sexual relationship with Ellie.'

'In other words, you both had dirt on each other.'

'Yeah,' Parry nodded. 'We had a long chat about what we were going to do. That's when Tammy said that she would do Ellie's hair and makeup to make her look a lot older than what she was. Tammy was good at that kind of thing. She did a makeup course at Pontypool College.'

Fagan pointed at the tablet. 'Ellie's diary tells a story, Sophie, do you understand? She was clearly miserable at what she was doing. She speaks of constantly arguing with you about wanting to stop.'

'I know and I wanted to, honestly.'

'What about the day Ellie was murdered? The last message she sent you was about her filming herself having sex with someone. Tell us about that.'

'A few months ago, Paul Decker contacted me and said he wanted to take things to the next level. He wanted Ellie to go with men. But I refused. Again, he said he would send photos and videos to the police and grass me up for what I'd been doing.'

Parry hesitated. 'He then said, if Ellie filmed herself having sex with someone, then it could earn us half a million quid. I was gobsmacked. I told Tammy, and she said if we earned that much money, then we could get away from here. Move out and disappear. I'd shut down my account and Decker would never find us.'

'How much money were you going to give Tammy?'

'I was wasn't going to give her anything. I was just going to disappear.'

'Did you tell Ellie what Decker wanted her to do?'

'Yeah.'

'What was Ellie's response?'

'She was livid. She didn't want to do it. I promised her, if she did this once, we'd move away and she doesn't have to do anything again.'

'I take it that did the trick?'

'Yeah.'

'Ellie sent you two messages before she was murdered. First, she informs you he'd arrived. Then, in the next message, she asks you if you want her to film it. Do you have any idea who Ellie was referring to?'

Parry took her time answering Fagan's question. 'Several weeks back, Ellie started talking to the boy on Cymru Teen Chat.'

'That's Shadowcaster.'

'Yeah,' Parry revealed. 'She'd been talking to him for weeks. Last week she said that he was the one she wanted to be filmed with.'

'Even though she'd never met him before?'

Parry was hesitant before she answered. 'Uh, yeah. Ellie said that she would invite him over and they'd have sex and film it.'

'If he was going to your house, then he must have been local.'

'I don't know,' Parry responded. 'Ellie never mentioned where he was from. About a week ago, Ellie got cold feet.'

'She didn't want to go through with it?' Stacey said.

'No.' Parry shook her head. 'We had a massive row about it. She said she'd rather be taken into care than keep doing what she was doing. We've been having massive rows all week about it.

Last Wednesday, the girls asked if I wanted to go to Cardiff with them. When Ellie found out, she went ballistic. She wanted to go with me. But I said she couldn't because she had to stay home and invite Shadowcaster round and film them having sex.'

'Is that why you were arguing all day?' Fagan asked. 'The day she was murdered.'

Parry nodded. 'Paul Decker messaged me three weeks ago and said I have to make the video by last Saturday night, otherwise he'd send information to the police.'

'But Ellie didn't want to go through with it,' Stacey said.

'No,' Parry replied. 'But come Thursday night she said she would, if it meant we could move away from the Sofrydd.'

'Where were you going to go?'

Parry shrugged. 'Anywhere, as long as it's not anywhere near here.'

Fagan took a long breath, considering the what Parry had told him. 'Okay, this is what we're going to do. We're going to release you for now. But you will be interviewed again regarding your part in all this. You will be charged with creating indecent images of children. I recommend you don't return to the Sofrydd. This will all eventually come out Sophie. I doubt whether anyone will want you living up there again.'

'I'll have to go to my mam's for now.'

'Okay, I'll arrange for some officers to pick up some clothes from your house.'

CHAPTER 37

Fagan massaged his temples, letting out a wide, long and loud yawn.

Brooks placed a mug of coffee in front of him. 'That will keep you going, sir.'

Fagan looked at him, flashing a brief smile. 'Thanks, Andrew.' He picked up the mug and took a large swig.

Watkins walked into the room with a box of Greggs.

'Just what I needed,' Fagan said, plucking a doughnut from the box. He bit into the confectionery whilst staring at the whiteboard. 'We've hit a dead end,' he finally announced.

'How do you mean, boss?'

'We're no nearer to catching Ellie's killer than we were when we first started three days ago.' He considered his options. 'We're going to have to release Woods. The most we can charge him with is intent to supply and sexual activity with a child. Which, I suppose, is a result in itself. Sophie Parry and Tammy Morris, who will be charged with creating indecent images of children. Which, again, is a result. Toby Morris will be charged with sexual activity with a child. And that's a bit of a grey area because the poor bugger has learning difficulties.'

'It's still a result though, sir,' Brooks said.

'Yeah, you're right Andrew, it's a result. But it brings us no closer to catching Ellie's killer. Besides Pamela Nash spotting Woods entering Ellie's house on the night she was murdered, we've no other witnesses who have come forward with any leads.'

'Unless you count the taxi driver who saw someone running down the Hafodyrynys road,' Stacey pointed out.

'What's the name of the taxi driver?'

Stacey looked at her screen. 'There's no name.'

'Not even the name of the taxi company?'

'No, guv, sorry.'

'Well, that's another dead end,' Fagan sighed. He looked at a map of the Sofrydd. 'Ellie's killer must have entered through the back of the property.' He glanced at Watkins. 'How far can you get a vehicle up that dirt track that runs at the back of the house where Ellie was found?'

Watkins called up Google Maps on his computer and studied the terrain for several moments. 'You can drive an off-road vehicle up there. Brookview Farm is around one point four kilometres. That's not even a mile.'

'Where was Ellie's phone found?'

Watkins clicked on a mouse. 'Three hundred yards away from the back of the property.'

'Do you think the killer could have come from a different direction, guv?' Stacey asked.

'He could have come across the top. You could easily get a four-wheel drive up there.' Fagan glanced at Brooks. 'Get a couple of uniform to visit the farm. See if they noticed any unusual activity the night that Ellie was murdered. They might have CCTV on their property.'

Watkins continued to study the map. 'The farm is connected to a lane that comes out on Cefn Crib Road. It's possible our killer could have come back into Hafodyrynys and joined the A472. Or he could have carried on along Cefn Crib.' Watkins paused and zoomed out. 'He could have come out at Wainfelin in Pontypool.' Watkin paused again, studying the map. 'There's a junction that leads onto the mountain. You then travel along Blaen-Y-Cwm Road, which brings you out at the bottom end of Six Bells.' Watkins puffed through his cheeks. 'You can go in several directions.'

'But all routes lead to a populated area,' Fagan said.

Watkins nodded.

'CCTV will be useless that time of night, guv,' Stacey said. 'All you get is the glare of headlights, and I doubt they have any numberplate recognition cameras in the areas where we need them.'

Fagan considered all the information. 'So our killer murders Ellie, wipes her phone. All her apps have been shut, but he leaves her personal diary, where she reveals all. Question is, why?'

'Isn't it obvious?' Brooks replied. 'He knew she was keeping a diary. He left it to incriminate Ellie's mam and Tammy Morris.'

'They've done a good enough job on their own, Andrew,' Fagan said.

'Yeah, but even our killer couldn't have predicted Sophie Parry throwing her phone in the bin at Cardiff Central. If Parry hadn't had thrown her phone away, then it would have taken slightly longer for us to find out about her FansOnly account. But the killer's motives were the same. Stall the investigation.'

'We've been focusing too much on Sophie Parry and her antics and not focusing on the killer like we should have been.' Fagan gritted her teeth. 'Shit!'

'He set us up to find out what Parry has been up to,' Stacey guessed.

Fagan nodded. 'In order to stall us.'

Stacey got to her feet. 'Excuse me a sec.'

'You okay? You look a bit green, Stacey,' Fagan said.

'I'm fine. Just a dodgy curry last night,' she explained, heading towards the door.

'So what do we do now, boss?'

'Our priority is to find our killer.'

'If he set all this up, then he's long gone,' Brooks said. 'He's a serial killer. He won't hang around to watch us struggle. Plus, he's operating online, which means he could be anywhere.'

Fagan's attention was diverted to his e-mail box on his laptop. He didn't recognise the sender's address. The e-mail had a video file attachment. The voices of Watkins and Brooks seemed to fade as they carried on discussing options.

Watkins looked across at Fagan, who seemed hypnotised by his laptop. 'Boss?'

Fagan clicked on the video which played. Fagan froze at the sight of Ellie smiling in front of her phone. She was brushing her long hair. 'Jesus Christ,' Fagan gasped.

Watkins and Brooks joined him at his desk.

Ellie smiled and waved at the Camera. *'Hi guys, finally, the day has arrived. Shadowcaster is five minutes away. He's been my rock for the last several weeks. I'm so sick of this life. I want to start a new life. Perhaps the next time around, I'll get a better chance. I know I will.'* Fagan paused the video.

'What's she talking about, boss?'

'He's convinced her she'll get another chance to live another life.'

'The killer has brainwashed her,' Brooks said. 'Like some kind of cult leader.'

'That's just what I was thinking.' Fagan clicked on play.

'I know many people will be pissed off with what I'm about to do. Especially mam, who doesn't give a fuck about me at the moment. All she gives a shit about is how much money I can make tonight for her. Well, sorry mam, but that's not going to happen. You'll just have to be content with showing your saggy tits to those perverts. God, I hate what I've been doing. What mam and Tammy have made me do. I hate those perverts I have to perform for.' Ellie closed her eyes. *'But no more. Today is the day when my suffering will come to an end. I'd just like to say sorry to those who will miss me. Gracie, Mia and Charlotte will join me. So at least I'll have company.'*

'What does she mean by that?' Watkins questioned.

Fagan paused the video again. 'What did Richards tell us when we interviewed him? He said when he left the park with his mates, the girls were talking to someone on Cymru Teen Chat.'

'Yeah,' Watkins replied.

'And that someone was Shadowcaster. Richards even said he had an argument over this Shadowcaster.' Fagan clicked on the mouse and the video continued.

'I'd just like to say thank you to everyone in our chat group. You've all been brilliant. And I can't wait to see you all on the other side, bye.' Ellie kissed the tips of her fingers before pressing them against the camera lens on her phone. The screen went black.

Fagan stared at his computer screen for several seconds. The phone on his desk rang suddenly, causing him to jump out of his temporary trance. He grabbed the receiver. 'DI Fagan,' he barked.

'Did you get the video?' A mystery voice asked.

For a moment, Fagan was like a rabbit caught in headlights. He tapped the loud speaker button on his desk phone.

'Well, what do you think do you think of my work?'

'I'm on it,' Brooks said loudly, marching towards his phone and calling for a trace.

'You don't think I'd be stupid enough to phone you, knowing you could trace me, do you?'

'I suspect you sent me this video to get my attention. Now that you have it, what is it you want?' Fagan asked in an even tone.

'What every master of their craft wants, DI Fagan, notoriety.'

'Notoriety?' Fagan repeated.

'I want to come out of the shadows. It's time I came into the light, so to speak. To let the world know of my intentions.'

'And what are your intentions?'

'I think I've made my intentions very clear, DI Fagan. What's I'm going to do now is watch as I make you and Gwent Police jump through my hoops.'

Fagan clenched his jaw. 'No one is going to perform for you. But we will do everything in our power to track you down.' Fagan looked across at Brooks, who shook his head. 'And now that we have your voice, we will eventually track you.'

The voice on the phone chuckled softly. 'You have nothing, DI Fagan. That's the best thing about artificial intelligence. I can make my voice sound like anyone I want, including you.'

Fagan's heart leapt as the voice on the phone spoke, just like him.

'I can make a phone call and pretend to be anyone I want. *Hello this is DI Fagan with Gwent Police.*'

'Is that cheap trick supposed to rattle my cage?' Fagan questioned, with a defiant tone.

'This is no cheap trick, DI Fagan,' the voice changed to a voice Fagan recognised.

'I can talk and sound like anyone I want. Today I could be Keir Starmer, our Prime Minister.' The voice of Starmer came through the phone's speaker. 'Or I could take on the role of our beloved king.' The voice changed again to King Charles. 'I will rule with fear over the South Wales Valleys, DI Fagan. You have ready seen what I can do with Ellie.'

'What I see is a sadistic bastard whose time is running out. You can use all the fancy gadgets you want. We'll hunt you down.'

'You can't hunt what you can't see, DI Fagan. That's the beauty of technology. I could be a hundred miles from you, or sat in the room next door. You'll never know who or where I am.'

Fagan looked at Brooks again, who shook his head solemnly.

The voice chuckled again. 'I know you're trying to keep me on the line for as long as possible, DI Fagan, but it's no use.'

'Fair enough,' Fagan said. 'Why Ellie?'

'Ellie was special.'

'Special, how?'

'She was my first.'

'First victim?'

'No, of course not. Ellie was a lost soul in need of salvation. I gave her that salvation. I gave her the peace she longed for.'

'What you did was murder her in cold blood.'

'What I did was save her,' the voice said.

'No,' Fagan interrupted. 'What you did was take the life of an innocent young girl.'

'I saved her from a life she hated. I found her pictures and saw the sadness in her eyes. The longing for death. I made her life mean something for the last few weeks. I made her feel alive again.'

'And how did you do that?'

'I made her feel she was worth something. Unlike that terrible mother of hers. Exploiting her into a world of darkness, for the sake of earning money.'

'And that justifies your actions, does it?'

'I don't need to justify myself, DI Fagan. These young vulnerable girls are crying out to be heard. I am that voice in the darkness they are looking for. I am their hope and their dreams. They know me, they trust me, they confide in me. Then they come to rely on me. And then I watch, as they die for me. That's the power I have, DI Fagan. What power do you have?'

Fagan remained silent.

'I will show you a power that cannot be bargained with, cannot be subdued. And I will wield that power. I will rain down terror on the South Wales Valleys, the likes never seen before. I will strike fear into the communities. And it all starts here. It's time the world knew who I am.'

'And who is that?'

'I am the Shadowcaster, and today is your first day at school, DI Fagan. I'd check your inbox if I were you, although it's already too late for little Grace, Mia, and Charlotte. They've all joined Ellie, they've all been freed.'

Fagan looked at the e-mail box on the screen. A new e-mail appeared.

'Don't bother trying to save them, DI Fagan. They've already gone.' The line went dead.

Fagan clicked on a video file called Gracie. 'Jesus, it's like Ellie's video.' He jumped to his feet, grabbing his jacket. 'Andrew, get on the horn to the incident room up at the Sofrydd. Tell them to send every available officer to the houses of Gracie Peacock, Mia Probert, and Charlotte Mason.'

CHAPTER 38

The Sofrydd

Fagan sprung from his car.

A stretcher was wheeled down the front path to the house. Residents stood on the other side of the street gossiping.

Fagan watched as the stretcher was hauled into the ambulance.

'The paramedics tried to revive her, but were unsuccessful,' Saddler explained. He looked further down at the road. Another ambulance was parked up. More onlookers stood across the street, watching the drama unfold. Another stretcher was being wheeled out. 'Charlotte Mason was also found unresponsive.'

'Jesus,' Fagan gasped.

Watkins Walked up the road. 'Boss, Mia Probert was found in her bedroom. Paramedics tried their best, but they couldn't revive her.'

Fagan closed his eyes briefly in silent prayer. 'He set this up, Sean.'

'Shadowcaster,' Watkins said.

Fagan nodded. 'He set this up to show his power. He said so himself.'

'He'll make a mistake, boss. We'll catch him.'

Fagan glanced at Saddler. 'I want you to interview Charlotte's parents. We need to know everything these girls have done over the past twenty-four hours.'

Saddler nodded before walking off down the road.

'Stacey and Andrew are with Mia's parents,' Watkins revealed.

Fagan looked at the property Gracie lived at. 'We better take a statement from Gracie's mam.'

Trisha Peacock was being comforted by a neighbour as Fagan and Watkins walked into the living room. A uniform was present, offering what little comfort she could.

'Can we have the room, please?' Fagan requested.

'I'll be back soon,' the neighbour reassured Trisha.

Fagan and Watkins sat down on a large corner sofa. 'On behalf of Gwent Police Trisha, we are sorry for your loss.' He inhaled. 'But at this time, we have to ask you a few questions. Can you tell us the last time you spoke with Gracie?'

Trisha's eyes were raw with tears. She struggled to speak through her grief. 'Not all that long ago, three hours, tops. Uh, Gracie said she wanted time alone. I thought she just meant she wanted time to process what happened to Ellie the other day. I didn't think she was going to do this.' Trisha broke down.

Fagan waited a while before asking his next question. 'How was Gracie before she went to her room?'

'She seemed fine. I don't understand any of this. Why would she?' Trisha couldn't bring herself to say anything else.

'It's okay, Trisha, take your time.'

'She seemed calm. I know the last few days have been difficult for her. They've been difficult for all the girls that knew Ellie.'

'Gracie was one of Elli's best mates, wasn't she?'

Trisha nodded. 'Gracie, Charlotte, Mia and Ellie. They were inseparable.'

'They did everything together?' Watkins asked.

Trisha nodded again. 'Gracie was in her first year at secondary school. Ellie, Charlotte, and Mia were already there. When she started last year, they said they'd look after her.'

'Did Gracie ever have any trouble at school?'

'No, not that I can recall. She was popular with both teachers and the kids.' Trisha glanced at a photograph on the wall.

'Did she say anything before she went to her room?' Fagan asked.

Trisha took deep breaths, trying to stay calm despite her emotions. 'She just said she was going to her room and have some alone time. I asked her if she needed anything.' Trisha stopped.

'Trisha, is there something you remember?'

Trisha stared back at Fagan. 'She said she had everything she needed. She also said she loved me and that I'd be fine?'

'You'd be fine?'

Trisha thought about the last thing Gracie had said to her. 'Yeah, she said I'd be fine. I didn't think anything of it.'

'Do you know what she was doing in her room?'

'I went up for a shower. I knocked on her door and asked if she was okay. Gracie said she was talking to Olivia Rodrigo.'

'Who?'

'Olivia Rodrigo,' Trisha repeated. 'Which I thought was odd because she's a massive popstar. I didn't think anything of it. I thought she was just messing around.'

'How did Gracie take Ellie's death?'

'As hard as everyone else, I suppose. I knew she was hurting. After you interviewed her the day they found Ellie, we went to get her nails done. When we were in the salon, she said that Ellie was at peace and that's what she wanted.'

'Do you know what she meant by that?'

'No, Gracie wouldn't let me in on her secrets.'

'So you had your shower. What did you do after that?'

'I popped into Pontypool. I went to Tesco. Met a friend for lunch.' Trisha broke down again. 'I shouldn't have left her. What kind of mother am I?'

'Trisha, listen to me,' Fagan said. 'You've done nothing wrong. You had no way of knowing what was going to happen.' He paused. 'Did you phone Gracie while you were out?'

'Um, no, I didn't. But I've this app on my phone that monitors Gracie's phone.'

'What was she doing?'

'She was talking to friends on Cymru Teen Chat.'

'Can you see what they were talking about?'

Trisha shook her head. 'The app I use allows me to monitor and block certain apps if Gracie is using them too much. But I can't block Cymru Teen Chat because it's run from another country. I can see who they're talking to. When I got back from Tesco, I went to check on Gracie to see if she wanted anything to eat. I knocked on her door and she didn't answer, but I could hear her music playing in the bedroom. And then I opened the door, and that's when I found her.' Trisha sobbed hysterically.

'Do you know who she was talking to?'

'She was talking to Charlotte and Mia. They have a private group.'

'Was it just Charlotte and Mia Gracie were talking to?'

Trisha to a few moments to answer Fagan. 'No, there was this new friend of theirs. Gracie seemed taken by him.'

'Him?'

Trisha fought her emotions. 'Shadow something or other.'

'Shadowcaster?'

'Yeah,' Trisha nodded. 'That's the one. I gave Gracie a row the other night, because I woke up at three o'clock and saw that she was talking to him.'

'Was it him she was just talking to?'

Trisha nodded

'Trisha, I'm sorry to ask you this,' Fagan said. 'I was wondering if we could have a look at Gracie's room.'

Trisha continued to sob, but nodded.

'We want to look at Gracie's room more closely. Do you think you could go to a neighbour for now who'll keep you company?'

'I want to go to the hospital. I want to be with my daughter.'

'Yes, absolutely,' Fagan replied. 'My colleague here, Detective Sergeant Watkins, will escort you to the ambulance.'

Watkins led Trisha out of the room, leaving Fagan to climb the staircase. He slipped on a pair of latex gloves and entered Gracie's room. The first thing Fagan noticed was Gracie's phone mounted on a tripod facing the bed, just like the tripod in Ellie's room.

Watkins entered the room. 'Ambulance is on its way to the Grange, boss.'

'He was here, Sean. The bastard was online with all three girls watching them.' Fagan noticed a bottle of vodka and a box of pills on a bedside table. He picked up the box and read the label. Jesus wept, Diphenhydramine. A powerful antihistamine. We'll get a team of CSI in here to recover the phone. Come on, let's see what Stacey and the others have found out.

Fagan had messaged Stacey, Brooks, and Saddler and told them to meet him in the community centre.

'This is going to spread like wildfire through the community. Give it an hour and the press will be all over this, so we need a plan. According to Gracie's mother, she was talking to her friends on Cymru Teen Chat. They were all talking to Shadowcaster. But Gracie's mam also said they were talking to a popstar called Olivia Rodrigo.'

'That's exactly what Charlotte's mam told me,' Saddler revealed.

'And Mai's mam,' Stacey added.

'This bastard has the ability to mimic anyone they want. Making his victims think they're talking to a well-known pop star. When in fact they're talking to the Shadowcaster. We need access to that Cymru Teen Chat app. We'll haul Russel Connor in. And question him further about misuse of that app.'

'You know Connor will surround himself with a wall of solicitors, boss,' Watkins said. 'You said so yourself.'

'I don't care two flying fucks, Sean. He can surround himself with a thousand solicitors. It still won't stop me from dragging his sorry arse down to Newport. I'm going to lay everything on the line to him. He either helps us or I'm going to trash his company all over the media.'

'I know you're pissed off, boss, but you know that won't work, and you're more likely to get in the shit for it.'

'I don't give a fuck!' Fagan bellowed.

Watkins shrank into his chair.

'I'm sorry, Sean,' Fagan apologised. 'Since day one of this investigation, we've been fed a pack of lies. The mother of Ellie Parry lied to us just to protect herself.' He glanced at Stacey. 'You were with me when we first interviewed her. She didn't seem to care that her daughter had been murdered.'

'No,' Stacey said.

'She was determined to protect that kiddie porn empire she was running. We've got to interview Russel Connor. If we can get access to his software, then we can track that Shadowcaster down.'

Watkins looked towards the door of the community centre. 'Shit,' he cursed loud enough for just them to hear.

Fagan turned around and spotted Griffiths. 'Jesus, this is all we need.'

Griffiths marched up to the group. 'Would you excuse us, please. I need to speak to DI Fagan alone.'

Stacey, Watkins, Brooks, and Saddler left the community centre.

'I want to know what's going on here, DI Fagan.'

'I'd like to know that myself, sir,' Fagan responded.

'I'm in no mood for jokes, Fagan,' Griffiths rattled. 'I got the message an hour ago. Three more young girls have lost their lives.'

'Why do you think my team is here?'

Griffiths looked at the mugs of coffee on the table Fagan was sat at. 'Drinking coffee isn't exactly helping solve the murder of Ellie Parry, is it? Or investigating three new suicides.'

'We've been given the runaround ever since this murder investigation started, sir.' Fagan could sense his temper getting the better of him. 'And now we have to deal with a serial killer who can manipulate people from a distance. Gaining their trust and their friendship and then convincing them to commit suicide. In all my thirty-six years in the force, I've never encountered anything like this. We are dealing with something totally new. Frankly, I am at a loss. So I'd appreciate it if you'd get off my back about this.'

'Do you realise the pressure we're under here now, Fagan? Once this gets out to the press, they'll have a field day. God knows what the public reaction will be. Ever since the incident in Southport, police forces across England and Wales have been treading on eggshells. The rumour mill is about to start and social media will be lit up like a Christmas tree.'

'I know what's at stake,' Fagan stated.

'Then what's your next move, DI Fagan?'

'I'm going to bring Russel Connor in for an interview.'

Griffiths shook his head. 'I can't allow that, which is why I'm here.'

'What do you mean, sir?'

'Connor's solicitor, that's what I mean. I just spent an hour on the phone convincing him not to file a complaint against Gwent Police. Because a certain detective interrogated him at a lecture at Cardiff University last night.'

'It wasn't an interrogation,' Fagan growled. 'The person responsible for Ellie Parry's death and the other deaths here today is using Cymru Teen Chat to target his victims. Russel Connor refused to give us any details about how to access his social media platform. He just spouted a load of bullshit about how his website is controlled by Artificial Intelligence. I just spoke to Gracie Peacock's mam. Gracie was using Cymru Teen Chat just before she died. As were the others. Whoever this Shadowcaster is, he has the ability to control people. He can manipulate them into taking their own lives. You're right about one thing: when this gets out, the shit is going to hit the fan. Unless we do something now.'

'Russel Connor is one of the most respected business people in Wales. He's done a lot for young people and local businesses.'

'Lloyd Bevan was also a great First Minister, wasn't he? But look how that turned out. I'm not arresting Connor, but we need to speak to him about his social media platform. He could be the key to bringing whoever killed Ellie and the other three girls to justice. I'm not going to ask him to shut down his social media platform. But we need access to it in order to catch this killer. I've seen what individuals like this Shadowcaster can do. You have two choices. Either you can stop me from questioning Connor. Then I'll just sit back and happily watch the shit hit the fan. Or you can just let me question Connor and hopefully we'll be able to catch this killer.'

Griffiths took a long breath, eventually nodding. 'Just a routine questioning, Fagan. I don't want any theatrics. Is that clear?'

'Crystal, sir.' Fagan spun on his heels and marched towards the exit.

CHAPTER 39

Newport Central Police Station

'For the record, DI Fagan, you are not here to throw any accusations at Mr Connor,' James Barlow, Connor's solicitor, stated in a firm tone.

'I wasn't going to accuse Mr Connor of any wrongdoing,' Fagan replied. 'The reason we've invited you here, Mr Connor, is because we need your help. Three girls have died today. They were all using Cymru Teen Chat.'

'Mr Connor has already explained, Inspector Fagan. He does not have access to the software. It's controlled by AI. That's why it was created, to prevent human tampering.'

Fagan maintained his stare on Connor. 'Oh, come on. Your company must have a way of accessing the software. Don't give me that crap about artificial intelligence controlling everything. I'm no rocket scientist, but I'm not stupid either.'

'You simply don't understand,' Barlow stated in a mocking tone.

'Then help me understand all this,' Fagan retorted.

Barlow inhaled. 'The software runs independently. It has learning capabilities so it can upgrade itself and write its own software. By eliminating human interaction, the software is perfect.'

Fagan ignored Barlow, maintaining his focus on Connor. 'The other night at your lecture in Cardiff, you said this software can root out cyberbullying and any other threat.'

Barlow continued to speak for Connor. 'Yes, its robust monitoring system allows the software to moderate the platform. It uses algorithms that can detect keywords used online associated with things like bullying, hate speech, violence and anyone wanting to incite a riot. You saw what happened at

Southport a few months ago.'

'This is why we have designed the software the way it is,' Connor finally opened his mouth.

'Ah,' Fagan interrupted, pointing at Connor. '*We have designed the software.* Which means there's a level of human interaction.'

'It's a figure of speech, Inspector Fagan,' Connor sighed.

'Well, it would appear, Mr Connor, that your software has been compromised,' Watkins said.

'Impossible. The software was designed to detect outside threats from hackers.'

'Again, *was designed*,' Fagan said. 'Was your software created by a human?'

Connor took a moment to answer. 'Yes, of course it was.'

'Who created it?'

Connor remained silent.

'Mr Connor, you're not helping the situation,' Watkins said. 'Do you have any idea what's at stake here? Three more girls have died. There's a killer using your social media platform as a hunting ground. He can manipulate those he talks to. Four girls have died in as many days. We need to catch this individual as soon as possible.'

'And that is a tragedy. But it has nothing to do with the software.'

'We're not talking about the software, Mr Connor.' Fagan rolled his eyes. 'We're taking about our suspect using Cymru Teen Chat. Now, who created your software?'

'Inspector Fagan, the identity of the software's creator is irrelevant to your inquiry,' Barlow cut into the conversation. 'Under the Trade Secrets Act, the processes and individuals behind our proprietary technology are protected by law. Revealing that information would open the company to legal liabilities, and we're not willing to take that risk without a formal court order.'

'I will not put the person who created the software in the line of fire,' Connor added.

'So you're not willing to help us,' Fagan said.

'What we're saying, DI Fagan,' Barlow continued in an even tone. 'Is that you need to go through the proper legal channels to get the information you need. This requires court orders and warrants.'

Fagan hadn't taken his stare away from Connor. 'Doesn't it bother you that four girls have died over the last week?'

'Of course it bothers me,' Connor grunted. 'I'm not a man without conscience, DI Fagan.'

'Mr Connor plans to donate two hundred and fifty thousand pounds to help the families affected by this tragedy,' Barlow revealed. 'This is a very generous amount.'

'Is that your answer to everything, Mr Connor? To throw money at a problem you can't solve?'

'Inspector Fagan, we will do everything in our power to help the police catch the person responsible for these horrible crimes,' Barlow promised. 'But the facts stand. The police need to jump through legal hoops to get the information they require.'

'That could take months and you know it,' Fagan rattled. 'You're just using red tape to hinder us in our investigation.'

'We are being cooperative, Inspector Fagan,' Barlow said candidly. 'We are sitting here answering your questions.'

'No, you're not. You're sat there with a smug attitude, using every legal loophole to stop us from catching a killer. This killer, incidentally, has been linked to a spate of suicides over the past two years. All the girls involved were using your social media platform.'

'All just hearsay and rumour, DI Fagan. No such evidence has been submitted that proves any of what you have just said is true. Third-party sources can be unreliable. Mr Connor has had many accusations aimed at him over the years.'

Fagan refocused. 'We need access to those girls' accounts so that we can know more about this killer.'

'Again, Inspector Fagan, you are missing the point. Our users' accounts are their own. Any data you're asking for is subject to the UK Data Protection Act. No personal data can be compromised, so no information will be shared without a court order.'

'And by that time, the trail will have gone cold.'

'That is your problem, DI Fagan, not Mr Connor's.'

Fagan glared back at Barlow. 'What if I issue a press release later on today? And tell the press that all the girls were using your client's social media platform just before they died. And that Gwent Police believe the killer is using Cymru Teen Chat to hunt his next victim.'

Barlow remained steadfast, returning Fagan's stare. 'I would advise you against that course of action, DI Fagan. If you release any statements like the one you just threatened Mr Connor with..'

Fagan held up his hand. 'No one is threatening anyone here.'

'Nevertheless, if you make any statements that could drag Mr Connor and his company through the mud, you'll be exposing yourself and Gwent Police to a defamation lawsuit. This alone will cripple your investigation. Not to mention jeopardising any legal cooperation we might offer, going forward with your investigation.' Barlow's eyes narrowed. 'Are you prepared for that, DI Fagan? I doubt whether your superiors are, when I launch a formal complaint.'

Fagan realised he had backed himself into a corner.

Barlow leant forward, pointing at Fagan. 'And what about the families of those poor, unfortunate girls? Imagine the further stress the parents of the three girls will have to endure when you make an accusation that has no substance. You'll not only be sullying the reputation of Gwent Police, but you'll be undermining the trust of the public. You need to ask yourself, do you really want to go down that road? We all saw how the events at Southport escalated because someone made a comment that was untrue. You are now playing with fire. And when you play with fire, there is only one outcome.'

'All I'm trying to do is catch a killer,' Fagan stated.

'And I fully understand,' Barlow continued his unemotional tone. 'However, it's my job to protect Mr Connor's reputation and the reputation of his business from people who are constantly making baseless accusations. You are very misguided if you think going to the press is going to sway Mr Connor or speed up your investigation. Mr Connor has cooperated fully within the bounds of the law, and we've provided you with all relevant information to help your investigation.'

'You've provided me with nothing. All you've done is spew legal and technical jargon.'

'We have shared everything we have been obliged to share. The one thing that is hampering your investigation is your inability to act within the confines of the law.'

'We were within our legal right to question Mr Connor,' Fagan argued, sensing his temper rise.

'That's the only thing we can agree on. You are welcome to proceed through the proper legal channels. Once you have done all that, we can proceed with aiding the police with their investigation.'

'In the meantime, our killer is free to carry out another murder.'

'We hope this isn't the case. So what's it going to be, DI Fagan? Pursue the necessary information through the proper channels, or through the tabloids?'

'Are you going to spend this entire interview hiding behind your solicitor, Mr Connor?' Fagan asked.

Barlow glared back at Fagan. 'DI Fagan, Mr Connor is unwilling to answer questions you put to him. And I'll tell you why. You are one in a long line of people who have targeted Mr Connor and his business.'

Watkins looked at his tablet. 'I see you are a very outspoken individual, Mr Connor. Especially regarding the war in Ukraine and what's happening in the Gaza strip. Criticising the UK government for their involvement. You've given several interviews in the local and national press.'

'I've a keen mind. I was thinking of running for the Senedd,' Connor explained casually.

Fagan seized an opportunity 'Why is it men like you, who have made a shitload of money, think they have the right to criticise the very government that gave them the freedom to make their millions?'

'Inspector Fagan, can I remind you that you are not here to

question Mr Connor about his political views or the ins and out of how he achieved success. Now, if there is nothing else, we'll be leaving.' Barlow stood and packed his briefcase.

Fagan smirked at Connor. 'I'm not quite done yet.'

Barlow stopped packing his briefcase. He fixed a steely gaze on Fagan. 'I'd think carefully about what you're going to say next, Inspector Fagan.'

Fagan threw Connor a mocking stare. 'I find it hard to believe that someone with *such a keen mind* can sit there and claim his social media platform is a safe haven for teenagers, especially for young girls. When in fact there is a predator trawling Cymru Teen Chat, profiling his next victim.'

Barlow spoke before Connor opened his mouth. 'Cymru Teen Chat has been credited as one of the safest social platforms around DI Fagan.'

'Four girls have died because of your bloody app.' Fagan's temper finally slipped. 'And you have nerve to come in here, claiming that you are helping us with our enquires, when, in fact, you've given us sod all.'

'I suggest you rein in your emotions, DI Fagan,' Barlow remained calm, his voice infuriatingly even. 'You've clearly moved beyond the scope of what's relevant. We'll be submitting a formal complaint to your superiors regarding your conduct.'

Fagan summoned as much restraint as he could muster. 'You can walk out of here with that smug expression, Mr Connor. But I promise you this. One way or another, the press is going to find out about your social media platform's connection to the deaths.'

Barlow couldn't help chuckling at Fagan's idle threat. 'There's a saying we have in the legal profession, DI Fagan. The first rule of holes states, if you find yourself in one, then stop digging. You've dug so far down it will take a miracle to get out. But go ahead and leak that information to the press. Because we'll know exactly where it came from. And when that defamation lawsuit hits your desk, we'll see how fast your case falls apart.' Barlow glanced at Connor. 'Let's go.'

Fagan could only watch as they both walked towards the door.

Connor stopped short of the entrance, glancing over his

shoulder. 'You think you can lay the blame on my doorstep because you're out of leads. You'll need more than political cheap shots and idle threats. Good luck finding your killer.'

The door slammed, leaving Watkins and Fagan in tense silence.

Fagan jumped to his feet. Rage coursing through him. 'Fuck!' he screamed, booting his chair across the room.

'Boss, clam down, will you,' Watkins urged.

Fagan jabbed a finger towards the door. 'He knows, Sean. He knows how to access the software. He can help us catch this Shadowcaster. But he's hiding behind law and regulation, just to protect his fucking social media empire.'

'He's playing the long game. You know that, boss.'

Fagan massaged his temples, his mind racing. 'Get someone from cyber forensics up to the conference room. We need to see if there's a way we can catch this bastard without Connor's help.'

Watkins grabbed his jacket from the back of his chair and left.

Fagan pulled out his phone, quickly messaging Melissa to see if she was available to head up to Newport. His eyes shifted to another number on his phone as he hit speed dial.

'Fagan, what's up?' Nigel Thomas asked.

'Nigel, I need a favour.'

'I'm in London for the next two days, Fagan.'

'Shit,' Fagan cursed under his breath.

'What's the problem?'

'Do you know Russel Connor?'

'Yeah, the Welsh entrepreneur behind Cymru Teen Chat.'

'That's the one. I was hoping you could grab an image of him and run it through that fancy face recognition software of yours. Connor used to work at Vine Road Music studios.'

'Interesting, but I only have a basic laptop with me. I won't be able to do it until I get back to Llanover.'

Fagan conceded. 'Okay, when you get home, run his face through your system and let me know if you find anything.'

'Will do.'

Fagan ended the call and stared at his phone, determination rising from deep within.

CHAPTER 40

Newport Central Police Station

Fagan composed himself as he faced his team. A member of cyber forensics was leaning against Brooks' desk. Melissa was at the back of the room. She threw Fagan a reassuring smile. He drained the last of his coffee, placing his mug on the table. 'Okay then guys, the situation is this. Russel Connor and his legal team are refusing to help us. All the accounts of the girls involved have been closed. So we need to figure out a way forward. I want to explore options that could help us catch this Shadowcaster that won't tread on the toes of Connor's legal team.'

'Sir, even if the accounts are closed, there are still a few possibilities,' the cyber forensics said. 'We can try to recover any shadow data from the platform.'

'What's your name?'

'Lee Harris, sir.'

'What does that mean, Lee, shadow data?'

'It's information that might still exist on their servers, even if it's not publicly visible. Data footprints can be stubborn. If we can't access the platform directly, we could try tracking external interactions such as messages, e-mails or other social media activity the victims had outside of Cymru Teen Chat.' Harris glanced down at his tablet before continuing. 'It's not foolproof, but it's something we can pursue while we wait for any court orders.'

'Connor's company is based in the Philippines,' Watkins said. 'Won't the servers be based out there?'

Harris nodded. 'If the servers are overseas, then it will make our job a lot harder. We'd have to go through international channels. Interpol, or the Philippines' legal system.' Harris displayed a frown. 'That could take weeks, maybe months.' He paused, tapping his pen against the table. 'However, there's a chance some data was routed through local servers here in the UK, especially if the victims were active at home. We could trace network activity and see if any of the data passed through here. It's a long shot, but if we find anything, it might cut through some of the red tape that Connor and his legal team are putting up.' He glanced at Fagan, waiting for his reaction.

'How long will that take?'

Harris scratched the back of his neck and puffed through his cheeks. 'If we're lucky and the data passed through UK servers, it could take a few days to a week to track and analyse the traffic. We'd need to coordinate with ISPs and get permission to access their logs, but given the urgency, we could fast-track it.'

'Would Connor's legal team suspect anything when we start sniffing around these ISPs in the UK?'

Harris thought for a moment before answering. 'Not necessarily, sir. We can access ISP logs here in the UK. As it's a fairly routine process for law enforcement in investigations like this. It could be done discreetly, and as long as we don't directly involve Cymru Teen Chat or mention his platform in the requests, Connor wouldn't have a reason to suspect anything.' Harris glanced at his tablet. 'The ISPs won't notify him, either. We're not touching his servers directly. So unless Connor has someone on the inside feeding him info, he won't know we're running this operation.' Harris tapped his screen. 'Trouble is, the more aggressive we get, the more likely we'll be discovered.'

'Fair enough.' Fagan nodded. 'The next thing I want to know is how the killer can use technology to mask his location.'

'Shadowcaster is likely using a combination of VPNs and proxy servers to mask his true location,' Harris explained. 'It means he's bouncing his signal through multiple servers across different countries, which makes tracking him like chasing a ghost. He's located here in Wales, but his digital footprint might show up in Russia, Singapore, or anywhere else. We need to trace patterns in his activity. Even with VPNs, there are sometimes slips, like when a connection briefly pings through an actual IP address before it's masked. We can monitor for those. And if he's using the same proxy services regularly, we might be able to triangulate his location by looking for repeating behaviours or specific time zones he's active in.'

Fagan inhaled. 'I'm too old school for this techno babble. His actual IP address. What if he's in a Wi-Fi hotspot?'

Harris nodded, acknowledging Fagan's concern. 'That's a good point, sir. If Shadowcaster is using a public Wi-Fi hotspot, it complicates things even further. It's a common tactic for those looking to evade detection. Drug traffickers are always pulling this trick. It can be a real nightmare to track their movements and link an individual to one address. You killer's actual IP address would be hidden behind the hotspot's network, making it harder for us to trace back to him directly.' Harris paused. 'However, it's not impossible. There are still some avenues we can explore. If we can identify hotspots he's frequently using, like libraries, cafes or other public places, we can set up surveillance or even use a decoy account to interact with him. We could monitor those locations for any unusual activity or patterns that might lead us to him. But,' Harris sighed, his brow furrowing.

'But what?' Fagan asked.

'He's brilliant at what he does. To stay truly invisible, he could choose a different Wi-Fi hotspot every time he logs on. You can check for Wi-Fi hotspots anywhere. There are thousands of them within a thirty-mile radius. For all we know he could drive a hundred miles away and log on. One thing is certain. He's not stupid enough to use the same hotspot more than once. He won't want to create a pattern.'

Fagan leaned back, massaging his forehead. 'So we're back to square one.'

The room suddenly plunged into silence.

'What about the technology he's using to disguise his voice? Is there any way to reveal his true voice?'

'I've heard the recording from when he contacted you earlier. Shadowcaster is using advanced voice modulation technology, which could make identifying his true voice nearly impossible. These tools can alter pitch, tone, and even inflections, making it sound like a completely different person. I have to admit, I thought his Keir Starmer and King Charles impressions were very good. Not that I'm condoning what he's doing,' Harris said, reading Fagan's expression.

'How was he able to mimic my voice?'

'He probably grabbed an audio sample from the press statement you gave a few nights ago. As for revealing his actual voice, we still analyse the audio for any anomalies that sometimes slip through the filters. If he's using a specific software or hardware, there might be telltale signs left behind, like digital fingerprints in the audio file itself. I'll run the recording through our system later on today. If I can isolate those anomalies, I might reverse-engineer them to expose the original voice. It's a long shot, but I could work with audio forensics experts to see if they can break down the modulation and give us something clearer to work with.'

'Well,' Fagan shrugged. 'It sounds like some sort of plan.'

Brooks raised his hand.

Fagan's eyes rolled. 'Andrew, we're not in school, mate. Jump in when you feel like it.'

Brooks directed his question at Harris. 'Could we set up a fake profile on Cymru Teen Chat? You know, try to lure the killer in.'

Harris was quick to dismantle Brooks' suggestion. 'Doing that is like throwing a stone into the middle of the Pacific and expecting a tsunami. This Shadowcaster is a seasoned internet user. The fact he's using all this kit demonstrates he's knowledgeable on all the latest technology. If we set up a fake profile, then he'll spot it.'

'Not to mention, Connor will probably look out for any move we might make. Then we'll have his legal team breathing down our necks.' Fagan glanced at Melissa. 'Doctor Knight, you are our expert on serial killers. What do you think Shadowcaster's next move will be?'

Melissa sensed the room focusing on her. 'This is a hard case to study. Mainly because he's not out on the streets hunting down his next victim. He using technology to his advantage. He knows he can stay anonymous, so he'll be full of himself. He'll be revelling in the latest events on the Sofrydd. I've also listened to the recording. He's obviously singled you out as the focus of his attention.'

'Why?'

'He's looking for someone in authority to antagonise. And because you're the leading detective in this case, he's chosen you. He'll view you as inferior. Someone whose buttons he can easily push. It's clear he enjoys the power he has over the situation. He's expecting us to follow conventional lines of investigation, and he'll continue to push boundaries to maintain control. If we apply pressure through any means, like tracking his voice or trying to set up a fake account, he'll most likely have the ability to adapt, maybe even change tactics.'

'So, what's our next step?'

'This is where it gets hard. He convinced three girls to take their own life today. The press has been on the Sofrydd for the past few days. They'll probably already know about the other three other girls and are just waiting for someone to confirm it.'

'They already have,' Watkins remarked. He walked over to Fagan, handing him a tablet. 'The South Wales Argus has just posted this on their website.'

Fagan took a moment to contain both frustration and anger before reading the headline out loud. 'Gwent Police Chief expresses concern about recent deaths on the Sofrydd Estate.' Fagan read the article. 'Chief Constable Paul Griffiths of Gwent Police expressed his concern over three more deaths that have occurred on the Sofrydd Estate earlier today. The three girls who cannot be named were found in separate properties. This comes following the murder of fourteen-year-old Ellie Parry three days ago.' Fagan glared at Watkins' tablet. 'Why the bloody hell would Griffiths do this?'

'Read the next paragraph down, boss,' Watkins encouraged.

Fagan carried on reading. 'Gwent Police released the statement an hour ago, following a statement from Russel Connor, the Welsh businessman behind Cymru Teen Chat. Mr Connor has stated that the girls were not part of a suicide cult started by someone on CTC. Speaking from his home in Newport, Mr Connor expressed sympathy for the families involved and has pledged a sum of a quarter of a million.' Fagan gritted his teeth. 'Barlow, that snotty-nosed solicitor of his, is behind this.'

'He pipped you to the post, boss. You did mention telling the press when we interviewed Connor.'

'Yeah, but you know I wasn't going to go through with it, Sean. Connor's legal team did this on purpose to deflect any negative publicity away from Connor's social media platform.'

'Connor's legal team put pressure on Griffiths,' Stacey suggested. 'Forcing him to make a statement before you had a chance to.'

Fagan's desk phone suddenly rang, causing Fagan to jolt. For a fleeting moment he stared at the receiver before grabbing it. 'DI Fagan.'

'Good afternoon, DI Fagan,' a generic voice greeted. 'I trust I have your full attention.'

Fagan tapped the loud speaker button. 'What you have is my determination to hunt you down.'

'We both know that will not happen anytime soon.'

Fagan glanced at Melissa, who was holding up a piece of paper with a note. *'Keep him talking.'* 'What do you think you're achieving by calling me?'

The voice took a moment to answer. 'I'm going to show you just how cruel irony can be. You see, DI Fagan, you have had a long and distinguished career. Over thirty years with Merseyside Police.'

'And how do you know this?'

'Your career is a matter of public record. Plus, I thought I'd create a Wikipedia page just for you.'

Watkins tapped away on his laptop and located the page. He stared at Fagan, pointing at the screen.

'You were part of the team that failed to bring the Merseyside Ripper to justice,' Shadowcaster said. 'You failed all those women. Your partner at the time kept secrets, and you covered for him. You withheld vital information from your superiors. Detective Sergeant Jack Daw was having a relationship with a prostitute. And you chose not to reveal this.'

Fagan glanced around the room, noting that everyone was

focused on him. Melissa scribbled another note. *'He's trying to push you.'*

'You know you can't do this forever. You'll eventually make a mistake and I'll be there to jangle a cell key in front of you before I throw it into the deepest, darkest hole.' Fagan paused. 'Eventually every serial killer makes mistakes.'

'Ah, there's that word, *serial killer,'* the voice purred. 'I've studied all the greats. From Jack of old London town to Ian and Myra. Did you know they made recordings of their victims? Screaming, begging for their lives before being murdered. Then there were Fred and Rose, the ordinary suburban couple who murdered thirteen women. What I wouldn't give to have been part of that. To watch Fred at work. Join in his crimes. I imagine myself and Fred torturing those women before ending their lives. That kind of thing excites me. What excites you, DI Fagan?'

'The thought of catching you, that's what floats my boat,' Fagan answered.

Melissa held up another piece of paper. *'Keep going.'*

'So, your inspirations are Fred and Rose, not the likes of Dalmer. Not really a fan of the Netflix series, myself, overrated if you ask me.'

'Keeping me talking will not gain you any kind of information as to my whereabouts, DI Fagan. But I'll tell you who I am a fan of,' the voice stated.

'Who's that?'

The voice suddenly changed to the chilling sound of Anthony Hopkins' character. 'I love Silence of the Lambs, both the novel and the film adaptation. The interactions between myself and *Clarice Starling.* Tell me, DI Fagan, what do you fear the most?'

'I don't fear men like you.'

'You should fear me,' the voice of *Lector* continued. 'Everyone has fear installed into them, DI Fagan. I will look deep into your soul. I will summon your greatest fear and turn it against you.'

'I'm not impressed by your theatrics,' Fagan said.

'Ah, theatrics,' the voice continued, the mimicry of *Hannibal Lector* unsettlingly precise. 'You dismiss me so quickly, DI Fagan. But fear isn't about what you see in front of you, rather what you don't. Fear of the unknown terrifies people the most. It's what's buried deep inside, waiting to crawl out when the lights go out, when you're alone.'

'Why don't we get to the point? I'm tired of your petty attempt to get inside my head.'

'Fair enough, after all. Time is of the essence,' the voice said. 'Tick tock, tick tock.'

'What is that supposed to mean?'

'It's time for another lesson, DI Fagan. A lesson in missed opportunity. You let Ellie Parry's mother go today. Why did you do that?'

Fagan clutched the phone receiver. A new sense of dread rose from within.

'Your silence, DI Fagan, speaks volumes to me.' The line went dead.

Fagan looked across at Stacey. 'When Sophie Parry was picked up by her mother the other day from Hengoed, where did you say her mam lived?'

Stacey did a quick search on her computer. 'Number 4 Commercial Close, Talywain.'

Fagan yanked his jacket off the back of his chair. 'Get uniform up to that address, now!'

CHAPTER 41

Commercial Close – Talywain – Pontypool

Fagan stared at the chaos in front of him. 'Where the hell is uniform to manage these lot?' he rumbled, eyes narrowing surveying the scene confronting him.

Watkins pounded on his horn forcing the crowd to park. A woman shouted an obscenity as they drove by.

Two ambulances were parked outside a terraced house. A woman was in the back of one receiving oxygen. The paramedic shut the back door and jumped into the passenger side. The ambulance's lights flashed and the wail of the sirens caused the assembled onlookers to scatter for a second time.

Fagan burst from the car and headed straight for an open doorway.

A CSI blocked his path. 'You can't go in there without full PPE,' he stated, standing nose to nose with Fagan.

Fagan bit on his lip. He took a moment to compose himself before walking back to the car to get changed.

A few minutes later dressed in full forensic PPE, Watkins stepped through the front door first. He glanced over his shoulder.

Fagan was like a statue, staring at the doorway.

'Boss, we need to do this.'

Fagan stared into the darkened hallway. 'It's all my fault, Sean,' he said.

'That's what he wants you to think.'

'I shouldn't have let her go?'

'Don't do this to yourself, boss. You know it's part of this Shadowcaster's sick, twisted game.'

'Was any of this her fault?'

'How do you mean?'

'This all started with the murder of Ellie Parry. The Shadowcaster found her online.'

'Yeah, and if it weren't for her mam uploading those pictures of Ellie, she'd still be alive. Okay, so Ellie wasn't perfect. We've all seen the reports. Residents on the streets have given their opinion on her. We've seen the messages her and her mam exchanged the day she died.'

'But I let her go, Sean,' Fagan said, his voice heavy with regret.

'Let me ask you this, boss. Do we feel sorry for the drug dealers we arrest? Or the paedophile who commits suicide because they've been caught? I don't, and neither should you. Yes, Ellie was the one who started it by uploading those pictures. But then her mam went one step further and uploaded more pictures and videos of Ellie. When we first interviewed Sophie Parry about her FansOnly account, she claimed she was skint, and that Ellie convinced her to upload more pictures and videos. How do we know any of what Sophie Parry told us is true? Ellie was dead by that time. Let's not forget, Sophie Parry lied to us from the start.' Watkins pointed at the house. 'We know what we're about to face in there, and we'll face it together.'

Fagan nodded before following Watkins into the dimly lit hallway.

The living room door was open.

Fagan stepped through.

Two CSIs were in the living room.

Sophie Parry was slumped in an armchair, her lifeless body drenched in blood. Blood soaked the fabric and dripped steadily onto the laminate floor, still pooling beneath her.

'She was declared dead at the scene,' the CSI reported grimly. 'Her mother found her when she got back from the hairdresser. A witness says she ran out screaming and collapsed in the street. A neighbour told one of the uniforms she has a heart condition.'

Fagan couldn't tear his eyes from Parry. Her stillness, the carnage. He could feel the weight of the scene pressing on him. When he finally looked away, his stomach twisted at the sight of a phone on a tripod, its lens coldly pointed at the chair.

'Oh my God,' Watkins gasped, staring at the wall.

Fagan followed his gaze and felt his chest tighten.

'It's in the victim's blood,' the CSI speculated, their voice a distant murmur.

Fagan's breath caught as he read the words smeared across the wall, each stroke thick with horror.

No children. No life. No future. No hope—no choice.
DI Fagan

For a moment, Fagan couldn't move. His eyes locked on the message that seemed to claw at his soul. Watkins' voice broke through the haze.

'Boss,' Watkins called, more urgently.

Fagan stood frozen, transfixed by the blood-soaked writing.

'Boss, we need to go. Now!' Watkins grabbed Fagan's arm, yanking him from his trance.

Just then, the phone on the tripod rang.

Fagan's eyes locked onto the ringing phone. The sound seemed to pulse through the room, echoing off the blood-stained walls.

'Boss, let it go,' Watkins pleaded, his voice sharp with urgency.

Fagan shook off Watkins' grip, his gaze fixed on the phone like it was pulling him in, a siren's call.

'Don't do this, boss. You know this is what that bastard wants,' Watkins pressed, his voice rising.

But the ringing had already taken hold of Fagan, drawing him closer, each chime pulling him deeper into its trap, like a moth helpless against the pull of a flickering flame.

'DI Fagan!' Watkins shouted.

Fagan unclipped the phone from the tripod. His heart pounded as he stared at the screen, the name glaring back at him.

Shadowcaster.

The ringing persisted, louder with each passing second, drilling into his mind, each tone more deafening than the last.

Finally, he pressed answer.

'Hello, DI Fagan,' the familiar voice of Anthony Hopkins character, *Hannibal Lector* greeted. 'I trust this concludes our last lesson today.'

Fagan slowly turned to face Sophie Parry's lifeless body in the armchair. 'You sadistic bastard!'

'Why? Because I gave her the ending she deserved. We both know this couldn't have ended any other way. She'd been abusing her daughter. Selling pictures of Ellie to unspeakable people who wanted to do unspeakable things to the poor girl. When I saw Ellie online, I saw the despair in her eyes, her tortured soul.'

'And what, that gave you the right to take her life?' Fagan seethed.

'Ellie had already taken enough ecstasy to end her miserable existence. I made sweet love to her. Gave her something that she'd never experienced, passion. As I watched her ebb away, I wanted to know what it felt like.'

'What?' Fagan rasped.

'What it was like to have my hands around her throat.'

'You bastard, you sick, twisted piece of shit!'

'I will leave you now, DI Fagan. I will dissolve back into the fabric of society. Live my normal existence and wait patiently, tending my flock. And when the time is right, like lambs to the slaughter, they will come willingly.'

The line went dead.

Adrenaline seized Fagan's body. He rushed out of the living room and into the hallway.

Watkins gave chase.

Fagan emerged out onto the street. He gazed in all directions.

Confused residents stared back at him. A deathly silence smothered the street.

'Boss,' Watkins coaxed. 'You need to let forensics have the phone. We need to go.'

Fagan stared at the phone's black screen.

Watkins held out his hand. 'Come on, give me the phone.'

CHAPTER 42

Two days later
Gwent Police HQ – Llantarnam - Cwmbran

Fagan stood outside Griffiths' office. Tension coiled tightly in his chest. The last forty-eight hours had been a nightmare of frustration and helplessness. His team had been ordered to halt all operations, leaving the investigation dead in the water. Police presence had been pulled from the Sofrydd estate after a series of damning leaks hit the press.

Social media was ablaze with fury. A storm of accusations hurled at the police, each post fuelling the public's rage. Fagan knew, deep down, that Shadowcaster had orchestrated it all. He'd already guessed Shadowcaster had convinced Sophie Parry to scrawl the message in her own blood. Before taking a picture and sending it to him. Now that same image was everywhere, spreading like poison through social media. The backlash was growing more vicious as the days went by. The national press had got in on the game, fuelling speculation that Gwent Police was yet another failing police force.

A protest was already forming in Newport city centre, an ugly wave of outrage ready to crash down on Gwent Police. Fagan could sense the whole situation was spiralling, and Shadowcaster was pulling every string. Griffiths had called a hasty press conference urging calm throughout the Valleys.

From what little information he could get, he had learnt that the phone that Sophie Parry used was a pay as you go phone she had brought the morning she had thrown away her phone. The phone contained just one number. The number that Shadowcaster had used to contact Fagan when he arrived at the house. The number was untraceable. Forensic had determined Shadowcaster probably used a cheap burner phone that he probably destroyed. Parry was also using her phone to upload more pictures of herself to FansOnly. However, that's all cyber forensics could determine. Her FansOnly account had been shut down a day later.

Griffiths yanked open the door to his office and summoned Fagan inside.

A tense silence hung in the air. Fagan's eyes darted around the office. His gaze focusing on the picture of Bob Benson Griffiths kept.

Finally, Griffiths opened his mouth. 'In light of recent events, DI Fagan, I'm transferring you and your team to Police HQ, here in Llantarnam.'

'May I ask why, sir?'

'I think the demonstration that was held two days ago in Newport town centre showed how fragile the situation is. For the moment I am not splitting you up. Since you joined Gwent Police last April, you have proved you are a competent DI.' Griffiths paused, choosing his next words. 'However, DI Fagan, I feel that you need to be reined in. I said to you the other day that your methods are a little too maverick for my liking. Which is why I've transferred you here to Police HQ.'

For a fleeting moment Fagan felt he was in the presence of Bob Benson. Griffiths' tone was similar to his grandfather. Fagan suddenly found himself in Abergavenny Police Station in 1985, facing the choice that Benson had given him.

'How are you holding up?'

'As well as can be expected, sir,' Fagan replied.

'I know this may be difficult for you, but I need to ask you about the investigation into the murder of Ellie Parry. Do you think in light of what happened, you could have handled things differently?'

'No,' Fagan said. 'There was no way of knowing what was going to happen. When we turned up at the property, it looked like a straight up murder.' Fagan inhaled. 'Looking back on it now, I realise Shadowcaster set the whole thing up.'

'How do you mean?'

Fagan considered the question. 'He was there from the start.

When he rang the phone, he told me he had found Ellie on FansOnly. Sophie Parry had lied from the start of the investigation. When we first interviewed her, she said that her phone had been stolen while she was in Cardiff the night Ellie was murdered. I had a feeling she was lying, so I asked Constable Flynn to trawl through CCTV footage from Cardiff Central. That's when my suspicions were confirmed. It was a minor detail that could have easily been missed. If we hadn't had found Sophie Parry's phone, the investigation could have gone down a different path. But had the same outcome. This person who calls himself Shadowcaster took Ellie's phone and deleted everything that could have helped identify him.'

Griffiths processed the information. 'What about your handling of witnesses and suspects?'

'What about it?' Fagan threw a question back.

'Your interviews with Sophie Parry. You weren't exactly sympathetic when you interviewed her regarding her daughter. I've seen the interviews, DI Fagan.'

'Sophie Parry had been pimping her daughter out on FansOnly. From the very start the woman didn't show any emotion regarding her daughter's death. You can clearly see that in the interviews we conducted. We have witness statements from various sources that Parry and her daughter didn't have a typical mother daughter relationship. Residents on the Sofrydd have commented how Ellie and her mam were seen constantly arguing in the street. Sophie Parry made herself out to be the victim. Said she was desperate for money.'

'I've read the report.' Griffiths nodded. 'Parry also claimed that the owner of the website was blackmailing her. Don't you think that could account for her vulnerability?'

'Sophie Parry was anything but vulnerable,' Fagan remarked. 'Last year, police were called to Parry's house following a domestic disturbance. We referred the family to Social Services. Parry then formed a sexual relationship with one of the social workers in order to undermine the investigation into the family. And it worked. The investigation was dropped and Parry was free to carry on her sordid activities.'

'What about Owen Woods?'

'Owen Woods in a convicted drug dealer.' Fagan inhaled. 'He found himself at the wrong place at the wrong time. He will be charged with sexual activity with a child. I would also like to point out that Toby Morris will also face the same charges.' Fagan paused. 'But it's clear he has learning difficulties and didn't fully understand that having a sexual relationship with an underage girl was wrong. His mam, Tammy Morris, was fully complicit in what Sophie Parry was doing. Officers have interviewed her since Sophie Parry took her own life. She's blaming everything on Parry.'

'What do you know about the man who runs FansOnly?'

'Paul Decker lives in the Philippines. He's also a former South Wales Police detective. Jailed for ten years in 1992 for being part of a grooming gang in the Swansea area.' Fagan glanced at the picture of Benson, but remained silent. 'But that's about all I know about him.'

'Well, I thought I should let you know. Russel Connor has launched a full complaint against Gwent Police, namely you.'

'Russel Connor is trying to protect his precious social media empire.'

Griffiths nodded. 'This Shadowcaster, what do you think his next move is likely to be?'

Fagan considered the question. 'I believe he will stop what's he's doing for the time being. He'll take time to gloat at the fact that we cannot find him. He's caused a lot of damage over the last week. Causing maximum impact in the local community on the Sofrydd estate. This isn't over. He will strike again. However, given his skill with technology, he's proving impossible to find.'

'Why do you think he convinced Sophie Parry to mention you when she killed herself?'

'That's a question that I've been asking, sir. Doctor Melissa Knight believes that he's looking for an adversary. A Batman to his Joker, so to speak. And he has chosen me.'

Griffiths pondered the moment. 'A serial killer stalking the South Wales Valleys,' he sighed.

'Will that be all, sir?'

'Just one more thing. The murder trial of Rebecca Jenkins will start next week. So this will be a difficult time for you.'

'It's an open and shut case, sir. Tim Davis murdered her.'

'True, but your past with the murder victim will be revealed during the trial. I just wanted to give you a gypsy's warning about what's ahead.'

'And I appreciate that, sir,' Fagan lied.

'Good, well, I'll let you and your team settle into your new surroundings.'

CHAPTER 43

Abergavenny Police Station

Fagan looked about as he entered the building. His conversation earlier that day with Griffiths had left him feeling uneasy.

'DI Fagan,' DCI Gethin Lewis called out from an office door.

Fagan walked briskly towards him and disappeared into the office.

Lewis reached into an office cabinet and took out a bottle of whiskey and two glasses.

'Not for me, thank you sir,' Fagan said politely. He hated whiskey. Too many of his former colleagues in Merseyside homicide would drown themselves in a bottle at the end of a day. He had seen three good detectives drink themselves into an early grave.

'When you've been in the job as long as I have, DI Fagan, you develop a knack for this. Question you have to ask yourself is, how much do you want it to destroy your life?' Lewis knocked back the first glass without a second thought before pouring himself another. 'I've seen the news, nasty business with this Shadowcaster.'

'My team has been taken off the case, and the investigation has been pulled out of the Sofrydd.'

'The news media will keep up their interest until another story comes along.'

'Whoever Shadowcaster is, he's in the wind. He's able to use technology to his advantage. Cyber forensics is working overtime on this.' Fagan shook his head. 'So far nothing.'

Lewis sipped from his glass. 'I see you and your team have been posted to Cwmbran HQ.'

Fagan nodded slowly. 'Orders of the Chief Constable.'

'So, have you had a look at the casefile I gave you?' Lewis asked, changing the subject.

Fagan reached into his laptop bag, pulling out the file. 'I've been through the statement of the girl you mentioned the other day. The pregnant girl who walked into the police station says there were two men who had raped her. One of the men was Police Detective Sergeant Peter Norman.'

Lewis nodded, sipping from his glass.

'But she doesn't mention the other officer who was involved in the crime.'

'The girl wouldn't say, not because she was afraid. But because Norman had become infatuated with her. They'd met frequently. But on the first occasion they met, there was another serving officer with him. They both engaged in sex with the girl.'

'Why didn't Norman name the other officer?'

'When I told my superior, Tony Blake, about that girl he held back arresting Norman. We persuaded the girl to help us set up a small operation to catch Norman. We arrested him, but he took his own life three days later. Norman was married and had three kids. Two other officers were arrested, along with Norman. Thirty-four-year-old Dafydd Roberts, a detective constable and Paul Decker. We gave photographs of both officers, but she didn't identify any of them.'

Fagan read Lewis' expression. 'You think there were other officers involved with the gang of paedophiles?'

'I'm certain of it. However,' Lewis sighed. 'Even though I had a theory, I couldn't prove it.'

'Who you think the other officer was?'

'I believe it was former Chief Constable, Owain Lance. At the time of Julie Mann's murder, Lance was a Chief Superintendent. He wasn't directly involved with the investigation into Julie Mann's murder. But he was good friends with all three serving detectives, Norman, Roberts and Decker. The pregnant girl told us she knew other girls who were involved with the three officers. She said that Norman would take her to places around Swansea and the surrounding area. One particular place which was a favourite was an orphanage in Port Talbot, St Mary's Orphanage for Girls.'

Fagan recognised the name.

'You've heard of it?'

'Yeah.' Fagan nodded. 'When I was investigating the Alex X case, I interviewed a woman who was raised there. She claimed that Dillon Powell raped her there. There was also a priest that used to abuse the girls.'

'Norman also took the girl to a hotel just outside Monmouth.'

'Would that be the Agincourt Hotel, by any chance?'

Lewis nodded.

'Bloody hell,' Fagan cursed. 'Quite the investigation.'

'Look, I'm not expecting you to make this a priority case, DI Fagan. For now, I want this kept strictly between the two of us.' Lewis glanced out of the window. 'This case has haunted me for over thirty years. And now my time is up in more ways than one. I want closure on it.'

Fagan glanced at the glass of whisky. 'How long have you got?'

'A year tops maybe.'

'I'll study the case file. I know how to stay under the radar with this.'

'Thank you.' Lewis polished off his glass.

The Cantreff

Fagan stared into his glass of beer.

'You going to drink that, or just gawp at it?' Jackie asked.

'Sorry, Jacks, I was deep in thought.'

Melissa put her arm around Fagan. 'Don't let him get to you, Marc,' she whispered. 'That's what he wants to happen. Serial killers will always try to play with the minds of others.'

'I know.' Fagan picked up his glass and took a swig.

Tyler and Evans walked through the door.

'Oh aye, started without us, have you, Fagan?' Evans ribbed, looking at Fagan's pint glass.

'It's not a competition, Jamie,' Fagan replied.

Stacey and Ricky walked in. Stacey was smiling at Fagan. 'Guv.'

'We're off duty, Stacey. It's just plain Marc.'

'The usual for you is it Ricky, my boy?' Jackie said, reaching for a glass.

'Not tonight Aunt Jacks, this is just a flying visit.' Ricky looked at Fagan. 'We've something to announce.' He cuddled up to Stacey.

Silence enveloped the room.

'Well, come on then,' Jackie barked. 'Don't keep us hanging.'

'I'm three months pregnant,' Stacey announced.

'Oh, my God!' Jackie boomed. 'That's lovely.'

Fagan stood and walked over to Stacey, hugging her. 'This doesn't get you out of being bumped up to Detective Constable.'

Stacey chuckled. 'I know.'

Fagan looked at Ricky, placing his hand on his shoulder. 'Well done. I'm so proud of you.'

Rickey stared back for a few moments, smiling. 'Thanks, dad.' He embraced Fagan.

'There's plenty of time for celebration,' Stacey said, 'But right now we have to get to Newport to tell my nan and grandad. We'll see you all later.'

Jackie teared up. 'Oh my god, Fagan, he called you dad.'

'I know.' Fagan beamed.

Evans slapped Fagan on the back. 'Well, it's time to wet the baby's head.'

'That's after it's been born, you idiot,' Tyler said, clipping Evans around the back of the head.

Jackie looked towards the pub entrance, spotting Nigel Thomas.

'Nigel,' Fagan greeted.

'I'm glad I caught you all,' Thomas said. 'I have something to show you, Fagan.'

They all sat in the corner of the lounge huddled round Thomas.

'I ran Russel Connor's face through my computer. There are quite a few photos of him at the Agincourt Hotel and Vine Road Music Studios where he worked. But there's one photo I found that all of you should find interesting.' Thomas called up the picture. 'It was taken at the Agincourt Hotel. It's a group photo in which Connor appears.' He handed his tablet to Fagan.

'Jesus,' Fagan gasped, pointing at the photo. 'That's Jimmy Saville, with all the boys that went to Forest Coalpit Dorms.'

Evans pointed at the photo. 'That's Bernard the Bummer Baxter, our old PE teacher.'

'And Bob Benson,' Fagan added.

'Look who's standing next to Benson,' Thomas said.

Fagan gritted his teeth. 'Benny fucking Nelson.'

'What does this mean?' Jackie asked.

'I thought all the boys that won the competition at school went to Forest Coalpit Dorms,' Tyler remarked.

'That's what I thought, but I just got off the phone to the photographer who took that photo. He says that they all went to the Agincourt, stayed for a few hours before heading out to Forest Coalpit.'

'What does this mean?' Jackie asked.

'I don't know,' Fagan answered, digging into his pocket to retrieve his ringing phone. 'Sean, what's up?'

'Sorry to bother you, boss. I'm in Trinity street, a body has been found at the back of a house. You're the only DI that's available.'

'Okay, I'll be there shortly.' Fagan handed the tablet back to Thomas. 'Hang on to that, Nigel, duty calls.'

Melissa stood. 'I have to get back and walk the dogs.'

'Hang on, you can't just leave,' Evans moaned, pointing at Thomas' tablet. 'It was just getting interesting.'

'I have to go, Jamie.' Fagan looked back at the gang. 'They've just found a body at the back of a house in Trinity Street.' Fagan headed towards the entrance.

'Fagan,' Tyler called out.

Fagan looked back.

'Trinity Street.'

'Yeah.'

'That's where Bernard the Bummer Baxter used to live.'

Fagan and Melissa emerged into the carpark of the pub.

'I'll see you for breakfast in the morning.' She kissed Fagan and turned.

'Melissa.'

She looked back at him.

'The dark,' Fagan stated.

'The dark?'

'When Shadowcaster asked me what I fear the most. I'm still afraid of the dark.'

A memory forced its way into Melissa's thoughts. 'The cellar you got trapped in.'

Fagan nodded. 'When we went looking for Danny Llewellyn in 1980.'

Melissa embraced Fagan and kissed him passionately. 'We'll talk more in the morning.'

EPILOGUE

Trinity Street – Abergavenny

Fagan climbed out of his car and looked down the narrow road. Uniform blocked off the road at both ends. Cars were parked all along the street, making it difficult for forensics vehicles to find a place to park.

Watkins approached. 'I had to leave my car in the Castle Meadows car park. A lot of the residents refuse to move their vehicles.'

Fagan pointed at a group of wooden huts. 'We'll contact the army cadets and ask them to open their gates.'

Both Fagan and Watkins walked around the back of Trinity Street. A group of forensics in white jump suits were milling around a garden renovation. Two tents had been erected. One containing objects recovered from the scene and another covering the trench where the body had been found.

Fagan looked down at the forensic, brushing away dirt from the remains of the skeleton.

'I spoke to the owners of the house, boss,' Watkins revealed. 'They bought the house six months ago. The owners knocked down the garage that stood here. They were planning a space for two cars and a patio. The builder who found the remains said that he was surprised the garage stood for so long. It was a crap build.'

Fagan climbed down into the trench. 'What have you got for us, Dia?'

'One body, buried in a shallow grave. I reckon the garage was built to cover the remains.'

'Any idea of age?'

'Adolescent,' Dia replied. 'If I were to hazard a guess, I'd say a ten-year-old male.'

'Male,' Fagan mused.

Dia pointed to the skull. A wire was wrapped around the neck.

Fagan spotted an object that was attached to the wire. 'It's a joystick,' he remarked.

Dia nodded. 'It's a joystick from an old Atari games system. The Atari 2600, to be exact.'

Watkins was checking his phone. 'The first Atari games console was launched on September 11th, 1977. It revolutionised the gaming industry. Had interchangeable cartridges, unlike earlier consoles.'

'I had one when I was a nipper,' Dai said. 'Used to spend hours on it.'

Fagan scrutinised the scene. 'There are no clothes on the victim.'

Dai nodded. 'Whoever murdered him stripped the body naked. Then dumped the clothes and the console in a plastic bag and buried them with the body. It's obvious our murderer ripped the cord from the main console and used it to strangle the victim. Pretty gruesome stuff, if you ask me. The items found with the body are in the tent.'

Fagan and Watkins entered the other tent that contained a table. Fagan spotted an old Atari games console immediately. A cartridge was still in the machine. 'Asteroids,' Fagan read the title. Another cartridge was placed next to the console. 'Pac Man.'

'Classic design,' The CSI remarked with a little too much enthusiasm. 'Collectors' items now.'

'And also used as a murder weapon,' Fagan responded. He spotted an old jacket spread out on the table. 'I used to have one of these,' he smiled, recalling his younger days. 'It's a Harrington jacket.'

'There's a name on the tag.'

Fagan slipped on a pair of latex gloves and picked up the jacket by the collar.

'It's faded, but if you stare hard enough, you can read the name.'

Fagan focused on the name tag. In an instant an emotional shockwave ripped through his body. 'Jesus, I don't believe it.'

Watkins looked over his shoulder. 'Who is it, boss?'

Fagan stared at Watkins, wide eyed. Memories forced their way into his thoughts. Suddenly it was summer 1980 all over again. 'I can't believe it's Sean, it's him, we found him.' Fagan paused, staring at the name tag. 'It's Danny Llewellyn.'

To be continued...

Detective Inspector Marc Fagan will return in Dead Reckoning.

Many thanks for buying a copy of The Dead Die Young. I would be grateful if you could spread the word about this book, social media, Goodreads, a local book club. Or just have a conversation next time you're in the pub or at work.

I don't have an email list, but you can click on the follow button on my Amazon page. They will email you when I have a new book.

Many thanks
Jason Chapman

Jasonchapman-author@hotmail.com

Hey avid book readers. Why don't you try my other books? They're also available on Kindle Unlimited.

Were you a fan of the X Files back in the day? You'll love my UFO Chronicles books if you like stories of alien encounters and government cover-ups.

Or perhaps you're a fan of fast-paced thriller. My Sam Drake series is perfect for those who like a bit of escapism and a bit of conspiracy.

The UFO Chronicles
The fallen
Codename Angel
The Angel Conspiracy
The Angel Prophecy

Detective Sergeant Samantha Drake
Dystopia
Avalon Rising
Signals
Project Genesis

Detective inspector Mark Fagan
The Dead Will Beckon
The Dead and the Buried
Melody from the Dead
The Dead Remember
Dead Reckoning (coming in 2025)

O F F W O R L D
P U B L I C A T I O N S

The truth is still out there...

Printed in Great Britain
by Amazon

50099059R00169